paper
heart

Also by Cecelia Ahern

PS, I Love You
Where Rainbows End
If You Could See Me Now
A Place Called Here
Thanks for the Memories
The Gift
The Book of Tomorrow
The Time of My Life
One Hundred Names
How to Fall in Love
The Year I Met You
The Marble Collector
Lyrebird
Roar
Postscript
Freckles
In A Thousand Different Ways
Into the Storm

YOUNG ADULT NOVELS
Flawed
Perfect

Cecelia Ahern

paper heart

HarperCollins*Publishers*

HarperCollins*Publishers* Ltd
1 London Bridge Street,
London SE1 9GF

www.harpercollins.co.uk

HarperCollins*Publishers*
Macken House, 39/40 Mayor Street Upper
Dublin 1, D01 C9W8, Ireland

Published by HarperCollins*Publishers* 2025

1

A catalogue record for this book is available from the British Library

ISBN: 978-0-00-860819-4 (HB)
ISBN: 978-0-00-860820-0 (TPB)

This novel is entirely a work of fiction.
The names, characters and incidents portrayed in it are
the work of the author's imagination. Any resemblance to
actual persons, living or dead, events or localities is
entirely coincidental.

Set in Adobe Caslon Pro by HarperCollins*Publishers* India

Printed and bound in the UK using 100% Renewable
Electricity at CPI Group (UK) Ltd

This book contains FSC™ certified paper and other controlled
sources to ensure responsible forest management.

For more information visit: www.harpercollins.co.uk/green

For Sarah-Jayne Tobin

Origami girl
hides inside herself
she tucks and folds
a pith in her peel
she expresses with shapes
    touches with corners
     feels with a concealed pleated heart
she whispers in ink

I

LIFE USUALLY TICKS ALONG, consistent as a drip from a leaky tap, but today is different.

The traffic through Ballybeg main street has stalled. Pip is a back-seat passenger in the car, her mother Josephine is behind the wheel, and Pip's daughter Bella is in the front passenger seat. Though this seating arrangement is the same as it ever was.

Josephine holds her hand down on the car horn. Bella laughs at her nan's impatience. Embarrassed, Pip slithers down in the back seat. Her mother's actions serve no benefit. There's something clearly wrong in the town, with a heavy line of traffic heading out, and nothing coming in. A dam in the flow.

Pip can't do anything about it, so she sits back, looks out of the window, and settles into a daydream. In her mind, she can be a million different people living different lives, with different loves. All the versions of herself that she cannot be in real life. Her daydreams are awash with true romantic love. The kind that will transform her. Even after everything she's been through, she still believes in romance. It seems a kind of a witchcraft that people fall under every single day. Why it eludes her is a great distraction to her. She wants something out of this world, in this world. She knows it exists, because she had it once, before they took it – him – away from her.

'Press it again, Nan,' Bella says loudly, playfully, her volume making Pip jump out of her head and back into the traffic jam.

Bella leans across and tries to press the horn herself.

'Stop it, you,' Josephine snaps. Then after a quiet moment she leans on it again.

The driver gets out of the car in front.

'Uh-oh,' Bella says. 'You've annoyed him now.'

But the driver doesn't come near them, he crosses the road to the nearest shopkeeper, who has come outside to see what's happening. Information is shared. Their discussion is too juicy for Josephine to ignore. There can be nothing she does not know about.

'Stay in the car,' she instructs, shutting the engine off and getting out.

She's all business. Five feet two, fifty-nine years old, dressed in her jeans, Nike runners and fleece jacket. Pip watches her from the back seat.

Head down.

Scurrying gait.

Small steps.

Tough.

Josephine inserts herself into the men's conversation without apology or introduction. They're momentarily put out by her, but move to make space. Then they do a lot of talking. She listens. She's good at that. Getting people to speak. The interrogator. She and Pip's dad, Philip, are made of the same stuff. They work as a team, like the Ballybeg investigative unit. Him silent, her probing, but he always in full support.

Bella opens her passenger door.

'She said to stay in the—'

Bella gets out and slams the door. Pip watches her sixteen-year-old daughter make her way confidently across the road.

Black leggings.

Crop top.

Swinging hips.

Assured.

The shape of Bella's thong is visible beneath her leggings. The confidence in her daughter marvels her. At her age, Pip was embarrassed to walk alone, past a line of traffic. She was self-conscious, felt the gaze of the judgemental world's eyes on her. Head down, apologetic, long shirt or jumper over her bum in case anyone was looking. Pip wanted to get to the destination as soon as possible, Bella relishes the journey. Her strides are long, her arms swing coolly by her side.

At that age Pip had covered her body with baggy hooded tops and oversized T-shirts because she was pregnant with Bella. She was ashamed and embarrassed to be female, by how her body was transforming. The first sixteen-year-old in Ballybeg ever to have a baby, it seemed. The burning shame of it, the guilt, the regret. With her stomach covered and her shoulders hunched, she was a walking apology.

Pip rests her head against the window trying to restart her daydream, but she's distracted by Josephine and Bella digging for information. People here in Ballybeg, a town in the midlands of Ireland, in the heart of the boglands, are always digging.

Whether it's the farmers who dig for peat, the quarry workers who dig to extract stone, or the astronomers in the observatory digging for information in the universe.

They dig down, they dig up.

At the bogs, the digging is ritualistic, it's generational, there's a rhythm to it, a self-identity to this place and thing. Peat-cutting for turf is their God-given right, they'd say. The land belongs to the people. The earth's resources are bountiful and provide with abundant energy.

At the quarry where her dad works they dig with fervour; it's hungry, greedy digging. It devours the earth and it feasts. It tears off the skin and goes straight to the bone. It feeds the growling hunger of another kind; pockets that can never be filled enough.

The digging upward in the local observatory is no less hungry. It's an intellectual hunger, a deep need to explore, to learn, to know the nature of the universe and search for revelations into our beginnings.

For the bog, the two-sided spade known as the *sleán*.

For the quarry, excavators, loaders, bulldozers, explosives.

For the sky, radio telescopes, satellites.

They're all hungry, inquisitive, digging down, digging up. Rock. Soil. Sky.

And heart. Time for Pip to dig in to matters of the heart. She dives into her imagination again, cooking up something steamy.

Josephine leaves the men and, head down, scurries back to the car, Bella behind her. The men look at Bella's arse. Pip looks away.

The traffic is flowing again.

'What was it?' Pip asks.

The response is Josephine starting the engine and Bella clipping her seatbelt.

As they continue out of Ballybeg town Pip sees cars parked alongside the road, blocking the lane on the other side. A

Garda manages the traffic while a crowd has gathered outside a house, an address Pip knows well. She sees Lorcan Murphy, Bella's paternal granddad, at the centre of it all, standing in his garden.

He's surrounded by more Gardaí.

Puce head.

Balled fists.

Twisted mouth.

Raging.

He's shouting something and repeatedly punching the air with his fist. She presses the button to lower the window but it has been locked from the front.

'Don't stare,' Josephine snaps, turning on the radio as if that will make them see less.

Bella's eyes widen, then she whips her head to face the front, examining her nails, as if nothing has happened at all.

Pip almost bruises her forehead pressing it up to the glass and twisting against it as they pass, looking to see if Jamie, Bella's dad, is there too.

'Philippa,' Josephine shouts.

It's a bark and a bite at the same time. Even at thirty-two years old she still responds to her mother's temper. She turns to face forward.

Her heart is pounding from what she has witnessed, she knows that Josephine will never explain it to her. She sits back and tries to drift away into another daydream.

But she can't be the back-seat passenger that does as she's told.

Today is different.

2

P IP IS DROPPED OFF at Ballybeg service station where she works, but if you call it that you're only a blow-in. The locals call it Crossroads station because it's positioned at one, and there once existed a hut and a single petrol pump Before Christ. Josephine's car barely stops for Pip to get out before taking off again in the direction of the observatory, where Josephine and Bella work in the canteen. Not long ago it was Pip's job, she gave it up for Bella a few weeks ago so that Bella could have a summer job.

Pip watches them speed off, looking back into the direction of town as if she will still see Lorcan Murphy. She's in shock. Was he arrested? She's ten minutes late for work, but it doesn't matter, her colleague Ronnie arrives just after her on his e-scooter.

Red mohawk.

Cocksure insecurity.

Local dick.

Trouble.

He lifts his helmet to reveal his flattened hair, which he self-consciously immediately pulls upward. The skinhead sides of his head are covered in tattoos. He reminds her of a rooster.

'Your criminal family causing mayhem out there,' he gobbles, racing by her and sticking out his pierced tongue.

Asking Ronnie about what he saw in town isn't an option, though its appeal reveals her desperation to know what's going on. The best way to deal with Ronnie is to engage with him as little as possible.

'Sorry I'm late,' she says to Krish, her boss, going to the staffroom to store her coat and bag.

'No problem, Philippa. When you're ready.'

She can hear the pressure in his voice. He has a queue of truckers lined up at the deli counter waiting to order their breakfast rolls.

Sikh.

Family man.

Trustworthy boss.

Solid.

'What did Farmer Murphy do? Murder someone and bury them in his bog?' Ronnie asks, lifting his T-shirt over his head to dress in his red polo shirt. His body is covered in tattoos and piercings. She looks away. 'Not a bad idea that, I've always thought it's a good place to dump a body. You'll have fun visiting him in prison. All the jailbirds will love the smell of you.'

He sniffs the air and wriggles his pierced tongue.

Disgusted, she puts her coat and bag in her locker, hiding the code, and quickly leaves. The lock is to protect her against Ronnie, after she found a slew of dick pics on her phone, a series of him sticking her phone down his pants. She'd sprayed her screen with so much hand sanitiser it had stopped working for a week.

She joins Krish at the deli, disinfecting her hands before sliding them into the too big plastic gloves that dwarf her.

'Sorry,' she says again.

'No problem, traffic is crazy in town today. Full Irish break-fast roll for the gentleman,' Krish says in his Punjab-Offaly blended accent, handing her the sloppy butter-covered knife. 'Do we know what's going on out there?'

'No,' Pip says quietly, taking it from him. Too much butter on the knife, she wipes it off on a paper towel. She's got her measurements down by now, knows just by looking at a slice of bread just how much she needs. She hates to scrape the left over knob back into the tub, it leaves crumbs in the butter.

'Some peat farmer sounding off about turf-cutting,' one of the customers says. 'Guards got involved.'

'Was it Lorcan Murphy? I know he missed his court hearing,' the third man in line says, pulling up his jeans and sniffing as he does. 'If you don't show up they come and get you.'

The first man snorts. 'They don't come and get you for missing it once or twice. If they're taking him into custody it's because he keeps avoiding court.'

'He's right to take a stand,' the second man says, straightening up. 'His land, his right.'

Ballybeg has had to reimagine itself since turf-cutting was banned for environmental reasons. Some can let go, others are holding on. The passion of those who cherish the traditional right to dig peat to burn as fuel for their homes and those who argue the high cost to the environment for extracting it. Some have wholeheartedly embraced the new rules and have conserved their bogs, allowing the carbon sinks to do their job for the environment, and protect habitats. Lorcan Murphy, who has a family patch of bogland that is now considered a preservation site, has had the tradition of turf-cutting in his family for generations, and refuses to let go.

'It's their livelihood,' Krish says, respectfully.

Krish shares a knowing look with her as he hands the reins over.

Pip's mind is stuck on the Lorcan Murphy revelation. Her heart pounds at the thought of Bella's granddad in jail, and she feels ashamed at the excitement and hope that builds at his expense.

Jamie will have to come home.

She hasn't seen Jamie for years. It was orchestrated that way, to keep them from making more babies with each other, as if they were rabid wildlings. The fear their parents instilled in them at being in the same room as each other at sixteen years old was pervasive. Terrified, they went along with their parents' demands, willingly keeping a wide berth from each other. For one measly hour a week they were granted time together, so that Jamie could have time with Bella. He would sit on the floor with her when she was a baby, while their parents and Pip sat on chairs against the walls watching him, as if it were a court-ordered meeting. It was agonising for Pip not being able to lie on the floor and play with them like a proper family.

Josephine in particular deliberately instilled a fear in her, *'If you so much as look at him . . .'* she'd say in an eerie teeth-gritted anger. The fear was omnipresent but never thwarted Pip's desire to be with him.

And then, as soon as Jamie had finished school, his family sent him away to Liverpool.

He came home as often as he could, but the pandemic introduced long absences that gradually became the norm. Now he only comes home for a few days at Christmas and Easter, and his and Bella's time together has transitioned to a designated time over the phone every Sunday. But if there's a hearing for Lorcan Murphy, and a trial, then that could go on for weeks or months, Jamie would have to be here during the family crisis, wouldn't he? She has to steady her nerves as she slices sausages for the breakfast roll with trembling fingers.

The deli selection is the same every day; the hot section, the cold meats and salads. A series of sauces in squeezy bottles. An all-day breakfast roll is their unique selling point, the double-sided display stand outside the station roars it to passing traffic as if they have found the cure to all evil.

Some customers like to talk, others don't, taking the break for a moment to themselves, to not have to speak, to get lost in the galaxy inside their phones. The majority of customers are the men from the quarry where her dad works and the construction site workers from the new housing development just outside of town. The station has a fancy parking bay around the back, along with a car wash, modern toilet and showering facilities, and a launderette, which attracts regular long-haul drivers. Sometimes they've forgotten the art of conversation and it all comes out at her at once, everything they've been thinking for hours. It's surprising the things people can come out with in the few short moments they have. Maybe it's because she's safe, a stranger in the middle of nowhere that they'll never see again who can help unburden them. Hairdressers, manicurists, barmen and sandwich makers.

She gets an idea of a person by their culinary decisions. Palates are as diverse as people themselves. She imagines, though there's no truth behind it, but it passes the time in her mind, that the sandwich choice reveals something secretive about them.

'What can I get for you?' she asks the next in line.

'Chicken and stuffing.'

Pip's about to slice his sandwich when he looks around him conspiratorially, then leans over the counter and speaks from the side of his mouth. 'Give us some of those pickled gherkins, will you?'

As she neatly slices the gherkin, she visualises him in lacy underwear beneath his jeans.

'Can I have a word with you?' Krish says, suddenly appearing at the newspaper stand and giving her a fright.

Even though she knows it's too early for anything to hit the local newspaper, she thought she'd see if she could find out anything about what happened with Lorcan Murphy this morning, maybe something about a court hearing.

He looks around, presumably for Ronnie. He speaks in a low voice. 'Philippa, I'm leaving here in a few weeks.'

'Why are you leaving?' she whispers.

'I've got a new job. Night security at the Wolverson quarry,' he says proudly, puffing out his chest. 'Mary's going back to work, so I'll be on nights and she's on days. Suits us both down to the ground. I haven't told Ronnie yet, you know?'

She doesn't really know. Ronnie is a pain in the arse, but she's not sure what impact telling him will have. He certainly won't be upset.

'Because they'll need a new manager here,' he says, filling in the gaps for her.

'Oh right.'

'And he'll want to apply.'

'Ohhh.'

'I know you've only been here a short while, but you're the best person for the job. You're the most dedicated employee I've had Philippa, perfectly reliable, meticulous in your work, and great with the customers. You show a genuine interest in them – I have to remind others to look customers in the eye.'

'Thank you. But I don't think I could be a manager. I wouldn't know what to do.'

'You just make sure everyone else is doing their job.'

Truthfully she doesn't really know what other people's jobs are. She just focuses on her own. Things tick over and Ronnie works on the till and then outside on the machines when they need attention, saying inappropriate things, and Krish moves around making things happen, and Pip just makes rolls.

She doesn't even handle the money. She wraps the sandwiches and rolls, weighs them at the deli counter, sticks a price tag on the wrapping, and hands it to the customer to pay at the cashier.

'You don't want to be making breakfast rolls for ever,' he says. 'Especially with that toad as a boss, and I'm sure you have plans for you and Isabella. I'd rather see it go to you, and I'll tell them as much.'

Which makes her stop smiling, not at Ronnie becoming her boss, though the idea of it is horrific, but firstly she doesn't just make breakfast rolls, there are a plethora of options she provides, but mostly because he assumed that this job was just one rung on a ladder for her and her 'plans for Isabella'. What plans does she have?

Pip thinks ahead to the end of summer, Bella will go back to school and Pip will probably have to take her old job back at the observatory canteen alongside Josephine. In daydreams her thoughts have wings, in real life, they are clipped, so that is as far as her thoughts are allowed to go.

At the deli counter there are two questions she asks everyone who seems amenable to a conversation, and that's, 'Where are you going?' and 'Where have you been?'

Everyone that passes through here, bar the locals that she already knows, are going somewhere. It's a stop-off point, it's never the final destination. There's a transient air, like at an airport or train station. Sometimes they elaborate, explaining why they're travelling or a bit more about the place they're going to if they're the chatty type. She loves those answers. She loves hearing about other places.

Because Pip never goes anywhere.

3

AFTER WORK, PIP'S DAD, Philip, is outside waiting for her in his car. He's still wearing his high-vis jacket from the quarry. She sees the luminous orange before she sees him, like another layer of his skin. His shirt is rolled up to his elbows, a thick forearm resting on the car door, the window open.

Shovel hands.

King Silent.

Quarry man.

Disappointed.

The disappointment is quiet but not a secret, and is directed at her. Philip has worked at the Wolverson quarry that specialises in aggregate, cement and blocks, ever since he left school at seventeen years old. It employs most of the men in Ballybeg. The quarry has been in the Wolverson family for generations. In with the politicians, and the community, the Wolversons are like local celebrities, playing a part in many families' lives. Philip reveres them, forever grateful to them for what they provide him, his family and the town. He won't have a bad word be spoken about them.

He's had just about every job in the quarry since he was seventeen years old, from a crusher labourer, to a forklift operator, to a digger and excavator, to an explosive blaster. Now he's a blast supervisor. The physical nature of his work has been tough on his body. He has problems with his back, repetitive strain injury from the heavy lifting. Pip recalls him sleeping on the floor on his back from early childhood. No wonder she's an only child.

Philip is big and strong, built like a rock himself, with hard skin, calloused and dry, craggy, lined face, cracks where he smiles, cracks where he frowns, like he is part-man, part-quarry. A limestone leviathan.

'What's that?' he asks, looking at the package in her hands as she gets into the car beside him.

'I had something delivered to work. I'd miss it if it was to go to our house. They won't leave it at the door.'

'What is it?'

'Paper.'

More specifically kami or koiy paper. A ream of 500 pages, clear, crisp, empty. Cotton white. Yet to be filled. A world of possibilities. It excites her. She hugs the package to her chest.

'What do you need it for?'

'It's photograph paper. For the printer,' she says, lying.

He has no interest in photographs, in taking them on his phone, nor in printing them. That'll be the last he ever asks about that. But he is like Josephine in that he wants to know everything. When either Bella or Pip want to leave the room they naturally say where they're going. If they don't, they'll be asked. No one just comes and goes. You don't just accept a parcel at the door without saying what it is. You don't just pop out of the house for a few hours without saying where you're going. It's always been like that, which is a natural way for parents to be with a child, but less so with a thirty-two-year-old.

She's aware of the constant monitoring, and yet speaking out only causes an upset that makes her life more difficult, and Pip is firmly a non-confrontational kind of person.

Pip strains her neck to look into Jamie's house as they drive by, but the nice, tidy, decent home with the perfect garden has returned to its quiet calm state. Hanging baskets by the front door, vibrant with colour. The garden bench under the front window. When Pip used to stand on the back of the bench, then used the windowsill to propel her to stand on the hanging basket bracket, to get on top of the front porch roof, she could climb in and out of Jamie's bedroom window unnoticed. Which is what she did many times when they were teenagers.

She bites her lip to hide her smile as she remembers when her foot missed the bracket and it had almost ended in death. She can still hear Jamie's strangled laughter as she slipped climbing out of his window and slid down the slanted porch roof on her bum, afraid of breaking her neck, but more afraid of being caught and so stifling her screams. She'd never seen him laugh so much. The memory of lying on the cold wet grass while looking up at the star-filled night sky, his head popping out of his bedroom window, his white teeth glowing in the darkness as he laughed hysterically, chestily and wheezily, makes her smile.

They took him away, but they can't steal her memories of him.

Josephine and Bella are home when she returns. Josephine's car is in the driveway of their newly built house. Philip built it himself, it took him four years, worn ragged after physical work in the quarry, he then spent all of his free time working on the house with whichever friend or tradesman he could find after hours.

It's the house of his dreams. His own plot of land, out of the hustle and bustle of town where they lived all of her life. You can't walk to town, the road is too dangerous, with no paths, and Pip doesn't know how to drive so she's at the mercy of her parents to drop her everywhere. She misses the freedom of being able to walk to where she needs to go.

Across the road from their house are five other houses, built fifty yards away from each other. Tom and Mary Fitzgerald own the land opposite. They divided it into separate plots and built three houses for their three daughters. One of their children moved away and sold the house to the Brennans. Then there is another house next to them, the Slatterys, an older couple with grown-up children and lots of grandchildren.

Their neighbour Aleksy gets out of his car as they approach their house, and walks with crutches to his front door. Pip prepares to wave, but he doesn't look their way. The neighbours never wave, they never look over, heads always down and avoiding them. If she's not being paranoid, she assumes they're angry that a house has been built on the land across from them, obstructing their view of the landscape. Who knows.

Philip goes to his garage at the side of the house, reaches into the hanging basket for his key to unlock the door, whistling happily. The garage is cluttered with car parts, machine parts, bits and pieces of everything. The end of something, the beginnings of something else. He hasn't completed the house yet, once he got it to a stage fit to move into, his work slowed. The exterior walls haven't been painted, wires jut out from the walls here and there. Some would see it as an incomplete concrete grey box, but Philip and Josephine see so much more. They see a dream come true, they see their future.

Pip sees the same; *their* dream, and *their* future.

'Right,' Philip says, rolling the house plans out on the kitchen table and not bothering about moving the things beneath it. Josephine looks at Pip pointedly and Pip scrambles to put away the milk carton, the jam, the butter dish that has already left its greasy stain on the house plans. By the time she returns to the table, the three of them have claimed their spaces and are all huddled around it.

Pip stands behind Bella, looks over her head, not looking at the plans at all, just happy to be so close to her daughter who, at twelve, finds physical closeness ick. She smells her apple shampoo, the hair that she washes herself now.

She tries not to breathe too heavily, not wanting to move, wanting to hold on to such a rare moment. Bella shudders dramatically at her mother's proximity to her, elbowing Pip away. She makes more room for her.

Pip understands the layout straight away, while it takes an excruciating moment for Philip to talk Josephine through it, slowly telling her which drawing is for upstairs and which is downstairs and where the front door is. They take their time talking about every single aspect. Pip tunes out, she doesn't care where the tumble dryer will be, she's looking at the upstairs layout.

Three bedrooms. Two double rooms. One single. Two en suite. One bathroom. She can tell just by looking at the drawing where Josephine and Philip will sleep. Their en suite has a bath. Philip loves his baths. He needs them for his aches and pains.

Which means the second double bedroom is hers. She imagines her room, the colours, the bed. She's never had a double bed before, like a hotel suite, like an adult. Her own shower, so she doesn't have to share as they all do now in the terraced house in town that was designed for living in the 1940s.

She has to act likes she's listening as they talk about electrical sockets and light fittings, all the time living in her new room, in *her big bed, so many pillows on it there's barely enough room for her. A space of her own.*

And finally they get upstairs.

'This is our room,' Philip says, prodding the back bedroom with the bath with his thick tree trunk finger, bigger than the double bed.

Pip imagines a giant finger emerging from the ceiling, exploding plaster, and landing on the bed, messing the tidy bedding, sending pillows spilling over the edges to the floor.

'Can I have this room?' Bella says excitedly, leaning over, her fingers with the chipped nail polish poking at the second double room that Pip is already currently living in.

Pip smiles, at Bella's excitement, at her sweet desire to have such an adult room.

'Indeed you can,' Josephine says, reaching out and running her hand through Bella's hair.

'Now yours doesn't have a bath like ours does, but you'll have a shower.'

Pip's smile is frozen, she doesn't want them to know how she'd already moved into that room and lived there in her head for the past ten minutes. Folded all her clothes away into the drawers, hung her new dresses in the wardrobes. She'd chosen her bed linen and plumped her pillows. She keeps her eyes down on the plans, her eyes getting hotter and wanting to kill the tears that threaten.

While they talk about bedside tables and placements for furniture, she tries to feel engaged. She should want this for her daughter. She should want the best for her. She wants to give her everything.

But her eyes grow hotter and she can't but think the opposite.

She has already given her daughter everything. She's given her her whole life, her teenage years, her twenties, her entire future.

All she wanted was that one room.

Pip carries the ream of paper upstairs to the box bedroom. Bella's door is closed, music is playing. Bella would lock her bedroom door if she could, but Josephine has rules. Pip hesitates outside, wondering what she could say to be deemed important enough to disturb her. Nothing comes to her.

She goes inside her room; a single bed along one wall, a two-door wardrobe and a small white desk. The desk and chair is Pip's favourite part of the room. Everything is white.

The window looks out to the front of the house, across the peatlands. She sees sky forever, and even though the view never changes, it's never the same on any given day. Sometimes the patchwork landscape is colourful and vibrant, the clouds above casting shadows and light below, sometimes the grey sky makes the entire landscape look grey. Ash-grey clouds, grey-blue grass, slate-grey bogs.

It's beautiful every time.

The smell of turf from every chimney in the town is the smell of home. The bogs have provided for the town, fuel for homes, fuel to sell, fuel for the soul. The bogs take, and the bogs give.

Her desk is pristine, everything in its place. She loves organising it, getting see-through plastic organisers for her desk drawers, for her pens and stationery.

She removes the new paper from the package and places it in the drawer beneath the desk. She places a fresh page on the desk.

She smooths the page out and focuses on it. Crisp paper on white desk. It's a moment, her moment, and she can make it whatever she wants it to be. The sunlight shines through the window on to her page, as if setting the spotlight, the light encouraging her, helping her words to blossom and flourish.

It has been a big day. Lorcan Murphy's arrest has brought Jamie into her mind for most of it. She'd heard about what happened in more detail later in the day from a customer travelling to Rosslare Harbour, with his car filled with family members and suitcases on their way to a camping holiday in France. Lorcan had been warned repeatedly to stop cutting turf on the land. He failed to show for two court hearings and so the judge issued a warrant for his arrest. He's back home under strict orders to appear at the third hearing.

Surely Jamie will return to join the family in this crisis.

Jamie's no longer a physical part of her life, but he hasn't left her heart for one beat.

She tilts the page on the desk diagonally, in line with the position of her hand, a ballpoint pen snug between her fingers, and in very small writing, she writes:

Origami girl
Has an origami heart
She folds it
And folds it again
Disguising it
As a triangle
Makes it so small
No one can see it
Or find it.
She hides it away
  For safe keeping

Pip carefully folds the paper in a series of movements that calm her mind. She never knows in advance what shape the paper will take, but as she starts to fold, all of a sudden she has folded her way into a new character, or shape. She takes her time and, as she goes through the hypnotic motions, her mind clears. She has created an origami heart, her writing hidden inside, along with a teeny triangle that she tucks into one of the folds.

She takes a box from the drawer and places the origami heart inside with the dozens of other origami shapes, and puts the box away.

In a safe place. So nobody can find it.

4

JOSEPHINE CALLS BELLA AND Pip for dinner at six p.m. Pip waits to hear Bella's door open and as soon as it does, she steps out at the same time so they're next to each other. She acts surprised to see her, what a coincidence. Bella's sixteen-year-old world momentarily seeps out. She closes the door behind her to stop it.

'Hi,' Pip says, smiling at her. 'How was your day?'

Pip enjoys this part of the day, the short moment she has to herself with Bella as they make their way downstairs for dinner. It reminds her of when she used to collect Bella from school and the walk home would be filled with Bella talking nonstop about her day all the way from the school gate to the front door of their house. If only Pip could have more of those moments of uninterrupted connection.

They sit at the table in the kitchen.

'Any news today?' Josephine asks.

The biggest news of course is Lorcan Murphy, being taken into Garda custody, but nobody will discuss that. The mere mention of Lorcan Murphy alludes to the terrible, terrible thing that Pip did to all of them, that they've had to suffer through; getting pregnant at sixteen years old. Bella's connection to that side of the family is an awkward Sunday dinner once a month, accompanied by Josephine. Bella would do anything to try and get out of going.

Philip is first with the daily news. Someone was injured at the quarry and was rushed to hospital.

'He lost the tip of his finger,' he says, crunching on a mangetout. He tears the tip off and tosses the rest into his mouth.

He mostly eats with his fingers, forgets his cutlery are tools.

'Another accident?' Bella asks with her mouth full, always ready to ask the very questions that Pip swallows.

'Don't talk with your mouth full,' Josephine replies, and that's the only response that Bella gets.

'Krish is leaving in a few weeks,' Pip says, filling the silence that ensues.

He'd said not to tell anyone, but she tells her parents everything. She wants to say that Krish is going to recommend her for the promotion, she's about to say it, but then doesn't. She doesn't want them to shoot down her hopes just yet, let her live with the dream for another little while.

'Where's he going?' Philip asks.

'A night security job at the quarry.'

His approval is instant and obvious. 'They'll take care of him there,' he says. 'And we need him.'

'His wife Mary is going back to work,' Pip says. She doesn't personally care about this news, but it's the kind of thing her parents like to hear. Tittle-tattle. Prittle-prattle.

'Five babies and a nurse, she's some woman,' Josephine says, taking a small fork of mashed potato. She has a tiny appetite, seems to exist on pure adrenaline.

Her comment feels like a jab to Pip. As though she's just a mother, but not 'some woman'. Barely a mother.

'Why did you two only have one child?' Bella asks suddenly, again asking a question Pip never dared ask them herself.

Bella dares, she oversteps the boundaries without seeing the barriers. She doesn't sense the tense silences, or if she does, she doesn't ever feel she belongs in them. If it's noisy, she shouts louder. This strained and contained existence that Pip lives in, is invisible, and she wrongly assumed Bella would live inside it with her too. To Pip's great awe and delight she watches her daughter growing older and unapologetically stretching to fill the spaces and shouting to fill the silences.

'More children?' Josephine asks. 'Sure wasn't Philippa as much work as five children? And don't we have you?'

Pip suddenly loses her appetite.

Josephine's voice on the phone sounds formal, strained. The type of voice she uses when she feels she can't get a word wrong. Like she's being interviewed at a police station or on the stand at trial. Every word is thought through in advance, every word is important. Pip immediately knows that she's talking to Maureen Murphy, Jamie's mother.

Pip pauses on the stairs to listen. She doesn't want to make a sound, or Josephine will halt the conversation.

'I understand that, but I think with everything you have going on now it's best that she doesn't visit with you this weekend. There was quite the stir this morning. It's best to wait until it passes.'

Josephine will use any event as an excuse to keep Bella to herself, even though the people in question are Bella's grand-parents. Josephine hasn't loosened her grip on Bella since she was born, if anything, she is grasping her tighter.

The chair leg screeches against the floor and Pip can

imagine her mother sitting rod straight at the kitchen table, the mind of an emotional schemer moving a million miles an hour as she tries to get into prime position.

Pip can only imagine what Maureen is saying. *We want to see Isabella. Why won't you let us see more of Isabella?*

It's Bella.

Pip had chosen Bella's name, and Jamie had agreed. They both loved the name.

Bella. They had agreed on Bella, and three weeks after she was born they're sitting in the HSE civil registration office to register Bella's birth. Josephine and Maureen sit between Pip and Jamie. They've barely been allowed to look at each other since news of the pregnancy broke. They haven't been in the same room as each other for two weeks. She gave birth without him, he'd been granted mere minutes with his own child. They could barely speak in the cubicle. He'd held Bella in his arms, in the armchair beside her hospital bed, the blue curtain behind him. She wanted to pretend her mother wasn't there with them, monitoring them, as if he'd jump into bed with her fresh after her giving birth.

He'd been so worried about her, kept asking if she was okay. He was so besotted with his daughter. She has his eyelashes. He'd played with her little toes, run his fingers over her fingers, as if counting them and marvelling at the miracle. Occasionally he'd look up at Pip and smile. And even though the situation felt hopeless, they'd been ripped apart from each other and their lives felt rotten, she felt such hope in his beam. He had so much love for Bella.

Pip feels Josephine's embarrassment at being at the civil registration office with her young daughter. When Bella cries, Josephine reaches for her immediately.

Josephine has filled out the registration form, Maureen oversaw it. Jamie and Pip merely signed it. Pip didn't even read it, Jamie was shoved roughly by his mother when he started reading from the top.

Jamie is handed a copy of the birth certificate.

'Bella,' he says, suddenly, the first word out of his mouth all day. 'Her name is supposed to be Bella.'

Alarmed, Pip tries to take a look at it, but Josephine pulls it away.

'You can't put that on the birth cert,' Josephine says, her anger flaring. 'it's not a real name. Officially it will have to be Isabella.'

'But that's not the name we wanted,' Jamie says, devastated. He looks as though he's about to cry. He looks to Pip for backup, but she can't. She focuses on the floor. She can't deal with the confrontation. Not in public, not ever. She's exhausted. Drained physically and emotionally. She hasn't the energy for another battle with Josephine, she hasn't the energy for another loss. Every moment of every day is exhausting. But in that moment, in looking for a place to hide, a moment of surrender, she feels she has betrayed him.

She is so exhausted she falls asleep in the car on the way home. She's woken by Josephine pulling at her shirt, opening her buttons.

'Isabella needs to feed,' she says, placing her tiny baby in her arms.

Back on the stairs, Pip listens to the one-sided phone conversation, to Josephine's final parting words.

'Will he come home, do you think?' Josephine asks, her voice going up a telltale octave. 'Well, let me know when you do know. It's important for me to know these things.'

They're talking about Jamie. Pip's heart pounds faster at the idea of him returning.

'Between us, Maureen, we'll work out what's best for Isabella.'

And that's the way it has always been.

Pip quietly retreats upstairs and, feeling jittery and power-less, she does one of the only things that calms her and gives her control – crafting words and paper. She sits at her desk.

Origami girl
Has an origami baby
Birthing her
Rips her delicate paper
She folds her baby
Once,
Then twice,
And tucks her inside
A fold of her own
So no one
Can take her
> *Away*

5

P IP LIES ON HER bed and looks at the 'Bridge over a Pond of Water Lilies' print by Monet on the wall above her desk. She could and has spent hours at a time studying it.

Art had been her favourite subject at school. She had enjoyed disappearing from conventional school and immersing herself in another world. She liked the paint on her fingers and stains on her uniform as she re-joined the other students in her next lesson. The woodwork boys emerged with sawdust on their jumpers and cuts on their fingers, the technical drawing crowd carried their T-squares over their shoulders as though they were back from digging a mine, the art students emerged as if they'd been on an adventure, on an outdoor excursion to examine shadow and light, or to find as many different shades of one colour as they could. These art wildlings, soul-slippers, sliding back into conventional academic life.

She was pregnant when she began writing the Origami Girl poems. She wanted to make herself smaller, but she kept getting bigger. She started to fold herself up in other ways, and keep everything in under layers, and the origami naturally occurred. Her pen finds words she can't say out loud, her fingers find the shapes, the shapes form feelings she can't express in any other way.

She doesn't need to open the box of poems to remember her first ever Origami Girl poem, it's in her mind:

Origami girl
Is a paper thin girl
So fine
And delicate
Made stronger by folding.
But underneath
She still hurts.

Her favourite artist at school was Monet and, while she didn't have the opportunity to finish school, or further her art studies, he was the artist she'd continued to be inspired by. Perhaps it was because his work reminded her of a time when she felt young, happy, free, without the shame and the disappointment. Having Bella had brought about many beautiful moments in her life, every day something new to celebrate, every giggle, every song, every word, tooth and first step were joyful unbeatable moments, she could never wish this child and this raw joy away, but it was also the event that altered her. Before, she was carefree, in love, naïve, confident. The woman that emerged after was heartbroken, afraid, apologetic, and lacked confidence.

A framed print of the water lilies painting hangs over her white desk and is the only splash of colour in her otherwise bleached bedroom. She likes the calm feeling her little space brings her, her only own thing in this house. Her mother is prone to clutter, filling every shelf and surface with something, and piling things up in corners and in drawers, even in this new house.

To Josephine, Pip's room seems unfinished. A blank canvas.

Perhaps Josephine is correct about that part – it is a canvas, for her to reflect her imagination, thoughts, dreams, desires upon. Not all of them visible to the naked eye. The projector is in her mind.

Pip watches the Monet painting for so long it seems to move. The water in the pond ripples. It spreads out to fill her canvas wall, she looks around the frame and imagines the wall cracking, the pressure of the water building against it and threatening to break through, spilling from the painting.

She frowns and sits up. She really does see a crack in the wall. She walks over and notices for the first time, a crack next to the bottom left corner of the white frame. She touches it and feels her way along it to the frame.

Did she make this happen with her mind?

She lifts the frame away from the wall at the bottom and her eyes follow the line of the crack, which travels all the way up to the nail she hammered into the wall for her print.

She can't tell Philip about the crack. She can't tell any of them. She'd been working so hard to remain under the radar, she had sent tremors through her and her family sixteen years ago, and they'd scrambled for so long after that. Moving house, building their dream home was a new beginning. She couldn't be responsible for any more cracks appearing.

She opens her top drawer and roots around for a sketch.

'Girls! Dinner!' Josephine calls.

Bella's music is playing, she won't hear. It will be up to Pip to call her.

'Okay!' Pip shouts.

With trembling hands she looks through all of the loose pieces of paper with her sketches and attempts at poetry. She is proud of them, which is why they're in the drawer and not in the bin, but she wants to keep her art private, not something else for Josephine to criticise, dissect and disassemble.

'Girls!' Josephine calls again.

Pip opens her door a crack. 'I'll get Bella!' she calls down, and then closes it.

Sketches of flowers. Almost matchstick-like. She likes rudimentary designs, her own style a complete contrast to Monet's. Her own are always sharp, pencil drawings. Flowers with corners and edges, which is why origami appeals to her.

She comes across a sketch of Pip's baby foot, in her own hand. It makes her smile.

She hears angry footsteps. The floor shakes as Josephine pounds up the stairs.

Pip pushes the drawer closed and tucks the sketch of the baby foot under the frame, where it just about manages to hide the crack.

Her bedroom door opens violently and hits her on the shoulder as she jumps away.

'Ow!'

'Well what are you doing in here?' Josephine snaps, getting a fright and moving directly to anger. Always defensive. Always right.

'I'm just finishing up.'

'Finishing up what?' she asks, eyeing Pip's desk as if it's going to attack her. Josephine does not like the unknown.

She opens the door fully and looks inside suspiciously, as if Pip is still a teenager smoking in her room. Pip's conscious of the crack in her wall, she feels it throbbing.

'I'll get Bella,' Pip says quickly.

Pip guards this part of the day. Calling on Bella and the two of them going downstairs together. Catching up on a little bit of Bella's life, having the freedom to possibly make an impact on her daughter. Plant something positive and guiding in her head, share something with her, learn something from her, crack a joke and enjoy hearing her laugh. Whatever she can get. It's two minutes.

'You get downstairs. Isabella!' Josephine calls, knocking on her door and waiting.

Huffy, Pip goes downstairs alone, her two minutes, on top of all the other minutes, stolen from her.

6

AT THE DELI COUNTER, at lunchtime, a man stands before Pip, arms folded, examining the salad bar. He has blond hair in a layer haircut, white shirt, rolled up sleeves to his elbows, black pants. He's tall, and lean. Ice blue eyes.

'Can I help you?' Pip asks.

'I hope so,' he says, looking so lost, she has to laugh.

'Let me guess, you're a Libran,' she says, and on his baffled look adds, 'Libra? The star sign? Librans are one of the worst decision makers.'

'My star sign?'

He's from somewhere outside of Ireland, she hears the hint of an accent, as if English isn't his first language.

'Or zodiac sign. A person's sign of the zodiac is the one that the sun was in when they were born. Astrologists believe that a person's personality can be predicted using their sign of the zodiac.'

'Fascinating!' he says, his eyes lighting up. 'You're an astrologist.'

She laughs, pushing her hairnet up from where it had fallen to her eyebrows. 'Clearly not.'

He smiles. 'But you're interested in stars?'

'I'm interested in which sandwich you'd like.'

He sighs, heavy with the load of indecision. His eyes scan the salads and cold meats, not looking any wiser.

'If you don't know what you want, I'll go first,' the customer beside him says loudly, overtaking him in the queue. 'Hello Philippa.'

Even now at thirty-two years of age, Pip feels the compulsion to genuflect to Sammy Wolverson, who is standing behind the counter of her lowly salad bar.

She looks to the customer apologetically. She can't tell a Wolverson off.

Since she was a child, if ever she was in the company of a Wolverson it was like being in the company of a god, such was Philip's deep respect for them.

'It must be hard to be a Wolverson,' he'd say, as if being them was a great gift but also an affliction, like royalty. With great duty comes great responsibility.

'Hello, Mr Wolverson,' she says. Chin up, stand tall, speak clearly.

Sammy smiles. 'Call me Sammy, please.'

She's not sure Philip would like her to call him that, but she's also sure he wouldn't like her to disagree with a Wolverson.

His teeth are perfectly straight and white. She focuses on them, wondering if they're veneers. He looks like those people on Instagram who filter their faces. He's in front of her, looking like a pore-less Desperate Dan, but very much real. Among the many useless facts and theories she'd read on social media was that men's physical appearances could be broken down into four animal-based categories; eagle, bear, dog or reptile handsome. Bear handsome is a round face and broad shoulders, reptilian handsome has a straight nose and sharp eyes, dog handsome men have big eyes and a cheeky grin, eagle handsome men have small eyes and a long nose. Sammy Wolverson is both bear and dog handsome; big, broad, round and cheeky.

Self-assured.

Pristine condition.

Threaded eyebrows?

Smooth.

'What can I get for you, Sammy?'

'Oh. Uh.' He straightens up and looks over her head at the menu. 'Gimme a hot chicken roll.'

'Brown or white?'

He leans his hand against the glass display unit. His nails are perfectly manicured, not a hint of dirt or grazes or cuts, unlike her dad's after a day in the quarry. His hands are huge, like the rest of him. He's broad, not muscular, but big. Big bones, big head. Bronze skin.

'Brown meat. I'm a thigh man.'

Her indecisive customer lifts the corner of his lip in amusement. She avoids his eye.

'I meant, brown or white roll?'

'Oh. Brown. Whatever.' He thinks she missed the innuendo. She didn't. She's not stupid, just polite. 'How's your girl, Isabella?'

This will be one of the rare times she doesn't correct somebody on her daughter's name.

'She's very well, thank you.'

'She must be what, twelve now?'

'She's sixteen.'

'Jaysus. I bet you don't take your eye off her.'

Because of what Pip did at sixteen. She blushes.

'She's a good girl,' she says.

'I'm sure she is. So how are you settling into the new house?'

'Great thanks. Dad has done a fine job.'

'I've no doubt. A brick of a man like him?'

She laughs. 'Would you like butter or mayonnaise?'

'Whatever you think.'

She pauses for a moment. She has no opinion on butter or mayonnaise, it's a question of personal taste. She eats a salad bowl, but this is a Wolverson and they are used to the best, in their country manor with their house staff, so she spreads butter on one side of the bread roll and mayonnaise on the other.

'Your dad has invited me over to see the house.'

She looks up at him, surprised.

'When's the best time for me to visit?'

She's conscious of her indecisive friend next in line, listening. She takes chicken from the hot section and slices it neatly and arranges it on the roll. Extra care for a Wolverson. Gourmet deli roll.

'I suppose I'd leave that up to you both to decide whatever suits yourselves. Would you like anything else on the roll?'

'No . . . uh. . .' he looks down as if seeing food in front of him for the first time. 'Tomato.'

She reaches for the tomato with her too big gloves, trying not to get her fingers and the plastic all tangled with the juicy tomato slices, she places them on top of the hot chicken.

'I'd like to go when you're there.'

He's a thigh man and he wants to visit her house when she's there. A Wolverson. She fights the urge to glance at her customer, she can feel his eyes searing into her.

'Would you like anything else? On the roll?'

He smiles. His eyes are soft.

'Yeah. Cheese,' he says, not looking down, eyes not moving from hers. 'And peppers. And egg. And red onions.'

He's just listing off anything he can think of to stay longer. 'And raisins.'

She feels heat rising in her cheeks. She smiles politely. 'We don't have raisins.'

He grins and watches her intently as she goes about applying all of those fillings to his roll. All of a sudden she's conscious of everything she does. She feels like she's under a microscope. Her long brown hair up in a hairnet. She's wearing the red service station uniform T-shirt, the red squirrel logo on her left breast. Suddenly her dad's rules feel stupid. Stand tall and speak clearly.

She places the wrapped roll on the weighing scales. It's a hefty price for a hefty roll. She prints out the price, sticks it to seal the wrapper and hands it across the counter to him.

'What about this evening?' Sammy asks. 'What time are you finished here?'

She hesitates, glances right, to her other customer.

He shakes his head.

'Four.' Mr Wolverson, sir. 'But my dad collects me.'

'I'll pick you up here and we can head straight there. I can tell him at work.'

She's torn as to what decision to make. She knows Philip wouldn't approve of her arranging lifts home with men at the deli counter, but it's a Wolverson. He wouldn't want her to insult him.

'Okay,' she says in a small voice.

Pip keeps her head down as Mr Indecisive slides along. She's barely able to meet his eye after what he heard.

'What would you like?'

'A lot less than him. Plus, you won't have to go out with me.'

She smiles and takes him in.

Tall man.

Slender build.

Reptilian handsome.

Kind.

'He's my dad's boss,' she says, feeling the need to explain the exchange.

'They should supply you with smaller gloves,' he says, watching her slide a fresh pair of gloves on, the tips hanging off her small hands.

She'd never thought of asking for them. She deals with what she has. Though in her first week she chopped off the tip of a glove when she was slicing a sandwich, and almost added the tip to the filling.

'Everything okay over here?' Krish asks, possibly excited that he'd just served his future boss Sammy Wolverson at the till.

'Your colleague needs smaller gloves.'

The customer has said it easily, good-natured, with a charming smile, nothing rude or spicy.

Krish looks down at her hands and seems to notice for the first time.

'My goodness Philippa, they are the wrong size. Did we change the box?'

'No, this is how they've always been since I started.'

'Why did you never say?'

He roots around in the cupboards beneath the deli counter. 'Katarzyna, who worked here before you was bigger even than me. We ordered them for her and, a-ha here we go.' He places a box down on the counter beside her. 'Small. That should be a lot better.'

'Thank you,' she says, surprised.

'Pump three needs to be reset,' Ronnie shouts out across the shop, in exactly the way they are not allowed to.

'Enjoy your food sir,' Krish says, and off he goes to solve the next problem.

Pip peels off her oversized gloves and throws them in the bin. She tries on the new size. Her fingertips reach the ends, her hands aren't swimming around inside, having to do extra work to grip the spoons or the knife. She will be far more efficient with these gloves.

'There. Wasn't so hard was it?' he says.

'Thank you.'

'I'm not looking for thanks. It's easy to fix things. Little things, bit by bit,' he says, surveying the salad bar closely. Each food type gets very careful consideration.

Sometimes people are indecisive, but there is something quirky about him, and Pip likes him instantly.

'I'm here for a few weeks,' he says. 'I want to ease myself into this. Where should I start?'

They settle on a cheese sandwich on brown bread without butter or mayonnaise. He doesn't like the look of the wet foods.

'Where are you from?' she asks.

'Don't you want to know where I'm going on holiday?'

She grins. He'd been listening to her questions to the construction workers in line before him.

'They're all from around here, I want to hear about somewhere else. I'd ask you where you're going, but I already know the answer to that.'

'And where's that?'

'The observatory.'

'How observant.'

She can see an ID badge hanging from his neck, the ID part tucked into his shirt top pocket. She recognises the black lanyard from the employees she served in the canteen. 'The options are limited around here.'

'I disagree,' he says, gesturing towards the deli selection.

She laughs.

'There's a canteen at the observatory,' she tells him, unsure as to why he's getting lunch here. 'They do hot food. You get two options every day. And a vegetarian option.'

'Which makes three choices.'

'Only one choice if you're vegetarian.'

'You could choose not to be vegetarian.'

She laughs, noticing how he has sidestepped answering where he is from, which makes her even more intrigued. She's charmed by him, he's put her in a good mood with her snug-fitting deli gloves.

'I used to work at the observatory canteen with my mam. She's the little one,' and then adds conspiratorially, 'with the temper.'

He grins. 'Don't tell her I'm here.'

Pip wouldn't dare mention that an observatory employee chose her deli bar over the canteen. 'You'll see her tomorrow. Top tip: if you're unhappy with any element of your food, just deal with it.'

'No, I'll see *you* tomorrow,' he says, lifting his sandwich proudly in the air. 'I look forward to hearing about your date with Sammy the boss.'

'It's not a date,' she says, laughing.

'My name is Io. And you're Philippa?' he asks, having heard Sammy say her name.

'Pip, actually.'

There are people you can spend a lifetime trying to warm to, and there are those who feel like old friends on a first encounter.

7

As soon as Sammy Wolverson's Range Rover pulls up outside their house, the front door opens. Philip fills the entire width of the door, with tiny Josephine peeking out from behind.

'You'd think you'd have built a bigger door for this big lad,' is Sammy's opening line as he approaches them with his hand out.

Philip responds with something technical about the door-frame, which isn't funny, nor is it supposed to be, and that ends that banter.

Last in, Pip closes the door. She sees her neighbour, Caroline, across the road in her garden washing her car. She lifts her hand in a wave, and Caroline looks away and turns her back to her. Pip slowly closes the door.

She follows them all to the kitchen where Bella is waiting, dressed in her leggings and crop top, her arms folded. Her skin glows, her long hair shines. Her daughter really is so beautiful.

Philip straightens himself up in the presence of a Wolverson. In his house. She can feel his energy, the pride, the excitement. Josephine steps in.

'This is Isabella, Isabella this is Mr Wolverson.'

'Sammy, please.'

'Hiya,' Bella says confidently, waving once.

'Nice to meet you,' he says, examining her.

'Are you all right?' she asks, cheekily.

'Isabella,' Josephine corrects her, embarrassed.

'That's okay. I'm trying to see her mother in her.'

'Okay,' Bella says, eyeballs going left and right as if he's a weirdo.

'I can see her all right,' he says. 'Across the eyes and nose.'

He's right. They're not obviously mother and daughter, most people think they're sisters, but people who know them can see the likeness. She's surprised, in a good way, that Sammy has recognised her in Bella. She can only imagine this has annoyed Josephine. Score one for Sammy.

'Isabella is the image of my sister Helen,' Josephine says. She just can't help herself.

Sammy looks around the kitchen. His eyes settle on the kitchen table, which is adorned with a tray of sliced gourmet wraps and a freshly baked apple pie.

'What a fine spread you have here,' he says.

Bella makes a face.

He pulls out a chair to sit down, dwarfing the chair. He reaches for a wrap.

'I wonder if this is as tasty as your daughter's.'

Bella makes another disgusted face.

Pip feels the corners of her mouth twitch.

'I had the greatest roll for lunch today,' he says to Josephine and Philip, before popping the entire thing in his mouth.

Josephine raises an amused eyebrow, as if she doubts that.

Philip and Josephine talk with Sammy about his dad enjoying retirement, about former employees and Philip's colleagues. Philip's not one for long stories, or for speaking generally, but once he gets started on a story about the quarry, it's hard to stop him. Sammy can though. Before Philip even gets halfway or is nearing the point he's about to make, Sammy jumps in and takes over, or changes the subject. If it bothers Philip, he doesn't show it.

Pip listens, the obedient child, while Bella occasionally takes her phone out of her pocket and scrolls before being smacked in the leg by Josephine to put it away.

'Any news from the Murphy side of the family?' Sammy asks, gulping his tea. Josephine has taken out her fine china, the set that usually sits in a display unit and is only taken out for Christmas or for special visitors. The fragile teacup looks comical in his large hand. He finishes most of the contents in one gulp.

Pip feels the family momentarily freeze at his question.

Sammy slowly lowers the teacup, eyes looking from one person to the next. Pip sees the amusement in his face, he's entertained by their awkwardness, thrives on drama.

'Is your dad going to come back for the trial?' he asks Bella.

Bella shrugs.

His eyes land on Pip.

She looks at her parents.

'It's a delicate situation,' Josephine says. 'Lorcan Murphy is a stubborn man.'

'It's his land,' Philip says, 'You can understand.' Man-to-man, landowner-to-landowner.

'It's not his land now. It's protected blanket bog. Don't they want more butterflies and bees on it now, isn't that the idea?' Sammy says with a grin.

Josephine is happy to drive a wedge between Bella and her other family. 'Didn't they give him another plot he can cut turf on for his own private use?'

'It's not the same,' Pip says, to everyone's surprise. 'When somebody tells you what you can and cannot do with something that's your own.'

There's a silence.

'Well,' Sammy says, slapping his hands on his thick thighs. 'Who's going to give me the tour?'

'Pip will,' Josephine says.

Startled, Pip snaps to attention. She clears her throat. 'Sure. So.' She stands up. 'This is the kitchen.'

Bella snorts.

After viewing the rooms downstairs, Sammy follows Pip upstairs.

'Where the magic happens,' Sammy says, looking inside Philip and Josephine's master bedroom with a grin. 'I once walked in on my parents. Scarred me for life.'

Pip smiles politely. Philip wouldn't be pleased how little attention Sammy has paid to his house. His eyes are on her the entire time.

'Another double bedroom,' she says, pushing open Bella's door and half expecting her to wail up the stairs like a banshee at them for invading her privacy.

'After you,' he says, holding his hand out.

Pip enters her daughter's room for the first time in many months, happy to take the moment to see inside. It is very much Bella, stuff everywhere. Nail polish, skin care, hair care, clothes, make-up, bits and bobs. The bed is neatly made, covered in pillows with satin pillow covers to prevent her hair from frizzing.

Pip looks to the wall that she shares with Bella, and sees the crack in the same place.

He follows her gaze. 'Bad plastering job.'

'Dad did it.'

'Yeesh,' he says, making a face.

She feels offended on Philip's behalf.

He picks up a bottle of perfume and smells it. Sammy is different in this room. He takes it all in. He rubs the surface of the vanity table. He's interested in what's on the walls, and on the shelves. He walks inside the en suite and turns 360 degrees before stepping out. He's taking too long, taking too much in. It's disarming. And then, as he stares at the double bed, she feels uncomfortable. This is her sixteen-year-old daughter's bedroom.

'Let's move on,' she says, making her way to the door.

She's almost at the door when he takes a quick step to the side, blocking her path. Sammy's hair-free beefy chest is inches away from her nose. She looks up at him. Not a nose hair in sight. After a day in the quarry, how is this man all polished marble and her dad is all dust and crust?

On the outside he is a beautiful man. Well-groomed, flawless, but he makes her feel nervous. Smooth on the outside, something restless inside him.

'My room is next door,' Pip says. She doesn't want to take this to her room, but she wants to get out of this situation.

He looks confused.

'This is Bella's room,' she explains.

He puts the perfume bottle down as though it's diseased.

He frowns. 'I saw the plans. The third bedroom is a box bedroom.'

She shrugs. She walks past him to the landing and pushes her bedroom door open. 'There's only room for one person in there, I'll stay out here if you want to have a look.'

The door doesn't open all the way because it hits the end of her bed.

He has to step in sideways. He stands in the thin gap between the single bed and the wardrobe and window. Josephine wouldn't have needed to do any tidying in here, it's perfect, nothing out of place. White bed linen, white walls, wooden floor with a small circular rug by her bed. White locker with a white lamp. White wardrobe, white desk. White ceilings. A blank canvas.

She's annoyed now that her sketch is on the wall held up by the frame of the Monet print.

'You like Monet?'

'Yes.' Mr Wolverson, sir.

'Did you draw this?'

He steps closer to her desk. Based on how he was in Bella's room, she hopes he doesn't start rummaging in the drawers with all her prized possessions, her box of origami words and shapes, her heart outside her body in various forms.

'Yes.'

He moves his face close to her sketch of Bella's baby foot, in her hand.

'What's going on, Cinderella? Why does a sixteen-year-old have the big double bedroom and you're in here?'

'This room was supposed to be bigger, but they had an issue with the tank in the attic, and . . .' she trails off. He's not really listening.

'You should have a four-poster bed, your own bathroom. A TV on the wall. A walk-in wardrobe filled with everything you want. That's how I'd treat you.'

It's as though he has reached into her imagination and plucked out the room she'd dreamed of. The room that was taken away from her and given to Bella.

Tears prick her eyes. The humiliation.

'My daughter is more important than me,' she says, trying to hide the tremble in her voice. She meant it to sound as if she was the one who had made the decision, who had put her daughter first. She meant it in a nice motherly way. Not in the way he interprets it.

'You shouldn't put up with that from them,' he says. 'You deserve better.'

She's shocked by the pity in his tone, by the affirmation of unfairness.

'Let's go back downstairs,' he says, placing a gentle hand on her elbow.

When Sammy leaves, Philip and Josephine say nice things about him, both so perked up by his presence in their home. It's as though he has christened the place, and now they can officially settle in.

'Does he wear those little shoes at the quarry?' Bella asks sarcastically with a smirk.

He'd been wearing slip-on shoes, his trousers turned up to above his ankles. Smooth skin, not a hair in sight.

'Did he dock his boat outside? Why is he orange?' Bella asks, pushing everyone's buttons.

'Isabella,' Josephine says, angrily.

'What? His face is an unnatural colour. I should know. He must do sunbeds, or spray tans. Spray tan Sammy.'

'Stop,' Pip says, quietly. She's conflicted; he was kind to her.

Bella looks surprised, Pip would usually laugh at that kind of thing.

Philip grips a cup of tea in his hand. Like Sammy, only one finger fits inside the handle.

'He's a good man, from a good family. The Wolversons are

good people. He would be good for Pip,' he says proudly. The first man he has ever endorsed for Pip.

Good, good, good. As opposed to the other decisions she made, which were bad. And she's right back there again.

What she put them through.

The sacrifices she forced them to make.

For as long as Pip could remember they'd gone to ten a.m. mass at the Mary Immaculate Church. Josephine and Philip would come alive in that hour and the thirty minutes that follow outside the parish church catching up with the community. Every week Josephine would say the readings and the psalm, and Philip would assist the priest in giving communion. But during Pip's pregnancy, Josephine stopped her readings and Philip stopped his communion steward role. They were in turmoil about Pip's sin, in talks with the priest searching for healing and forgiveness, and no matter the size of her bump they made her waddle down the centre aisle every Sunday morning without fail while Pip tried to hide herself in bigger baggier jumpers, melting in the heat and under the gaze of the congregation.

The shame, the fear, the utter helplessness.

Could she not just this once make a good, respectable decision?

8

Pip can't sleep.

She feels a tightness in her chest. She opens her curtains and opens the window to let some space inside. The sky is clear, the stars are out, the moon is bright.

She lies back down, breathing easier now.

The moon shines through her window and onto her wall above the desk. It illuminates Monet's water lilies and her sketch.

Sammy's comment about the crack comes back to her. It was rude to criticise Philip's plastering work knowing that he'd worked so hard on the house and had been so proud to show him. And yet on the other hand, here is a man that isn't afraid to be critical of her dad. She doesn't have that in her life. Perhaps he's a man who will have her back.

The crack, which had been hidden behind the sketch, now peeks out from the side of the paper, visible again.

Maybe the night breeze blew the paper aside. Or maybe the crack is growing.

Pip studies her sketch of Bella's baby foot, the messy strokes of someone trying to find a shape in the chaos.

Pip hears a baby cry. It pierces her dream, becomes a part of her dream. An alarm or a seagull, or both. It transfers itself to many different things.

Then the screaming stops and she feels a sharp sting on her breast.

She opens her eyes and feels her mother's fingers pinch her nipple. She latches the baby on to her. She sits on the side of the bed holding Bella in situ.

Pip awakes properly and tries to sit up, though locked into position by how her mother is pressing the baby to her. Bella is sucking greedily on her nipple, making breathy noises as she quenches her thirst. Her eyes are open wide and watering from her tears. They lock eyes and Pip smiles. She loves these moments, as exhausted as she is.

When Bella has fallen asleep and stopped sucking, she wants to keep holding her warm little body like a comforting hot water bottle. But Josephine immediately lifts her from her arms.

'No, no . . .' Pip starts, trying to hold on to her.

'I'll be back in three hours. Get some sleep,' she says, taking Bella back into her and Philip's room and closing the door.

Pip, now wide awake, cries herself to sleep.

Sometimes Pip lies awake at night still feeling like that powerless seventeen-year-old. The torment is always the same. How to deepen her relationship with Bella, how to pull her away from Josephine's tight grip. Which relationships, both romantic and platonic, can Pip forge while allowing her to keep her daughter, so that it's not a trade.

Pip tried to leave once before. Bella was two years old, and after another criticism of her mothering skills, Pip packed her bags while Josephine and Philip were out working, and left with Bella.

Josephine now refers to it as the time she'd 'run away', even though Pip was an adult and a mother.

She was gone for three days, but it was a spur of the moment, badly thought through plan. Pip didn't have the money, the organisation or the support networks in place. She couldn't last as she was, sleeping in a cheap B&B, missing work and ignoring life just so she could be with Bella.

Eventually, Pip reached out to her best friend Jennifer, her cousin, who'd told her that her mother, Aunt Helen, would welcome her in. She could give her a loan, help set her up somewhere and make a plan.

Pip had gone to them, grateful to have someone hear her. She'd opened the floodgates and shared how controlling Josephine was at home, how Pip couldn't bear to witness Josephine mothering her own child. Everything that had been building up inside came out, and it felt good to say it out loud to comforting sounds, gentle hand holding, strong tea and plenty of tissues.

Then, as their conversation ended at the kitchen table, late at night, with Bella sleeping soundly beside them on the couch by an open fire, Pip heard the front door open, footsteps in the hall, hushed voices, and there was Josephine. Back in her life. She felt she'd been thrown back into the arms of her captor. Her family had betrayed her. Her friendship with her cousin and aunt was never the same again. She realised that blood was thicker than water, that they would always be Josephine's loyal followers, and that Josephine's behaviour would always be considered as being for Pip's own good.

Pip had failed, and maybe Josephine was right, she couldn't do it alone. She doesn't know why it didn't occur to her to go to Jamie.

Many of Pip's fantasies have been of her on the boat with Bella, their lives in a suitcase, going to Liverpool. As the ferry approaches the port, a crowd stands on the dock, like something out of *Titanic*, and there he is, Jamie, waiting for them. It's never an aeroplane, she supposes he left on a boat, and that's in her consciousness. He's always excited to see them, waving at them wildly from the dock, weaving in and out of the crowd. It's all very dramatic. Pip never gets off the boat. The fantasy always revolves around his joy as he greets them, her inner hope that he still dreams of uniting the family.

Restless, Pip gets out of bed and sits at her desk. She hears Philip's cough through the walls. She sorts through her box of origami shapes and finds the origami boy. Jamie. She too knows this poem by heart. She holds it in her hands and recites in a whisper:

Origami boy
Has an origami heart
So large it doesn't fit inside his chest
He crumples it,
    Angrily
So tight it won't open
Ever again.
As it beats
The paper slowly opens
He crumples
It beats
He crumples
It beats
Opening and closing,
Until it's open wide

Like a moonflower.

She places a fresh page on her desk. And writes.

Origami girl
Is swept up in a
Swirling,
Twirling,
Dizzying,
Tornado.
She senses something else
Spinning in the air
With her
They twirl
Like autumn leaves.
'Is it you?' she whispers.
The whirlwind
Steals her words away
Falling alone is scary
But
There is something
So soothing,
So comforting
In f
    a
       l
          l
            i
               n
                 g
with someone else.

She folds it into the shape of a girl and stores the origami girl and boy away together. This is the only place they can coexist. Jamie is yesterday. She needs to look at her tomorrow. A shape is taking form in the chaos, a shape in the form of Sammy.

9

'HAVE YOU THOUGHT ABOUT the promotion?' Krish asks Pip, when Ronnie is out of sight.

She had fantasised about herself as the ultimate accomplished manager many times. 'No. I don't think it's for me.'

'Why not?' Krish asks, surprised. 'You'd be a great manager, Philippa. Better than him, he's not even an option. They'll have to bring in someone new, none of the part-timers are interested in more hours.'

'It's just . . . the hours would be longer.'

'Not by much, you'll be well able for the responsibility. You're a very conscientious woman.'

'This job suits me because Mam drops me in the morning and Dad collects me on his way home.' There's no public transport from their new house to town.

She continues her work, clearing out the dried-out eggs from the hot plate that didn't make it to this morning's breakfast rolls.

'You could drive yourself to work.'

'I can't drive.'

'You could learn.'

'I don't have a car. And can't afford to buy one.'

'You'd have a pay increase with the new job.'

She smiles and shakes her head. 'Thanks, Krish, but that all sounds too complicated.'

He shakes his head, baffled.

Pip looks up, seeing the indecisive scientist return. 'Io. Welcome back.'

'Thank you, Pip. I enjoyed the cheese sandwich.'

'Would you like the same again?'

'No, I'd like to try something different. Time to move on again. I'm going to build on the foundations of yesterday. What does cheese pair with?'

'Ham goes with cheese. Or tomato. Or some like it with coleslaw, but I don't think you will. Or all can go together.'

'Just two things,' he says, stopping her from getting carried away. 'I'll have three tomorrow.'

'I'm sure you have ham and cheese sandwiches where you come from. Where is that by the way?'

'Yes, your favourite question. Was the lack of answer yesterday burning into your mind last night?'

So he noticed that he didn't answer. 'Into my soul. I couldn't sleep.' She longs to be brought somewhere else, especially by Io, she has a feeling it will not be mediocre.

'I came here from the Netherlands. The hub is there, part of the same project at the observatory, but you know all about that because you worked there.'

'I worked in the canteen, I've never even been in the observatory,' she admits.

His mouth falls open in faux horror. 'You have to come see it. Let me give you a tour.'

What would Josephine think if Pip were to stroll through the canteen with Io while she's sweating over the steam of a hot shepherd's pie? The thought is inviting, in a naughty way.

'I'd prefer to see the Netherlands. What's it like?'

'Flat. With tulips and windmills.'

'And clogs?' she asks, amused.

'Yes,' he says. 'Clogs are everywhere. In all honesty I didn't see very much. The office and a lot of paperwork.'

This is disappointing. 'And the sky.'

'And the sky,' he agrees with a smile.

'What exactly do you do in the observatory, apart from look at planets?'

'We don't look at planets. It's an I-LOFAR telescope. It detects low-frequency radio waves from space. The current project is one of the largest astrophysics projects in Europe, tasked with finding a signal from a distant star.'

'A *signal* from a star?' she asks, fascinated, placing the ham on the bread with less care than usual, mind distracted. 'What kind of signals do they send?'

'Distant galaxies send out radio signals,' Io explains. 'But to hear more you'll have to come to the observatory. I can show you around. Do you get a lunch break?'

'Only thirty minutes.'

'Can you take longer?'

She probably could. Krish is accommodating like that, and she hasn't taken a day off since she started, but realistically, she'd never go, Josephine would see her with Io and ask her who she thinks she is, and make a fool of her and end it all.

'Why come to Ireland?' she asks. 'I didn't think we were the central intelligence for stars.'

'It's not. The Netherlands is the central hub. The radio telescope here is part of a network of similar telescopes, in twelve international stations spread across Europe; Germany, Poland, France, UK, Sweden and Ireland.'

'Do you travel to them all?'

'Yes.'

'Which is your favourite?'

'So far this service station is my favourite place of all.'

She laughs. 'How long have you been travelling?'

He clocks it up in his head. 'A year.'

'What?' She puts the knife down and looks at him in surprise. 'Have you been home since you left?'

'No.'

'An entire year?'

'One earth trip around the sun.'

She has so many questions. 'Have you received any signals yet?'

'If we had, you would have heard about it in the news.'

'Oh, so signals from stars aren't a regular thing.'

'They're not.' He frowns. 'Until I receive a signal, I can't go home.'

She's sad for him. 'I hope you receive your signal, Io.'

'Thanks. Me too. But I do really need to get back to work,' he says, looking down at the unfinished sandwich.

'Sorry.' She places the bread on top, slices it, wraps it and hands it to him.

'See you tomorrow, Pip.'

Philip picks her up from work. He's wearing his high-vis jacket.

'Sammy Wolverson had a word with me today,' he says, upbeat.

She feels her stomach flip.

'He asked if it was all right with me to take you out.'

She feels instant rage, that she can usually keep down. 'Nice of him to ask you first.'

His mood quickly darkens at her reaction, 'He's a Wolverson, Philippa. A fine family. The smartest in the county. They're respected by everyone. You don't get much better than that. It would be good for you, for your situation.'

Her situation.

'It would make people think better of me,' she says, slowly.

'Maybe he could get you a job at the quarry.'

'As what, a blaster?' She continues before he picks her up on her tone. 'I like my job.'

'You liked the other one too, but you left that.'

She didn't like the observatory catering job. She hated working with Josephine, going from home to a hot stressful kitchen, being barked at in front of other people. The only reason Josephine hadn't argued with her too much about her leaving was because she would be closer to Bella. Pip was not proud of sacrificing her daughter for her momentary freedom. It was the first time she had done it.

She's feeling dumbstruck. Her parents have always been domineering, they've talked her out of going on dates, they've talked her out of getting a place of her own, sitting her down and going through the numbers line by line: rent, utilities, Bella's food and clothing; she could never afford it, not on her wages. But they've never told her who to date.

'I told him yes, so he'll pick you up from the house at seven o'clock on Saturday.'

Her eyes widen so much she feels like they're going to pop out of their sockets. But still she holds her tongue. If she dares say one word now she'll say everything, and that scares her.

When they arrive home she wants to storm directly to her room and repeatedly bang her door shut so hard it smashes every window. She feels stifled. As soon as she places her foot on the first step, Josephine calls out her name.

Pip closes her eyes, takes a breath.

'Where do you think you're going? It's your turn to do dinner this evening.'

Her head is pounding. She wants to tell Josephine where she can put her dinner. She imagines making skewers.

'Yes!' Bella says, appearing at the top of the stairs, doing a happy dance that reminds Pip of a younger Bella. 'Fajitas?'

'If you like.' Pip smiles.

'Yes! Pip's fajitas are the best.'

When Pip cooks, she makes two meals, one for her and Bella with spice and all things nice, while she gives the bland version of the dish to her parents. It's one of the few times when she can make her and Bella feel like a family unit, splitting the four of them down the middle.

She takes her victories where she can. She always has.

As she chops the peppers for the fajitas, she thinks back.

Pip and five-month-old Bella are lying on Pip's bedroom floor. Bella, a plump marshmallow of a thing who has just begun eating solids and is inhaling each spoonful as fast as she can, looks and smells like a sweet potato. Pip can't stop smelling her skin, and kissing her plump cheeks.

Bella is enjoying lying on her belly and staring into the mirror on the playmat. A juicy ripe button nose and lips are reflected back. She drools onto the mirror and her finger moves to the drool and moves it around. She's been working on trying to get a zip into her mouth, flicking it back and forth with a podgy forefinger, trying to pull it from its seams.

Josephine would tut, no-no and move her hand away, which

would annoy Pip. Alone in her room she has the freedom to allow her daughter to experiment unimpeded. She will learn that she can't do it herself, or even better, Pip will watch her daughter as she figures out a way to do it herself. Then she will step in.

There is a chasm between Josephine and Pip's parenting styles, but Josephine doesn't like to be corrected, as the parent with experience. Josephine is taking the lead, which Pip was okay with at the beginning because the idea of a newborn baby terrified her, but now she's becoming more confident as a mother, finding her way, but Josephine is not stepping aside. If only she'd be allowed to find her way.

Pip lies on her back beside Bella, practically beneath her. Drool drips from her sore gums. These moments together are the most beautiful.

'Mama,' Pip whispers to her. She presses her lips to her double chin and kisses her. 'Mama,' she says again, her lips moving against Bella's skin so she can feel the vibration of the words.

She wants to hear that word so desperately. She'd had a disturbing conversation with Josephine about how Josephine would prefer it if Bella not call her Mama. Pip has just turned seventeen, looks fifteen, and she feels it would be inappropriate while out in public.

The door opens.

'What are you doing in here?' Josephine snaps. She has a basket of dirty washing on her hip.

'We're playing.'

'You don't have time to play. She's due her lunch.'

'It won't take long. I've it made up in batches in the freezer. And today is yummy carrot.'

Bella looks up at her and smiles.

'Oh you know what that is, don't you? Yum, yum.'

Bella rolls over on her back, shocked at first by her tumble, then smiles. Pip gently pushes her head onto Bella's belly and shakes it around. When she looks up Josephine is gone.

63

Of course Josephine had been doing her own baby-whispering, because 'Pip' is what had prevailed. Philippa had become Pip to Bella. Little by little Pip's title, and role, were taken from her.

'Christ of Almighty,' Josephine says, holding her hand to her mouth as if she's been punched.

They're sitting around the dinner table eating fajitas.

'What's wrong?' Philip asks, panicked.

Josephine reaches for her glass of water and downs it as if her mouth is on fire.

'What are you telling us?' Philip barks, unable to manage the situation.

'It's hot,' Bella says, smirking.

'Oh sorry,' Pip says innocently, lifting Josephine's plate and swapping it with her own. 'My mistake.'

10

ON SATURDAY MORNING PIP is more excited than she can remember being for anything. Not since her secret meet-ups with Jamie when she was a teenager, and it's not because of her date this evening with Sammy. She has teenage crush levels of excitement on spending time with her daughter, and it is divine.

Bella had surprised Pip the previous evening by inviting her to attend a Pilates class with her in the GAA club. Pip has wanted to invest time in herself on weekends for some time, but couldn't because weekends were for Bella, and her mission since her birth had been to reclaim time with her, not give it away. Doing something with Bella is simply a dream.

The only problem they have is Josephine, a roadblock Bella assured Pip she would traverse. Leaving such an important matter in the hands of a sixteen-year-old may be questionable, but Bella has more strategic methods of going about getting what she wants, and when Pip is on the good side of it, it's intriguing to watch.

Philip is in his garage pottering. The sound of his cough gives his whereabouts away.

'Good morning, Granddad,' Bella says, all sweetness and light.

Pip peeks from the window. If he sees her, she'll ruin it. That girl knows how to play everyone.

'You're up early,' he says, hands covered in oil that Pip imagines will be stuck in the fissures of his dry skin for at least a week, no matter how many baths he takes.

'I need to go into town for an hour or so. Could you give me a lift?'

No pleases, no thank yous, not even an explanation, she doesn't have to work hard for their trust or respect.

He instantly agrees, straightening up his back with an unforced groan. It occurs to Pip how old he looks, how crocked his body is. She hears him coughing in the night. She's so used to it now – when did they all get so used to it? He'll drive her to town, he needs to go anyway, to get something twiddly for another oily twiddly thing that he's moving around in his hand.

Philip and Bella get in the car. Bella is in the passenger seat as always and, as he starts up the engine, Pip chooses that moment to get in the back.

He stalls while clipping his seatbelt.

'Where are you going?'

'Pip's coming too,' Bella says. 'We'll be about an hour. Can you pick us up?'

'Where did you say you're going?'

It shouldn't surprise Pip that it is suddenly an issue now that she wants to come, but again it amazes her how brazen the transition is. Shouldn't it be better that Bella's mother is accompanying her to town, not worse? Or are they still afraid that their thirty-two-year-old daughter would run away with Bella?

'Pilates,' Bella says. 'At the GAA club.'

Philip looks at Pip in the rear-view mirror. 'Is your mother okay with this?'

'Why wouldn't she be?' Bella jumps in before Pip can answer. 'It's exercise. You're both always at me to move more. Now I'm moving.'

Pip should have said that. She's not sure what she would have said, but it wouldn't have been that. She should have spoken up when she was Bella's age, when her every move was monitored, when her baby stopped being her baby and became her parents' baby instead.

She'd never fought back then because she felt embarrassed, and unworthy, disgusting and ashamed, and she hadn't the first clue how to have a baby or what to do with a baby, and so she'd allowed Josephine to take the lead. But as the years went by, she was no longer the student, she was living it, she had her own instincts and experiences. By that time she'd already lost her voice, she'd given it away, and the treatment of a naughty sixteen-year-old had become the habitual treatment of a now thirty-two-year-old without being updated or reviewed.

They drive by Caroline, who's washing her car. Her child stands at the open door with a mask over his face.

'She's obsessed with washing her car,' Bella says. 'And what is with that kid always wearing a mask? They're weird. They're all weird.'

'Do they talk to you?' Pip asks, curious, watching them as they pass.

'I couldn't be arsed talking to them,' Bella says, turning the radio on.

Philip delivers Pip and Bella to the GAA club with a warning to be ready in sixty minutes. Pip looks up at the building, excited, as a few women enter. She has a feeling that this is a new beginning. New things are happening, life is changing. She's made a new friend, she has a date this evening. As Bella reaches this stage of her life, their relationship can change. They can blossom as a mother–daughter team. Her patience was worth it. She didn't let bitterness and spite poison everything. She played the long game. This is *it*.

'Let's do this,' Pip says. 'I'll pay for you. You should spend your summer job money on something nice. Have you anything planned for this summer? Other than getting your nails done?'

'Not really,' Bella says, sounding distracted, which sends warning signals to Pip. She stops fussing with her wallet and looks at her daughter. Bella is examining her watch.

'Okay, I'm going now. I'll meet you back here in exactly one hour. I think the class is fifty minutes, but don't tell Granddad that.'

'What? Where are you going?'

'I'm going to meet someone. Don't have a fit, it's no big deal, you know what they're like. But this way I get to do that and you get to do this, and you've wanted to do this for ages.'

Pip can't believe this. Bella has played her, just as she plays everyone else.

'Who are you meeting? Where?'

'A friend. Nearby. Don't worry, I'm not going to make a baby, I'm not doing drugs, and I'm not drinking alcohol. I'll be back in an hour.'

She takes off, leaving Pip standing outside alone.

She feels like an idiot. But worse than that, she's hurt. Stunned, she watches Bella walk away, uncertain as to whether to chase her down or do as she's told. Unsure of what to do, she goes inside to the class and spends the first five minutes trying not to cry.

Twenty minutes in and Pip has forgotten Bella isn't even with her. She gives herself completely to the class, to the movements, the stretching, pushing her body, controlling her breathing. She's so engrossed in the teacher's words that she is disappointed when she announces the cool-down is finished and the class is over.

And then the world comes back to her and she is once again sad. The change she has so desired has not occurred, she has just become a mat for one more person to walk on. She rolls her yoga mat up, imagining she is rolling herself up.

Around them, women spray their mats with anti-bacterial spray, and roll them away. They talk together, swapping notes on the body parts that hurt.

'Are you Philippa Sheridan?' a woman says, and she looks up from tying her shoelaces to see a familiar face.

'Yes.' She stands, trying to place her.

'I'm Kim, Kim Banks.'

As soon as her name is out of her mouth, the stranger before Pip transforms, and in her place is the teenage Kim she last saw when she was fifteen years old.

'Oh my God, Kim,' she says, throwing her arms around her.

Kim squeezes her back, laughing.

Pip is overcome by her teenage emotions. They had been such good friends, and in the same class at school until Kim's family moved to Toronto for her dad's work. Pip had been devastated to lose her friend and, while she had other friends, they weren't as close. They'd stayed in touch for a few months, writing letters furiously back and forth until they'd petered out as Kim slotted into her new life and Pip met Jamie and her life altered for ever. Nothing and nobody mattered to Pip after she and Jamie got together. She hadn't answered Kim's last, shorter than usual, letter, and their relationship had ended.

Kim is grinning. 'It's so good to see you. I kept looking at you during class wondering if it was you. You look amazing!'

'Thank you,' Pip says, unused to the praise. 'What are you doing back here? Have you moved back?'

'For the foreseeable.'

They pack up and walk as they catch up, following the women in front of them. While the majority of the group hurry back to the rest of their lives, they continue their conversation outside.

'Mum and Dad moved back when they retired. Anna and I both wanted to stay, we had university, and it felt like home. Dad recently had his hip replaced, and Mum isn't up to it, so I'm back for a while to help out. Anyway, what about you? You had a baby!'

'Not a baby anymore, she's sixteen. Her name is Bella.'

'Sixteen! Oh my God Philippa. I can barely take care of myself, how the hell do you do it? I still think I'm sixteen.'

They're talking a mile a minute over each other, their teenage giddiness has returned.

'Would you like to go for a coffee?'

Pip would love to. There's a café across the road, people are sitting outside eating brunch. But then the world comes crashing back to her. Her dad. Bella. The ticking clock. Where is she?

Philip pulls his car in. She looks around for Bella quickly, but there's no sign of her. Her heartbeat speeds up.

'Is everything okay?' Kim asks, placing a calming hand on her arm.

Philip lowers his window. 'Where's Isabella?'

'Mr Sheridan,' Kim says, leaning over and looking in to the car. 'My name is Kim Banks. A friend of Philippa's from school. It's nice to see you again.'

Thank God for Kim. She distracts Philip while they discuss her dad and his health for a life-saving moment until Bella appears with a smile on her face, cool as a cucumber, though slightly out of breath.

Pip throws her an angry glare.

Kim straightens up, her conversation with Philip over. Crisis averted, Pip's heart starts to slow down. The one thing her parents have not wanted her to be is a parent to Bella. Not on her own anyway, because they don't believe she's capable.

Perhaps they are right, perhaps she can't be a mother. In the one moment she had sole responsibility for her daughter, she'd run away for an hour, and Pip had no idea where she was.

'Bella this is Kim, a friend from school. Kim, this is Bella. My daughter.' The last words come out as a strangled gurgle.

'It's lovely to meet you,' Kim says, immediately hugging her. 'You're so beautiful. I can't believe you're Philippa's baby. The last time I saw your mam she was your age. I can't believe she has a sixteen-year-old.'

The awkwardness between Pip and Bella is uncomfortable. They don't talk about Pip having Bella so young, not with anyone. It's the terrible thing that happened in their home. It's not something they laugh at, it's not something that they are joyfully incredulous about as Kim is now. They'd rather people think they were sisters. Bella was raised to be embarrassed about it, to not talk about it with friends.

'It was so nice to see you Kim,' Pip says, hugging her again. 'And thank you for that,' she says quietly, pretty sure Kim stepped in to shoot the breeze when she sensed Pip's panic.

'That's what friends are for. Let's catch up, at a better time,' Kim says gently. 'Here's my number.' She hands her a business card.

Philip beeps, Kim jumps, startled.

'Wow. Okay, someone wants to leave.'

'Yeah, sorry. It was so good to see you.'

'You too.'

They hug again. Pip feels like she's clinging on to her fifteen-year-old self.

She doesn't want to let her go.

'So then we did this,' Bella says, doing an ungraceful downward dog in Josephine's face. Josephine looks away. 'And then this.'

A made-up move with her leg in the air. She looks like a dog trying to pee.

Despite her anger at Bella, Pip smiles.

'And how did you do?' Josephine asks Pip.

'Pip was amazing,' Bella says, jumping up. 'She was the best in the class and the teacher said so.'

'No need to exaggerate.'

She follows Bella up the stairs, waiting until they're far enough away to speak.

'Where did you go? You should have told me, or asked me first, not tricked me like that.'

'Would you have said yes?'

She's not sure. She would have been afraid to make the decision. She's never been the one that's had to make the decision.

'You see?' Bella says, rolling her eyes. 'We probably wouldn't have gone at all. You enjoyed it, you met a friend. That's good isn't it? So we're good for next week,' Bella says with a wink, and closes the door behind her.

Pip slowly sits down at her desk, exhausted. Perhaps having a shared secret is something, which is better than nothing.

She's excited to have met Kim, she and the Pilates class were the bright shining star in her otherwise dull and disappointing day, but she knows what happens when she finds something of her own, it has happened time and time again. Somehow things and people are taken away from her.

Pip studies Kim's business card. Chief Financial Advisor. She should call her, she certainly could do with her professional help, never mind a sympathetic ear. Her fingers hover over the numbers on her phone, but instead she opens the top drawer and files the business card away with her sketches.

She sits down at her desk, brimming with emotions after her morning. She's an overfilled teacup, the paper is her saucer.

Origami girl
Makes an origami friend
She folds her by herself
Sculpts her to create
The perfect friend
That she's always wanted.
Then she flattens her
And smooths out the creases.
Because she's afraid
They'll take her away too.

II

FEELING LOW AFTER HER disastrous morning with Bella, Pip has to dig deep to summon energy for her date with Sammy. She has no idea where they are going on the date, all communication had come through her dad.

She dresses in skinny black jeans and a black halter-neck top, and the internal struggle of a high or low heel begins. The high heel lengthens her already long legs, but they are undoubtedly sexier. Up, down, up, down, she stands up on her high heel and then down to her low heel as she examines herself in the full-length mirror on the back of her bedroom door. Sexy, or not.

She chooses the lower heel.

She hears the wheels of a car on the gravel outside, looks out her window to see a shiny black car, chauffeur-driven, with Sammy in the front seat. She kicks off her low heels and switches them with the high.

Any chance of leaving the house under the radar is blown as Bella waits at her bedroom door to check her out. Even Bella can't hide her surprised expression. The halter-neck top displays her toned shoulders and arms, feeling especially so after her morning workout. Her hair is down and in loose waves, after being back in a bun and hairnet for most of the week.

'Don't say anything,' Pip mumbles, still upset with Bella about earlier.

'Make sure his spray tan doesn't rub off on you,' Bella retorts, not in the slightest bit remorseful over her treatment of Pip.

Sammy is standing at the front door with Philip, wearing a tight black shirt with short sleeves and skinny jeans, revealing his buff physique. Josephine appears in the kitchen doorway to look at Pip when she gets down the stairs, and even her expression tells her that yes, she looks beautiful.

'You won't be walking anyway,' Philip says to Sammy, when he sees her shoes.

'Are we supposed to be walking?' she asks, worried, embarrassed.

'No,' Sammy says, taking her in while Philip isn't looking. 'I'll have her home by twelve sir,' he says jokingly to Philip, and they shake hands, which feels grotesque to Pip.

Sammy opens the car door for Pip and then sits in beside her on the other side. He smells clean, so much aftershave it tickles the back of her throat.

'You look lovely,' Sammy says, taking her in now in a way that he wouldn't dare in front of Philip.

His buttons are open two too many for her liking, revealing a shark tooth pendant in his hairless cleavage. His tan has been topped up. He's more a shade of tangerine than tan.

'Where are we going?' she asks.

'You'll have to wait and see.' He winks and opens the hand rest that separates them, revealing mini bottles of champagne and glasses.

They drive for forty minutes, and the conversation is easy. He likes to talk, about himself, and she asks questions because she would rather pass the time that way instead of having to think and talk about herself.

They arrive at an industrial estate. Warehouses with tile shops, fireplaces, kitchen showrooms. She's underwhelmed and confused, but can feel his excitement at having a secret up his sleeve. Sammy bangs on a metal door to a red-brick warehouse, and it's opened by a young woman surrounded by a black velvet curtain.

'Welcome,' she says, looking at Pip, who defers to Sammy.

He scrolls through his phone. Pip sees a QR code, which he holds out and she scans.

Pip is thinking it's a night club at this point, but there's no loud music.

'Right this way,' she says, sliding open the curtain.

Pip's breath is taken away.

Monet: The Immersive Experience. A 360-degree digital art exhibit.

She walks around in a daze, a winding corridor of Monet's works on screens, as well as projected directly onto the walls, and floors, as if being painted before her very eyes. Paint strokes appearing, layering up, Monet's garden in Giverny coming to life, the haystacks, the poppies. It's as though she has stepped into one of her own daydreams. This is really happening.

'Is this good? You're not saying anything?' His white teeth glow in the darkness.

'Sammy,' she says, grabbing his arm. She feels him flex his bicep beneath her touch. 'This is the best thing I've ever been given.'

'I saw the Monet print on your wall and then saw this coming up.'

He's like a peacock, all proud.

He tries to chat as they walk, but she's enchanted, in a trance, completely mesmerised by what's taking place around her.

'It's a little trippy,' he says, uncertain.

It's a dream, and she's overcome.

'I sometimes think,' she says, in a low voice, hand on her heart as she looks at a projected image of *The Magpie*, Monet's finest snowscape, while a sprinkle of fake snow falls lightly on them from above, 'that looking at art is like viewing a beating heart outside of somebody's body.' She thinks of the paper hearts she folds and tucks inside her origami girls, then realises, her entire origami collection is *her* paper heart. Her feelings and secrets, outside of her body.

'Giving serial killer vibes, Philippa,' he sings, looking around to see if anyone has heard.

She laughs lightly, embarrassed by his reaction and makes a note not to confide any further with her deeper thoughts.

They step through a doorway to enter the second layer of the space, and are faced with the Japanese footbridge from the print in her bedroom.

'Oh my God!'

She steps into another world, passes over the threshold where her imagination becomes reality. She walks over the footbridge, which gives her prime vantage point for the water-lily-filled pond that is projected on the floor below.

'This is the greatest gift,' she says, standing on the bridge looking out. Sammy leans against the wall, arms folded, watching her.

'Just call me Jesus,' he says, walking across the pond and ruining the mirage. 'What's in here?'

Then they enter an enormous space, a spectacular light and sound exhibit featuring projections of the artist's most compelling works. There are deckchairs in the immersive room. People sit, lounge, calmly taking it all in as the four walls around them are the canvas to an ever-changing painting. She watches one of Monet's first paintings, *Impression, Sunrise*, slowly come to life as stroke by stroke, the port of Le Havre appears all around her, on the floor, and on the ceiling. She holds out her hand to touch the ripples in the sea and sees it projected on to her hand. His paintings were a meditation on the relationship between humans and nature, and here she is fully connected. She is inside the paintings, she is part of it. From inside the sunrise to inside Monet's Japanese-inspired garden in Giverny, she watches the grass appear on her ankles. She experiences the movement and changing light of each one of his paintings, and it feels to Pip as though she's having a spiritual experience. She sheds a tear of happiness, so utterly moved and transported. Sammy is uncomfortable. She can tell he wants to move, by the fact he is pacing by the door. They watch from beginning to end, a projection of Monet's greatest works, and when it's finished, she wants to see it all over again.

The final thing on the tour is a VR experience. Sammy and Pip sit down opposite each other and place the head gear over their eyes, and once again she is transported. If she could have this VR head gear in her bedroom she would never leave.

She walks through the *Haystacks* in Giverny, changing light and landscape through the day and seasons. She travels through the *Bridge over a Pond of Water Lilies*, the arched footbridge over a pond of floating lilies surrounded by lush greenery. Maybe if she looks out far enough she will see herself in her white bedroom, lying on her bed, looking back at her.

Monet's use of light and colour and its reflection creates a peaceful dream-like atmosphere. His field of poppies is magical. She wants to lie down in the grass and feel it tickle her skin.

It has been so moving, an unforgettable experience, possibly life-changing as she considers re-discovering art, maybe looking into courses, or even just taking up painting again at home. She has the scenery around her to inspire.

She momentarily lifts the VR goggles to wipe the tears in her eyes and peeks over at Sammy to see how he's getting on with the experience, and finds him with the VR goggles on his lap, his phone in his hand. He's texting.

She subtly lowers the goggles back over her eyes.

'Sammy? Are you still here or have you left me?'

'I'm still here,' he says.

'I think mine is almost finished.'

'Yeah mine too, it's incredible isn't it?'

She lifts her device off. His are back on his head.

She sighs to herself. 'Mine is finished now.'

'Mine too.' He can't get it off fast enough. He makes a little act of rubbing his eyes and adjusting to the environment, as if it's been on for so long.

'Do you want to go around one more time?' she asks.

It takes him a minute to realise it's a joke. He grins. 'Let's get out of here. I've never had a date be so pleased about my choice.'

The conversation becomes all about how he chose the venue and not the actual experience itself. The analysis is all about him. She would love to be able to bounce off somebody about everything they have seen, but he's not that kind of guy. He's left it all behind already. Even so, she is so, so pleased that she said yes to this date. Io is right. Do one new thing every day, no matter how small.

'It was truly honestly, the best thing anyone could have done for me,' she says, genuinely. 'Thank you.'

'Can't wait to see how you'll repay me,' he says, with a wink, leading the way through the black curtains to the waiting car.

12

THERE'S MORE CHAMPAGNE IN the car on the way back home.

'I can't,' she says, refusing to accept the glass. 'I'm on a natural high after that.'

He fills it to the top anyway and pushes it towards her. The champagne spills onto her hand and drips down her arm. She sucks it up, and he watches her, with lazy eyes.

She wipes what's left on her hand on her jeans.

The date was a success. She's settling down, her tension finally leaving her at knowing she's made it, when the car stops in town. The chauffeur drives them down a narrow laneway, where they get out, and he reverses and disappears.

The restaurant is called The Suckling Pig. It's an award-winning fine dining restaurant, one of the very few in town, and she has never been inside it. Philip and Josephine are not culinary fans, despite her being in the catering business. Josephine can make lasagne for three hundred people, but she wouldn't know what to do with a box of spices, nor would the idea of change or bending herself to suit others ever be a consideration. Besides, they don't have the money to splash out on such things. Bella would love this. Pip would love to take her out. Pip *should* take her out.

'Before we get in there,' he says, pulling her away from the direction of the entrance door, away from the windows.

He doesn't give her a second to prepare, or to know what's coming.

His mouth is on hers before she knows what's happening.

His tongue is in her mouth, hard and probing. She tries to pull away, but he holds the back of her head tight to him. His arm around her body, crushing her. She's trapped.

She tries to make the kiss nicer. If this is happening, and it is happening, then she can make it gentler. At the very least she can make it more pleasant. But it's hard to move under his strong grip.

She feels stunned, shaken, as he finally pulls away from her and grabs her by the hand. She's desperate to wipe her mouth as he pulls her inside.

Her lips are throbbing, not in a pleasant way. Her arms feel sore. She feels like she's just been crushed by a human machine, and now they are sitting in a bistro, white table linen, a candle between them, the restaurant is oh so quiet. He's browsing the wine menu, then looks up to the waiter when he approaches the table.

The waiter looks at Pip and away again, and from his expression she feels like there's something wrong with her face. It certainly feels like it. Her lips are throbbing, she feels like Sammy has tried to eat her. She takes a sip of water, and the rim of the glass comes away red. She hasn't reapplied lipstick all evening. She lifts a linen napkin to her mouth and it too is stained with red dots.

Had he bitten her?

When the waiter leaves, she pushes her chair back from the table. Sammy's hand quickly grips her wrist, not roughly, but gentle.

'Leave it. It's fine. It's gone now.'

He returns his eyes to his menu.

'According to Kama Sutra it increases blood flow and makes a person more aroused.' He winks. 'I'm thinking the steak, what do you think? Monet certainly works up an appetite.'

It all ran together and she's confused. Lip biting is supposed to arouse her, or the steak is? His voice feels so far away. It's gentle and normal. But she feels anything but.

Right now she wishes she could be the type of super confident woman who can speak up for herself. She should stand up and walk out of there, because she knows what happened is wrong. But she's not that woman. She second, third, fourth guesses herself. She's confused by what happened, and if it even happened. Maybe she's a bad kisser and she caused it.

She feels the environment is conspiring against her to stop her from reacting in the way that she should. The too quiet bistro, the waiter avoiding her eye, Sammy gentle, almost tender. She can hear the sound of cutlery as people eat, the quiet murmur of deep conversation. She sees her neighbours, Tom and Mary Fitzgerald, in the corner out with friends. It's like a bad dream, opening her mouth to scream and nothing coming out. People are here, all around her, who could help her, but it's as if they're behind glass.

She quickly realises the other people with Tom and Mary Fitzgerald are all of her neighbours. Their two daughters, and the Slatterys and the Brennans. Ten of them are seated together from the houses across the road.

She tries to catch their attention, though what she would do, she has no idea. Somebody seeing her, acknowledging her, would be a good start.

She orders a starter for a main course, she has no appetite

anymore. She needs to sober up, and fast, though the last few minutes has been sobering already. She reaches for the bread. She's grateful he only orders a main course.

'Tell me about Bella's dad,' he says, casually. 'Do you see him much?'

'No. Not at all. He lives in Liverpool.'

'Why there?'

'He has family there. He was sent there—' she stops herself. 'He moved there after he finished school.'

'That's not very nice is it? Doing a runner on you?'

'He didn't. He's a good dad. Provides for her. They talk every week.'

'What does he do?'

She doesn't know exactly. 'He's in construction.'

'Is he married?'

'No.'

'Does he have other children?'

'No.'

Not that she knows of. Surely she'd know. Wouldn't she?

'So you two aren't . . .'

'No. God no. That ended before Bella was even born.'

She sounds exactly like her mother. Brainwashed to speak as if he almost didn't exist. The great love of her life. The father of her child. Nothing. In religion, the family is sacrosanct, but why weren't Jamie, Pip and Bella? They were something to be split up, not to celebrate.

'I heard a rumour he's coming back for the hearing.'

She shrugs. 'If he is, nobody has told me.'

'Not even Isabella?'

'No, not even Bella.'

'Isn't that a bit weird?'

He's right about that, the entire thing is weird. She can't think of anything to ask Sammy. She's no longer interested in any aspect of him. She refuses the red wine the waiter offers to pour for her. She eats her Caesar salad.

He eats one thing at a time; first the vegetables, then the potatoes, and then the steak, which bleeds as soon as he cuts into it. It reminds her of her lip, and she feels a wave of dizziness, certainly not arousal. She's relieved when Sammy puts the last bite of steak in his mouth. Relieved and scared, because she's not sure what exactly will happen next. She wants to go home. Sammy told her dad that he'd have her home by midnight and, though she knew it was a joke, she clings to that promise.

She looks over again to her neighbours. She tries to catch someone's eye. They're almost finished their meal too, if they're going home then Pip could ask them to take her home with them. It wouldn't be so odd, would it? It makes sense, a lot of people going in the same direction.

Caroline looks over her shoulder just at that moment and their eyes meet. Pip perks up and waves at her with a smile. Caroline throws her the most disgusted look she thinks she's ever received, and turns around to her family again. Now Pip knows all those other times she'd avoided her wave or smile since they moved there weren't an accident or a coincidence. Caroline says something to the others, who unsubtly turn around and stare at her and Sammy.

'What's wrong?' Sammy says, looking over his shoulder and seeing the group of them in the corner. As soon as he turns they all turn back around and focus on their meals. Heads down.

He stares at them a little too long. When he turns around he has a face of thunder.

'They're my neighbours,' she says, explaining. 'They've been very chilly with me. I don't know what's going on.'

He looks at her, reaches for a toothpick, and pokes the meat from between his teeth.

'Tom Fitzgerald was fiddling with his little girls for so long, that's why one of them left. Wouldn't want him involved with my kids. He should be banned from coaching football.'

Pip freezes. She can't believe it. She briefly glances at them to see if they've heard. They haven't. They're still huddling in, speaking in low voices.

'I think we'll leave the dessert and coffee, will we?' he says.

Feeling relieved to get out of there, Pip allows him to pay, and they leave. Her face is burning with shame at what he has said and she's grateful they didn't hear him. She can't even look at them. Outside she looks around for the chauffeur. He's gone, and Sammy instead presses the button on his key and his Range Rover lights flash further down the road.

'You're driving?'

'Sure am. I'll drop you home. Don't want Mr Sheridan to be angry with me now, do I?'

'But you've been drinking.'

A lot, he's been drinking a lot.

Instead of being angered, he looks at her in a sweet way. He wraps his arm around her shoulders and squeezes her gently. 'You, Philippa Sheridan, are like something out of an old-fashioned movie. A black and white one. I love it.'

He opens the door for her to get inside.

She looks in at the plush interior, blue strip lights line the doors. She could still suggest going home with her neighbours, they're all going in the same direction. But not after what he said about them, and the atmosphere between them. She feels the eyes of everyone in the restaurant on them. She gets into the Range Rover, using her hair to cover her face.

He drives her home without any drama, but she watches every turn in the road, waiting for a truck or car to come at them. Engine running, outside the house, she didn't realise how tense and frightened she was feeling until he unlocks the car doors. She is released.

'Thank you for tonight,' she says politely. Mr Wolverson, sir.

She opens the car door before he tries anything else.

The lights are visible beyond the drawn curtains in the living room, so Pip knows she doesn't need to look for the spare key. She's glad, as she wouldn't want Sammy to see where it's hidden either. Philip moves the positioning every few months for safety. It's eleven thirty: Josephine, Philip and Bella are all still up, watching TV. Pip's conscious of her lip, which feels hugely swollen, she kept catching it with her front teeth when she was eating her salad.

'Hi,' she says from the living-room door. 'I'm home.'

They all look at her. She feels self-conscious, her lip large and bulbous.

'Had you a good night?' Josephine asks.

She purses her lips and nods.

'Where did he bring you?'

'A Monet immersive experience.'

'What's that?' Philip asks.

'Art,' Josephine says, with an impressed raise of the eyebrow. 'Well, now.'

'I'm going to bed. I'm tired. Goodnight.'

'Goodnight,' they call after her.

She's only had time to sit down on her bed, not even remove her shoes, though she's in shock so she's not sure how long she's been sitting there, she feels numb, when there's a knock on the door.

'Yes,' she says, her voice shaky.

Bella walks in. Pip puts her hand over her mouth, as naturally as she can.

'Hi. Are you okay? You seem . . . I'm just making sure everything is okay.'

Even if she wanted to share what happened, Bella is her daughter, not her friend.

'I'm fine,' she says.

'Sorry about tricking you this morning,' Bella says awkwardly. 'It's just, I really like him.'

Pip looks at her, is so tired she can't think of anything else to say. 'Okay.'

'Well nighty night.'

'Goodnight Bella,' she says formally, feeling like a robot, keeping all her emotions locked up inside. Act, move, operate, function, don't think.

Head pounding, she sits at her desk. Even though the house is warm, she feels cold, she keeps her jacket on as she writes, and writes quickly, the words gushing out, as if she has to write before she forgets.

Origami girl
Meets a crocodile
Its teeth white
And gnashing
He snaps
She folds
He snaps
She folds

He snaps
She folds again.
'There's flesh caught
Between your teeth,'
Says origami girl
To the croc
In shock.
She's so minute
Her voice is tiny
His snap is loud
And bold
He pulls her close
And picks his teeth
Using Origami girl's
sharpened corners.

She sees the shape that she wants in her mind, and her fingers work with the paper to bring it to life. Whilst concentrating hard, mind completely focused, she still feels like it's a dance that just happens. As soon as her fingers touch the paper, they know what to do. She zones out for a while, and when she comes back, there it is in her hands, complete. An origami crocodile.

She drops the crocodile into the box with the rest of her collection. She thinks of it gnashing on all of her shapes and figures in the box, all the characters she has created, and on second thought, she removes the crocodile and places it in a box on its own so it can't hurt anything or anyone else.

13

ON SUNDAY MORNING HER body aches, as if she's been thrown around like a rag doll. Just from one crushing embrace. She feels tender and bruised, but when she examines her body she sees no marks. It's all on the inside. She remembers the way Sammy held her tight in his grip. Her head stuck in place, her body unable to move. It was like a nightmare, trying to run but not getting anywhere.

Or maybe she's being dramatic and the pain is due to the Pilates class.

She waits at the car before leaving for Sunday mass. She can hear her family rushing around inside, chairs scraping, the dishes crashing as Josephine loads them messily into the dishwasher and tidies away the Sunday breakfast that Pip couldn't eat, citing too much alcohol the night before, which is also true. Four glasses of champagne is four more glasses than she's used to.

Pip looks across at the neighbours' houses in the distance and cringes with embarrassment at what occurred last night. Was Sammy an absolute monster to say such a nasty thing, or was there any truth at all to the abuse allegations? Either way, something is unsettled, and she'd like to figure out what. Philip is first out, with his car keys.

'Dad, is everything okay with the neighbours?'

'Far as I know.'

'Maybe I'll go over later and talk to them myself,' she says, intending to do no such thing.

'There's no need for that,' he says, irritated now, and she knows that he knows something. 'Why?'

'Last night we were in The Suckling Pig for dinner, and all the neighbours were out together. Why do you think we weren't invited?'

'Because we're new. They've all been here since the beginning of time. Don't be taking offence.'

'Sammy, from kind of out of nowhere, said that Tom had . . . abused his kids and that's why one of his daughter's had left.'

'Deirdre,' he says, naming the daughter. 'I didn't hear anything about that. She got a job in New York. Lives with a woman. And what happened then?'

'We left. Thankfully they didn't hear what he said.'

He ponders this.

'Kind of cruel, isn't it? I thought they were good people, even if they don't acknowledge my existence.'

She plays it up, sees a way to get out of more dates. Philip doesn't like people who say cruel things about good people.

'A man can only take so much.'

'What do you mean?'

He throws his head back, as a horse would. It is Irish language for 'Sure you know yourself', which never means anything if you don't know and have to figure it out.

'I'm not saying that what he said was right, but a man like Sammy Wolverson doesn't say a thing like that unprovoked.'

'They didn't provoke him. If anything, Caroline seemed angry with *me*. She was scowling at *me*.'

'He was defending you then,' he says, a little bit happier about that.

'I didn't really see it that way.' She folds her arms. Is there nothing Sammy Wolverson could do to be seen as he truly is?

'Now you listen here, the Wolversons are a fine family. They've employed generations of us, Granddad John and Great-granddad Darragh, your uncles and your cousins now. We are grateful to them for so much, as is the community. They sponsor the GAA club, built that new all-weather pitch. We wouldn't have a stand if it wasn't for them. It was Mr Wolverson who funded the nursing home over in Kilmackin where your grandma was. They look out for their own. They've treated us like their own. I've been loyal to them all my life and they've been loyal to me. But this town doesn't know what good they've had. When you're a family like them you're an easy target for lies. People looking for their money, lazy gits who'd rather sue them than work a day in their lives. I've heard fellas talk at the quarry. Planning and scheming. A sore toe and they're suing. And look at what they've done for us with this house. They sold us the land. Wolverson land, Philippa. It's like gold dust. And they gave us a great deal on the stone. I'm telling you, everyone else had better watch themselves, because they'll get back what they give out. I know whose side I'm on.'

He's all fired up, emotional and angered. He couldn't be more upset if somebody insulted his mother. She wasn't expecting this.

'So you're saying that all of our neighbours are all looking for money from the Wolversons? That makes no sense.'

'Caroline's husband Aleksy had an accident at work. Hurt his leg. And they want every penny they can get now.'

She recalls seeing him limping in the garden. 'Maybe they're entitled to compensation.'

'Enough now,' he says, finished with the conversation.

But Pip isn't. 'Caroline's anger was directed at me, not him. What has it to do with me? Why do they ignore me when I wave at them?'

'You're Sammy Wolverson's girlfriend, aren't you?' he says, proudly. 'And if they didn't get the message before, then they know whose side we're on now.'

Her desire to reveal Sammy's true nature had backfired. Her dad now sits into the car thinking even more of Sammy Wolverson than he did before.

14

OVER THE SALAD BAR counter, Io looks at her swollen lip, then deep into her eyes. She feels like he knows. He has a look of pity. She feels like crying. She blinks the tears away. For some reason he sees her in a way no one else does.

'Can you take a break soon?'

She nods. 'I'm due one in twenty minutes.'

'Good. Tell Krish you're taking an extended break. I'm taking you out of here.'

Pip looks around Io's office, astonished.

'Not what you thought?' he asks, with a sardonic grin.

'No. Not at all.'

'Better or worse?'

'So much worse.'

He laughs, not taking offence.

The observatory is situated in Birr Castle Demesne, on 120 acres of science, botany, history, astronomy and engineering. It's home to tourists and walkers, nature lovers and historians. Pip is only familiar with the canteen, a separate outbuilding. She'd imagined Io working in an observatory with round dome-shaped windows, an astronomer perched on a ladder peering into the eyepiece of a giant telescope. The office is the very opposite; it's a windowless small room.

'Were all the other cupboards full?'

'Keep going,' he says, easy-going.

'Did Harry Potter not need it anymore?'

'One more.'

She thinks, and smiles, wanting to use her last one wisely. 'Any skeletons in here?'

'There you go.'

The room isn't messy, but it's cluttered, everything arranged in organised piles. But there are so many things, in such a small tight space. Information spilling out and off everything; stuffed file boxes, a computer, a laptop, books. Maps on the walls, stars, diagrams, instruments.

'For someone who studies the sky, I imagined you could at least see it.'

'I see it in here, on this.' He taps his computer. 'And this.' He prods sheets and printouts. 'And I communicate with the assistants and instrumentalists who make it possible for the rest of us astronomers to get data around this planet.'

'This planet,' she says, laughing at his phrasing. To him, earth is but a speck of dust in his vision of the world. To Pip, Ballybeg feels too big for her at times. 'Why come to Ireland at all if you can see it from your computer? Then you wouldn't have to spend so much time away from home.'

'My home is too remote to work remotely. But you're right. Astronomers don't have a routine presence in observatories, we spend most of our time working with computer analysis of data. Sometimes we visit when working with new instruments to better understand their data. And sometimes, I visit just to know what other people know.'

She narrows her eyes. 'Is that what you're doing? Spying?'

'This,' he says, displaying the room, 'is pretty much the same as every room in every country I go to. Same kind of room, same kind of data. Sixteen-hour work days. But I decided here would be different.'

'Why?' she asks, noting he didn't answer the question.

He perches on the corner of his desk, almost toppling a stack of files.

'I was about to submerge myself into another windowless room. I was driving into Ballybeg for the first time, another new country, another new town and I had to charge the car. While I was waiting, I overheard you at the deli counter.'

'Uh-oh.'

'You were asking customers where they were going, and where they'd been. Every single person. And you wanted details.'

She laughs, a little embarrassed. 'Did you get in line so you could tell me yours?'

'Maybe. We're here, aren't we.'

Pip decides to open up more. 'I work in a place where everyone is moving, coming and going from somewhere. And I'm completely still.'

Static. Stuck, she wants to add. She swallows, feeling emotion swell.

'But beneath the stillness,' he says, as if reading her thoughts, ice blue eyes holding her attention, 'there's a restlessness. Whereas with me, I'm always coming from somewhere, and going to somewhere. I don't settle anywhere, or connect with anybody really. They say when you've got motion sickness the best thing to do is focus on the thing that's not moving. So I guess that's what I'm doing.'

She wants to move, he wants to settle, they're drawn to each other because each has what the other doesn't.

He smiles. 'I like your groundedness. Earthiness.'

'You make me sound like a potato, Io, and you should be careful about discussing potatoes with Irish people,' she says with a smile, ready to escape his inspection. 'And I like your otherworldliness. Maybe you can help this spud grow towards your light. So where's this I-LOFAR thing?' she asks, looking around the cramped room. 'I'm guessing they couldn't squeeze it in here.'

He smiles and stands up from the table edge. 'This way.'

The I-LOFAR is also nothing as she expected. It's not a telescope as she would know it, but a series of solar panels on the ground in a field, with radio antennae.

'What exactly are these doing right now?' she asks.

'They're observing radio sources. Every time anything happens in the universe, like an exploding star for example, it releases enormous energy into its surrounding environment. In almost all events they have radio emissions, so in observing the radio band we can understand how and when these events occur.'

She nods. 'And why do we do this?'

'It's important for exoplanet research.'

'And what's an exoplanet when it's at home?'

It takes a moment for him to decode the Irish phrasing. 'Exoplanets are planets that orbit stars.'

'Like Earth?'

'Yes. We look for planets that are close to their stars and have a magnetic field, because if the star flare penetrates the magnetic field it emits bright radio waves. All of which are detected by the I-LOFAR.'

'Are we looking for other planets to live on?' She looks up to the sky, wondering if in this lifetime she'll be able to move to another planet with Bella. She'd do it. Preferably at the end of this summer.

'Habitable planets are part of it, yes.'

'Have any been found?'

'Not found, no.'

'But they're out there?'

'There are a few possible candidates for where life could conceivably exist, yes.'

'Will they invade us?'

'Not before Earth ends its own existence.'

'Well that's a lovely thought. Thanks for the uplifting tour.'

He laughs. 'I don't think invasion is on their cards. Spying, possibly.' He winks. 'Mostly what is at work is people here, looking out there, to understand what's going on here. You look out, to look in.'

She ponders that for a moment. The sky is beautifully blue in the summer evening. It has been another spectacular hot summer's day, but the heatwave is due to come to an end at the weekend. The air feels heavy and humid.

'I didn't fully explain earlier,' she says, ready now, as she looks up at the sky. 'I ask people where they're going all of the time because I've never been outside of Ireland. I've never been on a plane, though I've been told my head is in the clouds.'

His mouth has fallen open in an almost cartoonish fashion. If he could make his eyeballs pop out of his head to the sound of an Ahooga horn it would complete the effect.

'I fly planes, whenever you want, I'll take you up. I'll show you what it all looks like from up there. I promise you it will be life-changing.'

Now it's her turn to give him the cartoonish stare. 'You know how to fly planes?'

'And helicopters, and . . . other things. I have a licence to teach, but I just fly myself.'

'How would we get a plane?'

'The local airfield. I have a plane here.'

'We have a local airfield? I thought you drove here,' she says suspiciously, looking for holes in this tremendous piece of information.

'I flew. Then I rented a car. It's just a small plane. A two-seater. Propeller.' When she doesn't answer, he adds, 'The things at the side of the wings that go . . .' he makes a convincing propeller sound.

'I get it, I know, it's just . . . I've got no money.' She gives her parents half her wages, tries to put as much money aside for Bella as she can, for her future.

'No charge. My invitation.'

She tries to imagine herself in a plane. A two-seater. Her adrenaline is hopping.

'Where would we go?'

'Wherever you like. You can go anywhere you want to, Pip. You're going to go to a lot of places, I know it. And not just by living them through customers' stories. You're going to experience things yourself.'

A lump forms in her throat immediately. She tries to ignore her bulbous lip and the pain in her body and focus instead on his belief in her.

The clouds seem a million miles away and are racing by, with somewhere else to be, cotton-tails late, late for a very important date. The movement encourages thought, like watching a river running, or a fire crackling. The view reaches so far up it opens the mind to possibilities, ideologies, hopes and dreams.

Her sigh is tale-telling.

'The benefit of hindsight,' Io says.

'Tell me about it,' she says, thinking of Saturday night.

'I'm sorry about your date,' he says, sincerely. 'But I meant, looking up there. The light from all of the stars you see with the unaided eye takes four thousand years to reach us. So when we look up, we're actually looking into the past.'

It's daylight. The stars aren't revealed yet, but they're there, will come out at night like moonflowers, flourishing in the dark.

'So astronomers are more like historians.'

'In a way,' he says, smiling.

'I used to tell Bella a bedtime story about the stars.' It used to be Pip's favourite time of day, getting her little girl dressed into her cosy pyjamas, as snuggly as a teddy bear, and lying on the bed reading stories until the rhythm of Bella's breathing told her she was asleep. Pip would watch Bella for so long as she slept, her long eyelashes, her hot chubby cheeks, the rising and falling of her little chest, there was nothing more peaceful or calming than to be in the same space as her. Bella would fall asleep holding her hand. 'It was about a girl who lived on a star, Star girl, who was friends with a boy who lived on the moon.'

'Moon boy?'

'Correct. Every night they would have adventures together, but he would always have to go back to the moon and she would always have to go back to her star. "Goodnight

Moonboy," she'd say, "Goodnight Stargirl," he'd say. That's how each story ended,' Pip says, smiling.

'I wonder where Moon boy and Star girl are now. Maybe it's time to reunite them.'

She looks up at the sky, smile fading. 'Nah. That was thousands of years ago.'

15

A WHOLE WEEK GOES BY where Pip doesn't hear a thing from Sammy. She's on tenterhooks fearing that he'll call by Crossroads and insist on driving her home, or whisking her away somewhere on another surprise. She fears what will happen if she tells him no. She was practically monosyllabic by the end of their date so she doesn't imagine he'll be back for more, but she still dreads every time a customer walks in. She's relieved when it reaches Friday that there has been no contact. She feels lighter, having carried a heavy load all week, and looks forward to relaxing on the couch and watching TV.

On Friday afternoon Philip drives Pip home from work.

'I've a message from Sammy for you. He says he'll pick you up at seven tonight.'

Her heart sinks. 'Where are we going?'

'He didn't say.'

'Dad,' she says, gently. Then she drops it.

'What?' he asks.

'Never mind.'

'I mind, tell me.'

'You'll just get angry.'

He's silent for a moment. 'I won't get angry.' But he already sounds angry.

She speaks slowly. 'I want to like him, I really want to, but I don't think Sammy Wolverson is right for me.' She holds her breath for the lecture.

'I'm not going to pretend I'm not disappointed, but I won't force you to do anything you don't want to do. Not in these matters. You do whatever you think is right.'

You do whatever you think is right. It's a loaded sentence, she's supposed to understand it, she's sure of it, but she's so confused. 'Right for who?'

He frowns. 'Who do you think?'

He has no idea, all of the thinking she does, all the considerations she has to make every time she makes a decision. Do her parents think she only ever thinks of herself?

'For you, and for Mam, and for Bella. It's more than being just about me, about whether I like him or not.' She's exhausted at the mention of all the considerations she's been making.

'Your mother and I have been married for thirty-five years. Do you think I could stay married to her for that long if I married her for any other person than for myself?'

'No,' she says with a laugh, because of his playful tone and expression. Frankly, she doesn't know how he married her at all. 'But I thought this was important to you.'

'What's important to us is that you meet somebody that's not Barry the bartender.'

'He was a barista.' They could never understand that.

'Or Jason the married man with three children.'

'They were separated.'

'Or that bone surgeon that was as boring as watching paint dry.'

'You love watching paint dry.'

103

'That's true. It's never the colour you think it will be. But he was boring.'

'He was,' she agrees, but she doesn't think they'd like anybody she chooses for herself, boring or not.

When they park outside the house, Philip takes out his phone. 'I'll forward you Sammy's number. If you're cancelling, you should give him notice. It shouldn't be going through me anyway.'

'Will me saying no to Sammy affect your work?'

He looks appalled. 'Of course not. Better now than jilting him at the altar.'

His words have made her feel calm. Unpressured.

'Thank you, Dad. I'll give tonight a chance.'

He looks surprised, but shrugs and gets out of the car. 'As I said, it's up to you.'

There's no pressure now from anyone else. This is purely for herself. Up until Sammy kissed her on their date it was one of the greatest dates of her life. The Monet experience felt out of this world, and that's exactly what she'd wished for. Perhaps she should focus on that.

Sammy is handsome. He's interested in her. He's doing well for himself in business. Her parents approve of him. Despite the lip-biting hiccup, he's almost too good to be true. Maybe he could be the great romance she seeks so much, the one that can lead to her transformation.

16

Sammy and Pip go to a comedy evening at The Turf-cutter's Inn. She dresses in a floral mini dress with trainers. The June day is overcast and clammy, it feels as though the weather is about to break in a summer thunderstorm.

She's relaxed in Sammy's presence and laughs at the comedian onstage. As does he. And it feels normal. Everything is relaxed. It's nice to have company, to have somewhere to go with somebody, even if she's not serious about him, or very seriously not into him. It's better than sitting at home on the couch, or in her room alone.

After the comedian has finished his set they find a corner in a crammed space of the pub. Sammy's so big and wide he manages to clear the space around him. Maybe he's not so bad, maybe he's a kinky lip-biter and she'll just have to tell him she's not into that.

'Another nice surprise?' he asks.

'Yes. Thank you. But you can't keep going through my dad to ask me out.'

'I think he likes it like that,' he says, cheekily. 'Think he's got a bit of a crush on me. Yes, Mr Wolverson, sir, no Mr Wolverson, sir.' He signals to the barman to order.

Her smile fades. She doesn't like him teasing her dad. He

almost had her for a moment, but her wall goes back up. He's still a Wolverson, so she remains polite.

'Dad has great respect for your family. Your dad is a hero in our house.'

'My dad? What about me?' He pushes close to her, in her space. Not his fault, someone knocked against him, but he doesn't step back. 'I run the company now, I should be the hero in your house.'

'I'll let you know in another forty-two years when he's put the same time in with you,' she says easily.

He raises his eyebrows. 'With jokes like that you should have been on the stage tonight.'

She notices that he doesn't like it when she says anything other than respond to him or agree with him. He doesn't appreciate her humour, doesn't do banter.

'Who's the lad I saw you out with this week?' he asks.

She frowns, confused, then thinks to the only man she has been out with that's not her dad. 'Io? He's my friend. Where did you see me with him?'

'You drove by me in his car looking like a Passenger Princess. What kind of name is Io?'

'Dutch. He's working here for a few months.'

'Where?'

She takes a sip of her drink, pondering her answer, but she can't think of a lie quick enough.

'Do you not want to tell me?'

'He works at the observatory.'

He doesn't make any expression, she can't tell how he's feeling, she can't read him. 'Where were you going with him?'

'He took me to the observatory. Can you believe I worked there for so long without seeing it?' He's not in the mood for chitchat. She can see how much he has tensed and she hates how nervous and unsure of herself he has made her feel. 'It's nice to get out for my breaks, for a change of scenery. We're just friends.'

'I'm going to tell you straight, Philippa. I don't like my girlfriends being friends with other men. Nine times out of ten it doesn't stay that way.'

'Oh, well Io and I are really just friends. I could introduce you to him if that would make you feel any better.' Plus I'm not your girlfriend, she wants to add.

'No, that wouldn't make me feel any better,' he says, as though she has patronised him. 'I'm not asking to meet him. I'm saying that I don't like you meeting him.'

She's lost for words. She looks at the couples around them, the groups of friends. All smiles and laughter, in a good mood after laughing for an hour. And she has this to contend with.

Perhaps he notices this too, and switches gear. 'Did you enjoy the show tonight?'

'Yes.'

'Did you enjoy the Picasso show last week?'

'Monet,' she says immediately, without thinking, and laughs. His face darkens.

He moves so quickly she has absolutely no idea how her head snaps back and bangs against the brick wall. She sees stars. She holds her hand up to the back of her head, expecting it to be as split open as it feels.

Sammy's not even looking at her, he's reaching for their drinks over the bar and laughing with a couple beside them, paying no attention to her at all.

Again it's like she's the only person in the room, completely alienated, or invisible as everything carries on around her. Her head is pounding.

She looks around, it feels like everything is moving in slow motion. She sees so many people that she knows. It's a local gig, it's a small town. She sees one of Jamie's brothers, people from the town, these are all good people, surely she can ask them for help. Help from what?

'Tell him I was asking for him,' Sammy says, moving away from the couple. 'Here you go,' he says, handing her a vodka and Coke.

'No thanks,' she says, refusing to take it. Truth is she's so dizzy, she doesn't know if she has the strength to hold it. Her hand feels disconnected from her body. And she feels nauseous. 'I'm not feeling well, I'd like to go home.'

'Really? It's a bit early, isn't it?' He seems genuinely disappointed. 'I was hoping we could have a late night.'

She feels bile come to her mouth. She hunches over.

'Finbar,' he calls to the barman, who is, rather annoyingly, Jamie's younger brother.

There's no rule that he and Pip can't speak, but it always felt like there is one. He avoided her because he was younger and afraid of getting into trouble by talking to the naughty girl who got his brother sent away. But of the two brothers, he's the one that she sees around town the most because he works in the pub, and he's the only one that acknowledges her.

'Water, please. One too many scoops over here for my girl.'

She's having an out of body experience. Everything is happening without her say-so.

The people immediately around her are looking at her and he's down on his knees beside her with a glass of water in his hand and a stool for her to sit on, looking like the perfect concerned gentleman.

She sips the water, trying to figure it all out.

When they step outside the pub, it's ten-fifteen and darkness is closing in. She shivers in the night air. She's brought a small cropped denim jacket but it's not warm enough to protect her from the chill, even in July. Sammy presses the button on his car key and the Range Rover flashes its presence.

Her head is pounding.

'I need some air. I'm going to walk home,' she says suddenly.

'Walk home?' he asks, with a grin, and then realising she's serious, his smile fades. 'I'm not walking all that way.'

'It's okay, you don't have to,' she says politely. 'I'll walk alone.'

'Get in the car, Philippa,' he says, his voice low.

Two young women step outside the pub for a cigarette.

'I want to walk home,' she says, louder, feeling confident in their presence.

The women stop talking and watch them. He glares at her, deciding if it's worth it to make a scene.

'Get in the car,' he growls.

'She said she's not getting in, now off you go,' one of the women says, and Pip is so grateful.

'Shut up, you,' he says, irritated.

'Want us to go inside and ask for Angela?' the other woman asks. 'Maybe she wants to walk home too.'

'Who the hell is Angela?' Sammy asks.

Pip knows what she means. It's code for women, for letting bar staff know that a date isn't going well, that they need discreet help getting out of a situation that feels weird.

'Get in the car,' Sammy says, his lips close to her ear. She shudders.

Pip looks back to the pub door and sees that the women are gone. She's alone with him. He takes her by the arm, he squeezes her tightly. Suddenly the door opens and a bouncer steps outside, the two women behind him. Sammy lets go of her arm.

'All right, Sammy,' the bouncer says, opening a packet of cigarettes and lighting up. He looks up to the sky as if he's just getting some air. 'Anyone want one?'

One woman accepts.

His presence is subtle, but it's enough to make Sammy take a step back from Pip. 'Suit yourself. Why don't you call your Dutch boyfriend for a lift.'

He gets into his Range Rover and roars off down the road.

'Thanks,' Pip says, to the ladies.

'Don't thank us, thank Angela,' one says, nudging the bouncer and laughing.

'He's a prick,' the other says of Sammy, blowing smoke rings into the air. Pip watches them disintegrate against the star-filled sky. In the version of the world she looks at in the sky, none of this night has even happened, none of this life has even happened.

Walking home is not the smartest decision she's ever made, but getting away from Sammy was. The journey is almost an hour, on a road in the black of night, with very few street lights, on a Friday night, with cars racing by. A drink-driver could plough right into her, and on many occasions she has to jump quickly into a ditch as the traffic comes dangerously close. She fears Sammy driving by too. She considers calling Io, or her dad, but decides against it. The clouds move in quickly to hide the stars, and it starts to drizzle at first, then gets heavier and she's quickly drenched. Her summer dress clings to her skin, her feet squelch in her trainers, the denim jacket heavy and cold. Despite the danger, the walk is good for her throbbing head and racing heart and she enjoys the cleansing feeling it gives her. She's conscious she's walking beneath the stars and galaxies of the past even if she now can't see them in the rain.

When her house comes into view she lets out a small sob of relief. She walks up the driveway to the door, freezing cold, and shivering.

The lights are all out apart from the hall light, everyone is in bed. She squelches across the gravel to the mature trees. She feels along the bark with her fingers for the house key, which is hanging on a nail. With ice-cold fingers she tries to get the key in the door. She misses once or twice but it slides in on the third try.

The door opens before she has a chance to push it.

'What on earth,' Philip says, examining her.

'I walked home,' she says, shivering, lips quivering. Her hair is dripping down her back. 'He'd been drinking, I didn't want to get in the car with him.'

He looks at her with concern. 'Of course not.' A teetotaller, drinking and driving is an almost mortal sin.

'That was the last date,' she says firmly.

He nods. 'All right, love. You gave it a try. Should I put the kettle on?'

'I'm okay,' she says, leaving her wet trainers at the door. 'Goodnight.'

In the bathroom she peels her wet dress off as quickly as she can, her bra and underwear, hanging them in the shower. She towel dries her hair, her scalp aching where she hit her head against the wall. She is gentle with herself.

When she returns to her bedroom from the bathroom, there's a steaming hot cup of milky tea on her desk. She hears her dad coughing from his bedroom, a wild coughing fit where he sounds as if he's trying to cough up a lung before he goes quiet, then the snoring begins. She puts warm pyjamas on, rubs the fleece against her cheek for comfort. It takes a while before feeling returns to her fingers, and toes.

Her desk calls to her.

She sits down, and picks up a pen.

Origami girl
Gets wet one day
Big sploshes fall
On her paper arms
And paper legs
And paper head
And paper heart.
The ink secrets inside
Have run . . . away.
Too soggy to stand
She hangs herself out to dry
Dangles on a washing line
A peg piercing her shoulder
Swinging back and forth in the breeze
She transitions
Soggy to dry,
Crinkled
But hardened.

Pip folds her paper into the shape of an umbrella and hides it away.

17

THE NEXT MORNING THE lump on her head is about half the size of an egg. It hurts when she moves her head, it hurts when she sits still. It throbs, like a message in Morse code, sending a signal to all the other bumps on other women's heads.

She was worried about falling asleep after hitting her head. She tried to stay awake for as long as she could but she was so exhausted she fell asleep pretty much immediately, which at least prevented her anxiety seeping in.

As soon as Philip drives away from the GAA club where the Pilates class is held Bella turns on her heel.

'Come back earlier this time,' Pip calls after her daughter. Last week she cut it too close.

Pip enters the hall and sees the women on their mats stretching. She doesn't think she'll be able to lie down on her back because of the bump on her head. Kim is across the room and waves enthusiastically, but Pip's mind is elsewhere. She turns around and leaves, hurrying after Bella.

She'd seen her walk in the direction of the park. She finds her, walking towards a young lad at the entrance. She throws her arms around him and they kiss. He's young, like Bella, and Pip is happy to see this. She'd worried about it being an older married man or a weirdo.

She follows them into the park. They move away from the obvious places, to the dog walking off the leash area where the grass is long and they can have more privacy. She walks around the perimeter behind the mature trees, catching glimpses of them beyond the foliage. She finds a good viewing place where they can't see her. They sit on the grass. Him upright, her sprawled across his lap, they move around switching positions, but always their eyes locked on each other, fingers clasped. They talk a lot and then they don't talk at all, just staring deeply into each other's eyes. They kiss passionately and she doesn't need to look away. She thought this would be an uncomfortable thing to watch her daughter do, but it's not, because he's kind, and gentle, he's respectful. And she's so happy. They laugh so much.

'Oh my God,' Pip whispers, watching the line appear on the stick she has urinated on.

Jamie leans over and looks, so close she moves the stick away so that he doesn't wet his nose with her wee.

He looks up at her and he's smiling.

'What are you smiling at?' she asks, baffled, her mind racing.

'Am I supposed to pretend to be sad? Scared?' he says. 'Is this where I'm supposed to tell you to take care of it and I don't want anything to do with it?'

'I'm scared,' she says, smiling and blocking her mouth. She can't believe they're reacting like this. They're giddy.

They laugh and embrace.

'Bella for a girl. Maradona for a boy.'

She snorts.

'Pelé.'

'No chance.'

'We've time to discuss it.'

'Consider it discussed.'

'Georgie Best,' he says through a cough into his hand.

'I don't mind that one so much.'

He sits back on the floor of the bathroom. He takes her hand and gently draws her to him. She sits across his crotch, facing him. He places his hand on her flat stomach.

'This is how we got ourselves into this position,' he says playfully.

She laughs, and then suddenly nothing is funny anymore.

'My mam is going to kill me,' she says, the reality setting in, looking at his hand on her stomach.

'That's why we can't tell them.'

She thought he'd have wise words for her, tell her that she's wrong, not to worry, that everything is going to be okay. But Jamie is always honest.

'Who knows what they'll do? They'll make you give the baby up for adoption or they'll send you away or something messed up. And my parents won't be much better.'

'How can't we tell them? They're going to know pretty soon without me even saying anything.'

'We'll move away. I've got family in Liverpool. Mam and Dad have talked about me going to work with them some summers. They can help me get a job. I'll take care of you and the baby. It might not be easy for a while, but we'll be okay.'

She's so grateful that he's saying these things, that he's planning to stick by her, but her head is racing. 'Can we even move out of home at sixteen? Is it legal? Can you legally work? Can I just go to a hospital in another country and have a baby by myself and like, nobody will take it from me?'

He hadn't thought of any of that.

'Jamie,' she says, worried.

'Okay, maybe we will tell them. You're right, we'll have to tell them. But we have to be, like, firm. We have to be strong. We love each other, we want to be with each other. We both want this baby together.' He stalls.

'What?'

'Unless you don't.'

'Oh shut up, I flipping well do.'

She kisses him.

It's a terrifying place to be, but it's terrifying together. They are firm and strong, they are mature and honest with their parents. But no matter how indestructible and united they thought they would be, the guillotine still falls.

Pip watches Bella and her boyfriend for a while. Her head is thudding, really aching around the back and all around her head. She has no idea what happened. She didn't see Sammy hit her, or shove her, the only force she recalls is the brick wall behind her as her head smashed back into it.

She'd laughed at him for saying Picasso instead of Monet, which was amusing to her because they weren't remotely similar. Monet was the father of Impressionism, Picasso was a post-impressionist, a Cubist. She wasn't laughing at Sammy, she was laughing at the comparison. Snobbish she supposed, and he didn't like it. She knows that he didn't like it from the way his smile flattened, his eyes darkened. But was he really so insulted that he smacked her head, or did she get knocked in the busy pub?

She walks through the park back to main street, keeping her head down and hugging the shadows so that Philip doesn't see her in case he's hanging around waiting. When Pip and Bella's time is up, she makes her way back to the Pilates class. She stands inside the door so that Philip will see her walking out.

'Hey again,' Kim says, exiting the toilet in the hallway outside. 'I'm not gonna lie, I pretended I needed the loo just to avoid that last part. I didn't see you in there today.'

'No. I had to go do something, see someone, do, go somewhere, and I had a, have a headache.' Pip is a terrible liar.

'Oh,' Kim says, trying to make sense of that garbled sentence. 'I hope you're feeling okay.'

'Yes.' Pip blushes. 'Apart from my head that feels like it's cracked open. Probably the late night, I'm not used to going out.'

Kim doesn't laugh at her attempt at a joke. She looks concerned. 'Is everything okay?'

'Yes, yes. Perfect,' she lies, feeling her eyes fill up. Nothing is perfect, it's not remotely okay.

Kim looks concerned. 'I can sense there's something going on, maybe I'm wrong. But I'm here for you if you'd like to talk.'

Pip just nods, unable to force words out through the lump in her throat.

The class ends. Kim looks inside. 'Look, I'd love to ask you for a coffee today, but the girls have invited me out with them and I already said yes. It all feels a bit high school, but I've stepped into the middle of something with you guys and I don't quite know what to do about it. It's none of my business, and yet it kind of is because I don't want to take part in a mean girls movie.'

Pip frowns. 'What do you mean?'

'Caroline.'

Pip looks inside and sees her neighbour tidying her mat away.

'To be honest I'm in the dark about it myself. I've offended them and I've no idea how.'

'They said it had something to do with the man you're dating.'

'Ugh. Sammy. I'm not dating him. He's not good for me. He's not good.' She so much wants to tell someone, and Kim seems to be understanding and caring. She whispers, 'He's the reason I have this headache.'

Kim puts a supportive hand on her arm and the concerned look she gives her scares Pip.

'I don't mean it like that,' she says quickly, back-pedalling. 'I mean that the idea of him gives me a headache. The situation,' she says, gulping, 'is enough to give me a . . .'

'Headache,' Kim says, gently. 'Yes, I understand.'

'Hiya Pip,' Bella says, returning, out of breath.

Pip jumps to attention, assumes the mother position.

'What did you do in class today, in case they ask.' She completely ignores Kim, who's standing right beside her.

'Bella, remember Kim?'

'Hiya,' she says, chewing gum.

Pip is a terrible liar, but it doesn't mean she won't do it when she has to. She can't look at Kim. 'Uh, we did . . .'

'A fully body burn hit,' Kim says.

'Full body burn hit,' Bella repeats.

'And a lot of accessories,' Kim adds. 'Ball work, weights, the whole shebang.'

She reaches out to hold Pip's arm. 'Call me, Philippa, okay?'

'Yeah. Thanks.'

From upstairs, in Pip's room, she can hear Bella downstairs on her weekly phone call to Jamie. Her words aren't clear, just murmuring. She gets down on her hands and knees and puts her ear to the laminate floor, as close to Jamie as she can possibly be.

But she can't settle. She can't lie there as she normally would. She feels pathetic. She jumps to her feet, feeling the need to do something, feeling the urge to scream. Adrenaline is rushing through her, she paces her small floorspace. She thought that Sammy could be her way out of here. He's not. But the idea of a different future has been introduced to her, a brighter, clearer picture has emerged, and she can't get it out of her mind. There is no going back.

She stands at her desk to write. She doesn't sit down, she's antsy.

Origami girl
Practises opening
Parts of herself
While no one else is looking
Quarters into halves,
And halves back to quarters
Over and over again
Just to see what it's like
To unfold

Pip folds the square page into an origami butterfly. It sits on the tip of her finger pad and she examines it closely, expecting it to flutter, willing it to take flight. It bides its time. Not yet. But soon.

18

'Hiya Pip.'

Her heart flutters immediately at the sound of his voice.

Only two people have ever called her Pip; Bella and Jamie. And the only reason Pip encouraged Bella to say Pip is because it's what Jamie called her. If she couldn't have Mama, and she couldn't have Jamie, then at least she would have that.

He's here. Jamie is back.

She hasn't been this close to him in years, and now here she is, with her hair in a hairnet, in an unflattering red T-shirt, and an apron that's covered in twelve different food types.

Jamie.

Captivating presence.

Broad shoulders.

Doe-eyed.

Home.

'Jamie,' she says, her voice high-pitched and sounding fifteen years old again. 'Hi.'

Her heart is pounding so hard he must hear it.

Chin downward, he looks up now and then shyly through long eyelashes, his cheeks and the tips of his ears pink, matching his strawberry blond hair.

He's a little taller and a lot wider, built up in the shoulders from the physical work over the years on construction sites. He's had braces at some point, no more pointy little fangs on either side of his front teeth. She liked those fangs, liked to run her tongue over them.

He is more handsome than she could even have fantasised about. Her breath catches. She doesn't know what to say, or why he's here. It's a service station. Maybe he's filling his car, but he's at the wrong counter for that.

'Do you want a sandwich?'

'No, thanks.'

She feels stupid. She peels off her gloves to at least feel a bit more human.

'What are you doing here?'

'Sorry for coming over.'

'No, I don't mean it like that. I'm glad.'

'Are you? Good. I got diesel,' he says, looking over his shoulder to his car.

She nods. 'You have to pay at the till. I just make sandwiches.'

'Yeah. I know.'

She smiles and he grins and rubs his eyes, embarrassed.

'God, what are we like? I got the boat over today,' he says, sounding a bit more confident. 'So I could have the car while I'm here. A bit more freedom. I'm just arriving to town now.'

So Sammy's rumours were true.

'Does anyone know you're arriving today?'

'Finbar.'

'Does Bella know?'

'No. I didn't want her to say something, and for them to all . . . you know . . .'

She knows. He didn't have to say anything more for her

to know exactly how something simple can get so complicated when everyone gets involved. He's the only person who understands exactly how she has been treated, because he has been treated similarly too. Though he was allowed to stay in school and finish his state exams, get his education so he could have a career, and she wasn't. Nine months' maternity leave and she was sent out to work. She envied him that. And while he was sent away at eighteen years old, frogmarched to a boat to Liverpool, it felt like a prison sentence, she also grew to envy how he was allowed to start a new life, without anyone knowing all of his business.

'I suppose you know why I'm over.'

She nods sympathetically.

'Dad's got himself into some serious trouble. He missed court hearings that none of us knew about.'

'I heard.'

'Of course you did.'

Then suddenly she doesn't know what to say. He's right here in front of her, she's done all kinds of things to him in her imagination, and him to her. She's arrived at the docks in Liverpool over and over again, and he has greeted her with excitement and lust. But in reality, she doesn't know what to say. He's not the fifteen-year-old she fell in love with, the sixteen-year-old she was ripped from. The eighteen-year-old who had to leave the country. He's a man now, living in Liverpool, with a life she knows nothing about. He's become the object of her fantasies, but she doesn't have any idea about his real life.

The words fly out of him, fast, urgent. 'I want to spend time with Bella while I'm here.'

She loves how he says Bella.

'Of course. I'll speak with Mam and Dad.'

'No,' he says, angrily. 'I'm speaking with you. We don't need all the heads of state to come together, we can work this out ourselves.'

He must see her terror because he softens. 'I'm not angry with you Pip.'

Pip, Pip, Pip.

'It's them I'm angry with. It's criminal what they did to us.' His voice trembles with the anger coursing through him. 'The way they treated you, the way they sent me away.'

Alarm bells ring. The only other person who has referred to her treatment is Sammy, but he's not the moral compass she'd follow. Up until that point she assumed it was just all in her head. Hearing it from Jamie, is dizzying. He agrees. He has been her secret long-distance accomplice all this time.

'Maybe it's different for you because you live here, but as soon as I get here, as soon as I take the exit for Ballybeg on the motorway, I turn into a scared shitless kid who can be controlled. But not this time.'

He has raised his voice, and Krish comes over.

'Everything okay?'

She nods quickly.

'Krish, could Jamie and I talk in private please?'

He allows her ten minutes in the staffroom. Ronnie is leaving as they enter.

'Make sure you clean your jizz up after you,' he says, motioning with his hand.

'Watch your mouth,' Jamie says, giving Ronnie a shove. Ronnie is surprised as he falls over his feet and slams against his locker, steadies himself and then quickly leaves the staffroom. 'Who's that prick?'

All she can do is laugh. With relief. And surprise. And giddiness.

Her heart is pounding, her hands shaking. She hasn't been in the same room with Jamie for years, she hasn't been alone with him since the day they told their parents the news about the pregnancy. Their last sweet moment together. When they had so much hope, and bravery, filled with the belief that if they were together they'd be stronger. He thought he could protect her, she thought they could be a family of three. They were naïve.

Maybe he's thinking the same thing, maybe he's not. Maybe he's thinking about the hot woman he's left at home in Liverpool, keeping the bed warm for him. She has no idea who he is anymore, or what he does with his life.

'Is it okay with you if I see Bella? That's all I care about.'

He's trying to compose himself, but it looks as if he's about to break.

'And I don't mean spending time with her in a room with all of them watching me, like I'm some sort of court-ordered dad who's a danger to his child.'

'I don't think that,' she whispers, barely able to breathe in his presence.

'I feel as if they're listening to me on the phone with her. Judging everything I say; don't say this, don't mention that, you'll damage her. I have to watch everything I say. Sometimes I don't know what to say.' A trembling finger moves a hair out of his eye. 'And I've got so much to say to her, so much I want to tell her, and I can't because I keep thinking they're listening down the phone.'

She's astonished to hear that he has the same insecurities as she does. 'They're not, by the way,' she says, thinking of herself just last Sunday, ear to the floor listening to Bella's murmurs.

He looks relieved for a second. The anger subsides too and he calms.

'Bella doesn't know the real me. And it's like she's afraid to open up, we barely get more than ten minutes to speak, have they told her not to?'

This doesn't make sense, she hears Bella talking and laughing for thirty minutes every week. Pip sits upstairs in her bedroom, listening, yearning to be in on the conversation, feeling jealous.

He's staring at her waiting for the answer.

She shakes her head.

It's so difficult to explain. How can she explain that there wasn't a moment that they told Bella not to love her dad, not to open up to him. It was done from the beginning, the denigration of their role as Bella's parents began from the start. They were devalued from the moment she took her first breath, when Jamie wasn't allowed in the labour ward and Bella wasn't allowed to sleep in with her mother as soon as they went home. Ever since her escape attempt when Bella was a toddler, Josephine has watched her like a hawk. It's not a rule that Bella is following, it's a learned behaviour. When it's all you know, it becomes everyday.

But it has never felt normal to Pip. She's so nervous she can't figure out how to put the words together.

Jamie continues, his frustration rising again. 'I don't even have Bella's mobile number, I have to contact Josephine to get to her. Anyone I tell that to, and believe me there's not many I can admit that to, they can't wrap their head around it. They ask me what I've done? Is there some kind of court order? Is there some kind of legal custody arrangement, which there isn't, right? None of this has been done legally as far as I know.'

Pip shakes her head. She would remember signing something, wouldn't she?

'I'd love to be able to text her. Send her links to things I think she'll like. I have no way of getting to her, unless it's noon on a Sunday.'

He's twisted up with frustration.

'My own daughter doesn't even know the real me. I was shipped off to a family I didn't even know. I tried to tell her I didn't leave by choice, but whenever I broach the subject she says she has to go, and I want to talk to her for as long as possible so I stopped bringing it up. Does she ever ask? What do you tell her about what happened?'

Pip's head is racing. She can't think of a single discussion they've had about it. Bella has never asked, but of course she must have wondered. Perhaps it's Josephine who has done all the explaining, taking control of the narrative when it should have been Pip. Why has Pip let that happen?

'She doesn't ask,' she says, looking down at her hands, feeling like an utter failure. She has so desperately wanted to be a mother to Bella, but she hasn't even tried to do what is right.

'I wish I could have stayed here, and been her dad.'

This sentence instantly triggers her and angers her, because she had to stay here and still wasn't allowed to be her mother. She doesn't know why they bothered to let her stay home at all. She would have been better off going away with Jamie. She feels desperate for thinking that of Bella, but every memory she has of her, Josephine is inserted into it. Which could be lovely, that she raised her child with her mother, but it doesn't feel that way. She feels like her daughter was stolen right before her eyes. That it happens every single day over and over again.

'Sorry,' he says, retreating. The energy seems to leave him. He looks exhausted. He looks around as if suddenly surprised to be in a closet-sized room with her. 'I'm putting you on the spot. It's a lot to throw at you. I wasn't even going to say hi, then I saw you.' He looks at her and her stomach flutters, the way it always used to. Sixteen years, they can't steal that feeling away from her. 'And then I had to say hi. And then it all came out.'

Say something, Pip, say something that will let him know you feel the same. That you have sat in silence for so long, tell him that you don't know how to start speaking. Tell him that you can barely formulate the thoughts. Tell him that you have been teaming up with him in your mind for years now. Tell him.

'Where I live in Liverpool,' he says, anger reappearing, 'I'm considered a man. I make adult decisions, and get treated like one. I own an apartment. I have a job. A good one. I lead a team. Here, I'm a child. The family land was supposed to be mine. I'm the eldest son, it was supposed to fall to me. They're all fighting for it now, nobody's asking me to come and help, like I'm not even part of the family. They just struck me off straight away for doing something that wasn't even wrong.'

Her eyes widen.

It wasn't? He doesn't think it was wrong? Her heart pounds. These are huge revelations coming all at once.

'I let everyone in the family down and there isn't a day that goes by that I'll ever be able to make it up to them. No matter what I do.'

Her eyes are filled with tears, it's exactly how she feels. All her thoughts in words. Words she can't say, can't possibly speak out loud. She can't even think them. He can't come here and unravel her, he'll leave again, and she'll be stuck here without him, unable to pick up where he left off, or unable to continue it on her own.

Help, she wants to say. *Help me, I don't know where to start.*

He stands up from the crate. 'That's probably a lot for you. All at once. I'm sorry. I just vented at you. That wasn't fair. It's good to see you, Pip.'

He leaves.

No! This is not how it's supposed to go! She's not supposed to let him leave, and yet she's frozen in the spot by what he's suggesting – change, taking control, confrontation, upsetting everything. She'd told herself to start making a plan, but she'd been lying to herself. She's not brave enough. She hears all the Origami girls she has created over the past fifteen years yelling at her from their boxes, held captive with their secret desires and yearning to be free.

She hadn't even been able to tell him how happy she was to see him.

19

JAMIE IS HOME, JAMIE is home.

Jamie is here, and Jamie does feel like home.

But it has been days since she saw him, and she hasn't heard a thing from him, or from Josephine or Bella about him. Pip hasn't been able to stop thinking about him since she saw him, just like the old days, the same teenage feelings are still inside her and have intensified over time, ripened with age, and loneliness and desperation and neediness and neglect and abandonment. Marinating like decimated plants in a bog.

She wishes now she'd given him her phone number, that she'd been more eloquent and articulate. That she'd been appropriately funny and quirky. That she'd not been making sandwiches with a grinning red squirrel over her left tit. She now knows all the perfect things she could have said to him.

She thinks about him in bed at night, falling asleep and falling into dreams about him, and she thinks about him at length in the shower. Josephine had banged on the bathroom door both mornings to hurry her up as she was taking all the hot water.

She can identify with Io now, having to wait. Waiting for a signal from a distant star, is like waiting for a phone call from Jamie. When will he contact her? When is he going to make his move? What is his plan? Will he be strong enough for it or will he revert to the sixteen-year-old teen that he spoke about, the sixteen-year-old that Pip wasn't able to move on from. Until now.

She must continue with her plans while she waits to hear from him.

'Bella and I will be in town for a few hours tomorrow,' she says, at dinner.

Bella looks at her in surprise, then hides it.

'Why's that?' Josephine asks.

'I'm meeting a friend of mine for a coffee. Do you remember Kim Banks?'

'Her father had a double hip replacement,' Josephine says. 'Her mother's in a bad way. Early signs of dementia.'

'Yes. We're going for a coffee.'

'And why does Isabella have to go too?'

'I want Kim to meet her.'

Josephine doesn't say anything, but Pip can hear her brain working overtime. Does she think that this is a trick and that Bella is going to meet her dad? Jamie is in town and Josephine is especially jumpy. Pip expects some new event will coincidentally arise; a cousin's birthday party, an aunt they have to visit.

Upstairs, Bella pokes her head into her room.

'What's that about?' she hisses. 'I don't want to go for coffee with your friend.'

'We're not. I bought you three hours. Don't do anything stupid.'

Bella grins. She bursts into the bedroom and throws her arms around Pip. 'You're the best.'

Pip closes her eyes and savours the moment.

'Are you meeting Dad?' she asks, quietly.

Pip wishes. 'No. Have you heard from him?'

'I bumped into him at the shop. He asked if he could follow me on Instagram,' she says, making a disgusted face. 'And he wants me to teach him how to Snapchat.'

Pip has to laugh. She wouldn't even ask her daughter that.

'Nan says they're arranging a day for us to meet.' She rolls her eyes. 'First of all I have to work every day, and then on my time off I have to meet him, it doesn't feel like a summer at all.'

'Spending time with your dad is not supposed to be a punishment. You should get to know him, Bella. He's not what you think. He's wonderful. So funny, and kind, and sweet. He'd be thoughtful and respectful of your space. He really is the most perfect . . .' she trails off, as Bella is looking at her with one of her faces that looks like her head is screwed back too far into her neck.

'Do you still have a crush on him? Oh my God, you do.' Then she looks disgusted. 'This is so gross. I'm getting out of here.'

Pip laughs at Bella being unable to get out of her room fast enough, and as soon as she's gone, she ponders her words. Then falls back on her bed with a silly smile on her face.

Origami Girl
Has an origami heart
That flutters
In the wind
White
Slight
Paper light
She whispers:
I surrender.

As soon as Philip drives away from the GAA club and his car disappears from sight, Pip looks around for Io's car. He's parked outside the post office and flashes his headlights twice. She grins, then tries to conceal it. Bella looks at her, eyes narrowed, like her grandmother.

'What are you up to today?'

'Never you mind. Don't you have somewhere to be? You usually can't get away quick enough.'

Bella's not used to this side of Pip, the side of her that's trying to get rid of her. Pip's usually the clingy one, the one eager to please Bella. Typically, playing hard to get is attracting her.

'Meet you back at the café in three hours. Do not be late or you'll mess it up for the both of us, and believe me they'll never let you see him again.'

She nods, solemnly, knowing this to be true, suddenly looking young and nervous, not her usual cocky self. She's not in control this time. Pip is her mother and she has put her in this situation. Pip softens.

'You have three whole hours with him,' she says, gently. 'Enjoy it.'

Bella perks up, she kisses Pip on the cheek, taking her by surprise. 'Thank you. His name is Mark by the way.'

'Thank you,' Pip says, grateful to be let in.

'Who's the fella in the car?'

'Io. He's from the Netherlands.' She doesn't want to mention that he works at the observatory.

'Io is the name of one of Jupiter's moons,' Bella says.

'Is it? I met him at the station. I made him a sandwich. There's nothing in it. He's a friend. Don't mention him to Nan and Granddad.'

Bella looks over at Io, taking a photo of him with her mind.

'If you don't tell them about Mark, I won't tell them about Io. Spraytan Sammy might not be so happy though.'

'I don't give two fucks about Spraytan Sammy,' Pip says, without thinking.

Bella bursts out laughing.

'Tell Mark I said hi.' Pip grins.

'Okay,' Bella says, cheeks going pink. She walks away, the momentary glimpse of her teenage insecurity hidden again by a confident stride and a swing in her hips.

Io pulls up beside Pip in his car. He's wearing aviator sunglasses, and lowers them seductively down his nose as the window lowers.

He's blaring Frank Sinatra's 'Come Fly With Me', attracting stares from the breakfast brigade eating outdoors in the café opposite.

She laughs and gets in. As they drive away she passes by Kim, who gives her a wave. Pip's feeling on top of the world and rebellious, as they drive out of town leaving everyone behind. He drives them to an airfield that Pip never even knew existed, a six-minute drive away. No one asks him any questions as he drives around the hangar and parks beside the only other car in the car park.

Pip looks out at the grass runway.

'How are you feeling?' he asks, thoughtfully checking in with her.

'Excited.'

'You're going to love it.'

'I'm worried I might want you to keep going.'

A woman in khaki appears from the hangar. She holds her hand up to her forehead to block out the sun as she checks who has arrived.

Authoritative.

In command.

Boiler suit.

Ripped.

She reminds Pip of a soldier. Io lifts his hand in greeting, the woman recognises him and waves. She goes back inside.

'Who's that?'

'Stella. She's a friend. She runs the place, builds and fixes planes and other flying machines.'

'Other flying machines,' she repeats, smiling. 'Like what, a Tardis?'

'Helicopters. Rockets. Spaceships.'

Pip studies the hangar as they walk towards it. There are variations of small sized planes, and two helicopters. 'You don't seem to have the rockets and spaceships today.'

'Someone must have taken them out,' he jokes.

Stella is inside a small office inside the hangar. She's in the middle of a yawn as they walk inside.

'Morning, Stella. Late night?'

'The latest.'

Pip imagines her at a trad session in a pub banging a bodhrán until all hours, until she realises they meant at work. She didn't think the airfield would be open at night.

'This is Stella. Also known as Control Tower.'

'Nice to meet you, I'm Pip.'

They shake hands. Stella almost crushes her hand with the strength of her grip.

'This is Pip's first time in the air,' Io says.

'A groundling.' Stella examines her, then looks to Io. 'Does she know you're not a groundling?'

Pip isn't sure what passes between them.

'She knows that I fly planes and helicopters,' Io says.

'Please tell me that's true,' Pip says. 'Or I'm not going up there with him.'

'Io is one of the best pilots we have. You'll be in safe hands,' she says firmly. 'You'll go up a Pip and come down an Apple Tree. See what I did there? Though it's kind of cool down here on the ground. Gravity gives me a real kick,' she says, with a wink. 'Which one are you taking out?'

Io looks across through the office window to the hangar at the options. Everything's lined up neatly, sparkling clean and ready to fly. 'That's up to Pip.'

'I brought my passport,' Pip says, producing it. She has never left the country, but they all have a passport for ID purposes. It's her third one, and this is in as pristine condition as the first. It's never been stamped.

'Oh, we don't need to see that,' Stella says, taking it and reading her information anyway. She hands the passport back to Pip. 'So how is it going over there?' she asks Io.

'It's quiet,' he says. 'Too quiet.'

'It'll come.'

Pip tunes out of their conversation and leaves the office. She walks around the hangar, looking at the planes and helicopters. She's drawn to one plane in particular, at the far end. It reminds her of an origami plane, something she could easily fold together. Smaller than the others, it's tucked away in the corner. Neat, small.

She walks around it, reaches out to touch it.

'A Tomark Viper SD4,' Io says, suddenly beside her, making her jump.

'Is it easy to fly?'

'This for me is like a horse and cart for you. It's as rudimentary as they come.' He pats it as though it's a horse.

'I hope not, because I can't operate a horse and cart. Nor can I drive a car.'

He looks startled by this, as if she's an obscure being.

They climb onto the wing to get inside, just two seats, with a great glass lid closing over them.

They taxi out of the hangar, Stella watching them from her office.

Io speaks to somebody, presumably Stella, into the microphone attached to his headpiece about clearing for take-off. Pip can't hear their conversation as it's on another frequency.

They sit at the beginning of the grass airstrip, the engine on, the plane jumping excitedly as though it's on the boil, as the engine builds.

'Ready?'

'Up, up and away,' Pip says.

20

P IP FEELS AS THOUGH she's in a paper plane blowing around the sky. Origami girl in a folded-up plane, and it feels wonderful.

She leans her head against the glass and looks down at the town she has lived and worked in for her entire life. This large place that she often feels like she's drowning in, which looks like nothing at all. One main street and a few streets off it, amidst the peatlands and agricultural land, a patchwork quilt covering a lumpy mattress.

The boglands surround Ballybeg. They hug the town, nestle it, preserving the people who toiled them. They're seemingly calm, still and quiet, and yet just above and beneath the surface they are alive. Their moods vary wildly, they can be gloomy and secretive, thick and dense and hiding anything in there, swallowing up whatever dares to land or grow on them. They can feel like a sleepy hollow on foggy days, or playgrounds for wildlife on brighter days. Their mood is as contagious as it is inspiring.

'That's Jamie's land,' she says in awe as they fly over the recognisable peatlands. 'His dad's land,' she says, correcting herself. When they sent Jamie away he lost his right to the land, lost his right to everything that meant something to him.

But now he's back, and what can he change? Her stomach lurches.

'Not his dad's land anymore,' Io says. 'It's protected.'

'It's more complex than you think, Io.'

'Protecting the earth isn't complex. Earth is teetering on a planetary tightrope. You're plunging headlong into a disaster.'

'Please don't use those words while you're flying a plane. And why is it my fault? It's your planet too. I respect the tradition of turf-cutting,' she says, 'but I also respect the need to protect the planet.'

'Diplomatic,' he says, his lips curling at the side.

'But I understand more than anything,' she continues, 'that to constantly pick at something is to deplete it. To leave it alone is to let it grow. Josephine digs at me and Bella, while I like to stand back and watch my daughter grow. When you watch, you see how things change in new surprising ways.'

He smiles at her.

'Shouldn't you watch where you're going?'

'We're not on the road.'

'No, we're in the sky,' she says, nervously. Then grins and declares, 'We're in the sky! Woohoo!' She raises her arms up in the air, in the tight space.

Up here her small life is put into perspective.

Io points out Crossroads, a tiny, insignificant place in the middle of the spaghetti of roads. She always felt like she was on a desert island, completely stranded until she was collected by one of her parents. But it's not stranded, there are numerous routes leading out of there and away from it in every direction. Ways out and places to go. Roads that lead, not to nowhere, but to somewhere, because she can see the somewheres that they reach, which aren't that far away at all.

The quarry is impossible to miss, they fly right over. Like someone has taken a bite out of the earth, and left it to rot. An open ugly wound in an otherwise green vibrant world. The grey stone hole in the ground with little robots traversing it and digging and excavating, surrounded by green. Her dad works down there somewhere, the huge man, like an ant now. Her house is easy to find after identifying the quarry. The road to the quarry winds a long way around, with a small copse between their house and the quarry. They are far closer to the quarry than she thought, it looks as if the quarry is coming for their house, will get bigger and bigger until they topple right in, getting sucked into the rotten core.

The Wolversons, huge in Ballybeg, are kings of a very small kingdom. They fly on, out of there.

Io checks in on her.

She sheds happy tears.

'Thank you,' she says, reaching out and momentarily holding his hand.

As soon as they land, the real world comes back to her with a bump. She can see why Io likes it up there so very much.

Stella walks out to greet them, her silhouette against the hangar like that of a gymnast.

'How do you feel?' she asks, as Pip climbs out and Io helps her from the wing to the ground.

Exhilarated.

Overwhelmed.

Stimulated.

Free.

She currently feels completely incapable of slipping back into her normal life.

'I feel like, the world is big, and I'm trapped in a very tiny part of it.'

'No,' Io says. 'Your world is very small. The universe is big.'

He looks up, and she imagines he's looking past the sky, out of the stratosphere and into the space beyond that he loves so much.

'And you're not trapped, you're . . .'

He seems to cock his ear, listening for his signal.

'. . . Waiting,' she says.

'The signal will come,' Stella calls over her shoulder as she makes her way back to the office. 'And when it does, you might even miss the wait, so enjoy it while it lasts.'

21

SINCE ARRIVING HOME AND lying on her bed reliving it all, her adrenaline rush has ended with a crash. The invincibility field has worn off and now she feels slightly stunned. And stupid. Like the part in *The Truman Show* when Truman realises his world isn't real.

Flying has been life-changing. It has given Pip perspective. She has been shown the broader picture, a beautiful large landscape painting, and she has been living in one tiny brushstroke.

Origami girl
Folds herself
Into a paper aeroplane
Jumps
Glides
And soars
Before
Crash landing
On the floor

She folds the square page into a small paper aeroplane, similar to the plane she flew in today, and before she opens the box to store it, she has an idea.

She stands at her bedroom window with her origami girl paper aeroplane. She looks out at the agricultural and bogland that stretches out to the horizon.

'Good luck,' she says, to her origami girl.

She lets her go out of the window, and with a whoosh, she watches her glide and soar, hoping her origami girl will feel the exhilaration Pip felt in the sky with Io. Immense freedom. It swoops and glides, it even soars, but only momentarily, before being true to the ink written within, it crashes onto the bonnet of Josephine's car.

Pip hears the front door open seconds after it lands, and Pip races downstairs to get to it first.

Josephine picks it up. 'What on earth?'

Pip snaps it from her hand. 'I was just messing around.'

'Goodness, Pip, have you nothing better to do with your time? In fact, I smell a rat. What have you be doing with your time?' She puts her hands on her hips.

Josephine is petite but she has the ability to make herself bigger, and intimidating, inflating herself like a puffer fish when she feels under attack.

'You've been keeping something from me.'

Pip can't lie, so she's not going to start, or she'll be found out and everything will be taken from her.

'Can I show you something? In my bedroom.'

Josephine looks alarmed. 'What is it?'

'It's in my room.'

They go upstairs to her room and stand in the narrow space between the bed and the wardrobe.

Josephine looks nervous. 'Don't tell me you're pregnant. Please don't tell me you're—'

'I'm not pregnant.'

Josephine hears the bark in Pip's voice and remains tight-lipped.

'This is what I want to show you.' Pip starts to remove the sketches that cover her wall in an erratic line that now snakes to the ceiling.

'What kind of a mess have you made? Is it the Sistine Chapel you're going for?' she asks smartly, looking up at the sketches on the ceiling.

Pip sighs and works hard not to react to the criticism. There have been sixteen years of put-downs and insults. She was numb to it for so long, but lately she's starting to wake up.

Pip's sketches serve as stitches but do not get to the heart of the problem, which is deteriorating further. She removes the sketches from the wall one by one, revealing the crack. Finally Pip removes the Monet print, and the crack in its entirety is revealed.

Josephine gasps. 'What did you do?'

Pip's laugh is cutting. While she blamed herself at the beginning, the idea that she has done this herself is farcical, and Josephine knows it. Josephine appears scolded.

'It started a few weeks ago.'

'Why didn't you tell your dad?'

'This is his dream house. I didn't want to ruin it.'

This is true, but mostly it's because Pip has relied on wishing for nasty things to go away without actively doing anything to banish them herself. As if she needed any more proof that disassociating herself from the problem doesn't work, the cracks, which have become gory and invasive like an open wound, are confirmation that when you ignore something small, it grows.

The house looks as though it's about to be split in two.

22

WHEN PIP RETURNS FROM work on Monday afternoon with Philip, Josephine is standing at the door looking like she has witnessed a murder.

'We have a visitor.' Her voice is low and raspy, which means somebody is inside.

'What's going on?' Philip asks.

'I have no idea,' Pip says, genuinely confused.

All of a sudden Pip realises the number of secrets she has been keeping from Josephine, because she can't even guess what's coming. It could be anything from lying about the Pilates class, to Bella's boyfriend, to flying, to the injuries she received from Sammy, to her harmless origami girl art. Or it could be that she switched the dishwasher rinse aid with another brand without telling her mother. Anything on any scale could annoy her mother in equal amounts.

Pip steps into the house and sees Jamie sitting in the TV room on the couch, his back to her. Someone is beside him, she sees a leg, and assumes it's Maureen, his mother, she accompanies him on all of his visits to their house, or at least, she did before they moved Bella's visits with Jamie to his parents' house, and Pip wasn't invited.

Pip heads for the stairs.

'Where do you think you're going?' Josephine asks.

'I want to change.'

Josephine glances at her red Ballybeg service station T-shirt with the cheerful red squirrel over her breast and her mis-shapen stained black trousers.

'It's not a fashion show. Get in there.'

Josephine's raised voice has attracted attention already and Jamie has turned around to look at her.

'Hi,' she says.

He stands up respectfully. 'Pip, hi,' he says, reaching his hand out. She takes it awkwardly and he leans in to kind of give her a kiss on the cheek, but it's not a kiss, it's a kind of fleeting skin rub. His aftershave is strong, divine, but she also smells perspiration. Nervous sweat. Josephine watches the display and Philip ignores it entirely, walking around the room without greeting either of them and sitting in his armchair, out of the circle.

Pip looks at the woman beside Jamie, who has also stood and is offering to shake Pip's hand.

Long legs.

Dark eyes.

Cashmere aesthetic.

Sophisticated.

Pip guesses she's a lawyer, or someone official. Maybe because Pip was anything but helpful during their discussion at the service station, Jamie has decided to take the legal route.

'Tala,' she says, with a smile, taking her hand. 'It's nice to meet you, Pip.'

Pip smiles tightly. For once, Philippa would do just fine for her.

'It's Philippa,' Josephine says suddenly, sitting beside Pip, and she's grateful for her mother's backup.

Jamie sits, wiping his clammy hands on his jeans.

Jamie, on her couch, in her home. Pip will hug the cushions afterwards and smell the fabrics. She wonders where Bella is.

'They just arrived before you. You know, Jamie, with a bit of notice I could have something prepared for you.' She's telling them off in as polite a way as possible and she doesn't normally do polite. Perhaps the presence of the striking cashmere queen has her sitting more upright. 'Would you like tea?'

'No thank you,' Tala says.

'Water, please,' Jamie says, nervously, clearing his throat.

'Philip?' Josephine says.

He shakes his head. Neither of them wants to drag this on any longer than it has to. They're not welcome here.

Josephine looks at Pip. Pip tries to figure out what the look means. The hidden meaning, seeing as they're momentarily on the same team.

'Water,' Josephine snaps. 'Get Jamie a water.'

'Oh, yes, okay,' she says, embarrassed to be snapped at in company.

She leaves the room, cheeks ablaze.

She takes a moment in the kitchen to gather herself. She fixes her hair, her face, grabs a dry T-shirt from the clothes horse and changes, returning to the living room feeling slightly refreshed.

She places the water down on the coffee table.

'Thanks, Pip,' he says, as if she has given him the world.

Tala looks at him, a curious expression on her face, and for the first time, Pip reconsiders her take on her. A lawyer or social worker wouldn't look at him in that way. The look that passed across her face seemed personal. And she doesn't have any files or paperwork with her, just a grey Mulberry handbag on the floor by her feet. She's sitting close to Jamie, hips touching, personal space encroached on both sides.

Long legs.

Dark eyes.

Jamie's woman.

Grown-up.

Jamie watches Pip assessing Tala, she feels the heat of his gaze on her and she looks away immediately, to her mother, who presumably will start proceedings officially.

'Why are you here?' Josephine asks bluntly, and she's not looking at Jamie.

Tala looks at Jamie and smiles warmly, oozy, gushy. He barely looks at her. He leans forward to pick up his water glass.

'To introduce myself properly.' Tala smiles at Pip, speaking in a soft Liverpool accent, because Jamie has been pretty much monosyllabic since she walked in. 'I'm a relationship counsellor. Knowing Jamie and his story, your story, we thought it would be helpful if I came along on this trip, having experience in this area, to see if I can help smooth a path. While there are various therapeutic modalities that work for different relationships, I find emotionally focused therapy the most helpful. By focusing on the patterns and behaviours that create a disconnect in the relationship, people can begin healing and bonding. And of course that covers all kinds of different relationships, not just husbands and wives. Families, of whatever shape and size.'

Her voice is like honey, she doesn't stutter or say *uh* or *um* once. All flowing like caramel.

Josephine narrows her eyes.

Tala looks at Jamie. 'Sweetheart. Why don't you tell them why you're here?'

Pip tries not to allow her expression to change when she calls him sweetheart.

Jamie sits forward. His forehead is shiny, beads of sweat breaking out. Every atom of his body is alive. Pip wants to reach for him and wipe his sweat away, kiss him, hold him. At sixteen they had barely been able to keep their hands off each other, everything felt like electricity, but they're older now, she's a woman, she knows what to do with her body.

Their eyes meet.

Locked in.

She feels as if he can read her thoughts. She imagines he also feels the adrenaline coursing through her veins, shooting through her, out of her body and to him. She doesn't care who's sitting next to him or that her parents are in the room. There had always been this zing between them.

'I'm here because I want to see more of Bella. I'd like more time with her. Both,' he swallows hard, 'over the phone and in person.'

Pip can feel how difficult that seemingly simple sentence must have been for him to say.

'How can you see Bella more, if you don't live here?' Josephine says, as if that's the most absurd thing she's ever heard. Anybody else would welcome a father saying this, not in this house. 'How long are you planning on staying?'

'That depends on the situation with my dad. I'm not sure if you heard—'

'We all heard,' she interrupts him. 'It's been in the newspapers. And not knowing how long you're here for isn't very easy for us to work with.'

'It's actually not for you to work out, Josephine,' Jamie says, slightly too loudly, taking everybody by surprise. 'Bella is sixteen years old and can make that decision herself. And I would expect me and Pip to talk about this ourselves, but I was doing the courtesy of speaking to you first.'

There's an angry tremble in his voice, he's working hard to contain it. Tala places a hand on his thigh.

Pip was the first girl to kiss every part of him.

'*Pah!*' Josephine says angrily, looking to Philip for backup. She reads his silence as reinforcement. 'Isabella lives here with us, and raising her is still very much our responsibility and concern. You've been in and out for a couple of days here and there. She lives under our roof.'

Pip's throat is working to try to get the words out. She didn't say what she wanted to say to Jamie when he visited her at the service station, and she didn't support Jamie when she was supposed to when they were registering Bella's name, something she relives all the time. She has actual nightmares about opening her mouth and nothing coming out, or having her mouth stuffed with cotton, or so much gum in her mouth she can't speak.

Her throat works hard. Her mind works hard. She looks up at the ceiling. Jamie follows her gaze. There's a crack on the ceiling. She'd never noticed it before, running from the centre ceiling rose to the outer wall.

Jamie's eyes follow it too.

Neither of them says anything.

Tala steps in.

'I think we'd all agree that a stronger relationship with her father is of benefit to Bella. With support from everyone, with everyone working together, we can all ensure that Bella is happy and feeling safe.'

'But he lives in Liverpool,' Josephine says again, always more comfortable speaking about Jamie and Pip as if they're not in the room. 'How exactly could Isabella see him? And what on earth are you two looking at?'

Jamie finally lowers his gaze from the ceiling, as does Pip, and she tries to hide her smile. It's what they always did when they were being spoken about, during the awful dreaded time when they embarrassed their families, they'd pick a spot and stare at it because at least then they could feel united in the moment.

'Bella could stay with me for a weekend,' Jamie says. 'She could get the boat, or the plane over.'

'On her own?' Josephine is spitting feathers.

'From fifteen years of age teenagers can travel alone,' Tala explains. 'I assure you it would be a positive experience for Bella.'

'Pip could bring her,' Jamie says.

Tala looks at Jamie quickly, then away again. They might not have discussed that part. Unfortunately Jamie doesn't have the attitude of a calm, controlled father, he is more like a naughty student sitting in the principal's office, defensive and giving cheek to power.

'And we could spend holidays together. Go to Spain for a week. Like normal families do.'

Pip looks at her dad, who's looking at the floor. Her family has never been to Spain together, their daily time is him collecting her from work, but before all this, before this nightmare, was there a time when they had a normal relationship?

They camped. She used to love it. They would go fishing together, Josephine would stay back at the camp. They went to football and hurling matches. He was on course to raising the fearless daughter before she got pregnant.

Tala talks about healing and mending relationships. Pip admires her intelligence and her knowledge, but this word salad is not the language in this house. Tala's voice is gentle and hypnotic, with a light melodic Liverpool lilt. Her hands are expressive, usually landing in a fruit bowl shape together. Pip imagines Tala holding a pile of oranges in her hand-bowl and when she separates her hands to express something, the oranges all fall down onto her lap. They roll from her lap onto the floor, one goes in her fancy handbag, the other under the table. Her fingers move gracefully, they're long and elegant, nicely manicured nails. A kind of mushroom colour, very tasteful. Her jewellery is refined and classy. Yes, Pip can see why Jamie is attracted to her. She makes everything seem so easy, and sensible. She's a grown-up woman with logical thoughts, who can speak for herself. She might have opinions on the stock market and an appropriate anecdote for all occasions.

Pip would very much like to be a woman like her.

She catches Jamie watching her again. An intense stare. Her stomach flips, and flips again. Even with everything going on in the room, which she doesn't think she can fully grasp right now or process yet, she can't help but feel safer.

Jamie's here.

When he looks at her she forgets how to breathe.

'I agree with Jamie,' she says suddenly, and they all look at her.

It burst out of her in the middle of Tala's talk. A rush of words, nowhere near as sophisticated as Tala's, but every bit as meaningful.

Jamie's eyes sparkle as he looks at her. He knows what that took her, at least she hopes he knows.

Josephine is looking at her, confused. 'What?' she snaps.

Pip takes her time this time. She inhales and exhales before she says the glorious words she wished she'd said at the Registrar's office and on so many other lost occasions.

'I agree with Jamie.'

23

'HI PIP.'

Pip's adrenaline shoots through the roof. She almost chops her finger off while slicing a hard-boiled egg.

Jamie is at the deli counter again. It's like her fantasies have come alive and are creeping up on her when she's least expecting them.

'Jamie, hi, how are you?'

She puts the sharp knife down, an excited tremble running through her body.

He looks relaxed, unlike their last two meetings. It's hot outside, he's wearing shorts and a T-shirt. She can see the muscles rippling through the fabric, the hairs on his arm, the grown-up watch on his wrist. He's a man, but when she looks in his eyes it's still Jamie. She pushes her hairnet hat back off her forehead.

'Good thanks, busy. Dad's hearing is coming up soon. We're trying to convince him to turn up this time, he's ranting and raving about protesting it and being thrown in jail being good for the cause. But never mind all that, I'm feeling better after yesterday, after what you said.'

'It was about all I could say,' she says, cheeks flaming.

'I know how much it took for you to say it. I appreciate it.'

It should have happened a long time ago, but they're doing it now, and that's what counts.

'Can we meet tonight? To talk about Bella.'

'Yes of course. Do you want to come to the house again or . . .'

'No. I think, or Tala thinks, that it didn't go so well yesterday.'

'It went better than I thought,' she says, surprised.

He starts laughing. 'That's what I told Tala. Her family doesn't function like ours.'

'Ours functions?'

He laughs. Oh the laugh. The wrinkles and crinkles, the sound of it, the teeth with the tiny chip. His jawline. The kissable lips. He grew taller.

'So tonight suits?'

'Yes. But um,' she rolls her eyes at herself. 'I can't drive, yet, so . . .'

'I'll pick you up.' Then he notices the customer beside him. 'Sorry, I didn't mean to interrupt. I'll see you later, Pip.'

She watches him walk away, through the doors that part for him. She would gladly part for him.

'Ahem.'

'Stop. I'm watching him.'

'You're practically drooling.'

'You don't mind a bit of drool in your salad, do you?' she says, returning her attention to Io.

'So that's Jamie?'

'That is him,' she says with a grin.

'He didn't even see me standing here, he just went straight for you,' Io says, moving back to the counter after having given them a respectful space.

She can't wipe the silly smile from her face. She places the slices of egg on the lettuce in the salad bowl, barely able to concentrate. Her heart is pounding. How can anybody do anything when they're in love?

'You have it so bad,' Io says. 'I hope his girlfriend doesn't mind.'

She throws grated cheese over the counter at him.

Pip puts more effort into her outfit tonight. A drink in The Turfcutter's Inn with Jamie deserves more attention than a date with Sammy ever did. She's ready and sitting on the arm of the chair at the bay window watching when Josephine looks at her and tuts.

'One of us should be there,' she says, referring to her and Maureen; Pip doesn't think for a second Philip would sit in alone on it. 'I don't agree with this meeting.'

'We're just going to talk, Mam, it's been years.'

Josephine looks her up and down, knowing by her outfit choice that it wasn't designed for talking. The problem with her mother is that she knows her so very well.

'Jamie and I should be talking about our daughter,' Pip says, quietly.

'Don't you worry, plenty of people talk about Isabella. It's being done. Lots of discussion that you're not always privy to. There's a lot going on you know, Philippa, that you haven't had to bother about.'

'It wouldn't bother me to be involved.'

'And he has an awful attitude,' Josephine says, as if Pip hasn't even spoken. 'I didn't like it. He used to be quiet at least. There was a bolshiness to him. All those years on the building sites. And you didn't help matters by agreeing with him.'

'It's important for Bella to know her dad, how can you not agree with that?'

'It depends on the dad, doesn't it? We need to be careful. He's trying to take Isabella away from us. We need to get advice from a solicitor about custody.'

Pip doesn't think Jamie's trying to trick her, but if he is, she doesn't blame him. If she thought things were bad for herself, he wasn't allowed to be in the room with her by himself. And if he did take Bella to Liverpool and then disappear to another country like Josephine is panicking about, what would be so wrong about that? Bella would probably love it, it would most likely be her idea. She'd be away from here, she'd have her freedom.

'And what kind of impact will this woman Tala have on Isabella?'

She can only imagine how fascinating and wonderful Bella would find the sophisticated Tala. She wouldn't want Bella having another mother. She's trying to vie for her own attention as it is. As if sensing her thoughts, Josephine goes for the kill.

'He'd probably have her calling her mam.'

This makes Pip feel nauseous, but she doesn't react, she watches the road. 'I think they say Mum in Liverpool.'

Josephine tuts.

Instead of Jamie coming to get her at seven p.m. as agreed, a black Range Rover arrives outside the house.

'Is that Sammy Wolverson?' Josephine says, hands going to her hair.

Pip's confused.

Philip, who has been sitting in his armchair listening, stands up immediately.

'I'll go out to him.'

He goes to the door and they talk in the garden. She wills

Jamie to arrive now so that she doesn't have to have an awkward chat with Sammy. She hasn't seen him since their last date at The Turfcutter's.

'Philippa,' her dad says softly, coming back into the living room. 'He seems to think he's invited tonight. He met Tala last night and she invited him on a kind of . . . double date, as he put it.'

'What?' she whispers.

Philip shrugs, looking back at the door.

'Tala's coming too? I thought it was just me and Jamie,' Pip says.

'You obviously misunderstood,' Josephine says, clearly delighted. 'That sounds like a great idea,' Josephine adds loudly, so that Sammy can hear.

Philip closes his eyes. 'Josephine.'

But she's gone, out the door to Sammy.

'Come on now, Pip, you don't want to be late,' she calls in to them.

Pip honestly doesn't know what to do, it's a running train that she can't leap off. The cotton wool is back in her mouth, the mounds of bubble gum. She moves as if on autopilot, outside to Sammy, who looks her up and down. The outfit, the make-up, the hair, the high shoes. It's a far better effort than she'd made for him.

'I'll pick you up,' Philip says loudly, as they're getting into Sammy's Range Rover.

'There's no need for that,' Sammy says with a grin.

'I will of course,' Philip says firmly. 'I'll be awake anyway, and that way, you'll be able to have a drink.'

The drink-driving accusation is noted. Sammy doesn't answer, and gets in the car.

Once in The Turfcutter's they find Tala and Jamie in a corner, on leather couches. They greet each other, all kisses. Jamie is wearing a blue shirt, sleeves rolled up, his blue eyes popping.

Pip feels a little bit stunned by it all. That she's here, out with Jamie, but also with Sammy.

Sammy goes to the bar, Tala offers to help him carry the drinks.

Jamie looks at her, face open and ready to engage. He's about to say she looks good, the first few words are out of his mouth, but she jumps in.

'Why is he here?'

'Who?'

'Sammy Wolverson.'

'Because he's your boyfriend.'

'Says who?'

'My brother, for one. Finbar said he's seen you both out together. And Sammy. He was talking last night like you were both very serious. I'm happy for you,' he says gently. 'We were here last night and Tala got talking to him. They had a great laugh, and she said it might be easier for you if he's here.'

'Jamie!' She feels like exploding. 'We've had *two* dates. That I didn't want to go on. I tried for Dad. You know what he's like about the Wolversons.'

They've barely spoken for sixteen years and some things haven't changed, he knows exactly what she's talking about.

'Two dates?' he repeats, stunned. 'Why the hell did he come?'

'Jamie, he's . . . he's weird. Hot and cold. He flicks like this,' she snaps her fingers. She feels comfortable saying this to Jamie. Speaking to him is like speaking to herself, the honesty is pure.

'Shit,' Jamie says. 'I'm so sorry. Why did you get in the car with him?'

'He's a Wolverson, isn't he? I mean, I had to be polite. Chin up, speak up,' she says, rolling her eyes. 'Yes Mr Wolverson, No Mr Wolverson.'

Jamie laughs and covers his face with his hands.

'It's not funny.' But she's smiling now too.

'It kind of is.'

'Shit,' she says. But her panic is easing. Having Jamie here makes it feel less terrifying, less of a secret. He's the eye she can catch when she needs help. He would have seen her in the restaurant, he would have figured it out in the bar last week. He's the one who notices.

'Why the hell would Tala make this mistake?' he asks, angry now. 'I'm sorry we've put you in this position.'

'I wouldn't blame her,' she says, watching Sammy assist her at the bar. 'He's very charming when he wants to be.'

'I'll explain there was a mix-up.'

'No!' she says, almost leaping out of her skin. 'He'll take offence.'

'Sounds like he needs a wake-up call, Pip. If you're not interested . . .'

'I'm really not.' Does she see relief pass his face? Or does she just wish for it?

Sammy and Tala make their way back to them with drinks.

'What was so funny over here?' Sammy asks, handing her a drink and sitting down beside her. He pulls his chair closer to hers so that their knees are touching.

Jamie sees, and his jaw clenches.

'Nothing,' she says.

Tala is shaking her hand off and trying to dry it, after spilling a drink, and Jamie is helping her.

Sammy leans in. 'It obviously wasn't nothing.'

Jamie has one eye on Tala and the other on Pip. He catches Sammy's look and tone.

'We were catching up on old times,' Jamie says, firmly. He picks up his glass and holds it towards Pip. '*Sláinte.*'

'*Sláinte,*' Pip says, softly, clinking her glass against his.

'So, we thought this would be a great time to talk about Bella,' Tala says, beginning the talk.

'Another time,' Jamie says, with a quick shake of his head.

'Hmm?' Tala asks, moving her head closer to his.

He's not giving her anything more and she has the emotional intelligence not to push.

Pip takes a sip of her drink and almost retches as it burns her throat.

Jamie zones in on her, concerned. 'You okay?'

She coughs. She'd swallowed too much, expecting it to be vodka.

'What is this?' she asks, holding her throat.

'Whiskey and Coke,' he says.

'Whiskey?! Oh. Whoa. I usually drink vodka.'

'You were drinking whiskey and Coke all night the last time,' he says, with a smirk and a look at Tala. 'You must be losing it. Though you probably don't remember much about that night.'

Pip frowns. She's never drunk whiskey in her life.

'That's me last night,' Tala says, and she goes off on one talking about their night out last night and feeling tender today.

Jamie barely acknowledges what she says. 'Do you drink whiskey, Pip?'

'No. Never.'

She can see the shadow moving across Sammy's face. She can recognise it now.

His fist whips out and she ducks quickly, hands over her face, ready for him to hit her.

There's a terrible, awkward silence. Pip can't feel any pain, she wonders when it will come. He's usually so fast, takes her by surprise. She feels a gentle hand on her arm and she slowly lowers it.

It's Jamie.

'Are you okay?'

She looks around. They're all looking at her, stunned.

'Oh.'

Tala looks horrified, as if she'd actually witnessed Sammy hitting her. Jamie's face is soft.

And Sammy himself, who she's almost afraid to look at, has a smile creeping across his face. He starts to laugh.

'What the hell was that about?' He's incredulous, white teeth like a Cheshire cat. Then he reads the mood and his hand goes to her thigh in an effort to be more caring.

Jamie lets go of her.

'I was going to say. I'll get you a new drink if you don't like it,' Sammy says gently, slowly, as if she's a mad woman. He slowly reaches across and removes the drink from her hand.

That's what he'd been trying to do.

'Sorry,' she says, wishing she hadn't brought this embarrassing awkwardness upon them all.

'I just thought that . . . I don't know what I thought. Tala,' she says, trying to gather herself and hoping the burning embarrassment will leave her face, 'how long did you say you're staying for?'

'I'll get you a vodka.' Jamie stands and makes his way to the bar because Sammy still hasn't moved.

Tala composes herself quickly, and while Pip tries to

concentrate on her answer, her eyes quickly move to Jamie, who's glaring angrily at Sammy.

'And though I can do sessions with my clients on Zoom,' Tala continues, 'I don't like to do it for too long.'

'They're like your children?' Sammy says, now fully engaged.

'I wouldn't say that. They are adults. But I feel a responsibility to them. Everyone can have a break, but I just don't like to for too long.'

'Would you like children?' Sammy asks.

Tala's surprised by the direct question.

'Do you think you two will go down that route?'

'That's direct.'

'Am I not supposed to ask that? Who knows what you can say these days.' He laughs. 'How long are you two together?'

'Three months.'

'Will you get married?'

'We haven't . . . we're not . . . that's a very personal question and I don't know you that well, but if we do make plans I'll make sure we'll let you know.'

Sammy laughs. 'I'll have my hat ready.'

'So, to answer your question Pip, I'm going home on Monday. Jamie was due to leave then too, but in light of what's happening with Lorcan, he'll stay longer.'

Jamie returns to the table with a new drink for Pip.

'Thank you.'

'What's happening with your dad?' Sammy asks, pushing his big fingers into the small peanut bowl. His heavy hand finally leaves her leg and her leg is hot where his hand was. She moves her position so that it's harder for him to reach her. Jamie watches her leg.

'We shouldn't say anything until it happens,' Jamie says.

'Well, it's happening isn't it? But it's just a hearing. He'll get a fine. A slap on the wrist. They have to do it to make themselves look good to the EU.'

'He's pleading not guilty,' Tala says, 'which means it will go to trial.'

'But everyone knows he was turf-cutting. He won't be able to deny that.'

'His new lawyer seems to think that it's bigger than that. That it's a human rights issue and there are constitutional issues, so it could go to the circuit court.'

'Jesus,' Sammy says. 'Are you staying for the whole trial?'

Pip wishes he would, and feels bad for hoping his dad goes to trial. She's sure Jamie wants this over and done with as quickly as possible.

'I'll have to wait and see. I'm staying another week for the hearing.'

'Can you get that much time off work?'

'It's my own company, so yeah.'

Pip is surprised. She knows so little about him. 'What's your company?'

'Have you two never met before?' Sammy laughs.

'Plastering.'

'Did you do her house?' Sammy says, sending his thumb in Pip's direction. 'Shoddy job there.'

There's a silence, it was neither said in a joking way nor can it be taken that way.

'The release has already gone out from the Turf Cutters' Association about Tuesday,' Tala says to Jamie, as if asking for his permission to tell them.

He shrugs.

'Philippa should know for Bella.'

He looks at Pip. 'The TCA has planned a national day of action to highlight the spiralling cost of living and the turf ban. They've invited national media to watch them cut turf in the Clonboyle blanket bog. It's happening on Tuesday.'

'*Ooh hoo hoo,*' Sammy laughs, mischievously rubbing his hands together, gleefully. 'The plot thickens. Your old man's going to get himself locked up.'

Jamie looks at him sharply. His body tense, his jaw tense, his fists clenched.

'Come on,' Sammy says, 'you've got to be ready for the debate with people. I don't know if I side with the TCA on this one. Your dad took the government compensation, didn't he? And he's allowed to cut turf for himself and his neighbours. It seems like a good deal.'

'I suppose you would know about compensation,' Jamie replies. 'I've heard the quarry has had a lot of accidents, unfair dismissals, that kind of thing.'

Sammy glares at Pip as if she has done something wrong.

'It has nothing to do with Pip,' Jamie says, in a tone that makes Sammy look stupid.

'It's down to people's own bad luck and stupidity, not health and safety problems at our quarry. All everyone is looking for, is money.'

'Not in my dad's case.'

'No, but it's about money. The price of fuel is going up, these auld lads want to fuel their own homes. They can go on about their rights and their land, but it all boils down to money.'

'Or control,' Pip says, and everyone looks at her. It just popped out. She didn't mean to say it. She clears her throat and stumbles over her words. 'People want to be in control of their own lives.'

'Okay, calm down Sister Suffragette,' Sammy says, grinning and gulping his pint. 'Anyway, if anything does go to court we can always use our star witness.' He grins at Pip.

'I didn't see anything.'

'Always the best answer,' he says, roaring with laughter. 'I'm talking about your dad.'

'I don't think he'd be comfortable in a courtroom.'

'He's done it for us before. Gets a nice little bonus for it too. How do you think he built that house?'

'Come on,' Jamie says, quietly.

'Philip Sheridan is our courtroom hero. He's saved our arse on many occasions. When you have a guy like him come in, with all his experience, and his rules and regulations, the courts can see the quality of the place. All those old guys are the same. My granddad was a real stickler.'

This is followed by a silence in which Pip assumes everybody is thinking the same thing. Perhaps being a stickler is what will stop the accidents. Pip breaks the silence by finishing her drink, the ice crashing against her teeth.

'When did you start working at the quarry?' Tala asks. Sammy will love her interest in him, but Pip can tell Tala is more interested in digging into his personality which is slowly being revealed the more he talks.

'Another one?' Jamie asks Pip softly as the other two are engaged in conversation.

'Yes please. I'll help you this time,' she says, joining him on the walk to the bar. She looks back briefly and catches Sammy's look of disgust, before he hides it away and returns to talking about himself.

They stand close together at the bar. They have to squeeze in because it's so busy, and she likes their closeness.

'I'm sorry Tala invited him. I'll tell her as soon as I get a chance. What an arsehole, I can't believe you went on a second date. I can't believe you even made it to the end of one.'

'He kind of just shows up, and I didn't want Dad to be hassled at work.'

'Pip,' he says, coming closer, 'when are you going to put yourself first?'

Their faces are so close, there is so much warmth and care in his expression.

She looks away. 'I'm trying. I think. To start.'

'We should have just come out on our own.'

She gazes at him.

'To talk about Bella.'

She blinks and looks away. 'Yes.'

She watches Tala and Sammy in the mirror behind the bar.

'You ducked,' he says, anger in his voice. 'Did he hurt you before?' His eyes sear into hers. His face is a picture of concern. He cares. He sees her and sees everything, doesn't seem to miss a beat.

'Sorry, gay night is on Tuesdays,' Finbar, Jamie's brother announces, stopping in front of them. Finbar reaches across the bar and ruffles Jamie's hair.

'Nice to see you two love birds together. Try not to get into trouble again,' he says, with a wink. 'Watch out, or the boyfriend might drop a tonne of rubble on you.' He laughs, then it turns quickly to concern. 'Don't tell him I said that.'

'He's not her boyfriend you *amadán*. Why the hell did you tell me that?'

'They were here on a date last week.'

'One date,' Pip says. Actually two, but who's counting?

'Someone should tell him he's not your boyfriend. He comes

in here talking about you all the time. Thought you two were getting married by the sounds of it.'

'He probably thought you'd tell Jamie,' she says.

'Only too delighted to tell me, he was. Sorry,' Finbar says genuinely, hands up in surrender. 'No harm intended. Drinks on the house?'

'Two glasses of your most expensive champagne, please,' Jamie says.

Finbar growls at him, and with arms like an octopus goes about seeing to multiple orders at once.

Jamie turns to face her, his elbow on the bar, their faces are so close, he's fully focused on her and she feels like the only person in the room. She's pushed up against the man beside her, and she's screened by a crowd on the other side. She feels like she's in a cocoon with him.

'I want you to see more of Bella.'

'But?'

'No buts.' She hesitates.

'But,' he repeats.

'But,' she says, and he smiles, 'Mam thinks you're trying to take her away from me. That you'll try to get full custody and we'll never see her again. Or that she'll holiday with you in Liverpool and you'll whisk her off to a country with no extradition laws.'

He laughs, heartily. 'Did she really say that?'

'No, I made the last part up myself, but she probably does think it.'

He laughs loudly again.

Finbar places two glasses of champagne down on the counter in front of them, with a strawberry on each rim.

'The other two aren't getting a glass,' he says, with a wink.

They pick their glasses up. He holds it out to clink hers. She hesitates.

'You didn't say you're not going to take her away.'

He pushes his face even closer to hers, eyes comically wide, 'No, Pip, I'm not going to kidnap our child and take her to a jurisdiction with no extradition. I just want more time with her. Quality time. A life that looks a little more normal than this. I'm not trying to take her away from you. I don't want to do anything that makes you unhappy, but I've got to— got to start putting myself first sometimes.'

She nods and picks up her glass. 'I'll drink to that.'

They sip, the champagne is cold and fizzy down her throat. 'Oh my God, that's divine,' she says, closing her eyes. When she opens them, he's watching her.

'Wait till I tell you,' she says, excitedly leaning in to his ear. Her lips mistakenly touch his ear. 'Bella has a boyfriend.'

She tells him all about Mark and the secret meetings in the park, and they both become giddy with excitement talking about her.

'It's so cute, Jamie, I was watching them in the park, and they remind me so much of . . .' she trails off, feeling it's inappropriate now, she got swept away. 'It doesn't matter.'

'Of us. They remind you of us.'

She nods. 'It's lovely to watch. As a mother, it doesn't make me want to stop it, or block it, or stand in the way.' Not like their parents did to them. A dark cloud moves over their conversation and she wishes she hadn't brought it there.

'I can't believe our baby has a boyfriend,' he says.

Our baby. She watches his lips.

'Please say that again.'

He knows exactly what she means.

'Our baby.'

Realising how intimate they're being in public she suddenly looks back at Tala and Sammy. Tala is sitting alone looking at her phone. Sammy is nowhere to be seen. The drinks they ordered for Sammy and Tala are sitting on the bar, the head of Sammy's pint dead.

Jamie is still fixated on her, keen to continue the conversation.

'How long have we been talking?' she asks, nervously.

'Shit,' he says, gathering the drinks and heading back to Tala without another word.

She follows him.

'Is Sammy in the toilet?' she asks, unsure if she still wants him here or if she wants him to have left. Which is worse?

'No, he left. About fifteen minutes ago,' Tala says. 'I told him to calm down, that you both have a lot to talk about, but he didn't have the patience.'

Jamie squeezes her hand. 'Sorry.'

This action pops her bubble. Jamie's in a relationship, he lives in another country. She needs to stop pretending in her head. She needs to concentrate on building a father–daughter relationship with Bella, not be putting herself in the frame. She is not sixteen anymore.

Pip's phone beeps and she reads the message from Sammy. Perhaps her face changes, or reflects what she's feeling because Jamie takes the phone from her hand.

'Is that from him?'

'No,' she says, holding on to the other end of her phone.

'It is, let me see.'

'Jamie, don't just grab her phone.'

'Give it to me,' he says, tugging it aggressively, and it comes loose from her hand.

She's mortified. That he will read those words about her, that he will see what another man thinks of her.

YOU F*ING SLUT. YOU ARE PATHETIC.

That is just the first line.

Jamie reads.

'Jamie!' Tala says, looking at the phone in his hand, then as she catches the first few words her eyes widen. 'Oh my God.' She moves in closer to read more, then Tala is finished and Jamie is still reading.

'I'm sorry, but you can't take that,' Tala says, taking a long drink.

Jamie is still reading, face tight, jaw muscles working. The hand not holding the phone is opening and closing in a fist.

It doesn't take that long to read, she's a loser is the general gist. A bad kissing, disappointing, unattractive loser who still lives at home with her parents. Why is he still reading it?

He presses some buttons.

'Are you texting him back?' Pip asks, worried.

'No.' He presses a few more buttons and then hands her the phone back.

'Toxic relationships,' Tala says, and all of a sudden the pristine woman has been hit by alcohol and is slurring. Her hair slightly out of place and her eyeliner smeared.

Pip doesn't have time to see what Jamie has done to her phone, Tala is talking about toxic masculinity and relationships and, after abandoning her for twenty minutes, Pip feels she owes it to her to give her some attention. But after that point Jamie has disengaged, checked out. He seems bored by the conversation and is looking around.

He sees someone he knows from the olden days and leaves them both talking.

Tala moves to Jamie's seat so she's closer to Pip.

'I hope you don't mind me saying something about your situation. I'm the girlfriend. The very new girlfriend, so I'm still learning the dynamics, but when Jamie told me about what had happened to you both as teenagers and the arrangements that were made on your behalf, I thought he was exaggerating. Sometimes when you're in something it can seem so big, but really quite small and fixable on the outside. Having come here and met your parents and his parents,' she shakes her head, 'it's even more screwed up than I thought.'

'I thought you were going to say the opposite,' Pip says, feeling giddy at the surprise revelation.

'Now I've had a few drinks,' Tala says, swallowing a burp that makes her giggle. 'But I need to say it, I'm taking my professional hat off.' She removes an imaginary hat from her head, and tosses her hair in the process. 'When it comes to you both, two words. The Infantilisation Tactic.'

It's actually three words. Pip smiles, liking this version of Tala best.

'Jamie, don't get me wrong, he's great. *Great.*' She says it over-enthusiastically as if trying to convince herself. 'You know, you've been there. But his personality has completely changed since we got here. I knew the trip was going to be hard. It's actually our first trip away together and you learn a lot about a person when you go away with them; my friend Carys, easiest person in the world, nightmare to share a room with. She . . . no, where was I?'

'Jamie. Changing since he got here,' Pip says, sipping her

drink, urging her on, hoping Jamie doesn't return now that she can learn more about him.

'Oh yeah, I knew the trip would be difficult, but like, who is this person?' she says, irritated, then laughs airily to lighten it.

'What's the infant thing that you mentioned?'

'Oh yes.' Her eyes widen, so enthralled by her own knowledge. 'Infantilisation.' Hard to say when you're drunk. 'It's the process of treating someone older, an adult, as if they are much younger than their actual age. It can be a way to maintain power over someone and prevent them being a functioning adult. The narcissistic parent tells their adult child what to do and how to do it. It's their way to shame, belittle and make them feel incompetent so that the adult child won't become independent.'

Pip isn't smiling anymore. Tala's words are chilling.

'Sorry, I've had too much to drink, I love my job, I go on too much about it.'

'No, go on, please.'

'I can't remember what I was saying.'

'The parent doesn't want the adult child to become independent.' She won't forget a word of this. Her heart is pounding in her chest.

'Oh right. Yes. They're likely to feel threatened and resort to certain behaviours to regain power and control.'

'What type of behaviours?' she asks, swallowing.

'Oh like . . . attacking every kind of decision their child makes from school, to relationships, and jobs. They basically leave the adult child feeling like they're never worthy. It's exhausting for the adult child and it destroys their confidence.' She looks through the crowd for Jamie. 'Which is why, I'm trying to help him get it back. Also, a parent engaged in infantilisation behaviour perpetuates co-dependency, which means the adult child is at risk of becoming a narcissistic abuse target. Which may be why you were attracted to Sammy.' She says it all quickly as though it's a song, then her tongue feels around for her straw, as if she's a giraffe feeding.

'I'm not attracted to Sammy,' Pip says, quietly, feeling winded after hearing all of that. It's spot on.

'Good to hear it. Dump him,' Tala says. She sucks the remainder of her drink up until she's practically inhaling air. 'Is there somewhere we can go to dance? Jamie is such a fun dancer.'

Exhausting for the adult child, Pip recalls Tala's words, as she lies in bed, the vodka coursing through her veins. Tears roll down Pip's cheeks. Her T-shirt and pillow are soaked. Yes, having a mother like Josephine has been exhausting and confidence crushing and she feels the tiredness catch up on her now.

Her dad had picked her up as promised, he was sitting outside the bar when she walked out with Jamie and Tala. She appreciates his protectiveness. Of course, Jamie and Tala saw it differently, a grown woman being picked up by her dad.

Tala had winked at her inconspicuously. 'See?'

Infantilisation. There's a word for what Pip's experiencing at home with her parents, particularly her mother. There's a phrase for it. It's not just all in her head. It's not just a feeling. They've made it a phrase, a thing that people like Tala study. She lives it, they study it. She's waking up, seeing things differently.

The thought of Jamie and Tala out dancing, or back in their bedroom right now, makes her want to cry even harder. She tries to get lost in a fantasy. It's been a while since she created something juicy to disappear into. But she can't summon anything, she can't numb her mind anymore.

Her phone vibrates on the bedside table. She hopes it's not another angry text from Sammy. She doesn't think her nervous system could bear it. She picks the phone up and sees JAMIE on her display screen. She never had his number before, so that's what he had been doing when he was typing on her phone. She smiles.

She taps into his message and suddenly the world is softer again.

Sweet dreams x

24

ON SATURDAY MORNING WHEN Bella and Pip tiptoe downstairs for their pretend Pilates class, Bella excited to be with her boyfriend again and Pip excited to fly with Io for her second time, their dreams come to a shattering end at the sight of Josephine at the bottom of the stairs zipping her fleece up.

'No need to tiptoe,' she says. 'I'm awake and I'm coming with you.'

Bella stares at her, open-mouthed, her dreams visibly crumbling, while Pip tries to be less obvious, even though she's disappointed she'll be missing another flight with Io.

'My back is sore, I'd like to try this Pilates lark that has you both so changed. Maybe I'll have the same spring in my step.'

'You can't,' Bella says.

'Why not?'

Josephine knows. Or she thinks she knows something, she looks at Pip with a kind of satisfied smile, and for once the lie comes easily to Pip.

'You have to register in advance. Walk-ins aren't allowed, but we can arrange it for you for next Saturday, no problem.' She's cool, calm and collected. She's even impressed with herself. Catastrophe avoided.

'My name is already down,' she says, smug. 'I called them during the week.'

During the week. She's had this planned.

Bella can't hide her devastation. In the car, Bella and Pip furiously text on their phones. Bella to alert Mark to the fact she won't be there, and Pip with the heaviest of hearts texts Io to cancel their flying plans. The joy and fun of Saturdays, their mutual freedom day, has been sucked from them. Josephine's presence adds a heaviness to everything, today has nothing to do with spending valuable time with them, or fixing her back, and everything to do with a cat and mouse game of catching them out.

Bella is sulky, and Josephine watches them both as she drives, their moods closer to confirming her suspicions. How does she receive such joy from making people miserable?

Josephine parks. Pip is hoping the class isn't over-subscribed, she prays for this one small but important miracle, that there's room for her and Bella in the class. If the plan she came up with in the car doesn't work, she will have to pretend the app didn't work.

'There's no point in doing this,' Bella grumbles to Pip, as Josephine gets her bag from the car boot and they have a moment together. 'She's going to find out.'

'I'm not giving up yet.'

Pip and Bella, against all the odds, have managed to carve out some hours to themselves, moments in which Pip has only begun to start discovering herself. Especially with Tala's words about infantilisation ringing in her ears, she's not giving it up that easily. She also hopes that this is all a bluff, that as soon as Josephine arrives at the door to the Pilates class she'll realise they weren't making it up and she'll back down, feign an excuse and leave. Anything is possible right now, it's not too late.

They enter the club and join the queue of women. At the head of the queue Debbie, their Pilates instructor, ticks their names off a list as they enter.

Caroline, their neighbour is ahead of them.

Debbie looks up at Pip, who's leading her little group.

'Hi. Pip, Bella and Josephine Sheridan. My mam is joining me today.'

'Wonderful,' Debbie says, looking at her list, and Bella's heart pounds.

'Yes, yes, and yes. Welcome.'

The relief. They make their way into the hall and find a space, and as Bella has absolutely no idea what to do or where to go, she stays close to Pip, and copies her, trying not to look like it's the first time she's been there. Pip over-explains everything as she goes, what they have to do, where they put their water and trainers, making out it's for Josephine.

'How the hell did you do that?' Bella says from the side of her mouth as they're stretching.

'I got a friend to put our name down on the list before we arrived,' she whispers back.

Bella reaches out and squeezes Pip's hand. 'Thank you so much,' she says. 'You saved my life.'

The moment, and specifically the gesture, is so precious to Pip she could cry. She looks over at Kim, and mouths a very grateful thank you.

And everything goes smoothly. Josephine is irritated by most of the things she's asked to do, though she's still nimble, always on her toes anyway, and Bella is flexible and follows quickly. This is a relatively new class, so nobody expects them to be experts, but Pip feels her mother's inquisitive nature scrutinising her every move. She works hard to follow Debbie's instructions perfectly, so that her mother is impressed, so that she'll believe they've been there for the past few weeks. She tries to shake Tala's words from her mind, that she's trying so hard to impress her mother and not put a foot wrong, craving compliments. It makes her uncomfortable.

But everything goes smoothly.

Until, at the very end of class after they managed to get through it all, Debbie singles Bella out.

'Bella,' she says loudly, encouragingly, 'that was a great effort for a first class. Well done. I hope to see you back next week.'

Rumbled.

25

JOSEPHINE WAS RAISED BETTER than to argue in front of a crowd. She wouldn't want to make a scene.

She is so angry she demands they go straight home, even when Kim has invited them all for a coffee across the road. It's embarrassing how Josephine treats Kim, how she barks at her, voice rough like sandpaper, casts her invitation aside. Another instance of Pip's inner world being crushed. Pip has a checklist of Tala's infantilisation explanation in the forefront of her mind and she's watching her mother, her own life, and ticking it off one by one.

Suddenly Josephine stops charging around and turns back to Kim.

'Kim Banks,' she barks at her, suddenly remembering or realising something. 'You're just back from Canada.'

Josephine waits for more. She's used to people saying more. They talk to fill her silences, to please her, to cheer her up, to be polite, to make up for the awkwardness she can bring, but Kim leaves it there, unappreciative of the interrogation and the rude treatment.

Eventually, Josephine gets to the point. 'You were out with Pip last week for tea.'

Pip swallows hard. This is embarrassing, there is nothing

wrong with her meeting a friend for tea, but she wasn't with her friend then, she was in the sky with Io and she doesn't want her mother knowing that. She doesn't deserve to know. That knowledge, that freedom, that time is Pip's and Pip's alone.

She looks at Kim apologetically.

'No,' Kim says, and Pip's stomach drops. 'It was coffee actually. It's so nice to catch up with an old friend.'

Kim to the rescue again.

'I'm going to sit in the back with you,' Bella says at the car, afraid, but when she opens the back door Josephine lets out a roar.

'What are you doing? Get in the front.'

This angers Pip. Her daughter can sit in the back with her if she wants. None of them have assigned places, or at least she didn't think they had until now, it was more routine before that, habit, but not rule.

Pip, the adult, is defiant, thinking back to Tala's advice, running through in her head what she's going to say. She veers from telling the truth about where they've been spending their Saturday mornings to outright lies.

'Mam,' Pip says, trying to take control of the situation. She is not going to sit in the back cowering.

'Not now,' Josephine says, her voice trembling. 'Wait until we get home. Not when I'm driving.'

Josephine makes a few mistakes when driving, she's clearly distracted. She has to apologise a few times, is beeped at once. It's unlike her. She's usually solid on the road. The engine is barely off and Josephine catapults herself out of the car and is marching across the stones screaming Philip's name.

'Shit,' Bella says, tears in her eyes. 'Shit, shit, shit. I'm never going to see him again, am I?'

'This is bullshit,' Pip says, the anger rising, and she follows Josephine into the house, so ready for this.

Philip is sitting at the kitchen table with a cup of tea, his phone out with Tetris paused mid-game.

'I told you they were up to something,' Josephine says, pointing at them as they enter the house. 'I knew it. You're paranoid, you said to me but I knew it, Philip, and I was right. You should have listened to me. You dropping them off each week, would you not have checked?'

He's the target now. Everyone is the enemy, she's right and everyone's wrong.

'They weren't ever there, Philip. The lady said that Isabella had done a great job for a *first* class.'

'She just didn't remember me,' Bella says. 'Sometimes there are different teachers.'

Bella digs deeper, sounding feisty. Pip is proud of her, she always would have backed down.

'Don't you make it worse, young lady,' Josephine says, pointing a finger, and Bella shrivels.

'Where were they?' Philip asks, clearly confused by the fact he'd dropped them off and collected them in the same place.

'That's what I don't know yet.' She glares at Pip, her hands on her hips.

'What does it even matter?' Pip finally speaks. Her voice is gentle, the opposite of Bella and Josephine's, but she's firm. 'Why is this such a big deal? Why must you know?'

Everyone is surprised. Tala's words are floating around

in her head. Infantilisation. Pip is thirty-two years old, why should she have to be afraid of lying to her mother?

It's a strong opener.

'Excuse me?' Josephine says.

'Why is it such a big deal that we weren't in the class?' Pip's voice may be calm but her heart is hammering. 'Why should I have to tell you everything?'

Josephine looks as though she's about to explode. She looks at Bella.

'Where were you?'

'I was with—'

Pip can see she's about to cave.

'Me,' Pip says firmly. 'Her mother.'

Bella's eyes widen.

Josephine makes a quick decision. 'Isabella. Go up to your room,' she says to Bella who doesn't need to be asked twice. She runs out of the room.

'*Bella* and I were spending time together,' Pip says. 'Alone. Because we never get to be together.'

'Utter nonsense! You're together all the time.'

'I think you know that's not true. By design we have very little time together. You're always here.'

'Well excuse me for living in my own house.'

'If we told you that we were spending time together each week outside of the Pilates class, you wouldn't have let us go. You'd have stood in the way. As you have always done and always do. You would have created something for her to go to. A family visit, or a day trip. A sudden need to go to the butchers or the supermarket. A drive or something. It's been happening for years, since she was born. I don't know your reasons, but don't try to make me look crazy by denying it.'

Pip, of course, expects her mother to deny it, to make her feel like she's going crazy. Gaslighting, that's what they call it. Pip had only considered it a thing that husbands or boyfriends did to their wives, not mothers to their daughters.

She waits for the denial.

'I'll tell you my reasons,' Josephine says instead, her eyes narrow, her mouth pulled tight and wrinkled, all the muscles required called into action to say what she's about to say. 'At sixteen years old, you hadn't the first notion how to be a mother. I had to help you.'

No denial.

'I'm thirty-two years old now,' Pip says, loudly and firmly. She wants the whole world to hear. 'I've been mothering for sixteen years. I don't need you to continue trying to take my child for yourself. You wouldn't even allow her to call me Mam.' Her voice cracks. 'You made her call you Nan, because it sounds like Mam. Everyone always thought you were her mother, and that's what you wanted. You wouldn't allow us to christen her Bella. You changed her name on her birth cert. Bella. Her name is Bella.'

It's all coming out now.

'You barely let me have two minutes alone with her,' she says, pointing at her each time she says *you*.

'Don't point your finger in my face.' Josephine looks away, but Pip moves into her path again.

'You watch and listen to our every move. You never introduce her as my daughter, or your granddaughter. You have always wanted everyone to think she's yours. I felt like you never wanted me there, but you'd never let me leave. Nine months in, you made me get a job, while you stayed home to mind my baby. *My* baby.' Her voice wobbles. She breathes in. 'You race me to wash her clothes, you don't let me in her room, you criticise my ironing. You work with her every day. You tear apart every piece of advice I give to her. You've stolen her from me right before my very eyes.'

It all seems so petty now that she's saying it out loud, ironing and washing, but it all amounts to something so enormous that she's been burying for so long, that she's ready to explode.

She includes her dad now. He's the silent assassin.

'You broke me and Jamie up, you and Jamie's parents all stopped him from being able to be a dad. You sent him away. He would have been wonderful. He would have been the best. I'm here, you wouldn't let me leave, but I didn't even get to be her mam. You all tried to stop that too. Why did I have to pretend to be with her at Pilates? Because I want to be her mother. That's why!'

Her throat is raw.

She's trembling, and the emotion is caught in her throat, but she had to get through it, she had to say it. She hopes Bella heard every word, she's saying it for her benefit as much as her own.

Josephine's eyes are almost popping out of her head.

She'll try to deny it all, break it down point by point, she has an excellent memory, never forgets, doesn't let go of a grudge. There'll be nothing unturned, if Pip has exaggerated on one element it will be the thing that takes it all down.

Pip swallows, and braces herself.

'Yes,' Josephine says simply. 'Everything you say is true.'

Pip is in shock. She didn't imagine it. It wasn't all in her head.

'Josephine,' Philip says quietly, looking down at the kitchen table.

'What?' she says, looking at him briefly. 'It's true. Because I've never in all of my life seen anyone so incapable of being a mother. It's like you're not here at all sometimes. And what kind of example are you to her? Look at what you did when you were sixteen! I don't trust you for one second with Isabella, who is sixteen now. You've a bad track record. You couldn't have raised her alone, and still couldn't do it now.'

'I'm going for a promotion at work,' Pip says, raising her chin, trying to keep her voice confident. 'Krish is leaving and he's putting me forward for the job as manager. He thinks I can do it.'

Still trying to impress her mother. She's not sure what she's expecting or hoping for.

'Krish is a very good man and he has been kind to you and good to give you the job. I spoke to him before your interview, I knew he'd be good to you, but you make sandwiches, and becoming manager is quite the leap. I see your confidence growing because Jamie is back. You think Jamie is going to help you?' She laughs and wipes her nose with a tissue. 'He's going to try to take Isabella from us, because he's got a good job and he's in love with a very competent woman who will be able to help him mind a child. He can see how useless you are too, and you're too stupid to see it.'

'Now, now,' Philip says, louder this time, looking at them both.

'That's not true,' Pip says, but her mother has always voiced Pip's inner concerns.

'You want to go it alone? You tried it before and you lasted three days, but go ahead, try again. Move out on your own with Isabella. Sorry, *Bella*.' She exaggerates the name as though it's ridiculous. 'You can't even drive. You couldn't pay rent, never mind get a mortgage, with your salary. You haven't a trade and you haven't an education and you haven't any of that because of your shameful decision and carry-on. You proved to yourself and everyone that you weren't capable of behaving like an adult when you did what you did. When you embarrassed yourself and us. We've had to pick up the pieces, Philippa, and by God did we. With everyone saying the things they were saying about us, we kept going. You made your bed and you have to lie in it and now that you're unhappy you're blaming it on me.

'They won't promote you to manager because you don't know the first thing about managing a petrol station. You have a daughter and you can't even manage that properly because you don't have her respect.'

Gut punch. Every single word.

She feels like she's on her knees, doubled over, spitting out bloody teeth.

It hits because it is everything Pip's own nasty voice in her head has thrown at her over the years, and now said to her by her own mother in the silent acceptance and support of her dad, every single word feels true. His gentle protestations aren't enough to stop it or make Pip feel he's on her side.

'That's fine. Act the smart girl while Jamie is here. He'll be going home soon, back to Liverpool, and we'll see where you are then. I can see how you look at him Philippa, and it's no good. You have a perfectly good, successful man in Sammy Wolverson and you're treating him abominably. I'm embarrassed watching you with him.'

The mention of Sammy snaps Pip out of her self-loathing. Josephine's wrong about him and she's wrong about everything else she said. Pip won't be pulled back again.

Philip looks at Josephine sharply. His eyes are glassy. But he still doesn't say anything.

Pip slowly gets up and leaves the kitchen.

'Where do you think you're going?' Josephine asks. 'I'm not finished with you.'

'I am with you,' Pip says, leaving the kitchen and going upstairs.

26

ORIGAMI GIRL . . .
    Origami girl . . .
Nothing comes. There are no overflowing feelings spilling from her into the pen and through to the page. There is nothing. Emotional numbness. Origami girl waits to be spawned and fleshed out, but lies on her desk, on a white page cold and empty as bone. Pip crumples the page and throws it in the waste paper basket beneath her desk. But then she realises that the crumpled ball of paper of no words has expressed exactly how she feels. *Crumpled girl.* She takes it from the bin and places it in the box of origami girl poems. There's a gentle knock on the door and she hides her crumpled girl away in a drawer.

'Come in,' she says, knowing from the knock that it's not her parents.

Pip has to move from her desk in order to make way for Bella to step inside. Bella sits on the bed, places her nail kit bag down beside her. Pip spins the desk chair around to face her.

'Are you crying?' Bella asks.

'I was.'

'I've never seen you cry.'

'A wild exotic side of me you don't know,' she says.

Bella looks around the room. 'You're always so tidy. I wish I was tidy.'

'You once called it a prison cell.'

She looks hurt. 'That was mean of me.'

'I could help you sort your room out if you like, I like organising things.'

She groans. The effort.

Bella's eyes fall on the collection of sketches on the wall. The sketches travel the crack's track, like a vine snaking across her canvas wall. It wouldn't be the first fracture to be such a source of inspiration.

'You're so good at art.'

'It's what I wanted to study after school. Do you remember I used to draw pictures for you to colour in when you were little?'

'Oh yeah,' Bella says, eyes lighting up as she remembers. 'I loved them.'

Some of Bella's early works are stored next to the origami art, in a memory box Jamie gifted to Pip on her christening day, which also contains clippings of Bella's first haircut, the first tooth that fell out, and the grotesque umbilical cord stump that fell away. Proof of their connection.

'I wish I was good at art.'

'You could be if you put your phone down. Creativity can come from idleness.' Pip has boxes of origami art and poems in her desk to prove it. 'Anyway you are good at art, your nail art is incredible. I could never do such fine drawings on the tip of a nail.'

Bella seems pleased by the compliment. 'Oh yeah, I suppose I am great at art.'

Pip marvels at her confidence.

She picks up her nail kit. 'Want your nails done?'

'Sure.'

Pip wheels herself closer to the bed and holds her hand out. Bella reaches for a pillow and places it on her lap, to act as a table for Pip's hand.

Pip assumes Bella heard everything. The Wolverson quarry concrete is good, but it can't be that good to block out the shouts from downstairs.

'Thank you for not telling them about Mark.' She's practically whispering.

'That's okay.'

'I caused this. It was my idea to go to the class. It was my fault, and you got the blame. I'm sorry.'

Bella pushes Pip's cuticles back.

'Oval nails suit you. I want mine longer, but Nan won't let me because of work.'

Bella has what's called coffin shape acrylics, with a design and a jewel on each. She does them herself, and calls around to her cousins' houses to do theirs for them too. Pip needs to keep hers short for work, or her nails will pierce the blue vinyl gloves.

'I suppose you heard everything that we said.'

Bella shakes her head. 'I put my headphones on, I hate fighting. What happened?'

Pip feels weary, that all of those words intended for her and Bella went unheard. She feels something precious that she'd been hanging on to slip away. She had been shouting at Josephine, but all the time trying to connect with Bella, trying to let her know how she feels, how the past sixteen years have been for her.

Bella didn't hear a word.

Bella buffs her nails.

'We argued, but she doesn't know where we went. I'll tell her we went for walks in the park.'

'Why would we do that though?' Bella wrinkles her nose.

'So we could have time together.'

Pip can clearly see Bella thinks the idea of that is a bit weird.

'Do you think I'll still be able to see him?'

It's a good question. What exactly Pip has accomplished from the argument she's not sure. She feels as though she has come out of it battered and bruised, that she hasn't won. But she's stood up to Josephine and she's reminded her that Bella is her child, and hers alone.

'Of course you can see him.'

Bella drops what she's doing and throws her arms around Pip, which takes her by surprise and then fills her with joy. She closes her eyes and hugs her back. Bella pulls away and continues with the nails, excitement buzzing from her.

'And as boring as it sounds, sometimes I would actually like to go for a walk with you,' Pip says. 'I'd love to get to know you better.'

'But you already know me, you weirdo,' Bella says, concentrating on Pip's nails. She wipes them with rubbing alcohol.

'More importantly, your dad said he wants to spend more time with you. He said that ten minutes every Sunday on the phone isn't enough.'

Bella pauses for a moment with the nails, a give-away sign.

'Which is unusual because I thought it was thirty minutes every Sunday.'

The tips of her ears go red.

'I don't know what to say to him. It's so awkward. You lot are all around, listening. It's so boring. So when we're finished after ten minutes, I just keep talking.'

'To who?'

'No one. We end the call and I just keep talking. And laughing, like I'm a crazy person.'

All those times Pip listened to her daughter on the phone to Jamie, laughing, and there had been no one at the other end of the phone. Nothing is ever as it seems.

'Your dad definitely isn't boring,' she says, smiling fondly. 'Or he wasn't. Wouldn't you like to spend more time with him?'

Bella shrugs. 'I like things how they are.'

Pip is surprised. Pip and Jamie aren't happy and want to make changes, and the main player who they're trying to help, doesn't want change.

'You like things like this?'

'What do you mean? What's wrong with everything?'

Pip sighs.

'So I need to let you in on a little something I'm planning. Which colour do you want?' Bella says, calmly, opening her box of polishes.

Pip points to white and Bella wrinkles her nose again and picks up a silver.

'What are you planning?' Pip repeats.

'I haven't said anything to Nan and Granddad yet, so don't you say anything. I'm choosing my moment and tonight is not it.'

'What is it?'

'I'm leaving school. After the summer, I'm not going back.'

'What? Bella, why?'

'Because I know what I want to do and I don't need anything in school to help me to do it.'

'What?'

'This!' she says, hands out, displaying the nail kit. 'I want to be a manicurist. I can get work as an apprentice, you don't need your leaving cert, and they train you in. Then when I'm fully trained I can go freelance and work for myself.'

Bella is so excited, so certain, so confident, Pip doesn't want to burst her bubble. She appreciates that she's been let in on the secret, but she can't give her blessing on this bad decision.

'Don't tell Nan and Granddad yet, I'll tell them when I have it all worked out. And if they hit the roof then that's where you come in.'

'In what way?'

'Well, you didn't finish school, did you, and you've turned out fine. I knew you'd understand and that you won't be a killjoy like them.'

Pip wants to tell her that she dreamed of finishing school, but she doesn't want Bella to think she regrets having her. Earlier she wanted Bella to know all of her sacrifices, but it would not have been right to put all of that on her young daughter. There's no point making sacrifices if you then tell the person that you have made a sacrifice. It was her decision, her cross to bear. She's enjoying this moment so much she doesn't want to say something to anger Bella and make her leave. She will listen for now.

'It's so cool having you,' Bella says, chirpily, applying the base coat. 'Roisín, Catherine and the others are always saying they feel so bad for me being on my own and having no siblings,' she says, referring to her cousins. 'But I always tell them I have you, and that's like having a sister.'

Bella means it as a compliment, but it doesn't feel like that to Pip.

A friend, an accomplice, a sister. But not a mother.

27

For the rest of the day Josephine won't look at or speak to Pip. If it's supposed to be a punishment, Pip doesn't take it like that. It's a gift.

Nevertheless, Pip feels raw from Josephine's words, which replay on a loop, as though all the layers of her skin have been peeled back and the slightest breeze or thought stings. She feels fragile and shaken and stays in her room nearly all day and night, and on Sunday morning when Philip, Josephine and Bella get in the car to go to mass they don't call her to see if she wants to come.

She lies in bed looking at the growing crack in her ceiling. It's vicious, as though the house is separating. Like the ground after an earthquake. She imagines creatures appearing from the depths, from the belly of the house, peering out and crawling around.

She uses this quietness in the house to think.

When they should be home after mass and she's readying herself for more awkwardness, she receives a text from Bella to tell her they're going to an aunt's house for Sunday lunch. Josephine is already beginning to spin her side of the story to her adoring family members, getting the troops ready. Pip faces hours more alone. She wanders the house, so empty with everyone gone. She does the washing and notices a small crack in the utility-room window. The splinters are appearing and there has always been one consistent way for her to mend.

She has never drawn outside of her bedroom. She retrieves her sketchbook and pencils, and sits at the kitchen table, the kitchen door open, watching the front door in case they return home to catch her in the act.

It feels different drawing in another room, with another view. It feels freeing not having to hide. She doesn't know what she wants to draw, but as soon as the lead hits the page and she starts scratching back and forth, an image starts to take shape. She freezes and stops a few times when she hears a sound, which is just the crack and pop of the house settling around her, and then as she relaxes she gets into the flow she loses track of time. An hour later, she has finished her drawing and is feeling high on the adrenaline of doing something she loves, but also doing something daring.

It makes her hungry for more. She calls Io.

He collects her in his car and they go flying.

'You seem disheartened,' he says, when he is settled in the air after speaking with air traffic control.

'Sorry.'

'No need to apologise to me.'

'I'll be happier,' she says, trying to perk up.

'Not on my account. Happiness isn't for others, it's only for yourself.'

She ponders that for a moment. 'What makes you happy? Apart from flying?'

'That's an interesting question. I'm learning a lot on this trip, about myself, and I know now that happiness isn't a destination. It's not about leaving something or somewhere to find it, it's not at the end of something. Not in a car, or a pair of shoes.'

'Or in your job?' she asks.

'Or in my job. My happiness *is* the pursuit. It's the journey, it's in the discovering, the learning, the listening, the following, the trying, the hoping. The take-off, the flying *and* the landing.'

'The waiting?'

'Especially in waiting. Like this, with you. The people you meet, the friends you make along the way. Maybe it shouldn't be about the signal, maybe it should be more about what you do when you're waiting.'

She smiles. 'Io, that is the most romantic thing anyone has ever said to me.'

'I don't mean it in a romantic way,' he says, shifting uncomfortably in his seat.

'Yes you do, you love me,' she teases. 'I make you happy, that's what you were trying to say.'

He laughs. 'Shut up.'

'Seriously,' she says, 'that's a beautiful thought.'

'Yes,' he says. 'I think I just figured it out while I'm here.'

Today, they fly over Kerry. Stunning lakes and mountains, a clear bright day. They fly towards the Gap of Dunloe, a narrow mountain pass that separates the MacGillycuddy Reeks from the Purple Mountain. The gap between the mountains is narrow and beautiful.

'Are we going through that?'

He winks.

She closes her eyes.

'Open them,' he laughs.

She feels as if she has to breathe in. The gap is probably

over two hundred metres wide, but she feels like both wings are going to scrape the edges. Io has to be very exact. It's like a trust fall. Flying through, she's in awe, she feels as if she's immersed in the very essence of planet earth. Mountains, rocks, and lakes, such vibrant green. A car or two move on the road beneath them, but it's all land, no people, pure planet. She feels so calm.

As they fly over Coosaun Lough and Black Lake, she takes the time to process Io's words about finding happiness. His words aren't like Josephine's, which clank around in her head like a coin trapped and rattling in a piggy bank. Io's words are smooth like honey, slow and thick, running and rolling around her head to fill every part, to take the shape of her mind, and settle calm and still. Happiness has not been in staying still and keeping quiet. Happiness is not in reaching the end, but in the motion towards it. She at least must begin to try to set off.

She leans close to the glass and looks down, concentrating hard.

Even in the sky, fourteen thousand feet up in the air, she looks for Jamie.

As they fly back to the airfield over the quarry that resembles a sink hole, she's reminded once again of her house, which stands dangerously close to falling into the void.

28

O N Monday morning Pip wakes with an altered mind. She feels fresher. More alert. Confident and ready to be assertive.

First out of the house, she's ready to speak to her mother in a calmer fashion than her explosive rage of Saturday's argument. She's well aware that Josephine's pettiness can take weeks to dissipate and it does so slowly and unpredictably.

Pip waits by the car, her coffee in hand, smelling the sweet summer air, listening to the birdsong, somewhere in the distance a machine is cutting grass. It's a beautiful summer morning. The morning light is the kind that makes you stand taller, lift your head, lean towards it and grow. Ripe for fresh beginnings.

She watches her neighbour Caroline's husband Aleksy limping towards his car, followed by a little boy wearing a face mask. She keeps watching them, determined to wave as soon as they look up. He glances up and she waves quickly. He looks away, but is too polite to completely ignore her, resulting in a nod and a frown.

'Good morning,' she says to Josephine and Bella, as they come outside, dressed in their ill-fitting black trousers and white blouses for the canteen kitchen.

'Morning,' Bella says.

Josephine, head down, ignores her as she scurries to the car in her quick short strides, her car key the main focus of her attention.

'Good day yesterday?'

Pip had been in bed when they'd returned late.

'So much fun.'

Bella loves her cousins. They have grown up together, and are the closest people she has to siblings – apart from Pip – and are also her friends. Josephine is comfortable with Bella hanging around with family, family are safe and loyal, loyal being the operative word.

'What did you do?' Bella asks.

'Oh,' she says, looking up at the sky. 'I hung around, got some perspective. Would you mind if I sit in the front seat today?'

Bella is perplexed. 'Why?'

'Because I'd like to,' she says pleasantly. 'And I think it's my turn.'

Josephine hasn't unlocked the car doors yet.

'No,' Josephine says. 'And you can't sit in the back seat either.'

'Do you want me to drive?' Pip jokes, trying to keep her energy up.

'You said you didn't need me. You said you're thirty-two years old now and you don't need me. So that's fine.' Josephine finally looks her in the eye. 'You can make your own way to work. You'll have to figure it out anyway, with the new working hours, if you're looking for that promotion.'

'Nan!' Bella says, surprised.

Josephine unlocks the car.

'Are you serious?' Pip asks.

'Were you?'

It's the moment to take it all back, apologise for everything she said and to make everything right, and easier. To become passive again, and disappear into the background. To become a passenger, with her mother in the driving seat, and her daughter up front beside her. Pip's failure to engage in confrontation has always made life easier in the short term, but she knows it's not going to make anything easier in the long term. She has slid down the Rapunzel tower and has taken a shaky step onto the fresh grass, this time she has come too far to climb back up again.

Besides, she can't take her words back because she meant every single one that exploded from her mouth during their argument. She's only getting started.

Josephine is expecting her to walk it all back, to cower down and shelter from this menacing threat.

'You're right,' Pip says, stepping back from the car, taking both Bella and Josephine by surprise. 'I'll see you both later, have a good day.'

Her words seem robotic, but she's trying to keep the tremble out of her voice, stay firm and polite. So much to remember when she's naturally tuned to agree and then apologise.

'I'll sit in the back,' Bella says, trying to patch things up.

'No you won't,' Josephine snaps and turns to Pip angrily with a finger pointed at her. 'And don't you go asking your dad for a lift either.'

'I won't.'

The anger builds even more as each of her threats bounce off Pip.

'You'll spend what you earn in a day on a taxi,' she adds.

She's waiting for Pip to back down, to apologise, to realise she needs her. To thank her. To break.

'You're right,' Pip says, starting to enjoy the powerful moment she's taking for herself.

Josephine and Bella get in the car, Bella throwing her a WTF expression.

Pip watches them drive away and then lifts her face again to the morning sun. She breathes in the fresh, sweet, warm air. The morning air holds such promise. A moment of endless possibilities, hours of opportunity stretched out before her. She has always loved mornings, the enjoyable part of before you set out on your journey. She always felt that her days failed to rise to the occasion. She wants to break that chain.

Philip comes outside moments later, barely able to look her in the eye. He either heard the conversation from the house or Josephine has given him the blow by blow account from her car, which is more likely.

'You'd better apologise to your mother,' he says, opening his car door and sitting in. Before he closes it, he has a crisis of the heart. 'Jump in, I'll drop you over.'

'It's okay,' she says. 'Thanks, Dad, but I'll make you late. And she's right. I shouldn't rely on you both so much at my age.'

It's intriguing, that when people finally hear what they've always wanted to hear, they don't know what to do with it. After all their long-term investment in the idea, they can't trust it.

He frowns. 'I don't know what you're playing at.'

She watches him leave their driveway and turn right to the quarry.

She's due at work in fifteen minutes. She could walk, but it's a dangerous road, busy now, six kilometres of no pavement, and many potholes, thanks to the Wolverson quarry vehicles. She survived the walk once, she doesn't want to tempt fate again. And even if she didn't get flattened by an enormous wheel, it would take her almost an hour to get there and she'd be very late. She could phone for a taxi, but there's just one small taxi service run by the family that owns the florist, and she hasn't prebooked. They're usually busy in the mornings with bringing the elderly food shopping or the disability van for school pick-ups. Her mother is right about the price, too.

Maybe she'll take the day off, it would be the first of her holiday days she's ever taken off. Working with her mother every day in the observatory canteen for ten years meant she couldn't stay home no matter how ill she felt. Josephine didn't do illness, though she moaned and groaned about aches and pains, she would never surrender to it.

Pip rings Krish and asks him if it's okay to take a day off today. She expects to have to explain herself, but he accepts it easily. She hadn't wanted to let him down, she thought she was the only one propping him up, that to take a day off was a failure, a mark on her card. That's how Josephine had trained her. In reality, he can call somebody else in to take her place. Everybody needs a moment.

Before she hangs up, while she's feeling emboldened, she adds. 'Krish, I've decided I'd like to go for the promotion.'

'Yes Philippa, that is the spirit! I'll tell them.'

'When will the interview be?' she asks. She wants to move onto the next part of her life quickly. She's ready and motivated.

'Very soon, because I only have a few weeks left and they're already interviewing, but I will help you prepare. I will be Mickey Goldmill and you will be Rocky Balboa. Together we will help you achieve your full potential and you will be victorious. I will call you and let you know.'

'Okay. Thanks.'

'Enjoy your day off, Philippa.'

She goes into the house and does her washing. She does Bella's washing and ironing, getting to it first and feeling good about it. She's a better ironer and organiser than Josephine, who is angry at everything; the vacuum cleaner, the ironing board. She's an undomesticated domestic worker, uncomfortable in the household world, attacking it every day with unfulfillment and bitterness. Pip can imagine Josephine in so many other roles where she would be fearless and could flourish; a trader on the floor of the exchange going one hundred miles an hour with algorithmic trading info. Or Pip sees her at the horse races, as a bookie by the parade ring, doing Tic Tac hand signals to the crowd, taking bets and robbing them all. She's a scrubber, is her mother, a hard worker willing to get stuck in, taking a small number of ingredients on a daily basis and turning out food for hundreds of people like the old stone soup folk tale. Magic. But just not at home.

Pip is hanging her clothes out to dry outside when she hears the quarry siren go off. The siren is long, as though they're in a war zone and, even though she knows what it is, she instinctively looks up to the sky for a bomber plane. She has never heard it in the months they've lived here, as she's always at work midweek and the quarry isn't open on weekends. She stops to listen, imagining her dad in the quarry, the blast supervisor, shouting orders behind the cannon to the foot soldiers. The siren is followed by a rumble, that travels deep beneath the earth's floor, and then it's as though her imagination comes to life because the ground beneath her shakes and suddenly she feels like the world is ending. She holds on, stupidly, to the clothes line, thinking it's an earthquake or some kind of disaster. The rumble finally ends and there's silence again, though even the birds have momentarily quietened, holding their song in stunned silence.

She studies the house and sees the crack across the back of the utility-room window has gone from a small splinter to a spiderweb of broken lines, and it looks like it's about to shatter into a million pieces.

She walks around the house to the front garden, all the time surveying the house, her hands on her hips, studying the still unpainted exterior. She thinks about what the house has silently been through while they have all been away at work. It has tried to speak to them through its cracks. She feels a presence behind her. She turns around and sees Caroline watching her from her wheelie bin at the end of her garden.

'Hi,' Pip says, walking down the driveway towards the road.

She looks left and right and waits for a Wolverson cement mixer to pass by, going too fast on such a narrow badly surfaced road. She almost expects Caroline to be gone when it passes, but she's still there.

'Would you like to come in for a coffee?' Caroline asks.

29

THEY SIT IN CAROLINE's kitchen, a five-year-old house, built when her parents decided to share out their land and have their three daughters and their spouses beside them. The fridge is covered in kids' art, timetables and reminders of daily activities. Pip sits at the kitchen table, while Caroline makes coffee, looking out at their acres of land that stretch out to meet the sky.

Caroline places a mug of coffee down on the table before her.

'Fancy,' Pip says impressed. 'Quite the barista.'

'Aleksy got me a coffee machine for our anniversary, and I almost left him over it, but it's turned out to be the best present. Who knew I needed it in my life?'

Caroline pushes the plate of chocolate biscuits towards her. 'Move these as far away from me as possible.'

Pip smiles and pulls the plate closer to her, but doesn't take one. 'Thanks for talking to me, I'm glad we're doing this.'

'Our mutual friend Kim tells me I may have been over-reacting. And that I owe you an apology.'

'I adore Kim,' Pip says. 'But I think your overreaction is caused by the fact I have, or had, absolutely no idea what was going on between your family and the quarry.'

'I assumed you knew. What do you know?'

Her tone suggests, how could you *not* know?

'I've heard bits and pieces from my dad and from Sammy—'

'What did that arsehole say?' Caroline interrupts.

Pip puts her hands up in the air, in defence. 'How about you tell me everything so I have the full picture.'

Caroline takes a moment to calm down, her neck is red from her chest to her chin, a stress rash.

'I'm sure you've heard recently that the councils are to crack down on dodgy quarries, and let's hope the Wolversons are first in line because they're a law unto themselves. They're causing environmental and local damage, and we're trying to take them to the High Court to order a halt.'

This is news to Pip. Her eyes widen. 'You want to close the quarry?'

'We want to stop it until they can be taught how to run it properly. Old Samuel Wolverson was all right, and Rupert Wolverson was a good man, he ran things with an iron fist.' She watches her words. 'But new management has taken things to a new level.' She means Sammy. 'They've gotten greedy with all the new business ideas. And careless. Which is dangerous. The accidents are more frequent and more severe than those of any other quarry in the country.' She takes a breath and calms herself. 'Sorry. It's been so stressful.'

'That's okay. You should know that Sammy and I aren't together. We went on *two* dates. Mainly because Dad thinks so highly of the Wolversons he thought we'd be a good match. I thought I'd give it a chance. It didn't work.'

Caroline's face softens and the anger at Pip she'd still been holding on to falls away. 'Oh. I didn't know that. But that's good news. He's a monster. Apparently he hit one of his girlfriends, though normally I hate rumours, I don't mind a rumour about him. She moved out of town. I'm glad you got away from him in good time.'

Pip's stunned, and not for the reasons Caroline thinks. It wasn't all in her head, again.

'I know,' Caroline says, drinking her coffee, chuffed by the gossip reveal. 'All that airbrushed trendy exterior. He has a mouth on him like a donkey. He makes me want to throw carrots at him.'

She really hates him. Pip laughs, enjoying the release it brings her. The atmosphere has been so tense, for so long between them. Caroline finally drops her hardened shell and laughs too.

'It didn't have to be like this,' she says, more gently. 'This all began a few years ago, before you started building the house, with us noticing an increase in explosions.'

Pip readies herself again, feels her defences go up. Her dad is the blast supervisor, he is directly involved in the explosions.

'It used to be once a month, then it was once a fortnight. Then once a week. And now it's a few times a week. Ever since Sammy took over, things have changed. You're all at work every day, you wouldn't notice it, but I assumed you would know about it from your dad.'

If only people could understand, for all the talking they do in her house, there is no actual communication.

'The dust is affecting my son's asthma. He's had two asthma attacks this month, we've had him in A&E on nebulisers. We have humidifiers all around the house to clean the air, we don't open the windows. We make him wear a mask from the house to the car and from the car to the house. The house, which is only five years old, has cracks from the explosions.

The Slatterys down the road have a cracked window. My sister Helen, next door, has a toddler who's terrified of the blasts. They wake her baby every day. Little Bobby won't leave her side, and clings to her legs, in case the ground shakes when he's not with her. Our cars are covered with a thick layer of dust every day, I'm nonstop cleaning the windows, and I see you doing it too.'

Pip does clean the windows a lot, she'd assumed it was from the vehicles coming to and from the quarry, barrelling down the road in a puff of dust.

'Caroline, I had no idea about this,' she says, shaking her head.

Caroline takes a break and sips her coffee.

'The constant rock breaking is like torture. We asked them years ago to be more mindful of the community, we asked them to provide a schedule of operations so that we could work with them on ensuring we can live and work together side by side. They ignored every single letter, email and phone call. After getting nowhere with the quarry, we contacted the council. We asked them to install a seismograph in the house, as well as noise and dust monitors, and then we all got together to hire a solicitor. We thought that might be enough to get them to cooperate, and when we did that the quarry seemed to get worse.'

Surely Philip doesn't know about all this. How could he let this go on?

'And while all this was happening, Aleksy worked there. Aleksy was trying to balance working there, and deal with the legal side of it as a local. Then they started changing his hours, messing with his schedule, and his jobs. He'd be taken off one vehicle and put on another. Messing with his head.'

'They wanted him to quit.'

'Probably. But then there was the accident with his leg. He was refuelling when a pile of stones collapsed on him. He was working with young lads who weren't being properly trained, accidents were bound to happen. And they are. By the load.'

'Why hasn't anyone looked at that?'

'Maybe they don't want to look that closely. We need more housing, which puts pressure on the quarries. No one wants to shut it down and none of us are saying we don't understand the pressures, but what Sammy is doing is wrong, plain and simple. The workers are just getting paid off so their accidents don't go to court. Sammy knows that the quarry only has so long. He can only go so deep, or use so many acres before it's depleted eventually. He's quite literally running that family business into the ground.'

Pip thinks about the cracks in her house.

'Have there been any issues about the quality of their stone?'

'Not that I've heard. Why?'

'Just wondering.'

Caroline sips her coffee and studies Pip over the rim of her cup. Pip's not at the stage of trusting her with personal information about their house.

'How's your dad's breathing?' Caroline asks.

'Why?'

'Some of the old lads who've been there since the start have silicosis.'

'What's that?'

'An incurable lung disease caused by invisible dust particles known as silica. Long-term exposure can lead to heart disease, strokes, infertility and pregnancy complications.' Her eyes fill up suddenly. 'I'm not saying it's related, but I had a miscarriage last year. Gerry Slattery had a stroke last year. It could have nothing to do with the quarry, but our kids are small, we're all young, we want to protect ourselves.'

Pip thinks about her dad. He's older. Not as fast as he used to be, his body half-crocked, his coughing keeping him awake half the night, working in a dust-filled dangerous site that isn't what it used to be. Regulation man in a lawless company. She can imagine him feeling they need him, that they'd go down without him.

Caroline says, 'Aleksy says your dad is old school, he's one of the original good men. Trained as they all should be. He's their golden man. That's why they sold the land to him here, to take away our credibility. Because every time we say something, your dad denies it or comes back with something to the contrary. If he lives here and he's fine, then how can anything we say be untrue?'

She's not sure that's true. It seems far-fetched, though Sammy himself admitted to sending Philip to court as their best representative. 'I'm sorry.'

'I realise now, you don't need to be. You didn't know.' She studies Pip and says aloud what she's been thinking the entire time. 'How didn't you know?'

Pip almost takes offence at her directness. But Caroline is right, Pip has been walking through the past sixteen years with her eyes closed.

But she's waking up now.

30

BY THE TIME PIP returns home from Caroline's house, Bella and Josephine are back from work. She hears banging upstairs from Bella's room as she clomps across the floor doing who knows what, and a quick peek into the rooms downstairs tells her Josephine is also upstairs in her room, with the door closed. Pip could go to her bedroom as she usually does and fold herself away, or she could claim the space downstairs, and unfold.

When Philip returns from work Pip is sitting at the kitchen table with a cup of tea and a sandwich waiting for him. She's sketching, unafraid to be seen drawing in front of the others. This simple act seems daring. Philip seems pleasantly surprised to see her, and the food. He removes his high-vis jacket, and hangs it on the wall. His filthy steel-toe boots are placed on the floor outside the utility-room door for cleaning. He washes his hands at the sink, then joins her at the table.

'Good day?'

He grunts, and sits down into the chair, groaning with pain as he goes down. He eyes her pencils and paper on the table warily. Pip has put the radio on in the background to soften the tension. Josephine comes hurrying down the stairs to see him and is clearly disappointed to see Pip sitting with him.

Which is how Pip always feels when Josephine gets to Bella first.

'You brought her home?' Josephine asks.

'She was here when I got in.'

Pip bristles. 'Excuse me, *she* is in the room.'

They look at her.

'I took the day off.' Pip picks up a pencil and starts sharpening it. She has always felt it to be a relaxing task, sometimes she has wasted pencils entirely without even using them by paring them down too much, snapping the lead and then paring them again.

'Well for some,' Josephine says, looking at the graphite smudges on Pip's hands and then at the drawing in front of her.

Philip's huge hands had come to life in Pip's pencil drawing today, thick fingers, crusty and dry, wrinkled and calloused, a smidge of an oil stain, but sturdy and strong. Hands that break rock, the hands that built a home. The hands that have pushed her forward and pulled her back. The hands that have held her.

'What's that?' Josephine asks.

'Dad's hands.'

Philip looks at the drawing, eyes disappearing underneath his eyebrows as he tries to make it out. He holds his hand out beside the sketch to compare it, and she smiles.

Josephine opens the dishwasher and slides the drawer out. She gathers dishes together in a loud clatter that makes even Philip wince.

Pip had cut her dad's ham sandwich into two triangles. The first half he chooses is barely visible inside his shovel-sized hand. He takes a bite, half of it gone in an instant. It lives in his cheek, puffed out, while he chews. Then he takes a second bite of his sandwich despite not yet swallowing the first.

'I went to Caroline Nowak's house for a coffee today,' Pip says.

Josephine crashes a casserole dish into the drawer.

'Jesus Christ, Josephine,' Philip says, startled, through a mouthful of food.

'What did you do that for?' she shouts at Pip, hands on her hips.

'I wanted to go over and try to heal the relationship,' Pip says, feeling like Tala. 'I wanted to know what I'd done wrong.'

'Seems to me a pattern is emerging,' Josephine says, getting back to work.

'It was interesting to hear what she had to say.'

'Interesting, all right, like something out of a story book. Pure fiction,' Josephine says.

'I didn't know the full picture. Her husband Aleksy was injured at the quarry.'

'That was a farce,' Josephine says.

'Unfortunate what happened,' Philip says, a little more understanding because he can imagine the pain of what occurred and even worse, the inability to be able to work.

'Aleksy was injured *after* they all submitted their problems about the quarry.'

'So you're blaming the quarry for that too, I suppose,' Josephine says.

'I'm not blaming anyone. I'm just telling you what she said. They're planning on taking the quarry to the High Court.'

'And they'll lose,' Josephine says, Philip's best hype woman.

'Sammy says you're his best defence witness, Dad.'

He puts the second triangle down on the plate, appetite gone. 'I'm not keen on that description. I do it when I have to.'

'He's a good man. He's an honest man. That's why he does it. That's why they ask him to do it,' Josephine says.

Philip is appreciative of her support but he does look a little wearied by her interruptions.

Josephine empties the cutlery into the drawer, being more careful about the noise, probably so that she can hear their conversation.

'They're not just making it up, Dad, they installed a seismograph in the house, as well as noise and dust monitors. They have physical proof.'

He leans in, his elbows on the table, wanting to hear more.

She tells him about Caroline's son who has asthma, the terrified toddler and the baby's disturbed naps, the dust on the cars. 'They say that the number of blasts has tripled, that it used to be once a week and now it's three times a week.'

As she's speaking to the blastmaster, she's careful with her tone.

'Well that's true,' he says, shifting in his seat. 'Because we're under pressure to meet the aggregate requirements for the bypass.'

'Are you blasting more than you'd like?' she asks, softly.

Josephine spins and looks at them.

He nods. 'More than I'd like. But I can see why he's doing it.'

Surprised by his response, Josephine goes back to the cutlery. Pip feels like she's getting somewhere.

'Are they putting you under pressure?'

'It's my job, so I have to do my job.'

'Or else what?'

'Or else nothing. I have a duty to do. If there was anything wrong with anything we're doing, we'd know about it by now. The council wouldn't let it go ahead. Not in this day and age.'

'Caroline says the council are conflicted because they hired a firm that's using the Wolverson quarry for the bypass.'

'So you're saying the council is corrupt now?' Josephine says, getting involved. She turns around, drying her hands in a tea towel, twisting it around every finger, as if she's going to pull them off.

Pip ignores Josephine and speaks only to Philip. 'They formed a committee across the road. The Nurney Committee. They want to bring the case to court.'

'If the quarry gets shut down, then your dad will lose his job. He's five years away from retirement and getting his pension. Is that what you want?'

'Nobody wants the quarry to shut down. They want them to comply, to operate to the proper standards.'

'What do you know about proper standards?'

It's all Josephine now, Philip is listening silently. The argument seems not to be about the quarry at all now, but everything else, and Pip is ready for it. She feels a newfound confidence in contradicting her mother. Saturday night's argument has unblocked her, she can explain things to her mother without trembling, without fear of losing Bella.

'I know more than I knew this morning. I was here for a blast this morning. I was outside hanging the washing out and it felt like there was an earthquake.'

'Imagine what it's like for your dad in the quarry, sure it's nothing compared to that here.'

Pip ignores her. 'The blast was so strong the utility-room window shattered.'

'That crack has been there for ages, that didn't happen today.'

'What crack?' Philip says. The utility room is not his domain.

He wouldn't be in there or outside it where the clothes line is, to notice it.

'I didn't mention it,' Josephine says, folding the tea towel into a small rectangle. The corners don't meet, but she folds it anyway. It's imperfect. Perhaps this is what Josephine sees when she watches Pip; nothing but inconsistencies and flaws.

'It felt like a war zone. Have you ever been here when there's a blast?' Pip asks her dad.

'How could he be in two places at once when he's the one who's doing the blasting?'

'None of us are ever here to experience it,' Pip continues. 'Across the road they're here every day. With toddlers and babies. They're cleaning their cars every day, they're wearing masks. Trucks speeding by, destroying the road. It's filled with potholes, it was supposed to be resurfaced and they've been promised it for years, but it never has been. They see it, they feel it, and hear it. We should at least listen to them. Whatever you think about Aleksy's claim at work, at least be concerned about your own house. We're so much closer to the quarry than I thought.'

She stops herself from sharing how she knows this. From above in Io's plane, she can see that their house is so close to the deep pit. It looks as if they could topple in.

'Are we far enough away? How did we get the permission to build here? And if Sammy goes for planning for an expansion, then in which direction will he go? Why do you think he let you build here?'

'Oh stop with the conspiracy theories, Caroline must have put something in your coffee. It makes perfect sense as to why Sammy sold this land to your dad. He's a valued employee, the longest serving. He deserved it.'

Philip is quiet as he absorbs it all but Pip senses he is waking up too. It started with seeing how Sammy Wolverson was making Pip feel, and now this.

'Your dad is as loyal as they come and he'll be loyal to the end. Five years to go until his retirement, there'll be no boat-rocking.'

But her dad is listening.

'It's not just the utility window,' Pip says gently, ignoring her mother's orders. 'Did she not tell you about the crack in my bedroom?'

'Philippa Sheridan,' Josephine says, raising her voice, but Philip silences her with an irritated whip around on his chair to look at her.

'Josephine, would you please, for the love of God?'

Surprised and upset, she quietens.

'What crack?'

'I didn't want to bother you,' Josephine says, sniffing, insulted by the admonishment. 'I know you're stressed and busy with work and finishing the house.' She throws Pip an angry look.

Philip stands, taking a moment to straighten himself, and goes upstairs to Pip's bedroom. She follows him inside, leaving no room for Josephine. She doesn't have to remove the Monet print because the crack is quite visible now, but Pip takes it down anyway to give him the full picture. He puts his hands on his hips and surveys the crack that's a fissure now.

Josephine peeks her head into the room. She looks up, and her expression changes when she sees how much worse it is.

Without a word Philip goes into Bella's room. Again, hands on his hips as he stares up. It stretches across the wall like a climber.

'How long has this been here?' There's a kind of breathless incredulous tone to his voice. Not anger, maybe fear.

'It was here when I showed Sammy the house,' Pip says, and her mother throws her a dangerous look. 'Though it was much smaller.'

'What did he say?'

'He said it was a bad plastering job.'

She's slowly pulling back the curtain. He didn't want to look before. She's revealing things bit by bit. The Wizard of Oz is not as great as Philip thinks.

'Did he now?'

'What do you think?' Josephine asks. 'Can you fix them?'

He's silent for a moment. 'Some of them.' He goes back into Pip's room and they leave him there alone to look at the more dangerous gash on the ceiling. He comes outside to the landing and heads for the stairs. 'I'll start with the filler.'

Philip is busy in the house for the next few hours, applying filler to the walls and ceilings, and around the doors and window frames. He pulls the furniture away from the walls, and examines every corner, and the house is in a state, as he works his way around filling the cracks.

Later, at ten p.m., it's still bright outside, Pip hears boots on gravel in the garden. She goes to the bay window and sees Philip working his way around the house with filler. He looks as though he's in pain as he goes down to his knees to get the hard to reach parts. Not knowing he's being watched means he didn't bother to hide his grimaces.

'I hope you're happy with yourself now,' Josephine says, from behind, taking her by surprise. Pip hadn't noticed her sitting on the couch, curled up in the corner, her legs close to her body, hands hugging a mug of tea.

'If we ignore the cracks for any longer, they'll get bigger.'

It's what they've done for sixteen years.

'Maybe you can draw us a new house,' Josephine says, viciously. 'Maybe one of your little scribbles will save the day, seeing as you're filled with so many new ideas these days.'

Pip watches her dad, optimistically trying to stop the house from crumbling by using filler to plug the gaps. She doesn't know anything about building, but it seems as though this house has absorbed everything rotten about this family.

The best way forward is to knock it all down and rebuild.

31

THE NEXT MORNING PIP goes downstairs and her dad is taping up the utility-room window.

'Morning,' she says.

He looks up. 'Morning.'

'Did you know we had a washing machine? Is that your first time in there?'

'Ha-ha,' he says drily, but he smiles.

'Dad.'

'Uh-oh,' he says, hearing her tone.

'Jamie has a plastering company in Liverpool.'

He's silent.

'I could ask him to come around and take a look.'

He continues taping the window.

'I know you'd find it hard, but he wouldn't charge us.'

He looks tired. She'd heard him coughing half the night.

Bella and Josephine come downstairs.

'Morning, honey,' Pip says to Bella, giving her a hug and a kiss.

This surprises Bella as much as it does Josephine. It is slightly awkward and mistimed, but this is what she wants with her daughter. More physical interaction. More personal interaction. She wants to lead rather than follow, no more passenger princess.

'Right, I'm leaving for work. See you all later.'

Josephine and Bella look at her in surprise. Her mother thought she'd won the war, that Pip would be getting in the car with her today. Sitting in the back with her tail between her legs, a child-adult of thirty-two years of age. Not anymore.

'How are you getting there?'

'A lift from a friend.'

'At this hour?'

It's an hour earlier than Pip needs to leave, but it's the only time Io is available to collect her and beggars can't be choosers.

One day off work was a luxury, but she needed to return, and standing up to her mother and taking back the power could not be a one-off. She had to look ahead, and plan, for once.

She walks down the road and gets into the car. She'd asked him not to come to the house, still not comfortable with Josephine knowing about her friendship with a scientist from the observatory. She doesn't want her mother making problems for him.

'Thank you so much for this, Io.'

'It's my pleasure, really. I'm doing it for me. I need you back making my lunch. Your colleague with the mohawk hair made me eat coronation chicken.'

'Oh no. No, that's not what I would have suggested for you. It's a wet food.'

'No kidding. I vomited at work.'

'Oh Io, I'm sorry,' she says, trying not to laugh.

'You're laughing at me, after all I do for you, and you laugh.'

She laughs louder, hearing his playful tone.

'I'll get my own back. Loop the loops on our next flight.'

'Yes please.'

'Nothing in that plane scares you. I like it. What could I do to get you back?'

'Put my mother on the plane with us,' she says, then goes quiet.

'What have I told you since the day I met you?'

'One small change every day.'

'That's it. That's all it takes. And look where you are.'

She feels like she's walking a tightrope, one foot on the high wire, and is about to step off, but she can't quite reach the ledge.

He drives past the service station.

'You passed it!'

'We're going to the airfield.'

'We're flying?'

They'd hardly have enough time before her work begins.

'No. We're driving.'

He pulls into the airfield and Stella comes out of the hangar. Seeing it's them she waves and goes back inside.

'Does she live here?'

'Pretty much.' He gets out of the car and walks around to her side. He opens the door. 'You're in the driver's seat.'

'Driver's seat? What? I don't even have a permit.'

'I applied for one on your behalf.' He reaches over her and opens the glove box. He retrieves a book.

'The official Driver Theory Test Questions and Answers book,' she reads.

'Your theory test is on Saturday. I got you a cancellation.'

'How do you know someone at an Irish test centre?'

'I called them on the magic telephone.'

She is stunned, unprepared for this chain of events.

'You missed work yesterday because you couldn't get there,

and you told your mother you can do this on your own, so guess what? This is how you do things on your own. You get out of the passenger seat,' he says, taking her by the hand and escorting her out, and he guides her around the car, 'and you get your arse – to use your word – in the driver's seat.'

He's grinning.

'Why are you doing this for me, Io?' she asks, suddenly moved.

'Because I don't want your colleague to make my sandwiches anymore.'

'Seriously, Io. Not just this. The tour of the observatory. Taking me flying. Eating my sandwiches. Why are you being so kind to me? I've done nothing to deserve this at all.'

'I don't agree. I came here, as a scientist, to do what it is I always do. To look up, and to pay very little attention to what's going on on the ground. But you are giving me the human experience. And that, I'm discovering, is absolutely the thing that we should be trying to discover more of. You are it.'

Her eyes are filled with tears. She may have taught him to look around, but he has taught her to look up.

'Now get in the car and start the engine.'

32

Pip drives around the airfield under Io's patient guidance. She's not a bad driver despite having been a passenger all of her life. However, there's safety on the airfield, nothing to crash into, and she stays well away from the hangar. Stella sits out on a deckchair, her face lifted to the sun, taking a break from reading *The Complete History of the World*.

'You're sure a plane won't land on us?'

'Very sure. Nothing is scheduled, and I'm quite sure we'll see it and hear it in the sky first. Besides, control tower over there would tell us.'

'Are we the only people who use this place?' Pip asks, when she's feeling comfortable behind the wheel.

'No. Others use it at night.'

'Are you allowed to fly at night?'

'If you have a private licence you can fly when you like.'

She turns at the hangar and faces down the runway. She revs the engine and he laughs.

'Think you could take off?'

She puts her foot down and the engine cuts out. He roars laughing. Pip is revelling in driving, it's so much more fun than sitting in the back seat being driven, and she's disappointed when Io calls time. He has to go to work and so does she. They swap over and he high-fives her.

'I'll collect you each morning and drop you home until you learn to drive.'

'But Io—'

'No buts. If you feel like you're putting me out, that means you'll learn faster, right?'

As they drive by Stella snoozing in the sun, a cap lowered over her eyes, Io lowers the window.

'Stella,' he says, whistling, and she sits up, startled, confused, forgetting where she is. 'You heard anything?'

'No. Think I'd be snoozing out here if I had?'

He rolls up the window and she blows him a kiss as he drives away.

'Does Stella work with the observatory too?'

He pauses. 'No. Why?'

'Seems like you're both waiting for the same thing.' Pip watches Io. His expression is closed. 'If the signal comes, will she go home too?'

'This is home for her now. She's been here a long time.'

He's quiet for the remainder of the journey, and Pip is silently hoping he'll reconsider and stay here too.

As they drive towards Crossroads, Ronnie cuts them off on his electric scooter.

'Run him over,' she says, deadpan.

He grins and parks, because he wants to buy his lunch for later. As soon as Ronnie sees them, he whistles.

'What's this? Fraternising with the customers? I'm surprised by you, Sheridan, you seemed the quiet type, but isn't that who you have to watch?' He makes hand gestures and wet sounds with his mouth, before pretending to climax, and then goes inside the station.

Io watches him, confused. 'I should have squashed him.'

Pip passes Io's chopped salad over the counter to him and notices a van pull in outside, bearing the familiar logo of their national broadcaster. Two men get out, one is holding a television camera, and a woman with striking red hair climbs out. They take recording equipment from the back of the van and she emerges with a backpack.

'Look at this,' Krish says, excitedly. He's an avid TV and film viewer and Pip has regularly been forced to listen to explanations of scenes blow by blow, whether she's interested or not. 'TV has come to Ballybeg. You know my sister once met Shah Rukh Khan and got a photograph with him. He is one of Bollywood's biggest stars.' Krish's eyes are popping with excitement.

'That's cool.'

He reaches into his pocket and starts scrolling through his photos. She sees hundreds of photos of his five kids pass before her eyes. 'There he is.' He lifts the photo to her face. 'Anyway, it turned out not to be him, but his absolute doppelganger.'

Io laughs with glee and Pip smothers a smile.

Krish tucks his phone back into his pocket and concentrates on what's going on outside. 'Do you think the station will be on television?' He looks around the place. 'It could be cleaner.' He moves quickly and begins instructing Ronnie on what to tidy up outside.

Ronnie, who's standing at the till by the window, is holding his middle finger up in the air.

'The camera's not on,' Pip says to him.

He looks at her and makes sex sounds again.

Krish tells him off from behind one of the aisles, invisible but still all-seeing. He sounds like a tired father, exhausted with one of his children.

'They must be in town for Jamie's dad,' Pip realises. 'He's invited the media to watch him cut turf on Clonboyle Bog.'

'Jamie's going to need you there,' Io says. 'You should go to him.'

'I'm working.'

The TV news correspondent enters the station, looking frazzled. She looks around at Ronnie, then an unnaturally beaming Krish, who, if he had a red carpet, he'd have rolled it out for the crew. Then she sees Pip and heads straight for her.

'Excuse me, where are the toilets? I need to do my make-up.'

'Pip will take you to our service area,' Krish says grandly, as if it's something special. 'Pip, bring her through the back. Krish Singh, manager of the station, how do you do?'

She shakes his hand. 'Hi. Rachel Buckley. 4 News.'

'Ah yes, *For you, for us, for the world. Four*,' he says, repeating the news channel tagline in a deep voice-over accent.

'Follow me,' Pip says, waving goodbye to Io.

She takes her through the staffroom and exit, through their break yard, as if it's a VIP entrance. 'Watch out for the crates,' she says, 'and the broken glass.' She leads her to the service area in the back, near the car wash and truck parking bays. They're well kept, clean showers and toilets.

'Here you go,' Pip says, holding her hand out to display the service area.

'Thank you – I've been squeezed into a van with two very large men.'

'I know the feeling. I work with two men here too. One is a gentleman, the other an absolute imbecile.'

Rachel smiles. 'You can tell your boss I insisted on you staying, if you want to get a few minutes off work.'

Pip wouldn't usually, but with Jamie and the conflict with her mother on her mind she isn't as motivated to work in the same way as she was before. She's not looking for something to hide behind any longer.

Pip leans against the wall and watches Rachel. She pushes her fringe back with a hairband, and uses a pan stick to draw make-up on her forehead, cheeks and chin. She rubs it in with a sponge, massaging it in circular motions around her face. The transformation is instant. She has gone from one very pale woman to becoming very orange, before her very eyes.

'I thought you'd have a hair and make-up team.'

Rachel snorts. 'No chance. They tell me I have to look decent on-screen, then they rush me and tell me they need the shot. Then they give out about my hair blowing all over the place. I'm a journalist, not a model. The hair and make-up team are in television studios, but I've never been in. I'm a roving reporter.' She says this with sarcasm. 'Out and about capturing the hot stories on the road.'

'Are you going to Clonboyle Bog today?'

'Yes. You heard about it? Please don't tell me you've had the competition in here already. I was sure that lot wouldn't give a damn about this story.'

'I haven't seen any other reporters.'

'Well that's not good either. Means it's not a good story.'

Next, she turns to her eyebrows. She goes from angry to

surprised very quickly, as two thick black caterpillars dominate her forehead. In two weeks they will fly away.

'I think it's a good story. Will you be reporting live?' Pip would like to watch from work.

'No. We'll film, cut it together, it won't make the headlines. Probably three seconds of "in other news around the country", if it makes the news at all.' She sighs and drops the eyebrow brush into her make-up bag. 'Sorry for being such a grump, there was another story that I really wanted today. I missed out on it, and I'm here, in . . .'

'Ballybeg,' Pip reminds her.

'Right. Sorry.'

'It's okay. Are you from Dublin?'

Pip has never been there, they always holiday in a caravan park in Donegal – her parents have never had the interest to go to cities.

'No. I'm from Hurler's Cross. In County Clare. You won't have heard of it. Believe me, there's more happening here in this toilet than there was where I grew up. I moved out as soon as I could. Only thing that happened was someone murdered a cow. Put a steel pole right through its head, and they never caught who did it.'

'Poor cow,' Pip says.

'Oh, don't feel sorry for me,' Rachel says, and Pip laughs.

'Today isn't such a bad story you know.'

'Some old peat farmer doesn't want to stop cutting turf. We've heard it before all around the country.'

'There's a bit more to it than that.'

'Yeah?' She takes her hair down and backcombs it. She is thoroughly orange, and the light in the bathroom isn't the brightest. She turns to face Pip. 'Do you know him?'

'Krish, I'm so sorry,' Pip says, as he furiously makes breakfast rolls for the line of customers. 'The journalist is wondering if I can go with her to Clonboyle Bog, because I know Lorcan Murphy and she wants a word with him.'

His eyes widen. 'You must go, Pip. This is the opportunity of a lifetime.'

She doesn't know what he thinks will happen, she's not going to be reporting the news, but his obsession with television magic has him pushing her out from behind the counter. 'Go. Mention Ballybeg service station if you can get it into a sentence on-air.'

She removes her apron, stuffs it into her locker and grabs her coat, wondering what on earth she's got herself into. Her desire had been to get to Jamie.

'Break a leg!' Krish shouts after her, as she leaves and climbs into the van and squeezes in with the TV crew.

33

THE MEDIA VAN PULLS up to the Clonboyle Bog, and they aren't the first on the scene. A line of cars suggesting a decent turnout, and a Garda car is parked on the side of the road; the van pulls in behind it. A Garda stands at the car, arms folded, relaxed, and a second Garda stands further in from the road on the bogland. Clonboyle Bog was family-owned by the Murphys for generations but is now considered a preservation area. Lorcan Murphy was offered a site else-where for his use, but he is refusing to use land that's not his by his birthright.

The activity is taking place not far in from the road, so that the crew don't have far to trek. The land is rich with heather, the bog-building sphagnum moss and the bog cotton, with their fluffy white heads awaiting the dispersal of their seeds by the wind. A group of Lorcan's supporters, twenty to thirty people strong, gather with banners reading, 'Say No! to EU and Government bog restrictions!', 'Our land, our birthright!', and 'Freeze Prices, not the Poor!'

Journalists gather with notepads and pens, cameras in hand, photographers snap the scene. But it has an atmosphere of calm. It is gentle. Bog silence. There's nothing like it. The soil absorbs it all. The protest is silent. The only movement is Lorcan Murphy, in the centre of everyone, the calm in the storm, getting his tools and equipment ready for his demonstration. His court hearing is this week and this is his moment to shine, to try to make a difference; to protect his heritage, and his independence.

Rachel's energy changes as soon as they pull up to the bog. Pip can feel the adrenaline surging through the reporter, as she looks around and assesses the scene, finds her story. She's like a hunter. She has a limited amount of time to catch everything she needs, absorb every single thing around her and send the story back home. Even if she only gets ten seconds of airtime.

The sight is calm but the bog is teeming with life. Dragonflies and butterflies, the bog cotton sways in the breeze, lit by the occasional sunbeam as clouds pass overhead.

Pip sees Jamie standing with Tala. Her heart skips a beat. His brothers are standing off to the side, away from him, but not too far, maybe others wouldn't notice the disconnect, but Pip can see it. As the oldest son the land would have moved down to Jamie, but after the terrible thing he did, he was sent away, and the next in line, Domhnall was to inherit the land, before it was taken from them. Domhnall stands with his wife and four children, and with Finbar and his wife. Jamie hasn't been here for years to help with the family on the land, the backbreaking long days of cutting and drying, the stressful days of trying to protect the harvest, keeping the peat dry so that the winter's fuel can be saved.

Pip stands by Jamie's side, gently touching his elbow to let him know she's here.

'Pip,' he says, surprised, voice hushed in respect. 'I didn't know you were coming.'

'I'm sorry I didn't bring Bella,' she says, realising she got it wrong again. She should have planned this when they told her about it. She's slow to think for herself, but she's starting to crank up the machine.

'I'm glad you're here.'

Yes, this alone is progress. One small change every day.

'Hi Pip,' Tala says, leaning over, breaking their gaze.

'Hi,' she whispers back. She feels like she's at a funeral.

'How did you get here?' Jamie asks.

'I came with them,' she looks to Rachel and the TV crew, who are setting up their equipment. 'They came to Crossroads first. Do you think your dad will talk to them?'

He shakes his head. 'It's a silent protest, he wants the act of cutting to do the talking.'

She's not disappointed to let Rachel down, but is dismayed because in her experience silence has not been helpful. The silence in Pip's house has been mainly destructive; used to shut down communication and to create barriers, to discourage Pip from expressing herself. Jamie is watching her and, feeling her heart pounding at standing so close to him, she can barely concentrate on what she's here for. She blushes slightly, and focuses on Lorcan.

The Gardaí watch respectfully. The protestors are silent. The media stand back to observe and take photographs. It is a peaceful protest.

They all watch the ritual.

The paring had already been done in preparation, one foot of the top layer of bog, of sphagnum moss, bog cotton and heather has already been cleared. His cutting style is called stanking, usually done with two people and a wheeler. And he begins the hypnotic process of sliding the *sleán* through the wet peat, cutting a perfect rectangular shape, the turf coming out clean, and then placing it on the grasses where it will then be wheeled out to the spread field to dry.

Jamie watches his dad work alone. Usually there would have been the four of them, and together it would have taken them three days to cut enough turf to last them the full year.

'I always hated having to help,' Jamie says to her quietly.

'I remember.'

It clashed with football, with GAA training and matches. He was so focused on sport, being dragged out to help cut the turf was an irritant as a teenager.

Lorcan struggles for a moment, getting his footing.

Jamie jerks forward, as if to go to help him, then stops. He hadn't loved the family business as a teenager, but if he'd had the choice, maybe he would have stayed here and continued helping out with his brothers. He could have had his daughter and his tradition, but both were taken from him. Maybe it's not what he's thinking at all, but she feels a lump in her throat for him at his losses. Maybe it is like a funeral after all.

'Do you want to help him?' Pip asks.

He looks at her, lost.

'Go help him.'

He doesn't need much convincing. He marches through the crowd and picks up a sleán.

'Go on boy,' a protestor says, and there are mutters of support.

Finbar and Domhnall are fast behind him.

Jamie stands above the turf bank, cutting down vertically through the peat and nicking the back of the turf to help it come out clean. Domhnall places the already cut turf into the turf-barrow and wheels it to Finbar, who then unloads it on the field. Finbar builds the footing, standing the turf up to meet in the middle, like a tent, where it will stay off the wet ground and harden, and allow the wind to blow right through the cuts.

It's a well-practised, finely orchestrated movement. Hypnotic to watch them all working together, the unity of a family that was fractured and never really healed.

'What's he doing?' Tala whispers, snapping Pip out of the emotion of the moment. 'He came over here to stop his dad, and now he's joining in,' she says, genuinely frustrated. 'The police are right here.' She looks around, the wind blowing her hair into her eyes and mouth.

Pip takes a photograph of them in action.

When the display is over, the crowd splinters. The journalists have stories to write, the photographers have photographs to submit, the supporters gather in twos and threes planning next steps forward in their campaign. The Gardaí watch everyone leave, everyone's part played. Promises made, promises kept.

Jamie makes his way back to them, and Pip wants to wrap her arms around him with pride. Instead she grins and gives him a secret thumbs up.

'Pip,' Rachel says, making her way over, as if in a rush, mind always working, thinking ahead. 'Can we get a word with him?'

'This is Lorcan's son Jamie, it's their decision to make.'

'We don't have an angle here,' Rachel says to Jamie. 'We just want to hear what he has to say.'

'That's what he had to say,' Jamie says, nodding at the turf laid out, ready for drying.

'And I understand. It was a moving demonstration. But I think people at home will need to hear him. Actions don't always speak louder than words. We live in a world where words matter. I'll give you a moment.'

'I don't think his lawyer will want him to say anything,' says Tala, concerned.

Jamie looks at Pip. 'What do you think?'

She looks at Lorcan's grandchildren gathering around the freshly cut turf on the ground. Bella is also his granddaughter, she should have thought to bring her. It's not just Josephine that's the problem, Pip is also contributing to it. All of their thinking needs to change. 'When has being silent ever done us any good?'

She feels Jamie's hand on her waist, squeezing tightly, and his lips touching his ear as he whispers. 'It's going to change, I promise.'

When he leaves, her body is covered in goosebumps.

Later that evening, Pip sits to watch the news with Bella and her parents.

Lorcan, with the bog in the background, leaning on his *sleán*, says, 'I'm one man with a family patch that was taken away from me, and I want a shed full of turf so that I'm independent and can heat my home.'

'What do you say to people who believe that your acts are criminal? To the EU who would call this a crime scene, accuse you of a destructive assault on a precious natural resource?'

'I don't want to destroy the world. Our foremothers and forefathers fought for this land. It's not just about heating or money. When you've been doing something all of your life and it changes, you can become sentimental. It's not just soil. It's patriotic pride.'

It cuts to an interview with Krish at the fuelling station. He speaks in his special telephone voice that makes Pip smile, his moment of television glory. 'I've lived and worked here for twenty years. I've always bought the peat from local farmers and sold it right here outside the station, but I'm no longer allowed to do that.'

Rachel Buckley, standing in front of The Turfcutter's Inn. 'The peat farmers gathered here today believe that the government must take the reins of this burning issue and stand up to the EU. Some believe that turf-cutting should continue, others believe the government should pay turf-cutters to restore the bogs, and retro-fit homes that rely on turf for heating. And while there's a gulf widening between those who believe in the ban and those who don't, this will strike a chord with those who rely on it for their livelihood all around the country.'

The picture jumps to the fire inside The Turfcutter's Inn, which is bare.

'The turf fire has been integral to rural life and has become part of the national identity. Hailed as the smell of home, it has been burning in The Turfcutter's Inn since it first stood in 1879. The business can no longer legally buy turf, and today the fires are out in support of Lorcan Murphy and peat farmers in the area. From Ballybeg, County Offaly, I'm Rachel Buckley for 4 News.'

The piece is over and Bella looks at Pip with big sad eyes. 'Oh, poor Granddad. I should have been there, all my cousins were there.' And then the more telling sentence, 'I could have been on the telly.'

Pip imagines what it would have been like had Bella been standing at the bog with Jamie and Pip herself. A united family.

'You should have been there with your family,' Pip agrees, looking at Bella. 'I should have thought ahead.'

'I don't think an illegal demonstration would be the right

place for you love,' Josephine says, standing up, gathering the mugs to bring them to the kitchen. 'Next up they'll have a piece about peatland conservation, they'll have to keep it balanced.'

Philip is silent, deep in thought.

Pip receives a text message and immediately hopes it's from Jamie. Every time the phone rings she hopes it's from Jamie, but it's an unknown number.

More than twenty seconds. I owe you for today. So much better than The Four Courts. Thank you. Rachel Buckley.

A few weeks ago Pip wouldn't have got into a van with a reporter and gone to Lorcan Murphy's farm. She certainly wouldn't have urged Jamie to join in. She wouldn't have considered encouraging Lorcan Murphy to speak out and share his story, she would have been searching for information on what had happened, silently trying to find scraps of it to put the picture together herself. In a matter of weeks she had moved from the crowd to the sidelines.

She is fortunate for Jamie and Io's support, but both Io and Jamie are temporary. As soon as Jamie's dad's hearing is over, he will go back to Liverpool, and as soon as Io receives his signal, he'll also leave. Which will leave Pip alone without her two pillars, and nothing to lean on.

Origami girl
Do you hear that?
He asks
The signal from the star.
No,

She replies,
Tucking away her lie
And wanting to fold him up
Nice and small
To keep him with her
Because he makes her feel
So much bigger
And unfolded.

34

'WHAT ARE WE GOING to do about tomorrow morning?' Bella asks Pip, in her bedroom, doing Pip's nails.

She's panicking. It's the first Saturday since Josephine discovered they hadn't been going to Pilates and after the big argument between Pip and Josephine, and nothing has been solved. They've moved on without addressing or fixing anything, leaving another layer of unsolved issues to decay and ferment underground like the bog on which their town is built. The cracks around the house have been filled. They ooze with Polyfilla, like a yellow pus escaping a wound.

'We're going to do what we always do,' Pip says, unafraid of having another argument with Josephine. She's excited for tomorrow as she has an appointment for her Driver's Theory test.

'So I can meet Mark?'

'Unless you want to spend time with me instead?' Pip asks, hopefully. 'Then it wouldn't have to be a lie.' She would drop the theory test instantly in order to spend a few hours with Bella alone.

'No,' she groans. 'I really want to see Mark. It's been two weeks.'

Pip's feelings are hurt, but she keeps her sensitivities to

herself. She's all for speaking up to Josephine, but telling her parents about Mark's existence is a step she's not ready to take. She knows only too well how overwhelming forces can clamp down on something so precious. 'I'm not going to allow you and Mark to be broken up, but I would like to meet him. Can I?'

'Sure.'

'I can ask Io to drive us.'

Every day that week Io had collected her from her house and brought her to the airfield for a driving lesson before dropping her at work. He'd also driven her home.

'Are you and him together?'

'No. We're just friends.'

'What do you do together?'

Pip considers telling her about flying, but as much as she wants to bring Bella into her world, this is one little thing she'd like to keep for herself. Bella will inevitably tell Josephine, and Josephine would probably try to have the airfield shut down.

'Between you and me, he's teaching me to drive.'

Bella's eyes light up. 'I never knew you wanted to drive.'

'There are lots of things I want to do.'

'Really? Like what?'

'Travel. I'd love to travel. I'd like to see Giverny in the flesh. That's the garden where the Monet print in my room was painted. And other places. I'd like a beach holiday. A bunch of trashy books and a sunbed.'

'Me too,' Bella says, dreamily.

'We should go on holiday together,' Pip says.

'Nan and Granddad prefer staycations.'

'We're allowed to go without them, you know,' Pip says, with a laugh when really Pip's heart is pounding. What she's suggesting should be normal, but it's not in this house. The implication would be that she's trying to escape, when she's merely contemplating a holiday. 'A week would be nice. They hate beaches. We could eat spicy tacos and swim in the sea.'

'Oh my God, could we?'

'I'll start saving for next year. I think it's time to start doing things differently. Now that you're getting older.'

'I suppose.' Bella shrugs.

'Speaking of doing things differently. Your dad would like to meet Mark too.'

'I told you not to tell anybody!' She freaks out.

'He's your dad. He has a right to know.'

'That's so weird, Pip, no, oh my God.'

'What do you prefer, Bella, having grandparents who won't let you see him, or supportive parents?'

'Yeah, but you two aren't my—' she stops herself.

'Not your what?' Pip asks, eyes wide.

'It doesn't matter,' Bella says, standing.

'It does. Tell me what you were going to say!'

'Nothing!' Bella storms from the bedroom in a huff, leaving Pip with only one manicured hand, and tears falling from her eyes.

The following morning they don't need to ask Io to drive them at all because Josephine stays in bed, surrendering the fight, and Philip is ready to drive them into town without questions or heavy silences.

Pip sits in the passenger seat, which puts Bella out of sorts, but she pretends not to notice. It's not unusual for Pip to sit beside her dad in the car, they are always together on her way home from work. He drops them at the park, no need to pretend about the Pilates class anymore.

'Enjoy your walk.'

'Is three hours okay?'

It's a long time, but Pip will be cutting it tight. It takes thirty minutes to get to Tullamore test centre, an hour to do the test, and a half hour back.

'Maybe four hours.'

Philip doesn't even question it. This is not like him at all.

'Do you have something to do in town?'

'A bit, yeah. See you later.'

Fully suspicious of him now, she watches him drive away, away from the direction of their house.

'He's acting oddly,' Pip says.

'Come on,' Bella says, pulling her by the arm. 'Mark's waiting.'

'You know you have four hours with him.'

'It's not long enough,' Bella says, dramatically.

On the walk to meet Mark at the designated area, Bella talks Pip through a list of rules of things she cannot say to Mark. Questions she can't ask him, subjects that are deemed too embarrassing, too boring, and words she uses that are unacceptable.

'And don't say *cool*. You always say *cool*. No one says it. Not unless you're some surfer dude from the seventies.'

Pip frowns, and when they turn a corner there he is, on a pathway flanked by hundred-year-old trees, bowing and providing shelter and shade for those who walk beneath.

'Hello, Mark,' Pip says, holding out her hand.

'Mark this is Pip, my sister, Pip this is Mark, my boyfriend.'

Pip laughs at first, but when Bella looks at her with a straight face, and threatening eyes that only Pip can read, she realises this introduction as Bella's sister is for real. She stops laughing.

'Nice to meet you,' Mark says, shaking her hand. 'My sister Mary is ten years older than me, so yeah I get it. It was, like, one of the first things we had in common, wasn't it?'

Bella nods enthusiastically and looks at him dreamily.

Pip wants to cry. The urge comes to her so quickly that she suddenly needs to leave. The humiliation and the insult is too big. Bella is looking at her with flared nostrils, threatening her to perform like a monkey.

Mark isn't short of confidence.

'Isabella and I really appreciate how great you're being about us seeing each other and about next year and all.'

'Next year?' Pip asks, managing to find words, and thrown by him calling her Isabella. Even when given the choice to have a secret life with someone, she went with that name.

'Her leaving school,' he explains. 'We've both got plans, you know. We want to get started on life straight away. Isabella says you were totally the same and that you'll help smooth things over with her parents when she breaks it to them.'

Pip doesn't quite know what to say. Bella's rules have rendered her speechless. Frozen. Pip looks at her daughter, and from the one person she put up with everything in order to be with, all she can feel is betrayal.

35

PIP PARTS WAYS WITH them quickly, her head down as she wanders, in a daze, through the park, tears flooding down her cheeks as she tries to avoid having to face people who pass by on their morning walks and jogs, dogs out on leashes, children out on scooters, families on bicycles, taking advantage of the dry weekend morning.

Steel toecap boots and blue denim jeans come towards her. She moves to the left to pass by and so do the dusty boots. She weaves to the other side, as do the boots. She looks up and stops walking.

'Sammy,' she says in surprise, wiping her cheeks with the sleeve of her jumper.

'Are you okay?' he asks, face full of concern.

'Oh, yeah, I'm fine, thanks, I was just . . .' She can't think of anything at all that would explain why she's sobbing whilst out on a walk.

'Are you alone?' he asks, looking around. 'Whose arse do I need to kick?'

He's smooth and charming. Gentle when he needs to be, protective when she's feeling vulnerable. She could sink into his strong arms and sob her little heart out if she felt in any way safe, but she doesn't.

'I haven't heard from you.'

'Yeah, there's been a lot going on, since Jamie came back.' Then she remembers why she hasn't seen him. 'Your text.'

'I was angry,' he says, smiling, almost shyly. Is he pretending to be embarrassed? 'You left me, to drink champagne with your ex.'

'We moved aside to have a private conversation.' And still feeling the humiliation from Bella, and tired of being treated this way, she says exactly how she feels. 'Your text message was disgusting. I didn't deserve it.'

His smile disappears and the danger alert penetrates the pit of her stomach and she wishes the people she had been hiding her face from now would return so that she isn't alone with him on this tree-tunnelled path. She sees a man and a dog in the distance and she's relieved, until he cuts across the path into the off the leash area and they're alone again. How does Sammy do this? He shrinks her world every time he's in her company.

'I thought you were incredibly rude,' he says, folding his arms. 'You invited me out and spent more time talking to your ex-boyfriend.'

She hadn't invited him, but she doesn't bother getting into that.

'Just to be clear, I don't date women who have kids. I personally think it's disgusting. Going where some other guy has already been, having to spend time with some other fella's seed. But I gave you a chance on account of the fact she doesn't really seem like your kid, does she?'

Okay. He's going there. 'Look, Sammy, I don't want to get into this, I'm in a hurry to meet someone.'

She tries to walk around him, but he blocks her. She tries the other side and he's there again.

'Another date? There's Jamie, and Io, isn't it? I can't keep up with you. Are they getting all the action? Because you gave me nothing. You've been going since you were sixteen, Philippa, that's a long time now, I'm surprised your saddle is still intact.'

He disgusts her. She finally panic-runs and gets past him, expecting him to grab her, but he doesn't. He laughs.

She walks fast, expecting him to creep up on her. She keeps walking, getting faster and faster until she's jogging.

'Such a shame,' he shouts after her. 'Your dad was so close to retirement.'

She swallows, feeling sick.

She fills Io in about Sammy as they drive to the airfield, he has to pick something up on the way to her theory test, and he listens silently, and calmly.

He pulls in at the hangar and gets out of the car. While she waits, Pip wanders around the six planes and two helicopters. In the office she sees Stella wearing her boiler suit, the top down and tied around her waist, revealing a white vest. She has some kind of tool in hand, she has obviously been fixing an engine. Pip can see tools down on the ground beside a helicopter, and a hatch open revealing the engine.

Io and Stella talk in her office, and inside the office Pip sees another door, slightly ajar with a set of stairs leading down. There's a security panel beside the door to insert a code. Stella reaches out and closes the door, and Pip jumps, startled, as if Stella, who has her back to her, could read her mind.

She pretends to look at the helicopter that she's standing beside, but instead continues to look through the window into the office. Pip looks at the walls, and sees technical maps charting the stars and planets in the sky, with stars and measurements.

Suddenly both Io and Stella whip around to look at her. It's so fast she gets a fright. But they're not looking at her. They're looking behind her. She turns around and sees a black Range Rover outside the hangar. She's not one for remembering car registration numbers, but she's pretty sure that it's Sammy's Range Rover.

Black and menacing. A stalking, growling, prowling predator. It's crawling quietly, crunching over the ground, and then it comes to a stop at Io's car.

Stella walks out of her office, through the hangar, with the tool still in her hand. Her face is uncharacteristically cold and uninviting. She doesn't even walk to the Range Rover, but remains standing at the edge of the hangar. She stares intently at Sammy's car, as does Io.

Pip looks from one to the other.

Suddenly, Sammy begins to reverse, crawling back again slowly, to the hole he came from.

Pip watches as Sammy leaves the premises, and Io is beside her, at her shoulder, though she didn't hear him coming.

Sensing the tension, she fills the silence, feeling guilty. 'I'm sorry he followed me here.'

'No need to be sorry Pip,' Io says, looking at the empty space in the direction Sammy had disappeared. 'He followed me, not you.'

'If he didn't know before, he'll know now,' Stella says, before turning back and walking back to her office.

'He'll know what?' Pip asks.

'I might have sent an anonymous letter to the powers that be, accompanied by photographs taken of the Wolverson quarry. They have a few diesel generators in there that may require a permit under the Air Pollution Act. Far as I can see, they don't possess the permits.'

Her mouth falls open.

'The local authorities are responsible for enforcing the act in their area. They won't be pleased. He'll most likely be fined.'

'How would he know it's you now?'

'He might not,' he says, walking back to his car.

'Wait,' she says, trying to put it together. 'Were the photographs of the quarry taken from the sky?'

Io smiles.

36

JAMIE COMES TO THE house in the evening as arranged.
Everyone is out in the back garden eating strawberries in
the sun, Pip and her mother are drinking a glass of chilled
white wine. Bella is in a cerise pink bikini, tanning herself to
death. On the surface life is picturesque, but they are dispersed
around the garden, each in their own location, not talking.
Pip meets Jamie at the front door and steps outside to talk
to him before he's swallowed up inside.

'Hi Pip.'

Her name from his mouth.

He takes her in. 'You look . . .' he clears his throat self-
consciously, 'summery.' He seems embarrassed immediately.
'I meant nice. You look nice.'

She smiles. 'It is quite summery today.'

She's feeling more relaxed with him seeing her without the
hairnet and the unflattering uniform. She is barefoot and wears
a mini off-the-shoulder dress, as the summer day stretches
into a hot evening. All the doors and windows are open.

Jamie steals looks at her, and she enjoys his travelling eyes.

'How did the hearing go?'

'Dad pled guilty, to our surprise. I don't think he had it in
him to go any further. He got his message across to everyone,

thanks to you. He received a fine of €7,500. The judge had his say about nature conservation under law. The government took action. The EU will be happy. Everyone wins, right?' He leans against the wall tiredly. The sun hits his face, his nose is already sunburned and his eyes look ice blue in the light.

Angels could sing at this view before her.

'You look tired.'

He groans. 'I haven't been able to sleep with the thought of a trial looming. I'm so relieved now. I could sleep for a week.'

She has to fight the desire to run her hand over his forehead, to ease the tension she can see.

'Thanks for being at Clonboyle this week. We all really appreciated it, especially Mam and Dad. Especially me,' he says.

She lifts her eyebrows in surprise. 'Am I in their good books now?'

'Written in pencil maybe.'

They smile.

'I'm sure they appreciate you being here for them.'

'They do actually,' he says, standing taller. 'Which has been a welcome surprise.'

'Are you going to go back to Liverpool soon?' she asks, a lump forming in her throat.

'No. I'm going to stay a bit longer. A week or two.'

She wants to punch the air with delight, but instead crosses her arms.

'And Tala too?'

'No,' he says quickly. 'She went back a few days ago.'

It's an awkward moment.

'I want to implement the things I came here to do. Get to know Bella, let her get to know me. But I need your help. She keeps putting me off.'

'Don't take it personally, she's at that age that most things outside of her world bore her.'

'I want to be in her world. You know best. Should I take her for dinner or what?'

Pip thinks. Bella isn't displaying the sense of excitement for her dad that she'd like. And if they can barely sustain a ten-minute conversation over the phone then she can't imagine a dinner would be the best way to display Jamie's personality and win her over.

'I don't think dinner is a good idea,' she says, and his shoulders drop. 'Bella communicates best when you're not face to face. When she was little she liked having all the chats when she was on the potty, and then the toilet. It would all come out then, literally,' she says, laughing. 'We'd leave the door open and I'd sit outside and we'd talk about everything. She'd fill me in on the Montessori gossip. I'm not suggesting you do that.'

'Thank goodness! I was getting worried for a second,' he says, smiling.

'She's the same now in the car. She talks when my mam is driving, when they're side by side. Lately she talks to me when she's doing my nails. That's kind of new.'

'So my options are to talk to her while she's on the toilet, drive her, or let her do my nails.'

'Yeah,' she laughs. 'That's about it. I hope you like acrylics.'

'The fellas on site will love them.'

She laughs.

'I love hearing those stories. I want to know her like you do. Help me please, Pip.'

Her smile fades.

'What is it?'

She feels herself getting surprisingly emotional.

His blue eyes probe hers. 'Tell me.'

She keeps her voice down, and looks around to make sure it's just the two of them.

'I don't know her like you think I do,' she says slowly. 'I know you think it's been just me and her all this time, and I probably should, but I don't.'

Recently Bella has started opening up to Pip in a different way, but she's not sure she's comfortable with this either. Their new friendship doesn't feel right, and she can't explain it to him right now. It's built on secrets.

'It's difficult with my parents, to spend time with her, which doesn't make sense because I'm with her every day, but they've kind of managed to keep us apart. And I don't think I really saw what was happening until recently. It's hard to explain.'

'Try,' he says firmly.

At first she thinks he's angry, but his body language is supportive, his face gentle and open. He reminds her of Io: they're both willing her to come out of herself. She has curled herself into her shell, and they are the only two people bothered to encourage her out.

'Mam takes over. She took over from the second Bella was born.'

'I was here, I remember.'

'It never stopped. The same thing has been going on since you left. I'm sorry,' she says, tears welling. 'That I wasn't a better mother.'

'Stop it, Pip,' he says, holding her arms and standing opposite her, looking into her eyes.

'I'm sorry I didn't fight more for us, for myself.'

'I could say the same, Pip. Where was I in all of this?'

'You tried to push back, at the register office, at the

christening, I'm sorry I didn't help you. We promised to be a team, and I chickened out.'

'Can't say it didn't hurt. But you were exhausted. Every time I saw you you looked beaten down, so tired. I couldn't even make eye contact with you, we weren't allowed to connect.'

'I didn't have the energy to argue, all of my energy was going to feeding this little thing. And Mam was in my head all the time.' Her eyes are swarming with tears. She swallows and tries to blink her tears away.

'I'm sorry,' he whispers. 'I'm sorry I left you.'

'You didn't have a choice – neither of us did.' She wipes her tears. 'But since you've arrived I've been trying to change that. I'm trying to take me back.'

'Let's work together on it from now on? It's not going to be easy, but they're old now, I reckon we can take them on.'

She laughs.

They gather themselves in a comfortable silence.

'What about bowling?'

'What?' he asks, confused about the subject jump.

'Bella is competitive and would really like that, even though her nails are long and won't fit into the holes. She'll be distracted and won't feel under the spotlight to talk to you.'

'Will you come with us? It should be the three of us. She'll be comfortable with you there. The way it should be.'

'I'd like that,' she says, composing herself. 'When?'

'Tomorrow night? The sooner the better.'

'I can't tomorrow, I'm meeting a friend at the observatory.' She'd promised Io she would go to see a former NASA director doing an in-conversation event with an Irish astronomer. Pip is always excited for any night out, but the thought of a champagne reception is extra thrilling.

'Can you change it? I'm running out of time here.'

'I can't, I'm sorry, I promised him, and Bella isn't free anyway. She's working late at the observatory, serving drinks and canapés at the event.'

She's stuck on the *I promised him. Him.* Did she make it sound like it was a date? Is that what makes him pull back? He steps back.

'Sure,' he says, his energy changing. 'Of course.'

She wants to scream.

'Friday night?' she suggests quickly.

He agrees, but she hates how he has changed and she wants to bring the closeness back.

'So.' He straightens up, looking at the house with suspicion. 'Why exactly am I here?'

'Dad wants to show you something.'

'As long as it's not his fist, I'm game.'

She grins and steps inside the house.

The air between Philip and Jamie is different. The power positions have shifted. Philip is vulnerable, and Jamie is professional. He walks around the house examining the cracks. Placing his fingers on the wall, feeling it, with a serious expression that makes Pip smile.

Josephine stays outside with Bella.

Now and then Philip looks at Jamie, an expectant worried face, and Jamie asks to see the next room.

There isn't any room for Pip in her bedroom. Jamie and Philip take up the entire floor space. Philip steps outside onto the landing and leans against the wall, arms folded, as though he's in a hospital, waiting to hear about his firstborn.

Pip wonders what Jamie thinks of her room. Of course

she's worried because of how Sammy had ripped her private precious space apart. Where she hadn't wanted Sammy to get a single essence of her, she had put more of her own art on the walls for Jamie. She wanted him to see all of her.

When he opens the door to step onto the landing, Philip goes downstairs to have the conversation. Jamie looks at Pip. He has something in his hand. It's her sketch of Bella's baby foot.

'Did you draw this?'

She nods.

He studies it, for longer than it should take the human eye to see it. Just a series of lines.

'Can I have it?'

She nods.

37

'WE'LL BE WORKING LATE tonight, we need to set up
for this NASA fella's visit,' Josephine says to Philip
at breakfast.

'Who?'

'I told you five times.' She's annoyed, and tidying around
in quick motions but not really getting anywhere. 'Philippa,
you can put these in the dishwasher,' she says, looking at the
mess of dirty dishes gathered in the sink. 'There's a fella over
from NASA to do a talk with Professor Waters.'

Philip is distracted but feigns interest.

'Me and Isabella,' *Bella and I*, Pip corrects Josephine in
her head, 'have to set up the food. Canapés and champagne.
There's a champagne reception if you don't mind.' She badly
folds her uniform for the event, a black blouse, and places it
in a bag. Pip already has Bella's blouse folded neatly so that
it won't crease. Her mother shakes it out and folds it again,
which gets on Pip's nerves.

'There are three hundred and fifty people coming. A lot to
do. Not only do we have to do lunch, but we have to make
the canapés. There's no point in us coming back after work so
we're staying there until the event. Pip will make your dinner.'

Philip looks at Josephine, and Pip can tell he's taking none of it in. His head is absolutely elsewhere. The house plans are on the table, all the folders out for everything that had dominated their lives leading up to and during the house build.

'Okay, love, see you for dinner,' he says, as Josephine pecks him goodbye.

She stalls. 'I said we won't be coming home for dinner. I just explained.'

'Yes, yes, force of habit,' he backtracks.

Josephine stops buzzing about and takes him in, the plans, the paperwork. She looks as though she wants to ask him something but doesn't want to say anything in Pip's presence. Not in front of the child. 'Philippa will make your dinner,' she says firmly, to him and to Pip. 'Nothing spicy,' she adds.

'I can't,' Pip says. 'I'm going out tonight.'

'Tomorrow night is your night out with Jamie,' Josephine corrects her.

'It's something else.'

'Sammy?' she asks, hopefully.

'No.'

'Kim then,' she says with a sigh, stuffing her purse into her bag, not even looking at what she's doing and jamming it in over and over again.

'No.'

'Our Jennifer.'

'I have barely spoken to our dear cousin Jennifer since she tricked me into going to her house with Bella, and then called you to collect me. I wouldn't trust her as far as I could throw her.' Pip says it with all the venom she feels. She still hasn't got over it.

Josephine looks at her, eyes wide. They never mention the escape attempt. Not for fourteen years, apart from the occasional dig at Pip's expense that she couldn't survive without her.

Pip is enjoying this new honesty. Letting things out is hard, but it gives her freedom, makes her feel lighter. It might be addictive. It will all come flowing out.

'Whoever it is,' Josephine says, voice trembling with anger, 'you can cancel your plans. You have to stay here and cook for your dad.'

'And polish the silver and sweep the cinders?' Pip asks, feeling giddy.

'What on earth are you talking about?' Her temper flares instantly.

'I'm fine Josephine,' Philip says, irritated. 'Go on now, or you'll be late.'

She drops it and leaves.

'What did Jamie say about the cracks last night?' Pip asks.

Philip places two palms flat on the table and pushes his body up to his feet. The table wobbles under his weight. He leans heavily on the edge of the Belfast sink, gazing intently out of the window that looks out at the quarry. They can't see it from their house, but Pip knows now, from her flights, that the drop is dangerously close.

'Diagonal cracks,' he says in a low growl.

'Diagonal cracks . . . aren't good?'

'No.'

'Doesn't the house take time to settle after building? Cracks are normal.'

She'd googled a lot, as she'd watched the spider web weave across her wall and to the ceiling.

'Jamie said that diagonal cracks can't be confused with poor workmanship,' he says.

'Well that's good news.' Take that, Sammy Snake Wolverson.

'It only has one cause, and that's settlement, which is a nice way of saying sinking. The house, or part of the house, is moving in a downward direction.'

'But it's . . . fixable?'

He looks at her.

'I don't know the full extent of it yet. We're getting someone else around to look this afternoon.'

'While Mam is out.'

'Yes.'

She assumes this detective work is what he was up to on Saturday. There's nothing more to say about it and, knowing Io is down the road waiting for her, she gets her coat.

'I'll leave dinner out for you later.' She won't do it when ordered to by Josephine, but she'll do it because she wants to.

'Don't worry, I'll get a chipper.'

He goes back to the kitchen table and stands there staring at the plans, his jaw clenching and unclenching.

'She was beside herself with worry,' he says suddenly. 'When you left with Isabella. I've never seen her like it. She wouldn't eat, she wouldn't sleep. I brought her to the doctor, I didn't know what else to do. The doctor gave her pills to help her calm down, and sleeping pills. But she wouldn't take them in case you came back and she didn't want to miss it. Her whole world is you two girls.'

'What you see in her isn't what I get from her.'

'That's why I'm telling you.'

She tries to figure out how she feels behind all the anger that it summons in her. Mostly rage. She can't find her way to appreciation or gratitude. If this is her mother's way of love, she would have preferred to be unloved.

'Dad, we should go fishing again together. It's been a long time.'

His face de-ages for a moment as he looks at her in surprise. He agrees. 'I'd like that.'

'Are you not going to work?' It's the latest he has ever left. He looks at his watch. 'Going now.'

She walks down the road, constantly looking back over her shoulder, watching for him to leave the house, lock up and drive away. It doesn't happen, and she thinks she knows why.

He's staying to feel the blasts.

38

THE RECEPTION FOR THE former NASA director is in the event centre, and all Io has to do is flash his ID, and doors are opened. They enter the green room where guests mingle in sharp suits. Io is casual as usual, his shirtsleeves rolled neatly midway up his muscular forearms. He's wearing slacks, and stands with his hands in his pockets as he introduces her to electrical, mechanical, optical and software engineers, technicians and astronomers. The star of the show is the former NASA director Cashel Brown, alongside Professor Waters, who will be interviewing him onstage. A crowd gathers around him, waiting for their moment to speak with him.

'Oh my God, look at you,' Bella says, arriving with a tray of champagne. She looks Pip up and down in shock.

Pip had been excited about the mention of a champagne reception and had possibly overdressed. She's wearing a black slim-fit mini dress, long sleeved, glittering like the celestial sky. She's on theme. Her long toned legs are polished and shining to perfection and now, with a few sips of champagne, she is feeling absolutely sparkling.

'Do you like it?' Pip asks, but can tell her daughter loves it. Her mouth is open, her eyes wide.

'You look amazing. How the hell did you get in here?'

'I'm Io's plus one.'

She looks across the room at Io, who's deep in conversation with two men.

'I so don't believe that you two aren't dating.'

'We're not.'

'Whatever. I'm sure you're still "driving",' she says, with inverted commas, rolling her eyes.

'I am. I passed my theory test, actually, so now I have a learner permit. In six months I can take my driving test and get a full licence,' Pip says proudly.

Bella is in awe. 'That's so cool. Then you can drive me around. I can be your passenger princess.'

'You shouldn't say cool, it's not cool,' she says with a wink. 'And you need to get your own licence so you can drive yourself around. Maybe we can share a car.'

'Yes!' Bella says excitedly. 'I love this new you.'

'Where's Josephine?'

'Getting more canapés. She's going to cack herself when she sees you here, looking like this.'

'Keep your voice down.'

'Hey, down that glass and take another one, I've something to ask you.'

'I can't drink too much. It's Krish's last day tomorrow and I've got him a cake. Why do I get the impression you're trying to get me drunk?'

'There's a house party tomorrow night, and Mark wants me to go and I really, really, really want to go.'

'You can't. We're going bowling with your dad tomorrow night.'

'Oh come on,' she says, sticking her bottom lip out.

'Remember what it was like for you when you were my age, wanting to be with Dad.'

'Don't play that card.' Because it will work.

'I can see Dad any other night.'

'No you can't, he'll be leaving soon.' Her stomach feels sick at the thought. He's been here for so long, and she's barely seen him. Why can't Bella have the same excitement?

'*You* go out with him, you're the one who's so excited to be with him,' she says, annoyed. 'Come on, please. Mark and I haven't been anywhere together, we're always just stuck in the park, and we want to go out and have fun.'

Pip remembers that feeling. 'I don't even know whose party it is or where it is.'

'His best friend's house. We can pretend to Nan and Grand-dad that we're all out bowling, and you can let me go to the party.'

'Absolutely no way.' Though the thought of meeting Jamie on her own is enticing. 'The answer is no. Now I'm going to mingle.'

Despite her grumpiness, Bella watches in surprise as Pip makes her way over to the NASA director and introduces herself. Pip is feeling buoyed by Bella's reaction to her, by the fact her mother is now staring at her, gobsmacked, with a tray of canapés in her hand.

She speaks with the NASA director, all the while feeling her mother's eyes on her, but Pip never once meets her eye. She knows that Josephine's expression will read, *Stop what you are doing right now, you're making a fool of yourself, there are more important people in the room that he needs to speak to. Be small, hug the walls.*

Josephine's voice sounds so very much like her own internal voice, the one she needs to stop listening to.

She's also conscious of Bella watching her. Bella keeps her topped up with champagne, removing a not yet empty glass from her hand and replacing it with a full one.

Io isn't a social bunny. He's quiet, he stays on the periphery, orbiting conversations. He listens to what others have to say, moving around slowly and listening intently. He hugs the same champagne flute to his chest, barely sipping it, warming it in his hot hands. The room is warm, the conversation is interesting, she's talking to people she used to serve lunches to, ending up speaking to technicians and astronomers. Pip feels utterly divine. Wearing her sexy dress, drinking champagne and feeling fuzzy. Sparkling conversation, with fascinating people on subject matters that are entirely new to her.

She has her driver's permit, and she has been practising for the promotion interview that could give her enough money to rent a place of her own. She's building a way out of here, from the road to the sky, and she feels the fizz of possibility and excitement in her life for the first time in a very long time.

'Are you having fun?' Io appears by her side. 'Everyone's asking me who you are. You have the attention of every man in this room.'

'Not yours.'

'No offence.'

'None taken. I know. You're in love with your long-distance lover. Tell me about her.'

At that point she notices her mother glaring at her. No one else would see it, maybe they'd see a hassled woman, busy, rushed, flushed, but Pip can see her anger about to explode from her, unable to unleash it because of the situation they're in. All hell will break lose later, and Pip simply can't worry about it now. She can't summon the fear that would usually form in the pit of her stomach and freeze her. She's having a good time, she's not doing anything wrong, she feels protected in this room by the company, not like at home, where she's made to feel young again and small and quiet.

'Should I introduce myself to her?' Io asks, amused.

'I think not.'

Bella arrives over with a tray of canapés.

'Hello,' she smiles brightly, the perfect hostess in her all-black ensemble. They'd switched the white blouses for black shirts. She's wearing a lot of make-up, too much in Pip's opinion, but her daughter is beautiful, with her hair slicked back into a high pony.

'I'm Isabella, nice to meet you,' she says to Io. 'I do not believe that you two aren't dating.' Then to Pip, and speaking through a pleasant smile she says, 'Nan says to tell you to get the hell home. Something about Granddad's dinner.'

'These look nice,' Pip says, disobeying, and surveying the tray of canapés. 'What are they?'

'This is deep-fried brie.' Bella points with her long acrylic nails with metallic tips. 'Tastes like crap. And this is goat's cheese with red onion. That's not so bad. She's seriously fuming, Pip.'

Pip pops a deep-fried brie ball into her mouth and then points to her mouth to signal she can't talk.

When it's time for the interview to begin, the guests in the champagne reception stream into the event space. The audience have already taken their seats. Those seated at the back turn to look at them. Pip's high sandals are slippery on the wooden floor, and Io encourages her to link his arm as they walk together.

All the seats are full, there are people standing at the back, and she has to push her way through them to get to the aisle.

'Excuse me,' she says to one tall man blocking her way.
He turns around.

'Jamie!' she says, surprised.

'Pip,' he says, equally surprised, taking her in, with a look
that makes her stomach flutter. Then he clocks Io and steps
aside. She's leading the green room gang, feeling Jamie's eyes
on her as she walks all the way up the centre aisle.

The front row is reserved for them. Io takes a seat at the
edge and she sits beside him, looking around for Jamie.

Josephine and Bella move out of the green room and take
their places at the side of the hall, ready to pour more drinks
for the reception after the talk. Bella grins proudly at Pip
seated in the front row, and Josephine still looks hot-headed.

'I'd like to start by quoting Professor Stephen Hawking,'
Professor Waters begins. '"I don't think the human race will
survive the next thousand years unless we reach out to space.
There are too many accidents that can befall life on a single
planet. But I'm an optimist. We will reach out to the stars."
At the observatory, focusing on the stars is what we are all
united in doing.'

Pip is enthralled by the fascinating discussion that takes
place over the next forty-five minutes, and when they end
their conversation the floor is opened for questions from the
audience. A woman stands up and is given a microphone.

'Thank you for such an interesting talk,' she says. 'I wonder
if I can lower the tone a little and ask about aliens.'

The audience laughs.

'How likely do you think it is that there is life on other
planets? And how likely is it that we will intercept a signal
from them, here in Ireland?'

'It's a good question,' Cashel says, 'and it's a valid one. Years ago, we thought we had our first signal, it came from the Parkes radio telescope in Australia. We are now pretty much convinced that it was caused by interference, but it is just as likely that the next one will be from the I-LOFAR here in Ireland. It's virtually certain that we're going to find life in our solar system. We have a number of places we're looking, and I predict we'll find a life-bearing planet around one of the nearby stars within a decade,' he concludes. 'Why shouldn't Ireland be the first country to intercept that message?'

There's a grateful cheer.

They answer some more technical questions about space exploration, and then Professor Waters brings the talk to a close. 'I began this evening by quoting Stephen Hawking, and I'll end it with him too. "Remember to look up at the stars, and not down at your feet. Try to make sense of what you see and wonder about what makes the universe exist. Be curious. And however difficult life may seem, there is always something you can do and succeed at. It matters that you don't just give up."'

Pip's eyes have filled with tears and she's working hard to not let them fall. She feels the heat of eyes on her. She looks around and sees Jamie, leaning against the wall at the side of the room, looking at her.

After the interview, it's time to mingle again. There's a table stocked with red and white wine where Josephine, along with two other colleagues, are busy serving guests who line up for their glasses while Bella works the room with trays.

Bella comes toward Pip with a tray of white wine, and speaks like a ventriloquist through her smile. 'Take the one at the edge, that's champagne.'

'Bella, I don't want to get you in trouble.'

'I won't get in trouble. Can I have a glass too?'

'No! Absolutely not.'

She's quickly grumpy again. 'What's happened to you? You used to be more fun.'

Pip is afraid of her slipping through her fingers. 'I don't mind you having a drink, in my company, but not while you're at work.'

She smiles slyly. 'Please let me go to the house party tomorrow night.'

'I've already said no. Your dad is here, by the way, try and talk to him if you can.'

'I'm *working*,' she says, suddenly employee of the month.

'Hello,' Jamie says, joining them.

She pities him his timing. She's sure he built himself up to approach them.

'Hello, Jamie,' Pip says, brightly.

'Hi.' Bella sounds rather flat. For the hostess with the mostest, she's not performing for her dad.

'Did you enjoy the talk?' Pip asks.

'Yeah, doesn't everyone love an alien story? I think I'll prefer the bowling though,' he says, trying to sound perky and interested. 'I hope you girls are ready to lose. I'm going to bring my A-game.'

Bella is close to rolling her eyes. 'I have to get back to work.'

'Yeah, see you tomorrow night,' he says, all eager.

He groans as soon as she's gone. 'I'm the biggest loser dad in the world,' he says, and she wants to hug him. 'I came because you told me Bella was working. Thought I'd hang around and try to talk to her. Now I don't know if that's considered making an effort or being weird.'

'I think it's sweet,' she says. 'Tomorrow night, she'll get

to know you, don't worry.' She puts a hand on his arm, his thick bicep, and he stiffens. She lets go quickly. Somewhere Josephine is watching them, she senses it, and that intensifies the moment even more, heightens every single glance, touch and breath they take in each other's company. But Josephine's powers to tear them apart won't work in this room, or in any room anymore.

Jamie's eyes run over her again. 'Wow. You look incredible, Pip.'

Her heart races. 'Thank you.'

Suddenly Io is by her side. He doesn't even look at Jamie. 'We have to go,' he says to her, urgency in his voice.

She'd rehearsed this in her head a dozen times during the talk. *Jamie this is my* friend *Io.* Extreme emphasis on the friend. 'Io, I want to introduce you to Jamie—'

'Nice to meet you, Jamie. I'm sorry, we have to go,' he says firmly. Then with troubled eyes he says, 'Pip, we have to leave.'

39

PIP IS DEVASTATED TO be torn away from Jamie. She was finally feeling confident, not dressed in a hairnet and a mayonnaise-stained polo shirt. She felt sexy, like the woman she wanted him to see. The woman who could speak freely and not get confused about her words by the time they'd worked their way from her mind to her mouth.

Now, thanks to the champagne and the socialising, her head is hopping. She swipes through the evening's conversations in her head as though she's swiping through social media on her mobile phone.

Io had been abrupt with Jamie, he'd swept her away like a jealous boyfriend. She will never forget Jamie's face as she was led away. Io had called her Pip, nobody but Jamie and Bella call her that, it's an intimate name that implies so much more between Io and Pip. But perhaps none of that matters. She was reading it all wrong. Io obviously saw what Pip couldn't. That she was making an absolute fool of herself.

He hasn't said a word for the past few minutes, as he drives from the observatory through darkening country roads.

'I'm sorry,' she says, finally blurting it out.

'For what?'

She's confused. 'I've embarrassed you? I said something

wrong? I asked the NASA guy a lot of stupid questions, I know I did. It's the champagne, I've been talking too much. Did I throw myself at Jamie? I felt like I did. I touched his arm and he kind of recoiled, or did I imagine that? Or is it the dress? I realise I got the dress code wrong, but I was so excited. You said champagne reception and I . . .'

'Pip. Stop.'

She falls silent.

'You've done nothing wrong. You were beautiful in there. But you're beautiful behind the deli counter because you just are beautiful. Inside and out. I'm glad you came with me, you made a stressful work night so much more pleasurable. You get people talking, I could listen, and there's no such thing as stupid questions. People tell you important things, did you ever notice that?'

She did notice. People tell her things at work because they don't know her and they're passing through. She poses no threat. Sometimes it's a quick and silent exchange, other times she hears a life story or a whopper of a revelation in five minutes.

'Where are we going? Why did we leave?'

'Stella called me. The police are at the airfield. But I promised you I'd get you home.'

She wants to protest that her mother and daughter were there, as was Jamie. She groans inwardly, she could have been driven home by Jamie, but she appreciates Io thinking of her in the middle of an emergency.

'Is Stella okay?'

'I don't know. I hope so. Do you mind if we stop by the airfield first?'

'Of course not.'

They turn into the airfield and he slows the car as they roll in. Io switches off the headlights. A Garda car is parked beside the hangar, and Stella is standing outside talking with two Gardaí, with paperwork in her hands. They take the documents from her and study them.

She looks up in their direction, though she couldn't possibly see them, or so Pip thinks.

'You stay here,' Io says, quietly. 'Anyone asks you anything, I teach you how to fly okay?'

'Okay,' she says, confused.

Io is about to open the door, but Stella looks up suddenly, sharply, and subtly shakes her head, as if telling him to leave.

Io slowly reverses, leaving the grounds and going back on the road again.

They're quiet as he drives her home.

'What was that about?'

'I don't know.'

'I know,' she says, finally, a deep loathing building inside her. 'My mother. She saw me with you tonight and she couldn't stand it. I knew it. This is exactly what I was afraid of happening. That's why I didn't want her to know about you. She doesn't like me having friends. I wanted to fold you up and put you in the box for safekeeping.'

Io frowns. 'You wanted to do what to me?'

'Nothing,' she mumbles, head racing.

'Pip, I'm quite sure it wasn't your mother.'

'Well then who else would . . .' she stops herself, remembering how they'd been followed to the airfield. 'Sammy.'

40

Origami girl
Is a firework
A powerful,
Sparkling
Metamorphosis girl
Who can unfold
Unwind
And shine.
Origami girl
Is a cork
Exploding from a bottle
Released and free
Once she's out
It's impossible
To fit back in.
She has unwound
She can't rewind
Has unfolded
And won't re-fold.

WHEN PIP GETS HOME she leaves her dress on the floor and crawls into bed, sleeping naked. Her head is swimming with everything from the evening. The way Jamie gazed at her in her dress, the pride Bella had for her, Josephine witnessing her as a woman in her own right, the tension in Io's face as he drove to the airfield. The Gardaí examining the paperwork Stella gave them. The door in Stella's office that leads downstairs, what's downstairs? She'd assumed it was a paperwork issue, licences and permits, but what is Io so worried about them discovering? Jamie's expression when Io pulled her away from him. Back to the nicer thought of how Jamie looked at her in her dress.

She hears Bella and Josephine return as she's drifting away, but she's too far gone into the next realm to come back.

Pip wakes up confused. Something feels different.

Her, yes, because she's hungover, her head pounding and foggy, a sick taste in her mouth.

But something in the room feels different. The light.

She had forgotten to set her alarm for the morning, but she doesn't usually need it because she always wakes around six a.m. She sleeps with her curtains open, she likes falling asleep to the stars and for the natural light to wake her, even in the summer. She'd read it was good for the circadian rhythm. But the morning light and the birds' chorus failed to rouse her as they usually do.

She hears car doors banging and an engine running and she knows deep down that these sounds should be cause for alarm, but she disappears again below the surface.

Then she shoots up with a whoosh. It's not a weekend. She was out last night, on a Thursday. Her mouth is so dry, her breath rank, and her head thuds as soon as she sits up.

She takes deep breaths, in through the nose, out through the mouth to help the nausea to subside. The breaths also help her brain to catch up with her surroundings.

The dress on the floor. She's naked. Hungover. Last night. Her mother's scorn. Bella's pride. Jamie. Leaving early with Io, how that must have looked.

She reaches for her phone. She'd forgotten to charge it last night and now it's dead. She plugs it in and it takes a while to come on.

She stretches, gets out of bed. The room moves as if she's on a ship. She looks out of the window. The two cars are gone. She scrambles to her phone, it's still not on, the apple sign on the display screen.

She waits impatiently, her heart pounding.

Her parents wouldn't have left early, unless something had happened, and in that case, wouldn't she have been informed? Her phone is the only clock she has in her room.

Her Origami girl poem is left open on her desk, unfolded. A mistake, but perhaps appropriate. Anyone could have read it.

She puts it away in the drawer, embarrassed.

Finally her phone lights up.

Io must be waiting down the road for her. She looks out of the window at the same time as putting the code in. Finally the screen comes to life. Bella and Pip as the screensaver, a baby photo. And the time. Nine twenty a.m.

She swears.

There's a lot of missed calls. A message from Io at three

twenty a.m. saying he's sorry but he can't drive her to work. He hopes she can work something else out.

'Ohmygod, ohmygod.'

She has never been late for work. She had taken her first day off the previous week, but she and Josephine had never been late, apart from when Lorcan Murphy had held up the traffic.

She panics, rushing around the room but not really getting anything done. She needs a shower. She plays her voicemails on speakerphone as she runs to the bathroom.

It's Krish. She swears. Why was he calling her at six a.m.?

'Good morning Pip, sorry to call you so early. I didn't tell you yesterday because I didn't want to make you nervous, but Mary says I should have, so I need to let you know that the interview for manager is this morning. They'll be here at nine a.m. to meet you. They're very nice, a woman from HR named Alison who loves Labradors and a man named Trevor. He, like me, is a big fan of the television series *Buffy the Vampire Slayer* and enjoys talking about each episode. A top tip in case you want to bring it into the conversation. He has a particular fondness for Xander's comical impact on the story. They look forward to speaking with you. Tom Twomey will be here too. Remember everything I talked to you about, just repeat what I told you, and everything will be fine.'

He had been training her what to say since she'd told him she wanted the promotion.

Pip has no time for a shower now, she needs to get there immediately. Hopefully they will wait for her. She runs back to her room, pulls on a pair of skinny black jeans and a bra. She runs back to the bathroom to retrieve her phone.

She dials Cathy the Florist-slash-taxi driver.

'Cathy, it's Pip Sheridan.'

'Philippa, hi.'

Does nobody hear her even when she tries? IT'S PIP, she wants to scream. 'I desperately need a taxi to work.'

'Dan is gone out in the taxi, I'm afraid. He has the minivan for the school bus.' Dan, her husband, provides the school bus for children with special needs, as the minivan has wheelchair access. 'He'll be finished at ten.'

'No, that's too late.'

'I'm sorry, Philippa.' Not sounding sorry at all but affronted by Pip's harsh tone.

'Could you bring me? Please?'

'I can't, I'm working in the shop now.'

'Can you close it for a little bit?'

'I can't just shut it down to drive you. I'm the only one working here.'

'But it will only take you ten minutes.'

'It will take me more than ten minutes!'

'Six minutes to my house and eight minutes to the station. That's fifteen minutes max. Put a sign up, back in ten minutes. I've seen you do it before. How busy are you going to be at this hour? I will pay you for every bouquet you don't sell in that time. Charge me double, triple. Whatever!'

'Philippa, I can't—'

'Please, please, please Cathy. Please. It's important to me. Really, really important.' As she says it, she realises just how much it is. She can't keep going with the job she has. She can't afford to move out, look after Bella on her own, provide for her future. Her mother is absolutely right. She needs this promotion. She needs to start thinking smart. Io will leave, as will Jamie, and she will be back on her own again.

Cathy sighs. 'My God. Okay. I'll be there in ten minutes.' She hangs up, not happy about it.

Pip washes her armpits roughly and quickly, splashing water everywhere. She sprays deodorant. Everywhere.

She puts her voicemails on speakerphone and continues.

She runs back to her room and puts her work T-shirt on, hearing the messages echo in the bathroom.

'Philippa it's Krish. They're here now. It's nine a.m. I hope everything is okay?'

And then a less understanding tone ten minutes later. 'Philippa? Philippa? They're going to leave if you don't get here in the next few minutes.'

She runs back into the bathroom and starts brushing her teeth again, vigorously.

At 09:15 he sounds angry.

The last phone call is at 09:22, right about when she woke up and was scrambling to turn on her mobile phone. Resigned. His speech is slower now. 'They've gone Philippa. They've left. They were just squeezing you in before they had another meeting. As a favour to me.' He sighs. 'This is so unlike you. I hope all is okay.' And then, as if flicking a switch, he returns to his managerial role. 'Fiona is on her way in now to cover you, so don't bother coming in. Ronnie told me you got cake for today so we'll have that later. Thank you.' He pauses. 'I don't know when I'll next see you once I start work at the quarry. Take care, Philippa.'

She drops her toothbrush into the sink.

She spits and wipes her mouth. Pinches the bridge of her nose as it all comes crashing down.

She calls Cathy, who is driving and on her way.

'Cathy, I'm sorry, but I need to cancel the taxi. I'm too late. I'm sorry.'

She receives such an angry sweary tirade down the phone she knows she can never, ever use their taxi company again. She ends the call.

She removes her T-shirt and bra, peels off her skinny jeans. She runs the shower, gets inside and sits on the shower tray.

It's over.

Origami girl
Is a silly girl
She thought
She could
> *Unfold*
> *Stretch*
> *Grow*
> *Shape*
Herself into anything she wanted
But
She can't.

41

JOSEPHINE, BELLA AND PHILIP won't be home for hours. Pip takes Krish's advice and stays home. She doesn't have the energy to face what will be her future. She's too ashamed to call him back. She went from being a high-functioning, aspirational, dream-maker with hopes, notions and ambitions, to nothing overnight.

She calls Io again, desperate to find out what happened at the airfield and why he has to help Stella today, but his phone is off. She has already left two messages. She's hoping Sammy wasn't successful in getting their business shut down. As well as having friends in the council, she wouldn't put it past him that he has a friend in the Gardaí too. In the sober light of day she decides she'd given Josephine too much credit and it couldn't possibly have been her. Pip is lying on the couch watching *Homes Under the Hammer* when there's a key in the door. She immediately knows from the heavy boots and heavier breathing that it's Philip.

She sits up, feeling caught. 'Dad?'

He pauses, equally caught out. 'Philippa?'

He peers inside the TV room. Bushy eyebrows and hooded eyes. Bags under his eyes, enough to carry everything they own.

'Why aren't you at work?' Pip asks.

'Why aren't you?'

'I asked you first,' she says. 'And you better tell me the truth or I'll tell Mam.'

He sighs and comes into the room. He sits on the arm of the armchair in the bay window. He rubs his eyes tiredly, the bags moving floppily.

'My hours were reduced.'

'What?' Her brain can't compute. She's hungover, thinking more slowly than usual, and it's a nonsense sentence. 'They can't have been.'

He shrugs. It's no joke.

'But you've worked there for forty-something years, five days a week, you're their longest serving employee. You've barely missed a day.'

'I know.'

'This is my fault.'

'Don't be daft.'

'It is. Sammy threatened me last week. I was afraid he'd punish you.'

'What do you mean, he threatened you?'

'Because I wouldn't date him. He said, "pity your dad is so close to retirement".'

Philip is having none of it, and barely listens to the end of her sentence. 'That's got nothing to do with it.'

'I'm telling you, he's a psychopath.'

'He may be that,' he says, to her surprise, 'but you have nothing to do with it. It's because I was asking about the blocks. I think they're bad blocks. It wasn't my plastering that did it. There's something in the cement that's causing the cracks. Jamie had a look at them, and he's an expert.'

She can't believe he's saying this about his precious quarry. Or about Jamie. Sammy bad, Jamie good. It should be cause for rejoicing, but not at the expense of her dad and their home. He built his dream, and now it's crumbling around them. Dust to dust, ashes to ashes.

'I bought the blocks from the quarry. I sat down with Sammy and told him he needs to check the blocks going to the new housing estate because they're not good. Something's not right. It's either that or the blasts. I told him about the effect they were having on our house. I'd seen it with my own eyes.'

'What did he say?'

'He was a gentleman about it.' This surprises her. 'He said he appreciated my feedback and that he'd look into it. And then the next day I was informed that they only need me on a three-day week. They're bringing in a blasting contractor, and my role will be revised.'

His eyes are watering. He folds his arms to hold himself in.

'But, Dad, I don't understand. Can they do that, legally?'

'I told them that we were blasting too much. I told them that the crowd across the road have a point, that Sammy should listen to them, at least investigate it. I told him that the number of blasts isn't safe, and to look at the effects it's having on the surrounding environment. I told him about the lack of training on site, that he needs to start training the young lads in properly or there'll be more injuries. Told him that I can't testify in court any longer. I'd say that gave him reason enough. He can't fire me, but he'll make life hard enough for me that I'll want to leave, it's what he does. I've seen him do it with a dozen lads ahead of me. I just thought they all deserved it at the time.'

'What made you change your mind?'

'You.'

She's shocked into silence.

'I don't think you've always been the best judge of character, love, but I can't forgive him for letting you walk home in the rain on that road at night. It made me take a good look at him. Made me take a good look at everything.'

If only he knew there was more to it. She supposes he senses that too, or he wouldn't have taken a closer look.

He looks around the room, at the growing cracks, his eyes filled. And this is where his composure unravels.

'My house,' he says, losing his ability to speak. He gasps, trying to get the words. 'My house is falling apart.'

She watches him crying, in shock. She has never witnessed this before. She gets to her feet and awkwardly comforts him. When he doesn't pull away from her she hugs him tighter, and he sobs.

'I built it with these hands.' He lifts them up in the air. Two shovels that could lift the world.

'I know, Dad.'

'I spent every minute of my day, planning it, executing it. I didn't cut one corner. I saved every penny.'

'I know, I know,' she says gently.

'I did this for us. To keep you all safe. To give you a future. A home for you and Isabella. And now . . .' His voice goes up an octave with the emotion.

She goes to the toilet for tissues, which she does so she can compose herself as much as assist him. He blows his nose and dries his eyes.

'What are you going to do?'

'I'm going to Mr Wolverson. He's a good man. A fair man.'

Pip isn't sure about this. They're all the same, Sammy didn't lick it off a stone. Games and tricks. The good people lose out. It's like the Wolversons are playing a game of chess with other people's lives.

'Will you come with me?' he says. 'He always liked you.'

She could think of nothing worse and she's surprised to be asked. But she'll do anything she can to help her dad.

As if sensing the danger in the air, the quarry sirens sound. Brace for impact.

Philip and Pip drive to the Wolverson mansion on the outskirts of town, a manor at the end of a long yew-tree-lined driveway. At the end of it is an eighteenth-century country house with a lake and stables.

Their visit is expected and they're greeted at the door by a housekeeper who leads them from the large entrance hall through to double doors on the left. The house smells of leather and brass polish. Mr Wolverson, Sammy's father, is so very old. He's almost dust, and very pale, his body is frail, but he's dapperly dressed.

If Philip was wearing a cap he'd have it in his hand, scrunched tightly like a steering wheel. He stops short of genuflecting. They're in the library, with walls filled with books, slippy burgundy leather couches in the centre of the room. They sit together facing Mr Wolverson.

They catch up, and Pip feels like a twelve-year-old again. She speaks clearly and loudly, also because he's hard of hearing, about where she works and how old her daughter Bella is. She feels childish answering in such a way, the patriarch at work, but she falls into her role so easily. Yes Mr Wolverson sir, No Mr Wolverson sir. She's still hungover, filled with fear about the opportunity she has missed out on today at work, her head is pounding, as is her heart. It has so far been a very bad terrible day.

'Good girl, good girl,' he says, returning his gaze to Philip. 'Let's hear where we are now, Philip, you have something to tell me.'

'Yes sir.'

Mr Wolverson is eager. He tells Philip to take his time and tell him everything, not to leave a word out. He stops him occasionally to clarify his understanding and never moves on until he has the full picture. He listens keenly, he frowns and nods along, as though he's a priest taking confession. And then, when her dad has comprehensively explained everything, calmly, clearly, with his chin up; the blasts, the house, the concrete, the cracks, he finally stops talking and watches Mr Wolverson expectantly. Hopefully.

Mr Wolverson's elbow is on the burgundy couch, his finger running across his lips as he listens to the full story.

Philip has not spoken with an accusatory tone, he has not named names. He has been professional and diplomatic. Pip would have personally loved to hang Sammy out to dry, but she supposes the reality of what is happening in the quarry is enough to do so, and being told by their most senior, most respected employee will be hard for Mr Wolverson. Pip and Philip await his response with baited breath.

'When I left the company I told the family that I wouldn't get involved after my retirement. There was a reason for that. The outgoing boss doesn't always agree with the changes being made, that was certainly the case with my father, who, as you know, Philip, ruled that quarry with an iron fist.'

They share a look and a chuckle. Mr Wolverson leans in,

elbows on his skinny legs, his knobbly knees poking through his corduroy chinos. He mirrors Philip's position.

'I have always seen it as passing the baton. One generation passes to the next, with the promise to build on the foundations of what his father has done before, with the freedom to create and build his own.'

Pip's imagination moves to Sammy and Mr Wolverson on a running track. Mr Wolverson, frail, out of breath and crumbling, turns to dust as he reaches the exchange zone and holds his hand out to Sammy, who catches the falling baton and runs on without looking back.

Philip nods, understanding. 'A system we've always benefited from.'

'With Sammy there has certainly been an evolution within the quarry. Business is booming. He's a smart boy.'

He thinks for a time and then the judge is ready to rule.

'I can't meddle in Sammy's affairs,' Mr Wolverson says, after some thought, and Pip feels her stomach twist, as she senses where this is going. 'The quarry is thriving under Sammy's care, the country is crying out for aggregate, we can't have enough houses, and Sammy has made Wolverson quarry key to benefiting Ireland's social infrastructure. With increased productivity unfortunately we have seen more incidents, that is true, and Sammy is focused on increasing training—'

'He has cut back on training, Mr Wolverson,' Philip interrupts him, which he does not like to do. 'It's nowhere near the level that we used to undertake.'

'Times have changed. My father was a bulldog.'

'And there were fewer accidents.'

'As for the quality of the stone,' Mr Wolverson says, sitting up, no longer mirroring Philip's position, putting himself back as top dog. 'There has never been a whiff of mica or pyrite in our aggregate. We send it all around the Midlands.'

'You should test it, sir. Something is certainly not right.'

'I understand it's difficult to view your own work in the right light, particularly someone trained as you are, but—'

'It's not the quality of my work Mr Wolverson,' Philip says sitting up now, taller than him. He's a bear of a man who looks as if he could crush the older man with one squeeze of his hands. 'And if it's not the building materials then it's the quantity of blasts that are affecting the houses over at Nurney Road.'

'So you've joined the committee of angry neighbours now, have you? The Nurney Nine,' he says, with a smirk. 'I thought by offering you that land we would have an ally. I thought that it was understood what we would want you to do. You can't have such complaints taken seriously when the blast supervisor is sharing the land.'

'That was your idea?' Pip finally finds her voice, and the disgust in it can't be hidden. 'You wanted to use my dad to scare them off?'

'Philippa,' Philip says quietly. He sounds beaten, broken.

'Not so dramatic as that,' Mr Wolverson laughs. 'Your dad is a long-standing respected employee, we were happy to do what we could to help him out.'

'Help him? You offered him the land and he paid you. You came to him with the bargain of a lifetime. He didn't come to you for help. He could have built anywhere else. He chose Nurney Road because of his devotion and respect for Wolverson quarry, of you and your father, of the family he felt he has served dutifully for the past forty-three years.'

Philip looks at her, tears in his eyes. She'd only ever seen him cry at the funerals of his parents, and now twice in one day.

Mr Wolverson for some reason finds her words humorous. The little lady has spoken.

'With great respect uh, uh . . .' he searches his mind for her name, and she's not about to give it to him. His words become clipped and staccato. 'Your father *worked* at the quarry and was *paid* for it. He hasn't *served* us. Though we have appreciated the years of, of, of . . . efficiency.'

'Loyalty,' Pip says, not afraid of Mr Wolverson now, and with great joy she stands up to leave and says, 'No, Mr Wolverson. No.'

Philip bows his head.

Big as a quarry.

Could crush a rock in his hands.

Cap in hand. Broken.

'What were you doing on the weekend?' Pip asks quietly as they drive home, in what had been up until now a kind of stunned silence. 'You were planning something, what was it?' She wants to know that he has a plan, that he's going to do something about this, not take it all lying down.

There must be a plan C.

'It had nothing to do with the house.'

She frowns. 'What was it then?'

His silence is heavy, but it's not final, she can sense him weighing it up in his mind.

Finally he sighs. 'Doctor's appointment.'

He coughs, as if to let slip the secret, then he's annoyed he has, and tries to cover it up by turning on the radio. She turns it off. No more secrets.

'For what?'

'He wants to refer me to hospital for some tests on my lungs.'

His livelihood, his pension, his job, his home. And now his health. Her blood boils. If he's not going to do something, she will.

42

Pip practically barges her way into Caroline's house as soon as the door opens. She has to squeeze in because it's barely opened to prevent the dust from travelling inside. Kim and Caroline's sister Helen sit at the kitchen table, avengers assembled for her urgent meeting. Aleksy limps away, sensing woman danger.

'Sit down, would you like a—'

'No,' Pip snaps. On a mission.

'Ooh,' Kim giggles nervously. 'Okay.'

'I have an idea of how to catch Sammy out and end this thing once and for all.'

'Oh goodness,' Caroline claps her hands and exclaims.

'Yes!' Helen agrees.

Kim looks worried.

'I'm going to ask him out on a date. I'm going to wear the sluttiest dress I can find.'

'You can go to Helen's wardrobe for that,' Caroline teases, and Helen makes a face.

'I'm going to ply him with alcohol, and promise him the world, and I'm going to make him talk. About everything. About what he's doing at the quarry, about the accidents, about the shortcuts in training, about the increase in blasts, about the noise and the vibrations and the dust, about *everything*.'

'Helen, get the paperwork,' Caroline says, all business. 'We'll give you a lesson on all the issues we're talking to the solicitor about so you know exactly what to ask him.'

Helen hops up and goes for a thick file on the kitchen island, always at hand, it has become so much a part of their lives.

'Whoa, whoa, whoa.' Kim holds her hands out, stopping everything. 'What is happening here?'

'You heard, she's going to seduce Sammy and get him to talk. You'll have to record him, Pip.'

'How?'

'Voice recorder on your iPhone,' Helen says.

'I didn't know I have that on my phone,' Pip says.

They huddle together to show her the app.

'Stop!' Kim says again, and they freeze. 'This is crazy. It's dangerous. We're not sending her to this maniac. What if he finds out she's recording him?'

'It works from the handbag, I've done it before,' Helen says, surprising them. 'But not in the pocket, all you hear is rustling.'

Eyes wide, Kim continues, 'It's not safe. We should leave this to the professionals. Your solicitor is dealing with it.'

'It's taking forever with the professionals,' Caroline says. 'The solicitor seems to work on this for five minutes a week, before sending it off to the Wolverson solicitor, who sits on it for two weeks. Nothing is being done, they're dragging it on and on. In the meantime, Aleksy can't work and the kids are suffering. We'll have lost all our money on legal bills by the time it even gets to court, and the Wolversons will be richer, and by then who knows if our houses will be standing. It's impossible,' Caroline says, her voice breaking. She collapses into the kitchen chair and presses a hand across her eyes.

'Our house is cracking,' Pip says. Which stops Caroline crying. It gets their attention. 'Dad thinks it's either the explosions, or the building materials were defective.'

This is new information, nobody has ever questioned the quarry's rock.

'He raised the issue with Sammy and he's suddenly reduced to working a three-day week. He's not the blast supervisor anymore, he's going to be given a new role.'

They gasp.

'We just got back from the Wolverson house where Mr Wolverson said there's absolutely nothing he can do. They're throwing their full support behind Sammy.'

'Oh, this is terrible,' Kim says. 'I understand why you want to corner Sammy, but let's be rational about this. This Sammy guy, I don't know him personally, but he sounds like an arsehole, a dangerous arsehole. You can't just try to catch him out.'

'Yes I can,' Pip says, with tunnel vision. She is going to get Sammy Wolverson.

Kim sighs. 'Okay then, if you have to meet him, then make it a public place and we'll be there too. We'll be at another table, out for my pretend birthday, and we'll be able to keep an eye on you. And you'll have to bring me real presents to keep it legit,' she adds to lighten the tension in the room.

'Kim is right,' Helen says. 'He has a violent side. Laura who does his spray tan said she dated him for a month and she didn't go into detail, but he scared her. He still goes back to her for the spray tans, and she's terrified of him.'

'Is that why she deliberately makes him orange?' Kim asks, and they smirk nervously.

'A public meeting is a great idea Kim,' Caroline says. 'The Turfcutter's Inn. We know everyone in there. It will be a safe space.'

'I was thinking somewhere more private,' Pip says, not liking this idea.

'That is not a good idea,' Kim says.

'What's wrong with The Turfcutter's?'

'Everyone will see me with him,' Pip says, biting her lip. 'I don't want Finbar to tell Jamie.'

And, as if they're all twelve years old, the three woman sing a teasing *ooooh* in unison until they're all laughing and Pip's face is beetroot red.

'Oh my God, stop the lights, Philippa Sheridan is in love with Jamie Murphy,' Kim says, gently, 'again.'

'Not again,' Pip says with a smile, her adrenaline surging at the sound of those words aloud, shared with others, with friends, new friends. 'Still.'

Pip leaves Caroline's house all fired up. From the time it takes her to get from Caroline's front door to her own, her confidence has waned. But it just takes her stepping into her bedroom and seeing the fissure in her ceiling, to be motivated again.

No time like the present.

She calls Sammy.

It rings for a long time, and just when she thinks she's safe, and she's about to hang up, he answers.

'Hiya.' He sounds out of breath.

'Hi Sammy, it's Philippa.'

'Philippa,' he sings her name. 'Now there's a surprise. How can I help you, Philippa? Are you calling to give me a piece of your mind?'

'Why would I do that?'

'Have you spoken to your dad?'

'Have you?' she asks, in a teasing voice, and he laughs, liking it.

'I have.'

'So you know and I know, and let's leave that aside.'

'Oh?'

'I wanted to ask you out. On a date. As you said, I owe you one.'

For some surprising reason, the flirting is coming easily to her. She despises him so very much, it's easy to lie to him.

'You want to ask me out because your dad is angry with me?'

'That's not what I said.'

'I'm reading between the lines.' He speaks as if he's a super detective.

Of course that's what she's expecting him to do.

'Well, take from it what you like. You brought me out on two dates and now it's my turn.' She speaks with a smile on her face because it changes her tone.

He's quiet for a moment, and the nerves trickle through. She never for a moment thought he'd say no. He has always been so keen, but maybe Sammy Wolverson has always just wanted what he cannot have.

'Where?'

'The Turfcutter's.' Even though she doesn't want to meet there, she'd given in to the girls, who felt being in a safe zone was the best idea. She would have to explain to Jamie if word ever got back to him, which it no doubt will, thanks to his brother Finbar.

Sammy pauses. 'Okay. When?'

'Tomorrow night?'

'How about tonight?'

'I can't tonight, I'm sorry, I'm going bowling with Jamie and Bella, it's kind of important.' It is important.

'I'm only available tonight.'

The scut. She's quite sure that's not true, but he likes to play games, be in control. It gives her more impetus to play her game with him.

She thinks fast. She can't cancel Jamie and Bella, she doesn't want to let them down as they both need her there to help their relationship move forward, but maybe she can move it. Bella certainly won't mind, and Jamie is so eager for a relationship that he'll take any date given. She pushes the thought aside that they're running out of time, Jamie's leaving soon, back to Tala, and she could see Sammy Wolverson any day.

'Well?' Does she hear a chuckle in his voice?

'Okay. Tonight then.'

'Eight p.m. at The Turfcutter's.'

'See you then,' she sings, trying to keep her voice perky. 'I'll book a table and meet you there.'

She ends the call, drops the phone, and washes her hands, to get him off her. And then she texts the girls. Tonight at 8 p.m. She realises this gives her very little time to prepare. She thought she would have time to work her way through the file of documents, but she'll just have to hit record and get him talking.

Her heart sinks as she dials Jamie's number and prepares to disappoint him for a second night running. She hopes he doesn't incorrectly read into it, they need to continue to act as a team. She let him down before, she can't let him down again.

43

WHEN BELLA AND JOSEPHINE return home from work, Bella runs straight up the stairs and knocks on her bedroom door at the same time as pushing it open and barging in.

'Whoa, that's a bit much for going bowling, isn't it?'

She's referring to Pip's make-up, which is most definitely a bit much. For the previous two dates with Sammy, Pip was unsure, this time she's doing everything to give him signals so that he'll talk. Her lips are blood red, she's wearing fake individual eyelashes, her eyebrows preened to perfection. Her hair is down and blow-dried in loose waves. She knows he appreciates things like that.

'So, here's the thing. We're not going bowling tonight.'

She's saddened at how Bella punches the air. She wishes for her to be excited to be going out with her dad. And with her for that matter, but she's used to that.

'But we need to tell Josephine and Philip that we're still going bowling.'

Bella grins, loving the scheming and deceit 'Where are we going?' Bella whispers.

'You're going to that party with Mark that you've been going on about.'

She squeals with delight, bounces in the air and hugs her so tightly, if it weren't for the particular circumstances, Pip would be overjoyed by the physical closeness.

'And where are you going?'

'Somewhere else.'

'You are so mysterious lately. Is it Io?'

'No.' He still hasn't called her back, and she's worried.

'Dad?' She makes a disgusted face, as though the thought of them together makes her physically repulsed. Sixteen years of Josephine separating Pip and Jamie would do that to a mind.

'No.'

'Please tell me it's not Spraytan Sammy.'

She doesn't say anything.

'Ugh, Pip, no. He's gross. He gives me the ick.'

'He gives me the ick too,' Pip says, whispering. 'But it's not a date. It's . . . business.'

Bella's eyes widen. 'Are you a prostitute now?'

Pip is naturally insulted, until Bella starts laughing. 'Okay, whatever. I'm not going to ask any questions, I'm happy to be going to my party. Mark is going to be so happy.'

'He better take care of you. No drinking.'

'None?'

'One drink, no more. No drugs, no sex.'

'Oh, gross, shut up,' Bella says, not used to hearing this from Pip.

'Don't tell me to shut up,' Pip says, firmly, and Bella is shocked. Pip has shocked herself too. She sounds like a mother. Bella's mother.

Pip tries to shake off her worry about the party. Her gut told her no, and she's ignoring it, but she's not going to watch their house crumble around them, watch her dad, who has worked so hard all of his life, lose everything. As for Josephine. Perhaps she's doing it to prove that she's not worthless, she doesn't have to rely on her family, they can actually rely on her.

'What about Dad?'

It's not Jamie's fault, but it's curious how he has the honour of being called 'Dad' when he wasn't physically present for most of her life, and yet Pip has never been called 'Mam'.

'Jamie's very disappointed of course. We're going bowling tomorrow night instead, don't make that face, and he's offered to drive you to the party, and don't make that face again please. We're going to have so much fun pretend-bowling tonight that we'll all go again tomorrow,' she says, sweating at the web of lies she finds herself in. 'I'll be in the car too. We're leaving in an hour.'

The disappointment in Jamie's voice was heartbreaking when she cancelled their bowling plans. She's eager to show him that it doesn't mean they're shutting him out, but the opposite. She appreciates his involvement in getting Bella to the party, she needs another watchful eye.

Bella watches Pip stuff a dress into a backpack.

'What's that?'

'Nothing.'

'What are you wearing tonight for your *business meeting*?' She makes inverted commas with her fingers. 'Why aren't you wearing it now?'

'Because.'

Bella folds her arms. 'What's going on?'

'I'll tell you when it's finished. Now get changed, and dress like you're going bowling.'

'I will. I'll change into my dress later, like you.' She winks. 'Oh,' she stops at the door, 'I just remembered why I came in. Why weren't you at work? We stopped at Crossroads and Krish said you didn't come in and he hasn't heard from you all day. Nan is raging. She wants to speak to you downstairs.'

Pip slowly walks downstairs, in jeans, a T-shirt, and her face fully made up. She's too focused on what she has to do tonight with Sammy to be distracted by a dressing down. The house is quiet, Bella is in her bedroom, door firmly closed, probably wearing her headphones to block out any arguments. Philip is outside, tinkering in his garage, with much on his mind after today's meeting with Mr Wolverson. It's silent, just the hum of the dishwasher and the sloshing around of water. Josephine is sitting alone at the kitchen table. There's a mug of tea in front of her, and a mug of tea at the opposite seat.

'I made you tea.'

'Thank you.'

The tea is like a flashing neon sign pointing her to where to sit. She sits. Good dog.

Josephine looks tired. Pip has no idea what Josephine knows about the house and Mr Wolverson. She should assume that her mother knows everything, but Josephine should stop assuming that Pip doesn't know anything.

Josephine begins with a beleaguered sigh. She's tired.

'When there was all the . . .' she finishes her sentence with a dismissive wave of her hand. The hand is not nothing, the dismissive wave that her mother uses so much has a language. It is the signal for Pip's pregnancy. The unspoken horrendous mistake.

'When I became pregnant,' Pip says.

Josephine is stopped in her tracks.

'Let's say it like it is.'

'When you fell pregnant at sixteen years old,' Josephine snaps.

Pip has always hated that expression. She didn't fall pregnant. She didn't stumble into it. It wasn't planned, but it happened in the most beautiful, tender way, in one of the greatest moments of her life. She was fully in control, with the man she loved, even if nobody else yet saw him as the man he is.

'I was filled with self-condemnation. Father McDonagh told me and your dad a story from the Bible. Luke 15:11–32. The story of the prodigal son, he said, was about parenting. In every parent-child relationship there's a struggle. A struggle for control.' She breathes in deeply and straightens up. 'I can see from the entitled way you behaved last night and today that you're rebelling.'

Pip stops her right there. That word boils her blood. 'I am not *rebelling*. I am not a child. I am not a teenager.' Pip speaks slowly and clearly. She repeats it so her mother hears her. 'I am not a child. Look at me.'

She lifts her eyes from her clasped fingers and looks Pip in the eye.

'I'm thirty-two years old. I'm an adult. I am a woman. I have a child of my own. You have to let me go.'

Josephine starts trembling.

'You think I don't know anything,' Pip says steadily. 'You think that the way through this change is to sit me down and preach to me, keep me in line so that I go numb again, back into a coma for another ten years. But it's not happening. I know what you're doing. I know what you did and why you did it. You feel like you failed with me, don't you?'

'Well, of course. It's hardly a secret, Philippa. I did fail with you.'

Pip knows it, but hearing it still hurts Pip's feelings.

'It was a horrid embarrassing affair for you,' Pip says. 'And it was all about you. How my actions made everyone view you. So you took that baby from me, stole her from my arms, gave her a name you wanted, a life you wanted, moulded a child that was completely loyal to you so you could get it right second time round. You made sure that her dad had nothing to do with her. So that you would be obeyed. So that everyone would think what a great mother you were after all.'

Josephine's fingers are trembling. She's fidgeting in her chair, physically unable to take this confrontation.

'Do you know what would have been a better way to redeem yourself as a mother? You could have continued to mother *me*. You could have taught me how to be a mother. Learned from your own mistakes and passed the lesson on to me. But instead, you tried to take that from me too.'

Josephine has had enough. She doesn't want to hear another thing and stands up. She reaches out to hold onto the handle of the chair, to stay upright. Pip speaks again.

'I am a mother. Bella is my daughter. Not yours.'

Pip is finished. She doesn't want to hear anything else and she has nothing more to say. She leaves the kitchen, passing a stunned Bella in the hallway, headphones off, this time having heard every word.

44

'I'M SORRY ABOUT THIS Jamie,' Pip says, when she gets into the car beside him outside her house.

'It's no problem. I don't want her missing anything cool on my account. I want her to like me,' he says with a wobbly smile.

'Jamie, she does like you. She loves you, that much is . . . automatic. But you're not allowed to say "cool" apparently, I'm under strict orders.'

'Jesus,' he says. 'Is there a rule book you can give me?'

'If I had one, I'd be following it myself.'

'If driving Bella to a party will make her love me then I'm in.'

Pip's guilt comes to the fore. 'I'm honestly a little worried about this party. She's never been to a house party before. Mark is older, there'll be drinking . . .' She bites her lip. 'Have I made a bad decision?'

He thinks about it, doesn't naturally back her up, which concerns her, but she appreciates it. 'Why don't we say she can go until eleven p.m., and if she proves that she's trustworthy, then the next time she can stay longer.'

She hadn't even thought of that. 'That's a great idea. Or it would have been, only . . .'

'You can't take it back now.'

'No. Damnit. Look at you being the better parent.'

'Stop being so hard on yourself.'

'I will if you will.'

He groans.

It's as if they're starting from the beginning as parents, skipped the baby part and are learning from scratch with a teenager. There is something comforting about being completely clueless together.

'I'm sorry about running off early last night. My friend needed me.'

'Yes,' he says, looking at her in a way that she can read so obviously.

She laughs. 'His name is Io. He's my friend. He works at the observatory. He's here for a few months and then he goes back home. He's just my good friend. He's been teaching me to drive.'

Jamie smiles, his eyes crinkle at the side. They didn't do that when she knew him before. She wants to reach out and touch the lines. She hates that she missed seeing them form.

'What are you laughing at?'

'Is he just a friend?' he asks, a giggle caught in his throat.

'Yes. He's just . . .' Wait. He's teasing her.

'It's just that you mentioned it a few times.'

'I wanted you to know.'

'Okay, well now I know.'

'Good,' she says, grinning, turning to look at the house.

Bella appears at the door with a concerned Josephine.

'She looks nice,' Jamie says, surprised.

'She has her dress in her bag. You won't think that's so nice. It's about the size of your dad's handkerchiefs.'

He laughs.

'She's changing into it when she gets to the party. Josephine and Philip think we're going bowling.'

'Right.'

Bella bounces into the car.

'Enjoy bowling!' Josephine calls uncertainly to Bella.

'We will!' they all say in various tones of deceit.

Bella waves at her nan until she's no longer in sight. 'Right bitches, let's party.'

'Bella!' Pip admonishes her. Jamie starts laughing.

They crawl along the road as they approach the house that's clearly the venue for the party. People spill out into the garden, and the music is audible from the end of the road. There are small French flags planted in the grass out front, fluttering in the breeze.

'Why are there French flags?'

'Mark's friend is French. It's the fourteenth of July.'

'Right,' Jamie says, concerned by the look of some of the people crossing the road and entering the house. 'Will there be cannons?'

Pip bites her lip to stop herself from laughing.

'Are his parents here?' he asks.

'They live in France.'

Pip turns around.

'Don't look,' Bella yelps, 'I'm getting changed.'

'If his parents are in France, then who's in charge tonight?' Jamie asks, and Pip winces as each of his questions highlight her bad decision. She only agreed because of her plan to trick Sammy, but in doing so she has left her daughter in a very unsavoury position.

'He's in charge. He's, like, twenty-five. It's his house.'

Jamie and Pip look at each other, uncertain. Neither of

them wants her to hate them. Both of them want to be her friend. Both of them should be parenting.

'Bella,' Pip says, turning around and ignoring Bella's cries. Her daughter has her foot on the back seat as she tries to close the clasp of a ridiculously high shoe. Her legs are an unnatural bronze from the fake tan, and her dress is up so high and is so tight she can see the shape of her thong beneath. Pip has a very, very bad feeling. She toughens up.

'Okay, Bella, listen to me.'

Bella lifts her other leg up to put her second shoe on, giving Pip an eyeful of what's beneath the dress. At least she's wearing underwear.

Pip looks away. 'You know that I'm nervous about you going to the party—'

'I told you not to be.'

'Listen to me now, please.'

Bella closes her mouth.

'And you know that I said no every single time that you asked me if you could go to this. I'm still not comfortable with you going. The people look,' she glances out of the window at the crowds, and is pleased to see a group of girls that look Bella's age in matching dresses and equally ridiculous shoes, 'slightly older. And odder. Watch your drink. Somebody could slip something into it. Don't roll your eyes, it's a real thing and it happens. Stay with Mark. Do not leave his side. If you need me, call me and I'll be here straight away.'

'Or me,' Jamie says. 'I'm not doing anything tonight, I'm free to pick you up.'

'Thank you,' she says quietly. 'But you guys don't need to be so worried. It's just a party.'

'And you're just our sixteen-year-old daughter. We love you and we're worried about you.'

She seems to look at them differently then. For once, they're her parents. Not outnumbered or diluted by others in the room. It's just the three of them in a small car, and Pip has the feeling that for the first time their presence is powerful for Bella, while it feels slightly more terrifying for Pip and Jamie. There's no one else to blame if it goes wrong.

'Okay,' she says softly.

'I'm allowing you one drink. One drink. That's it. Make it last. Do not get drunk. Do not have sex.'

'Pip,' she says, embarrassed by Jamie's presence. He looks away, faces front as if he has nothing to do with the conversation.

'But if you do, make sure he wears a condom,' Jamie adds.

'But don't . . .' Pip says, her eyes widening at Jamie.

'Exactly, don't. But if you do . . .' he continues.

'Jesus,' Bella says, dying of embarrassment.

'Anything else?' Pip says, more to herself.

'Drugs,' Jamie says quietly.

'Don't do drugs. No pills, no cocaine, don't put any crap up your nose. It can kill you. And if that's not bad enough, it can give you a deviated septum, no one wants a squished nose. Be the amazing girl who can go to a party and have the confidence to be herself.'

She rolls her eyes. 'I don't want any of that stuff.'

'Good. Okay.' Pip breathes out slowly. 'Have fun.'

She opens the car door and gets out. She wobbles in her shoes as she takes a few steps. She turns around and waves her hand, tells them to leave.

Mark comes running from the house to meet her.

'So that's Mark,' Jamie says, leaning forward to hug the steering wheel. His shoulder muscles expand as he examines him.

Mark looks at Pip and waves with a grin, then he looks at Jamie and his smile quickly fades. Uncertainly, he takes Bella's hand and they walk to the party.

Pip starts laughing.

'What are you laughing at?'

'Your face.' She can't stop. 'You look like you want to kill him.'

'Maybe I do. Cocky little shit. He needs to know.'

'What, that her sister's friend will get him?'

He sighs. 'You shouldn't allow that.'

'I wanted her to like me.'

'I know.' He rubs his jaw. She hears the sound of his fingers on his unshaven skin. She wants to kiss where he rubs, she wants to feel his bristles on her. 'We'll figure it out.' Then he starts laughing. 'Deviated septum? No one wants a mushed nose?'

Pip joins in with his laughter. 'Honestly, she cares more about how her face looks than dying.'

When they've both stopped laughing, he turns to her. 'Why does she call you Pip?'

She sighs. 'Josephine didn't want a baby to be calling her teenage daughter Mam.'

His jaw tenses. He watches a few more groups enter the house.

'Would you like to go for a drink while we wait? Or we could sit outside the house all night and really ruin her fun.'

Her heart sinks. She would love nothing more than just to sit here with him, but she has a date with a demon.

'I'm so sorry Jamie, I can't tonight. When we cancelled bowling I made plans that I can't change, and I wouldn't do it if I didn't have to. It's something for Dad. About the house.'

'What's going on?'

'I promise I'll tell you when it's all finished.'

'It's not Io.'

'It's *not* Io.'

He seems disappointed, but they talk as they drive back to town, despite the years of not knowing one another, being in his company is so easy. She feels safe.

'Sure I can't change your mind?' he asks again easily as he pulls over to let her out of the car on the main street.

'I would prefer to be with you than where I'm going, trust me, but I can't.'

'Okay,' he says, with a look that breaks her heart. 'Where will I meet you in three hours so we can pick up our daughter?'

She smiles. 'Meet you back here in three hours.'

She throws her bag over her back and, when his car has left, she walks towards The Turfcutter's, ready for her showdown with Sammy.

45

AFTER TELLING HER MOTHER she wasn't a teenager and she wasn't rebelling it feels difficult to back that up when she's in the toilets of The Turfcutter's Inn changing into a dress and heels at thirty-two years of age. She'd borrowed a very little black dress from Helen, who is shorter than her, making the dress a micro mini. Sitting down is going to be tricky.

When she exits the toilet she sees Caroline, Kim and Helen in place, sitting at a table by the wall. They've even gone so far as to wear party hats for the pretend birthday. Kim looks at her with wide eyes and mouths *wow*, which Pip tries not to laugh at because they're pretending not to know each other, or at least to be seen as no more than acquaintances. She finds a table away from the girls, but close enough so that they can see her clearly. It's private, tucked away in the corner, she sits with her back to the room so no one can see her with him. Sammy hasn't arrived yet, but she's already ordered the drinks and they're sitting on the table, she took the lead from her mam's tea placement earlier, his pint is sitting before the chair she wants him to sit in. She wanted to make sure she has enough time to set up her phone. She searches through her apps for the audio recording.

'Boo!'

She jumps and drops her phone.

Sammy has sneaked up behind her. She shudders at his breath on her neck.

He's laughing.

'You almost gave me a heart attack,' she says, trying to manage picking up her phone without him seeing what's on her screen. She stands and gives him a half hug and peck on the cheek.

'Wow,' he says, looking at her dress, eyes lingering on every part of her body for a creepy amount of time. 'Yes. That's more like it.' He moves her hips so that she's turning around for him.

'More like it?' she says, pretending to be insulted. She couldn't give a crap what he thinks of her.

'Yeah, the last two dates were a bit, you know, is she a nun or what?' He laughs.

She laughs too. Yes Mr Wolverson sir, no Mr Wolverson sir.

Her fingers are trembling as she tries to concentrate on him and look at her phone too, to get the voice recorder back. But of course he notices, he notices everything if she so much as looks away if he's mid-sentence.

'Is everything okay down there?'

'Sorry,' she says, thinking quickly. 'It's my daughter Bella. She's gone to a house party tonight and . . .' she looks down and presses record, puts the phone by her hip and leans in towards him, giving him a full view of her cleavage. 'I'm so worried about her. She's dating an older guy. Eighteen. And this is her first house party. There'll be drinking and God knows what else.'

'Sounds good, what's the address?' he jokes, and she laughs.

'Seriously though, I'm worried about her, hence having

to check my phone now and then. So don't take offence,' she says, warmly, reaching out and touching his hand. 'You have my full attention, but I do need to make sure I don't miss her call.'

He seems to believe that. 'This is the problem with dating mothers. I can't have your undivided attention.' He says it playfully, but she believes every word.

She smiles. 'Oh believe me you'll have my undivided attention.'

'Why can't her dad be on duty?'

He nods over her shoulder and, confused, she turns around and sees Jamie sitting at the bar, talking to Finbar. Just as she's turned around he looks over at her. At first he smiles, but when he sees Sammy the smile quickly fades.

She feels like jumping up and telling him it's not a date, it's not what he thinks it is, but instead she swallows back the emotion, the frustration and anger, and turns back to face Sammy. If she's going to lose Jamie's respect for this, at least she needs to make it worth it. She can see Sammy's thrown by the interaction, and she needs to get him back onside again.

'Sammy, it's been a while, I distinctly remember the last two dates being very much about me.' This is absolutely not true. The conversation on both dates was entirely about him. 'Let's talk about you.'

She thought he'd devour this opportunity, but instead he studies her, eyes narrowed.

'Hmm.'

'Hmm what?'

'You seem different.'

'I'm wearing more make-up.' She bats her eyelashes.

'Different in another way.' He looks around the room. He clocks Caroline, Kim and Helen in the corner, and Jamie at the bar. She's afraid he's going to bolt.

'Okay, you're right. I am different. You guessed it over the phone, but I'm tired of living the way I'm living at home with my parents. It's time for me to take a step away from them. I want to do my own thing. I want to be more like me. Hence, the make-up, the hair, the dress.'

It's almost all true.

'I'm surprised you called me after the things you said to me in the park.' He sticks his bottom lip out.

'Poor baby,' she smiles, placing her thumb on his lip momentarily.

He quickly grabs her thumb and sucks it. She tries not to squirm. Her smile is pasted on her face. If Jamie is watching this, she has just dug her own grave.

'And after what happened with your dad,' he says, releasing her thumb.

After they took Philip's job away, sold him bad building material, destroyed their home, took his savings, ruined his future pension, perhaps his health too.

She smiles as if she hasn't a care in the world. 'Like I said, I've decided my parents' problems are their own problems. Do you not ever feel like that in your family? Did you ever want to do anything else apart from work in the family business?'

'It wasn't an option. All of us from as far back as I can remember were told that we'd be going into the family business, and that's what we do.'

'You've all been so successful, your granddad and your dad, is that not pressurising?'

He leans forward, leers at her boobs, happy to be in the

hot seat. 'You'd like to think that you can bring something different to the company, you know? I have lots of ideas that my dad and granddad didn't have. Even though you know what the job is going to be for the rest of your life, doesn't mean you can't be creative.'

'In what way?' She drinks from her straw, leaving red lipstick all over it.

He looks at it. Then at her. 'I've come up with a lot of new ideas. Grown the company. We have vehicles and equipment and already do the site clearance service, so it was my idea to add tree felling, scrub removal, stump grinding . . .'

'Stump grinding.' She laughs. 'Sounds kinky.'

He grins, then as quickly as his smile appears, it fades again. It's disturbing how he swings so quickly without ever trying to disguise it.

'Something's going on here.'

Her heart pounds.

He looks at the girls over in the corner table, they're smiling and laughing, deep in conversation, gift wrap strewn across the table, not at all seeming to be clued into what's going on with Sammy and Pip. He looks over in Jamie's direction, she doesn't want to turn around to see if he's still there. Her heart thuds. If Sammy has clocked what's going on then she will join her friends, she can go to Jamie, she's safe. If he doesn't figure it out, then she'll be able to help her dad and her neighbours' case.

Sammy seems to consider everything in a long thoughtful silence. He slowly rubs his finger pads together as he ponders.

He looks over at Kim, Caroline and Helen again, in thought.

She leans in, and lowers her voice conspiratorially. 'What's going on with that lot? None of them will speak to me, they ignore me every single time I say hi. Dad says it's because they think I'm your girlfriend.'

'Is that so?'

'I'm happy not to tell them otherwise.'

'The Nurney nitwits.'

'Hey, I take offence to that. I live in Nurney.'

'Not you,' he says, flicking her arm with his finger. It's supposed to be playful but it stings.

'They're going on about dust and vibrations, I haven't noticed anything. What's the deal?' She checks her phone to see that it's still recording. She'll run out of storage at the rate she's going. She needs to get something from him, fast.

'*Ach*,' he looks away, 'between you and me, there is something in it. The tests the council came back with aren't in our favour. But I shouldn't be telling you that, with your house being so close.'

'Not my house.' She shrugs. 'And I'm planning on moving soon.'

'To where?'

'Whoever ends up being the lucky guy,' she teases. 'So what are you going to do about it? Is it going to court?'

'Not a hope. I have a friend in the council. He'll make it go away.'

'You can do that?'

'With money, you can pretty much do anything.' He rests his chin on his fist. 'I'm bored.'

'Oh.' She sits up, insulted.

'Let's get out of here.'

'And go where?' The plan was to stay here, not go somewhere else with him, without her protection squad.

'You've asked a lot of questions about the quarry, why

don't I take you there? It's a lot of fun at night. I can show you around.'

'Maybe we should stay here. I don't think this dress and shoes are made for walking around a quarry,' she says with a smile.

'I thought you wanted to know more about me. I don't want to keep talking about myself here,' he says, looking around. 'Besides, there's a new security guard starting tonight, I want to check in on him.'

His face does that thing again where the smile disappears and a stormy version of himself takes over. Immediately darker, like a shadow passes across his face. Has she got enough from him on the recording? The fact that he's paying off a council member – but is that enough? There is so much more to discuss. She doesn't want to be alone with him so far away, but maybe at the quarry she can get more information.

'Let's go,' he says, standing up, grabbing his coat.

The girls look over as he leads her away. Kim's eyes widen in alarm and Pip tries to stay calm. Jamie is sitting at the bar drinking coffee. Their eyes lock in the mirror behind the bar and they stay on her as she walks towards him.

All she can feel is his judgement, her betrayal. She doesn't know if he'll ever understand what she's doing here, it all looks bad.

'Is the quarry even open at this time?' she asks loudly, as they walk past.

Sammy completely ignores Jamie. A hand on her lower back as he guides her outside into the night, leaving her protection squad behind.

46

S AMMY STANDS BEHIND HER as she climbs up into the Range Rover, which is quite the feat in her short dress and one he takes time admiring. He gives her the creeps, and she has to fight the urge to call the entire thing off, to run back inside the pub to her friends and Jamie.

As he drives, his left hand slides across to her leg. He runs his fingers up and down her thigh, which gives her goose-bumps, and not in a good way. One hand on the steering wheel and one hand on her, trying to work its way in to her.

'Now, now,' she says, trying to keep it light, and crossing her legs. The dress is so short this only causes it to ride up, giving him greater access to her entire thigh.

'So what's fun to do in a quarry at night?' she asks, trying to take his attention away from her legs, but realising that the question sounds more leading than he'd intended.

He looks at her and grins.

'Oh right. Is this where you take your dates?'

'Some of them, sure. Who doesn't get turned on by a digger?'

She's not sure if he's joking – it's hard to tell with him, he doesn't have a sparkling sense of humour – but she hopes he is.

They arrive at the entrance gates to the quarry, which are locked and Pip could leap for joy at the sight before her eyes.

Krish steps out of the security hut, with a clipboard in his hand. He looks at Pip first and is confused, and then he sees Sammy, and it's like the king is visiting.

'Mr Wolverson, hello! Good to see you this evening. Let me get the gate for you, sir.'

They drive down into the quarry and, while Pip has never been to the grand canyon, she imagines it's something like this. At ten p.m. it's still a bright July night.

She looks around, the vehicles are paused in their work, as though they're sleeping horses. It feels eerie without people here, just rock that seems to reach the sky and giant robotic creatures. They drive to a portable site cabin in the thick of the quarry. He stops the car and gets out.

'Here?'

'Want to see where your dad works? Or should I say worked?'

This angers her, gives her the fuel she needs to continue. 'Sure.'

She gets out of the car, trying to slide her legs to the side so she can get out in a more ladylike manner without revealing everything, but Sammy is standing there for the view. The dress and the high heels all feel very silly in this environment as she lands on the concrete.

'Do you train all your workers here on site?'

Her phone is in her bag, she's not sure how clear the recording will be, so she speaks up.

'Yeah. We used to have to send them off site, my granddad was a stickler for that, but I changed that. It was costing a fortune to have our guys go to training all around the country, so now we do it in-house. Cut down the hours they have to spend. All training happens here.'

'So they do less training than before? I remember my dad having to go off and re-certify for this and that over the years.'

'Yeah, he was old school. We don't do it like that anymore. I bring a lot of guys in who aren't permanent, just to do days here and there, so they don't have to do the same training as they're not employed by us full-time. There's always ways around it.'

She looks in the direction of her house, knowing that it's not too far away.

'What happens when you're all quarried out, will you expand?'

'I've a new idea,' he says with a wink. 'I've applied for a Waste Licence.'

'A what?'

He keeps walking, but she pauses in shock. He turns around, and she hurries to keep up.

'If the application is successful we can use this space for landfill. The quarry is the perfect way to fill the void. See? I'm always thinking of new ways to expand. So it doesn't matter what objections your neighbours raise about this quarry, I'll keep going regardless.'

She thinks of living next to a landfill site, how devastated her parents would be, and wonders which is worse. Is he threatening her? For a moment she feels fearful – is he toying with her?

He points at the cabin. 'This is where your dad has his tea breaks. Where they have the morning meetings.'

He unlocks the cabin and climbs the few steps up inside. It's a small square Portakabin, she doesn't know why she needs to go inside. She prefers it outside where she can see the sky, where she's not in a tiny room with him. She knows exactly what he's planning and she's not going there with him, particularly not in a dusty cabin where her dad has his tea breaks. Maybe that's what's a turn-on for him. Doing his daughter on her dad's lunch desk.

Her phone rings, disturbing her recording. She reaches into her bag, looks at the screen. 'It's Bella.' She answers straight away. 'Hello?'

'Pip,' Bella says, sobbing down the phone. 'Can you come and get me? I want to go home. Now. I need to get out of here.'

'Sweetheart, what's wrong? What happened?' She's so distracted by Bella that she steps inside the cabin. Sammy watches her.

'I hate him,' she sobs, barely able to get the words out. 'I . . . I . . . I hate him.'

'Who? Mark?'

'Yes.'

She sounds drunk. Everything Pip had feared. 'Okay I'm coming to get you straight away, don't worry, I'm coming for you okay?'

'Okay,' she sobs.

'Are you safe? Are you with someone?'

'I've locked myself in the bathroom. He's trying to get me out.'

Pip hears banging on the door.

'Okay, sit tight, I'm coming for you. I'll be fifteen minutes. Don't worry sweetheart. Stay in there until I get there.'

She hangs up the phone, her heart pounding and her fingers trembling. She can barely think. Jamie. She needs to call Jamie. She searches through her phone for his name and presses dial, when her phone is plucked from her hand.

Sammy has taken it from her.

'What are you doing?'

He ends the call.

'What the hell are you doing?' she asks angrily.

'What the hell am I doing?'

He steps towards her, he lifts a hand to her face, runs a finger down her cheek.

'Sammy,' she says firmly, 'now is not the time for this. My daughter is in trouble at the party, I have to go get her. We can do this another time. Please. Can you take me to her? Or back to The Turfcutter's? Jamie can drive me to her.'

Suddenly his fingers squeeze her face so tightly it hurts.

'Ow, stop.' She can barely move her jaw to speak.

'Do you think I don't know what you're doing? Do you think I'm stupid?'

While holding her tightly with one hand, he scrolls through her phone with the other. Suddenly his voice is playing back to her on the recording. He squeezes her face even more tightly.

He lifts the phone up so she can see what he's doing as he presses delete.

She starts crying. 'Ow. Sammy. Stop please. Help! Krish help!' she yells out of the open door. Sammy covers her mouth with his hand.

'Shut up,' he says angrily. 'Who did you send this to?'

He looks through her phone and, seeming satisfied that it hasn't been forwarded, he returns his attention to her.

'You think I didn't guess your little spy game from the start? The state of you in that dress. You think I'd be interested in you, you prick tease. And all your little friends around you for backup. Well they're not here, are they?'

She can barely breathe, his hand is tight across her mouth.

He suddenly lets go.

'Ow,' she cries. 'Okay then, keep the phone, let's go and I'll never bother you again. You won't see me again. I have to go to Bella,' she says, making her way to the door. He gets there first, leaves and slams the door in her face. He locks it. She starts banging on the door, then looks around for her phone. Sammy walks to the window, which is dusty and stained, and waves her phone at her. It's ringing again. Bella's name pops up on the display screen. Pip starts crying.

'Let me out!'

She bangs on the window.

He props the phone on the narrow windowsill outside so that the display screen is facing her. The call ends and then it starts again. It ends and then it starts again. She watches it, tears spilling down her cheeks, the panic in her chest. The feeling of claustrophobia. Her daughter is alone, locked in a bathroom, in a house party, drunk and afraid, ringing her for help and she can't respond. It's the worst kind of torture. It's Pip's fault. She desperately wanted to be Bella's mother and she'd made the worst decision, proving Josephine right, that she can't be trusted to make the right, safe decisions. She bangs on the window, angrily. It reverberates and knocks the phone to the ground.

She waits for Sammy's game to be over. How long will he keep this up for? He has her where he wants her. Panicking, crying, afraid. He's won.

Grinning, he walks towards the Range Rover.

'No, no, no,' she says, watching him. 'No.'

He gets in the Range Rover and drives away.

'No!' she yells, banging on the window. She tries the door again, but it's locked. She looks around the cabin for a phone, searches through drawers and shelves, but there's nothing. She picks up a chair and she launches it at the window, but it just bounces right back off. Blast proof. She sits down, feeling utterly hopeless and useless, sobbing.

She has achieved absolutely nothing for her family, if anything, she has made it worse. How can her dad ever return to work here after this? What has she done to her daughter?

She sits and waits.

The cabin clock reads ten forty-five. She's been in there for forty minutes. She has been looking out for Krish, hoping that he'll do his rounds, but there has been nothing, no one, and now it's dark and she can't even see past the darkness of the window. She fights the claustrophobia that comes in waves along with the desperate urge to pee. She needs to toughen up, she's not going to get through this by panicking. She takes deep breaths and tries to think her way through this rationally.

She turns the lights on and off. Surely Krish will have to see them from his security hut. The hut is the only bit of light in the dark quarry. On-off, on-off, she does it for so long and waits, searches for headlights in the distance or a torch. Blackness stares back at her.

She takes deep breaths and slowly but surely calms down. She looks around the cabin. She opens drawers and finds paperwork, work schedules and quarry maps, bits and pieces, but nothing that could help her break her way out of here.

She opens a cupboard and sees mugs, coffee, tea bags, sugar and biscuits. She instantly recognises her dad's mug. Bella had given it to him a few years ago for Christmas, it's black and reads 'If Granddad can't fix it, we're all screwed'. The handle is in the shape of a spanner. She smiles, taking it out of the cupboard and holding it, the presence of Bella and Philip giving her strength.

Then she thinks of her dad. The space where he fixes everything is his garage. She hears him whistling happily, taking a hidden key from the hanging basket by the garage door. He always hides a spare key to the house, at the new house and the old. With four of them coming and going, keys were going missing and people were getting locked out. He would come up with new and inventive ways to hide the key. This is his workspace. He has worked here for forty-two years, surely he has taken his work habits home with him and vice versa, and if this is his cabin, she's pretty sure he'll have a key hidden somewhere.

She looks under the desk, runs her hand over the wood, she opens all the drawers, empties out envelopes. She searches in the mini fridge, checks in cartons.

She's been through so much over the past few weeks, what could she possibly have learned that could get her out of this? Jamie taught her to stand her ground. She searches on the ground, under everything, under the chair, the bin, the fire extinguisher.

Io taught her to look up.

Pip looks up. There are lights on the ceiling, circular LED ceiling lights. They aren't flush to the ceiling, there's a ridge around the outside leaving a gap between the ceiling and the light. She pulls a chair from the table over to the doorway, removes her high heels and stands on it. She reaches up and feels around the rim of the light. She feels dust and cobwebs, and then her hand hits something. She knocks a metal key from the rim and sends it to the floor. She jumps down and immediately grabs the key. With trembling fingers she slides the key into the lock and cannot believe it when it fits in perfectly and turns. She pushes the door open and the cool July night air fills her lungs.

Now that she's out safely, she's terrified Sammy will come back. She looks around for his Range Rover, expecting the headlights to come on suddenly from the darkness at any moment.

She runs for her phone that's on the ground, the screen shattered. Eleven missed calls from Bella makes her cry out in fear.

She dials Krish's number, carefully, trying not to slice her finger on the smashed screen. She needs his help to get out of here, but it's too mangled to make a call.

She sobs, looking around for ideas, panicking that Sammy will return. Her best hope is to try to get out of here herself and make her way home. She's not far, but can she bring herself to tell her parents what she has done?

All of a sudden there's a loud sound, like thunder. She's afraid that Sammy is letting off explosives, her imagination runs wild, and now she's genuinely concerned about her safety. She didn't think it could get any worse, and it has. There's a bright light and the whole quarry is lit up. It's the sound of a helicopter. She looks up and sees it hovering over the quarry.

She recognises the helicopter from the hangar at the airfield. It's Io!

She starts jumping up and down, waving her arms. And then she runs back into the cabin and switches the lights on and off so that they can see her.

The helicopter slowly starts to descend into the quarry. There are sleeping vehicles everywhere, but there's still enough space for it to land. Dust is flying everywhere, spraying and hitting the cabin. She stands inside, where she's protected and hears stones hit the metal walls. It's like she's under attack. She watches as the helicopter lands and the door opens.

Jamie!

Jamie gets out, ducking low to avoid the blades, and runs towards her. Io remains inside the helicopter, the rotary blades still spinning.

She runs to Jamie and throws her arms around him for the tightest hug of her life.

'Are you okay?' he shouts over the noise of the helicopter.

He tries to move to check her, but she won't let go.

'I'm fine,' she says into his shoulder, fingers gripping him tightly. 'I'm fine.' But she's in shock.

'Did he hurt you?'

She squeezes him even tighter, and he gives in and rocks her gently.

Krish suddenly comes running towards them with a torch in his hand, out of breath.

'Pip! What on earth is going on? I'm going to be fired, and it's only my first night.'

Pip finally lets go of Jamie.

'Krish, I'm so sorry. A stupid plan of mine went disastrously wrong. Where's Sammy?'

'He told me to go home ten or fifteen minutes ago, but I'm not due to finish until six a.m. I couldn't see you in the car and I got worried. Something was off. Then I remembered Sergeant Al Powell in *Die Hard* played beautifully by Reginald VelJohnson who left the premises of Nakatomi Plaza thinking everything was okay, but realises there is in fact an emergency when the dead body of a terrorist lands on his car, cleverly thrown there by John McClane. So I drove away and pretended to leave, but I turned back.'

'Oh Krish, thank you so much.' She's so relieved to have such support. It has been around her all of the time disguised as something different. And then Pip's eyes widen. 'So Sammy didn't leave the quarry?'

'He drove to the security hut to send me home, then went back in again. I haven't seen him exit.'

She clings to Jamie again. 'He's still here.'

'I can find him,' Jamie says, pumped up, looking around, ready for the fight.

'No!' She holds on to his arm, to rein him in. 'We have to get Bella. Krish, do you want to come with us?'

'No,' he says, standing taller. 'I will remain at my post and deal with Mr Wolverson.'

She hugs him quickly, taking him by surprise. 'Thank you.'

She and Jamie duck and run towards the helicopter. Io takes her hand and helps her climb in.

'Are you okay?' he asks, concerned, searching her eyes.

'Thank you,' she says, kissing him on the cheek.

As the helicopter lifts, Pip sees a Range Rover racing through the quarry. Jamie watches it with anger, his jaw clenched. She watches Sammy get out of the Range Rover and look at the helicopter in shock and anger, the blades sending dust and rock his way. He runs towards the cabin for safety and Krish slams the door closed, protected. Sammy has to run back into his car, rocks flying against it, denting the paintwork.

Io flies towards the airfield, Jamie wraps his arm around Pip and she feels so safe.

'Thank you, Io. I've been so worried about you, I've been calling you all day. What's going on?'

'A friend of Sammy's in the police wanted to search the airfield. He didn't have the right paperwork, but he's going to get it. Stella and I decided to shut it down and clear it out. We were busy all night and day.'

Jamie quickly looks at Pip, then away. She can't read his expression.

'And now this,' she says. 'I'm so sorry. It's all my fault. If it wasn't for me, Sammy wouldn't have pursued you.'

Jamie strengthens his hold on her.

'It's not your fault. Our paperwork is all in order, he won't find it easy to get a warrant, but I don't trust him, he'll be watching us. And don't you worry, I gave as good as I got.'

Though Io has illegally landed in the quarry, and Sammy won't let that go.

'But you can't leave yet,' she says, 'You have to wait for your signal.'

'Signals come in different forms,' he says, grimly. 'Maybe this is mine. We can relocate.'

They land at the airfield where Stella is waiting and watching. The hangar is empty, as is her office. The maps are gone from the walls, the books are gone from her desk. The door with the security code is shut. Stella lifts a hand and waves at Pip, and it feels very final.

Pip's relief at being rescued is short-lived as she and Jamie get in his car to race to Bella. It's been an hour since she called. Too much can happen in an hour.

'I'm so sorry,' Pip says, teeth chattering as they race there. 'This is all my fault. I'm so so sorry.'

'We'll get into it later, let's just get Bella,' he says, full of concern.

'Jamie, if anything has happened to her,' she says, starting to cry again. 'It's all my fault.'

He races, far too fast through the streets, and pulls up outside the house. The music is blaring, vibrating down the street, people have spilled out into the front garden. Pip and

Jamie get out of the car and make their way into the house, of course everyone is staring at them.

'Where's Bella?' Jamie asks a teenage girl holding a brightly coloured can. 'Isabella?'

Pip looks around, and the entire gang are holding them, and they're littering the garden. Canisters, not cans. Nitrous oxide, also known as 'Fast gas'.

The girl shrugs and moves away to her circle.

'Try the toilet,' Pip says. 'I told her to wait there.'

They instantly know where it is because they hear banging.

'Isabella, get out now, come on!'

'Out of the way,' Jamie says, shoving Mark aside, like he's a whippet. He grabs him by the collar and pushes him away.

'Bella, I'm here,' Pip says. 'Open the door, let's go.'

The door is unlocked and Bella appears, looking so young. Her make-up has worn off from crying. Her eyes aren't focusing, she's drunk.

Pip gives her a hug. 'Are you okay?' she whispers in her ear. 'Did he hurt you? Did he touch you? Did anyone?'

'No, nothing like that,' she says, embarrassed now that they're here and people are staring. 'I just want to get out of here.'

She ignores Mark as she makes her way out of the house, people staring and laughing, as she's escorted by her parents to the car. She can barely walk in a straight line, they both prop her up. She gets in the back seat, and slams the door.

Pip looks at Jamie.

'Don't look at me, this is new territory for me.'

'She says nobody touched her. Do we believe that?'

'Why don't we go back to my hotel room and talk to her. If we think we need to do anything then, go to the hospital or call the Gardaí, then we'll do it.'

'Okay, good idea,' she says. 'Why are you staying in a hotel?'

'It's better than staying at home.'

She understands that. 'I'll sit in the back with her.'

Pip wraps her arm around Bella, and Bella rests her head on Pip's shoulder. Pip kisses her on the head, wrapping her arms around her tightly. She smells like a brewery.

'What took you so long?' Bella mumbles.

'I'm sorry,' she whispered. 'I was trying to do something good, but I made a stupid mistake.'

Now that the adrenaline is wearing off and things are calming down, Pip's jaw is starting to hurt. She remembers how Sammy had gripped her tightly, squeezing his thumb into her cheek so forcefully she thought he'd break it.

When she looks ahead she sees Jamie watching them both in the rear-view mirror.

His eyes are soft.

'I feel sick,' Bella says suddenly, breaking the moment. She sits up suddenly and moves to the door.

'Wait, wait, wait,' Pip says. Jamie pulls in quickly and Pip gets out and rushes around to Bella's side of the car. She holds her hair back as Bella vomits into the bog by the side of the road.

47

I N JAMIE'S HOTEL ROOM, Jamie and Pip sit on the bath-room floor. Bella has been so sick, the last few times have just been retching, nothing left inside her stomach. She's exhausted and is lying on the cool tiles of the bathroom floor, her head on Jamie's lap. He's leaning against the bath, his long legs stretched out in front of him and crossed at the ankles. Casual as can be. His hands are running through Bella's hair, slowly smoothing it down over and over again. It's relaxing to watch.

Pip has taken her high heels off and is sitting on a towel in the ridiculous mini dress, feeling like a tart.

They smile tiredly at each other across the room.

Fingers laced together, Pip's head in his lap, looking up at Jamie. He's beautiful from every angle. He smells of grass and sweat after football.

'Lush lashes.

Apricot pits.

Thunder thighs.

Lips.'

Jamie laughs. She occasionally, and randomly, sums up attributes about him that she loves. Always in that rhythm, like a drum. She does it about other people too, as they spend a lot of time hanging around in public places with each other, watching others.

'Apricot pits?' he laughs.

'Your deodorant smells of apricots.'

'How do you even know what apricot smells like. When's the last time you had an apricot?'

'I had a peach last week.'

'You are a peach,' he says, leaning over, lips grazing hers. 'If we had a girl, what would we name her?'

Jamie is never afraid to talk like this, not embarrassed by what others think. She doesn't know any sixteen-year-old couples talking about marriage and babies in their future, and yet Jamie is confident that's what their future holds. They're locked in on each other.

'Bella,' she says, not even needing a moment to think about it.

He laughs at her certainty. 'You've thought about it.'

'Of course I have.'

'Bella,' he says, slowly, gently, lazily, the name escaping his pillowy lips like a breath.

She kisses him.

It starts gently, but as always builds to hot and heavy, hungry for each other. They want each other so badly, it's exciting but terrifying.

He groans, frustrated at having to stop. They're in a park, on the grass, in public.

'Bella,' he says, fixing his trousers. 'I love it.'

'I love you,' she says, easily.

He looks at her, deep in her eyes. 'I love you too.'

He looks down at Bella and runs his hands through her hair again. 'How did she get so big? Our baby.'

Pip's eyes fill with tears. 'Our baby.'

'Hey, it's okay.'

'It's not okay, Jamie. I let them take over.'

'We let them, it's not your fault. We were so young.' He's emotional too. 'If I could do it all over again I swear I would still get on that boat all over again.'

This surprises her, disappoints her.

'But with you. And Bella. As soon as we found out you were pregnant, we should have just gone and raised her ourselves. Together.'

She smiles. 'Could we have?'

'We could have tried. I don't know.'

He smooths down Bella's hair.

'We'll never know now,' Pip says sadly.

'That's not necessarily true,' he says. 'We could try it now.'

'All move to Liverpool?'

He's embarrassed by the suggestion.

'I'd love to,' she says quickly, before the moment is lost. 'I'd really love to.'

His face lights up.

'But my life is here. They need me at Crossroads. Who will make the sandwiches? Will I ever find another place like it?'

He looks at her in surprise, until he realises she's joking and he throws his head back and laughs. It's so loud it wakes Bella.

She sits up.

'Sorry,' Jamie says.

She looks around at the unfamiliar surroundings, at where she's been lying on her dad, and where they are in the bathroom. She seems more sober now than during the last vomit explosion, that have been followed by the whiny mantra, 'I'm never drinking again.'

'Where the hell are we?'

'In your dad's hotel room. Bella, sweetheart, I need to know what happened tonight. If Mark hurt you or tried something, we need to know now so we can act quickly.'

'Nothing like that,' she says. 'We had an argument. He was an arsehole. I said I wanted to break up and never see him again.'

'What happened?' Pip asks.

'He was different to who I thought I was. He was calling me a liar. It was about you.' She looks at Pip. 'I told him you're my mam, it didn't feel right lying about it, and he just flipped out. I told him if that was a problem then we're finished.'

'Oh,' Pip says, breathily, relieved and feeling guilty for being so pleased. She's trying not to smile. Jamie grins at her.

'What the hell are you wearing? You look like a prostitute,' her daughter says, back to being Bella again.

'You're right. I do. Do you have anything I can wear?' she asks Jamie. 'A T-shirt?'

'I'll get you one.' But he doesn't move. Pip thinks he quite likes the closeness with Bella.

'Are we staying here?' Bella asks.

'I'm not bringing you home like this,' Pip says.

'Nan will have a conniption if we stay out.'

'I texted her to let her know we're not coming home tonight. From your phone,' she says, looking sadly at her smashed phone screen.

It had been followed by nine missed calls. All which she didn't answer, though she did text her dad to tell him they were fine and Josephine's phone calls stopped.

'I'm wrecked. Can I get into bed?' Bella doesn't wait for an answer, she staggers away and falls onto the bed and goes to sleep immediately.

'Do you mind if we stay?'

'Not at all. I was really hoping for a family night all along. This is a dream come true.'

They both start laughing hysterically, exhausted by the dramatic events.

Jamie stands, reaches out his hand and pulls Pip to her feet. He goes into the bedroom and roots around his suitcase for a T-shirt, which he hands to her. She changes in the bathroom.

When she comes out, he's sitting on a chair by the TV.

The way he looks at her, dressed in his T-shirt. She walks to him and sits on the floor, leans against the bed, her legs tucked up. She welcomes his stare, it's not a devouring look like Sammy's, it's gentle, it's wanting. Her stomach is filled with butterflies.

'I wasn't on a date with Sammy.'

'I know. I knew.'

'The way you looked at me.'

'I was trying to figure out what you were doing. Why you were doing it. I thought it was something dangerous. Turns out I was right. Kim told me as soon as you left, the girls came over, panicked, and filled me in. They were worried, they didn't know where you were going, but I heard you say you were going to the quarry. Clever of you.'

She smiles. 'How did you meet Io?'

'He was sitting in his car outside The Turfcutter's. He said you'd left him a voicemail telling him what you were planning.'

'He's always a good sounding board. Even if he didn't answer the phone.'

'Well he thought it was a bad idea. So he was waiting outside just in case. I followed him in my car to the quarry. We couldn't find a way in. I tried to scale the fence. There's barbed wire at the top,' he says lifting his T-shirt and revealing scrapes across his chest.

Pip sucks in air at the scrapes. And she notes the toned torso.

'Io had the idea to land inside with the helicopter.' He shakes his head. 'Crazy night.'

Io, Krish, Jamie, the girls, she is surrounded by care and love. She is not alone.

He studies her as he speaks. 'You're right, Io is a very special friend.'

'I told you, not like that.' She smiles. 'He's like my fairy godmother flying in to save the day.'

'Hey, I'm the one who leaped out of it, I was pretty chuffed with myself for that.'

'You were awesome.' She laughs, then becomes serious again as the pain takes hold. 'Sammy nearly broke my jaw,' she says, moving it from side to side, testing it.

'He hit you?' He sits up, action man again.

'He grabbed me. He was rough. I've decided I'm going to report him tomorrow. Lead by example, you know?' She looks at sleeping Bella.

'Good. I can come with you. I was going to have Finbar get someone to beat the shit out of him.'

'No. We need him in one piece. We're going to bring him down another way.'

She fills him in about what had happened with her dad since Jamie viewed the house and the photographs of the diesel generators that Io had taken.

'What's the deal with Io?' Jamie asks. 'Do you think it's drugs?'

'What?!' The word explodes from her. So that's what Jamie's look to her was about in the helicopter. 'No way! What makes you think that?'

'Why would Sammy send the Gardaí there?'

'Because he's a bully and he was trying to scare Io off,' she says, angrily, detesting every inch of Sammy Wolverson. 'He told me he didn't like his girlfriends to be friends with men.'

Jamie curses and shakes his head. He looks as though he's about to say something, then drops it.

'Go on,' she urges him, needing to hear what he has to say.

'Why would Io and Stella relocate so that the Gardaí don't search the place? What are they trying to hide? It's a remote airfield, a large building, maybe there's a grow room in there, plus they can pretty much fly wherever and whenever they want.' Before she explodes again, he adds quickly, 'The business is suspicious. Finbar didn't know anything about it when I asked him. I don't know if they actually teach anybody to fly there, other than you.'

She's been pondering that. She thinks of the room in Stella's office, with the security panel. 'I think it's bigger than that.'

'Bigger than exporting illegal drugs?'

'No,' she says, laughing, because she just can't see it. 'I mean bigger than we can comprehend. I get the feeling it's more out there. Government stuff. Secret mission space stuff.'

Jamie laughs. 'Your imagination hasn't changed much, but what do I know about what happens around here anymore anyway?' he says, growing weary of it and dropping the subject.

But Pip does agree with Jamie about the airfield business being suspicious. For a flying school, they don't seem to do much teaching. She hadn't encountered another person or aircraft in all the times she'd been there, and Stella seemed to be busier by night than by day. She feels Io had let her into his world a little, had given her a glimpse, and she'd assisted in landing him in trouble.

She yawns and winces in pain. 'What time is it?'

He looks at his watch. 'Four a.m.'

'We've talked all night.'

'Just like old times.'

'Thankfully I don't have work tomorrow.'

'You don't have to go back to the station ever again. You're going to get a new job. In Liverpool.'

'Jamie,' she starts, what feels like a very awkward question. 'This idea about living in Liverpool together. Do you mean *together*? Or just in the same city? Because you have Tala, and . . .'

'Tala and I broke up.'

'Oh.'

'She felt my life was too complicated for her, which I understand. And to be honest, my heart wasn't in it with her, and she knew that. Because it's elsewhere, with someone else.' He slides from the chair to the floor, in one eloquent graceful move, he's beside her. He brushes his thumb against her jaw. 'Does this hurt?'

She gives the tiniest shake of her head because she doesn't trust her voice to work.

He kisses her jaw, gently, a butterfly kiss. Then around her chin, all the way up the other side. Kissing away the pain. Then his lips find hers. So softly, they connect. It's been a long time, it's familiar, but so very different and so much better with time, with age, with experience, with pain, with healing, with a love that never died.

On the bed, behind them, Bella starts snoring. And they laugh.

Origami girl starts to unfold, safe with her Origami boy.

Paper Heart

Origami girl
Tumbles
    Down
        Down
            Down
She lands with a thump
Upside down and
Crumpled
'Hello,' Origami boy says,
'I fell here too.'
She knew he was there
All this time
Tumbling downward
With her
She couldn't see
But she could feel him.
'What now?' she asks.
Origami boy
Stands and shakes out his creases.
He holds out his pointed hand
To her
She takes his hand in hers
And they move to the ledge
Together
And
    Jump

48

Jamie and Pip sit down with Josephine and Philip, two opposite two, at the kitchen table in their home.

Josephine is fidgeting, eyes red from crying, nervous. Philip reaches across the table and holds her hand.

Pip and Jamie are holding hands, they both sit up straight, Pip has not a hint of nerves, or regret, or fear. She feels more confident than ever, more certain that she has found her place. It couldn't be more different to the meetings they've had with their parents in the past, bowed heads and slumped shoulders, barely able to find the words to defend themselves.

'I'm moving to Liverpool,' Pip says, 'to live with Jamie. I've quit my job. I'm leaving next week.'

Josephine gasps with shock. It takes her a moment to figure out what to say next. 'You can't take Isabella.' Her voice is a trembling whisper.

'Actually I can, because Bella's my daughter. She's our daughter.'

Jamie rubs her hand with his thumb. His grip is solid, his touch is soft. He is everything she needs.

'But I'm not going to.'

Josephine sighs with relief, and Pip understands how much she truly loves Bella, perhaps more than she ever loved Pip.

'You helped me raise Bella, and I'm grateful for that. I may not agree or like how you accomplished it, but I'm grateful for the love you have for her. I'm grateful that you gave us a place to live, that you didn't cast us out. Bella loves you very much and she's lucky to have you.' She takes a deep breath. 'We spoke to Bella about all of this first. She wants to stay here with you, at least until the end of the summer. She wants to leave school, but I'm not allowing that to happen. Maybe she can have a fresh start in a new school in Liverpool. She likes the idea of studying at Liverpool University, but she's not deciding anything yet.'

Philip looks at Josephine. 'It makes sense, love. We have to move out of here, we have to move in with Helen while we fix the house. It's too dangerous being here while it's like this. There wouldn't be much room for Isabella.' He corrects himself. 'Bella. She's welcome of course, but it would be a tight squeeze.'

'I have a two-bed apartment,' Jamie says. 'We have room for her and of course want her with us. But it's not up to me or you, it's up to Bella. It's her life.'

'But she's too young to make that decision, she's only . . .'

'Sixteen,' Pip finishes for her. 'Nearly seventeen. A year away from school ending. She has some big decisions to make about her future. But it's up to her. I'm not taking her voice away from her.'

Josephine is shaking her head. 'And what are you going to do?' Her eyes are narrow, scrutinising Pip.

'I'm going to take art classes.' Pip lifts her chin, trying to compose herself. The mention of her own future, of entering an undiscovered world of art, brings tears to her eyes. She had pressed pause on the woman she could be, she has no idea who she would be now if she could have continued her education and flourished, but she is also acutely aware that the pain she suffered over the past sixteen years inspired her to continue her art journey in an intense and personal way, as private as it was. Origami girl and all her secret wishes and fears kept her afloat.

'Art classes won't pay the bills,' Josephine snaps.

'Now,' Philip says gently. 'We support Pip in her endeavours.'

'I'll support Pip,' Jamie says, and she grins.

She has no fears, no qualms, no thoughts that it will be smooth and plain sailing, but she's ready for the adventure, for the lessons life is about to teach her. But she has learned her lesson, she doesn't want to have to rely on anyone else for her life to function as she wants it to.

'The art classes are in the evening, I plan to get a job too.'

Josephine wriggles in her seat, uncomfortable. 'You criticise me, for everything I did. For every decision I made. But who else was going to make them?' she asks. 'I was only doing my best,' Josephine says, firmly. 'I did my best.'

'For you,' Pip says, trying to keep her voice even. They planned on this meeting being adult, responsible, argument free. She's trying very hard to stick to that plan. 'You did the best for yourself. You told yourself it was for me and for Bella, but you only managed your pain, your embarrassment. You did everything for yourself.'

The doorbell rings.

Bella runs down the stairs and answers it.

'Are you expecting someone?' Josephine asks Philip.

He shakes his head. 'I'm going across the road for a meeting after this. We're working on building a Grant Scheme to provide financial support to those who have to fix damaged properties due to the quarry, like us. Every penny of this shouldn't come from our own wallets.'

'That's great, Dad,' Pip says, supportively.

'It's Io,' Bella calls.

'Who's Io?' Philip asks.

'The scientist from the observatory,' Josephine says. 'What's he doing here?'

They all go to the door. Io is practically dancing, his eyes are filled with tears.

'It happened. Pip it happened. The signal.'

Pip gasps and runs to hug him. They both dance around. Then she stops dancing.

'That means you have to go?'

He nods. 'Time to go home.'

She kisses him on the cheek. 'Thank you so much for everything.'

'Thank you, Pip.'

'When are you leaving?' Jamie asks.

'As soon as possible. The world's media are about to descend on the observatory. This is big news. Big, big news. So,' he says, changing the tone, 'I need a lift to the airfield, please. And Stella wants to say goodbye.'

She frowns. 'But you drove here. Your car is right there.'

'It's a rental and it's all paid up for the next few months. I don't need it where I'm going, so I'm leaving it with you. You can have it. Get some more practice in.'

Her jaw drops. 'No way.'

'It's not enough, not after what you have given me – true friendship. I told you you could go anywhere in the world you want. Go, Pip.'

343

'But she doesn't know how to drive,' Josephine says, smartly, breaking the moment.

This is enough to spur Pip on. She takes the car key from Io's hand. She hugs him again, then runs to the car.

'Bella baby, want to come?'

'Absolutely!'

'Hop in the back,' she says with a wink.

Pip, the girl in the back seat, sits into the driver's seat and starts the engine.

49

'Indicate,' Jamie says.

'I did.'

'You sprayed water on the rear window.'

'This car is weird to drive.'

'I'm sorry my car isn't as fancy as Io's kingpin car,' he says with a laugh.

'Stop it,' she says. 'You can't speak about him like that.'

'Right, I meant his secret government agency car.'

'That's better. And you can stop laughing at me.'

'You've a cute little face when you're concentrating,' he says, grinning.

Pip laughs, breaking her focus.

She drives into Ballybeg service station. They're driving to Dublin, where they'll catch the car ferry to Liverpool to start their new life together. Jamie's car is filled to the brim with all the possessions Pip could squeeze in, memory boxes and origami girls included. Bella will join them in time, and is already looking at courses at the University of Liverpool.

'It's diesel,' he calls across to her before he goes into the shop.

'Okay,' she says, not sure exactly what to do. All this time working at the service station and she never once used the pumps. She figures it out herself, pressing the button until she hears the machine whirr into action and the numbers race up.

'What the hell are you doing?' Ronnie asks, coming out of the station. 'Who asked you to work the pumps?'

'No one,' she says. 'Just thought I'd try while no one was looking. It's kind of like sex, isn't it, sticking it in.' She rattles the pump around in the fuel tank suggestively. She laughs at his expression.

He frowns, confused. 'Where have you been all week?'

'Didn't they tell you? I quit,' she says, grinning, loving the feeling of freedom. 'I'm getting out of here. Out of Crossroads, out of Ballybeg.'

She watches the numbers climb to fifty euro and she stops, pulling the pump out, tapping it to get the drips off and placing it back in its holder. She closes the cap on the fuel tank, feeling his eyes on her, his mouth open in surprise, feeling wholly independent. 'Good luck with everything, Ronnie.'

Jamie comes up behind her and wraps his arms around her waist and buries his face in her neck, with kisses that tickle. She laughs and kisses him back.

'I paid for the fuel. And I got you coffee and a croissant.'

He leans into the car and places the coffee in the cup holder and the bag on the passenger seat.

'Just when I thought you couldn't be more perfect.' She pulls him close and kisses him, long and meaningful, not caring who's watching, which is Ronnie.

'That was nice,' he says, pulling her closer, wanting more.

A truck honks, urging them to move on and they both jump, startled.

'Okay, we should get moving, we don't want to be stuck in rush-hour traffic.'

'Maybe I do, then it won't be as fast,' she says, anxious about her first long drive.

'We'll take it easy, no show boating. Slow and steady wins the race.'

'Obviously,' she says, kissing him again.

The truck honks.

'Okay, okay,' she says, waving at the driver.

'Look what's in the news,' Jamie says, handing her the newspaper, before walking around to the passenger side.

'It can't be Rachel Buckley's story already?' she asks, in surprise.

Pip had visited the Garda station and reported the incident with Sammy on July 14th, when he had hurt her and locked her in the Portakabin. Then she had sent Rachel Buckley a copy of the Nurney Road file, everything that had been compiled by her neighbours about the Wolverson quarry over the past few years, plus more information supplied to her by her dad regarding the sub-standard building blocks. She'd included a handwritten note: 'Here's the scoop you were looking for.'

'No, it's good news,' he says with a grin, and she knows he's teasing her. 'Maybe part of your secret government mission stuff. Page four.'

Pip opens the newspaper to page four, and reads.

UFO investigated in Ireland after multiple aircraft sightings

The Irish Aviation Authority says it is investigating the incident after Shannon Air Traffic Control received multiple reports of an unidentified flying object off the coast of Ireland.

In a statement, an IAA spokesman said: 'Following reports from a small number of aircraft on July 16th of unusual air activity, the IAA has filed a report. This report will be investigated under the normal confidential occurrence investigation process.'

'Io,' Pip whispers.

He went home.

She looks up at the sky, at the stars, at the millions of possibilities.

She starts the engine, she indicates, waits until it's clear, and instead of turning left to go back home, turns right into a world of possibilities.

Epilogue

'BRACE YOURSELF,' THE SONOGRAPHER says. 'This will be cold.'

She squirts the ultrasound gel onto Pip's stomach and smears it across her skin with a probe. Goosebumps rise on her tummy and an image appears on the screen in black and white.

'There we are,' the sonographer says. 'Hello, baby.'

Jamie takes Pip's hand, he's seated on a stool beside her.

'Oh,' Pip's voice warbles as emotion immediately overwhelms her. 'Hello,' she whispers to the image on the screen.

Jamie grips her hand more tightly.

She looks up at him in time to see him wipe a tear away.

'There's one baby in there,' the sonographer says, 'and there's Baby's heart.' She taps on the keyboard, zones in on an area and zooms in. 'You see there? That's the heart, flickering.'

Flickering like a beacon. It says *Here I am*.

We see you, Pip wants to say aloud.

'How many weeks do you think you are?'

'Eleven,' she says.

The sonographer carries out measurements to establish the gestational age.

'That looks about right.'

'But I've only known you eight weeks,' Jamie says, letting go of her hand. The sonographer looks up at them quickly.

'Don't listen to him,' Pip says, smiling, 'that's just his humour.'

The sonographer doesn't laugh and returns her attention to the screen while Pip and Jamie share a look, and try not to lose control of their giddiness. Jamie takes her hand again.

'Is this your first?' the sonographer asks.

'No, our second,' Pip says, unable to believe it. She can't take her eyes off the screen, off the little bean with the flashing heart.

'Boy or girl?'

'A girl,' Jamie says, 'Bella.'

'Beautiful name. Big sisters can be helpful.'

'I'm not sure this one will be too helpful, she's very busy with her own life,' Pip says, feeling emotional at the idea of Bella's new role.

The sonographer smiles. 'I've a two-year-old girl, she's all business. She's into handbags now, she keeps stealing mine and filling them with a jumble of all kinds of things. But she's good at doing little jobs and getting nappies and wipes for my baby. They like to be helpers. How old is your daughter?'

'Eighteen,' Jamie says.

'Eighteen months?'

'Eighteen years. She's in university.'

The sonographer swings around in her chair to get a good look at them. 'And here was I thinking you're newbies.'

'We kind of are,' Pip says quietly.

'I've heard all kinds of age gaps between siblings, but that's the biggest,' she says with a grin, returning her attention to the screen.

'We wanted to make sure we really liked each other,' Jamie jokes.

The sonographer laughs this time. 'I don't suppose you kept any baby gear from eighteen years ago?'

Bar a few items of baby clothes and shoes in a memory box, they have nothing. Josephine has stored Bella's cot in the garage, but Pip doesn't want anything from the past. 'No,' Pip says. 'We have to buy everything from scratch.'

'So it really is like starting again,' the sonographer says.

'Yes.' Pip looks at Jamie. 'It really is.'

'I'll print a few of these photos out so you can show the big sister.' She taps on a button and a ream of photographs roll out.

'I can't wait to see the look on Bella's face when we tell her,' Jamie says.

'She's going to think it's disgusting,' Pip says, and they laugh.

'But she's going to be so happy,' he says, and Pip agrees.

Pip takes the scan photographs from the sonographer, remembering back to the first time she did this eighteen years ago, lovesick without Jamie, her mother beside her doing all the talking, her voice gone, her body changing, her light dimmed. Life has corrected itself. No, she has corrected her life.

Jamie leans his head against hers as they study the photographs. 'Congratulations, Mama,' he whispers, then kisses her.

She looks up at the screen one more time, to the flashing light of the heartbeat, like a twinkling star first arriving in the night sky, its beam having taken years to travel. A signal from her distant star.

Acknowledgements

My motivation and inspiration for this novel came from wanting to write about the various ways in which our curious, investigative souls dig – physically into the earth, mentally and spiritually into the sky and universe, and emotionally into our own hearts. Bog, Sky, Heart. The bogs of Offaly, its radio telescope and Pip's secret passion for origami helped me depict the ways in which we dig and unpeel the layers that are within us and all around us. We are constantly folding and unfolding ourselves and the world around us.

Enormous thanks to HarperCollins UK; my editors Lynne Drew and Laura Palmer, Charlie Redmayne, Kate Elton, Frankie Gray, Anna Derkacz, Liz Dawson, Susanna Peden, Olivia Robertshaw, Jo Kite, Indigo Griffiths, Vicki Watson, Fleur Clarke, Tony Purdue and Patricia McVeigh.

Thank you to my phenomenal literary agent Abby Koons at Park Fine & Brower Literary Agency in New York.

There is an I-Lofar radio telescope at Birr Castle in Co. Offaly, Ireland, and it is home to the Leviathan telescope which was once the world's biggest telescope for seventy years, and so setting the story for Io to await for his signal from a distant star in this location seemed apt, but that is where the similarities end – everything in this story, including the town

353

of Ballybeg, is entirely fictional. A few real-life elements which have been diluted and mixed, stirred up in my fictional pot, made their way into the novel and so I acknowledge them here. A real-life conversation with former NASA director Professor Worden with Professor Peter Gallagher, the head of the radio telescope in Birr, inspired the fictional conversation between my fictional professor and former NASA characters. The opening paragraph of the news article regarding reports of an unidentified flying object in the region is a real Sky News article by Lucy Binding in November 2018.

Heartfelt thanks to the supportive booksellers, for your passion and love of books. So much has to happen to get the books from the printers, to the warehouses, to the shelves, and into the hands of readers, I'm grateful for all you do. To the libraries and Literary Festivals for welcoming me and supporting my novels. To my readers, thank you for reading and listening, thank you for coming to my events, I love meeting you and hearing your stories. Your feedback and encouragement is a shining star during every novel writing process. Thank you to my fellow authors who are an inspiration and support.

Thank you, my loving, supportive family and friends.

David, Robin, Sonny, Blossom, I love you.

Cecelia Ahern

Stay in touch!

To hear about my new
books first, all my news
and special deals, sign up
to my newsletter at cecelia-ahern.com.

About the Author

Cecelia Ahern is an Irish novelist whose work was first published in 2004. Her debut novel *PS I Love You* was an international bestseller and was adapted to film starring Hilary Swank. Her second novel, *Where Rainbows End*, was adapted into *Love, Rosie* starring Lily Collins. Her books have been published in over thirty-seven languages, and have sold over twenty-five million copies. In addition to her novels, she is also the author of a highly acclaimed collection of stories, *Roar*, which is now an Apple Original series starring Nicole Kidman on Apple TV+.

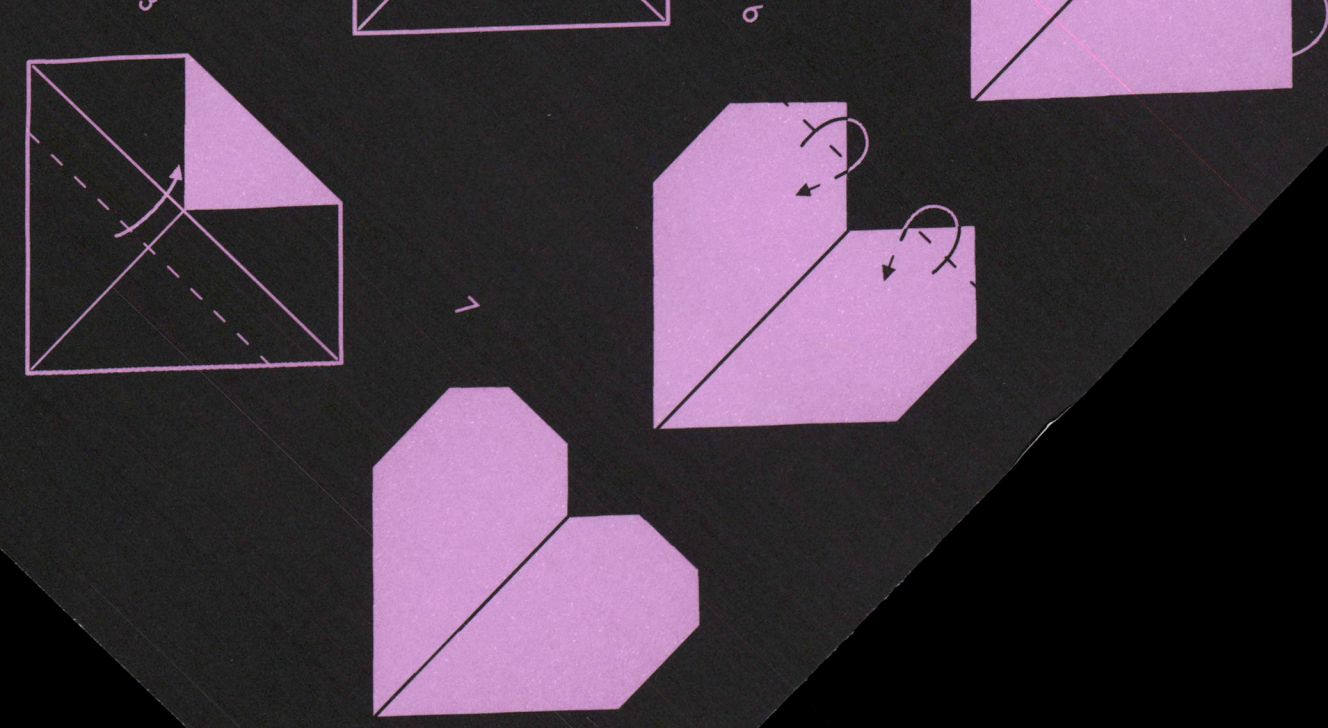